# GAY EROTICA ADULT STORIES
# THE SPINNING CLOCK

Hot Sex Short M/M, Explicit Dirty Rough Family, Taboo Age Gap, Daddy Men, Threesome, Dark Romance, MM First Time, Stepdaddy

**RICK JOSHUA**

# TABLEOF CONTENT

# CHAPTER 1

Warren is sweaty and disheveled from the work, but this machine has been leaking water all week and he's sick of mopping the floor and waiting on Giles to call for an actual maintenance worker, so he's decided to fix it himself. He may or may not be currently regretting that decision.

Minnie is sitting on the top of the machine, her small paws gripping the edge as she peers over it, head tilted curiously as she watches him work.

"It's a little farther back, I think," she says helpfully. "On your left, Warren."

"I've got it."

Warren grasps the hose, pulling it toward himself. A thin stream of water sprays out, and his daemon scrambles back, her nails clicking on the metal surface.

"Watch it!" she cries.

"Sorry, Minnie," Warren says, wrapping his palm around the leaking part of the hose to keep the spray contained. The front of his button-down shirt is soaked.

Warren sighs. The night shift at the Blue Wave Laundromat is typically quite slow, especially once the university students trickle off after midnight. His fellow night shift comrades or the occasional insomniac on a productivity spree are sporadic patrons at best, so Warren hadn't anticipated being interrupted before solving this problem.

"Does anyone have some change?"

"I'll be right with you," Warren calls back. He has finally managed to locate the loose joint that's the culprit behind this whole thing, and he is not stopping now. To Minnie he murmurs, "Can you—"

He doesn't even need to finish speaking; she's already nudging the wrench toward him. Warren reaches up and grabs it. He fits the wrench to the bolt connecting the joint to the hose and begins tightening it in increments. His hands are slippery from the leaking water, so it takes a bit longer than he'd like, but he manages. When he's done, he watches the hose, willing it not to drip. After a moment he smiles, satisfied with his success, and rises from his crouch behind the machine.

Minnie hops down to the floor, brushing familiarly against his calf as Warren bends to wipe his wet hands on his jeans. He pushes his curls back off of his forehead, wrinkling his nose as he uses his forearm to swipe the sweat from his brow. Then he looks up.

A man is leaning against the counter, regarding him with an amused expression, a large bundle of cloth sitting on the floor by his feet. He is tall, with deep brown skin and tight black curls that are faded into a close shave around the sides and back of his head. He has an eyebrow piercing, and he's wearing a highlighter yellow hoodie and lime green track pants, which somehow work on him, despite every misgiving Warren has ever had about the color lime green. He is deeply, absurdly attractive.

His daemon stands beside him, some kind of canine with tawny grey fur and a black-tipped tail that's swishing just slightly behind her. Her ears are pricked forward and her gaze is sharp as she regards Warren and Minnie, the counterpoint to her human's relaxed slouch.

"Hi," says the man. He's grinning now, and Warren's eyes get caught on the gorgeous curve of his lips.

He knows that he's staring, but he is seven hours into his eight-hour shift, and exhausted, and he doesn't know what to make of this man, who is the most beautiful person he has ever seen, inside this Laundromat or out of it.

Minnie nips his ankle.

"Uh," Warren ekes out. "How can I help you?" He tears his gaze away from the man's lips to meet his eyes, which, he can't help but notice, are a stunning shade of grey. *Is everything about this guy perfect?*

The man raises an eyebrow, and Warren's eyes are drawn to the amethyst-studded barbell that adorns it. "I need change. For the machines?"

"Right, yes," Warren says, flustered. "You said that." He gestures for the man to move away from the counter so he can open the gate, heading around to the till.

Minnie follows, jumping up to sit beside the cash register, her tail tucking neatly around her paws.

"I need detergent too."

Warren nods. "Sure, no problem."

The man gives Warren a five dollar note and he exchanges it for coins. Then he pulls out the store's selection of in-house detergents, a variety of small, colored bottles with hand-written labels. The man points to one, seemingly at random.

Warren hesitates, before saying, "I wouldn't choose that one. It's not very good."

"No?" The man seems surprised by Warren's forthrightness. "Then which would you recommend?"

Warren grimaces. "Actually, none of them are very good. My boss waters them down." He's not sure why he says it. Giles would fire him on the spot if he overheard.

The man huffs a laugh. "Well, aren't you just a ray of sunshine?"

Warren shrugs at him, trying to ignore the heat in his cheeks. "The red bottle is the best of the lot."

"I'll take it."

They exchange money again, and then the man kicks his pile of cloth over to the closest washer, his daemon ambling after him. He bends to start loading it, and Warren sees that the pile appears to consist entirely of drop cloths, stained black in places with what might be soot.

"You should use the industrial washer for those." When the man looks up, Warren points to the end of the row where the biggest washer sits. "It'll work best for canvas."

"Okay," he smiles at Warren. "Thanks for the tip." He pushes the pile down the row to the machine Warren indicated and loads it, fiddling with the controls a bit before inserting his coins.

Warren quickly looks away as the man turns back around. He sits on the tall chair behind the counter and tries to focus on the half-finished Sudoku puzzle he'd been working on from the book he scavenged from the lost and found bin earlier in a fit of boredom. The font swims a bit on the page in front of him, but if he concentrates enough the numbers make sense. He's always enjoyed the challenge of logic puzzles— along with music, they are some of the few things that his brain doesn't make more difficult for him. Though he's finding it very hard to concentrate at this particular moment.

"Wolf or dog?" he whispers to Minnie, who is standing on her hind legs with her paws resting on his shoulder so that she can see the puzzle too.

Her whiskers tickle his cheek as she shakes her head. "Neither. Too small to be a wolf, and that is definitely not a dog. Coyote."

From the corner of his eye, he watches as the man folds his lanky frame into one of the cheap plastic chairs that comprise the waiting area and pulls out his phone. His daemon— a coyote, apparently— flops down on the floor in front of him, resting her head on her front paws. The man's feet start to tap on the floor in a quick rhythm that Warren wants to hum along to, a staccato beat that echoes a little in the otherwise quiet room. Warren's eyes track the man's long fingers as he runs them through his hair before settling them over his kneecap, where they immediately take up drumming along to the tempo of his feet.

Warren drops his eyes as the man looks up. He wills himself not to blush, gnawing on the side of his thumb as he attempts to focus on the puzzle. He feels unmoored, blindsided by an instant attraction that he's never felt before, for anyone. He is acutely aware of his wrinkled button-down, its damp sleeves haphazardly rolled up his forearms, of his winter-pale skin and the dark bags he knows are visible beneath his eyes.

*Stupid,* he thinks. *What does it matter what you look like? This guy is going to finish his laundry and walk out of here, and you'll probably never see him again.*

With a defeated sigh, Warren abandons the Sudoku puzzle, shrugging Minnie off his shoulder. She sniffs a bit at him and curls up in a fluffy ball on the counter as he pulls his headphones out of his messenger bag. In the twenty minutes he has left before his shift ends he figures he can at least start listening to the readings for his next 'Introduction to Control Systems' class, even if he isn't likely to absorb any of it at the moment.

A little after six, Evana comes in for her morning shift, holding her phone in one hand and a takeaway coffee cup in the other, her pigeon daemon perched sleepily on her shoulder.

Warren stands in relief when he sees her, donning his coat and slinging his bag over his shoulder. He bends a little so Minnie can leap onto his shoulders, where she proceeds to drape herself like a particularly soft and furry shawl.

"I fixed the number four washer," Warren tells Evana on his way to the door. "It shouldn't leak anymore."

"Great," she says, without looking up from her screen.

"Yeah, great," he echoes. "Bye, Evana. Have a nice day."

No response. Warren shakes his head a bit, and pushes open the door, steeling himself against the chill January wind. Minnie tucks her face into his neck.

Before he exits, he can't help casting a quick glance toward the man on the chair. He is startled to find him already looking back, his grey eyes crinkling at the corners as he smiles at Warren, small and lopsided. Cheeks flushing pink, Warren gives a quick nod in response before hurriedly stepping outside.

As he walks away along the darkened sidewalk, something tugs unhappily in his chest. It feels like regret.

------

Warren makes it back to his apartment just as the sun is beginning to rise. He toes off his sneakers in the entranceway, and trudges down the narrow hall to his bedroom with every intention of collapsing into bed for a few hours before he has to go to his afternoon classes. Minnie pads wearily along behind him, her tail drooping.

When he reaches his room, Warren sees that Karl has taped their most recent utility bill to the door. It's meaningless scrawl, especially when he's this tired, but

Karlhas helpfully written a number on a blank corner of the page in large, clear digits. He's circled it twice in red ink, and Warren gazes at it in despair, knowing he will be scraping the bottom of his meager savings to pay his half this month.

He pulls the bill off the door and takes it into his room, dropping it unceremoniously on the desk. He shrugs off his messenger bag and coat, before crawling onto his bed and curling up into a ball. Hiding his face in his pillow, he takes deep, measured breaths, trying to quell the rising tide of panic. Minnie jumps onto the bed and tucks herself into his chest, a warm ball of comfort and love. She licks tenderly at his cheek, and he grasps at her, digging his fingers into the silky, dark fur on her back.

"Listen," she murmurs softly. "What can you hear?"

It's an old game, a strategy they've developed from years of carefully managing Warren's anxiety together. It helps center his thoughts on the here and now, rather than on the uncertain future.

Warren listens. He can hear the sounds of traffic outside his bedroom window, the hum of the television in the apartment above, the shower running in the bathroom down the hall as Karl gets ready for his morning lecture.

He doesn't know if he'd call Karl a friend, exactly. They don't hang out at the apartment or on campus, but they are in the same engineering cohort at university, and they have some shared classes, despite specializing in different fields. Karl had been his chemistry lab partner last semester when Warren's father had dropped the bombshell that he was disowning him, effective immediately.

JosephDalton is a man obsessed with his own legacy, and Warren had never been under any illusion that he was the child his father had envisioned to uphold it— his father had always been very forthcoming about that. So when Warren found out that his father's second wife, Janis, was pregnant, he had understood it was unlikely he'd be receiving any inheritance. But he'd never imagined that he'd be cut off completely.

Left abruptly with no income and no place to live, two years into a mechanical engineering degree he was distraught at the thought of not being able to finish, Warren had panicked. Desperate for someone to talk to, he'd ended up confiding in Karl during lab one day.

Karl had rolled his eyes at him and told him to get a student loan. *You know,* he'd said, *like the rest of us.* Warren had been embarrassed that he hadn't thought of it himself. Then, to Warren's astonishment, Karl offered him a room in his apartment, unoccupied since his previous roommate had graduated and moved out the summer before. Warren gratefully accepted. The apartment turned out to be small, thin-walled, and uninsulated— but affordable, even on a minimum wage budget, and that's all that had mattered in those first few terrifying weeks.

Warren hears the water shut off just as he is starting to doze, his eyelids heavy. In his last moments of lucidity, he sets an alarm on his phone so that he doesn't sleep right through his afternoon lectures. Minnie is already asleep, and he can feel her heartbeat under his palm, steady and familiar, just like her.

The noise from the television in the upstairs apartment cuts off and someone turns on music instead, a joyful melody with a thumping beat that makes him think of the man from the Laundromat.

Warren drifts to sleep to the memory of tapping fingers and smiling grey eyes.

------

Warren has been working the night shift at Blue Wave Laundromat for going on five months now.

While the student loan takes care of his tuition, and the DSA he receives from the university covers his audio textbooks and the specialized software he uses to complete his coursework, he needs to work to pay for his rent and everyday necessities. He works here four nights a week, Monday through Thursday— because Giles refuses to give him enough hours to earn full-time benefits— and has Friday and the weekend off, which he typically spends holed up in his room studying and attempting to reduce his perpetual sleep deficit. Every week has been the same since September: school, work, study, sleep.

Warren is lonely.

He's never *alone*, not with Minnie, but he does miss other people sometimes. At first, he hadn't noticed, too busy teaching himself to cook, clean, use public transit, and a plethora of other basic but necessary skills he hadn't had cause to learn before. He'd never had many friends, isolated by his wealth and his disability, the situation exacerbated by his father's demand that he hide his dyslexia as much as possible— but even the few friends he'd managed to make at school have disappeared since he started working the night shift, his lack of time and funds breaking any tenuous bonds that had started to form between them.

Now it's mid-January, and his social interactions are limited to the polite small talk he shares with his classmates, and the transactional back-and-forth exchanges he has with the late-night customers at the Blue Wave.

As far as Warren knows, this is the only 24/7 Laundromat in the whole city, strategically located a block away from the university on a busy street with an entrance to the subway close by. It's an older establishment, and he doubts its interior has been updated since it opened. The walls are a depressingly dingy powder blue. The aging washers and dryers, dented and dulled from years of abuse from uncaring patrons, form two rows across the black and white checkered linoleum floor. Inexplicably, there is a beach scene painted across the back wall featuring palm trees, golden sand littered with seashells, and what he's pretty sure is supposed to be a dolphin jumping out of the ocean in front of a tacky orange sunset.

Warren spends a while staring at the static palm trees, head resting on his folded arms on the countertop, before turning his gaze to the dark sky and drizzling rain outside. Next to him, Minnie is grooming herself, licking delicately at the top of one paw before rubbing it vigorously over her ears. The neon sign hanging by the door casts the grimy plastic chairs lined up against the windowed wall in flickering blue light. Nothing in this place has changed since he started, only the weather outside the window marking the passing of the seasons. He wonders if this is what the next few years of his life are going to be like, trying not to fall asleep at this counter every night, struggling through his coursework every day, until he graduates and gets a real job.

Unless he can't find a real job. His stomach clenches at the thought. He does well in his classes and his grades are high, but it's the same for many of his classmates, and they don't share his affliction. *Why would anyone settle for you when there are plenty of better options? What do you have to offer that they don't?* But that's his father's voice, and Warren is quick to bury it. He has his doubts about the future, but one thing he knows for certain is that he is done listening to JosephDalton.

When Giles walks in at the end of his shift, his bulldog daemon trailing obediently behind him, Warren grabs his messenger bag— which Minnie happily burrows inside— and is out the door as quickly as possible, barely pausing to toss a quick greeting over his shoulder as he goes.

A woman with a long black braid and half a dozen piercings in each ear is unlocking the door to the coffee shop across the street, her cat daemon keeping a vigilant watch nearby. When their eyes meet, the woman gives him a close-lipped smile, and Warren nods his head at her, smiling politely in return. They've done this routine before— more mornings than not it seems her shift begins just as his ends.

Warren watches her slip inside the shop, catching the moment her guarded smile transforms into a bright grin as she greets whomever she sees inside. His chest aches with loneliness and he looks away, pulling his wool cap down further over his ears against the icy rain.

------

The second time they meet, Warren is bent over his thermodynamics problem set. He's simultaneously studying for a test in his morning class and attempting to ignore the headache he is developing from staring at equations in the stark fluorescent lighting. Minnie is lying on her back on the counter beside his textbook with her eyes closed, and Warren absently runs his fingers through the fur on her stomach while he works.

It's early in his shift, almost half past midnight, and the Laundromat is as busy as it ever gets at this hour. A boy wearing headphones is dozing in one of the plastic chairs, head tilted back against the tall glass window, his dog daemon resting on the floor nearby. On the other side of the waiting area, two girls giggle over something on their phones as they wait for their laundry to dry. One of them has a squirrel daemon who is chattering away to the other's butterfly daemon, and the pitch of its squeaky voice is definitely not helping Warren's headache.

He glances up absently when the door buzzes, expecting another bleary-eyed student. His heart jumps in his chest.

It's the beautiful man from a few nights ago. He holds the door open for his coyote daemon before strolling into the Laundromat like he belongs there, carrying a small bottle of detergent and a cloth laundry bag that he's slung over his shoulder. He seems to emanate joy, his gait loose-limbed and his expression cheery, as if there's nothing, he'd rather be doing than laundry in the middle of the night. Tonight, he's wearing a fitted purple t-shirt under a black and gold bomber jacket, and tight grey jeans that accentuate his long legs. His black combat boots thud dully as he crosses linoleum, and Warren tries not to stare too obviously as the man approaches the counter where he's sitting.

"Hi, there," he says in the rich, warm voice Warren remembers. "Can I get some change?"

"It's you," Warren blurts before he can stop himself, cheeks pinking in mortification. Minnie flips abruptly onto her belly and digs her nails into his forearm.

The corners of the man's mouth tick up into a smirk. "Made an impression, did I?" he says. "I'm not surprised— who could forget this face?"

Warren blinks at him. He could only dream of having that kind of self-assurance. "Are you always so confident?" he asks, taking a paper note from the man's outstretched hand. He opens the cash register and begins counting out change.

"Usually," the man replies, and Warren can hear the amusement in his voice. "I try to capitalize on my strengths: I pull a damn fine shot of espresso, I am excellent at throwing darts, and I look *good*."

Warren ducks his head to hide his smile. "I'll have to take your word on the first two," he mumbles awkwardly.

The man lets out a burst of laughter. "Wow, that was almost smooth. I honestly didn't think you had it in you."

Warren wrinkles his nose, feeling his cheeks go pinker. He must be practically magenta by now. He passes over the coins, trying not to fumble them when their hands brush. "Here you go."

"Thanks, sunshine," the man says with a wink. He hitches his laundry sack higher on his shoulder and turns toward the machines. His daemon gives Warren and Minnie an open-mouthed canine grin, tongue lolling, before following after him.

Warren watches as the man dumps the contents of the cloth bag into a washer. It appears to be just regular clothes this time, no drop sheets in sight.

"Warren, you're starting again," Minnie whispers, nudging his shoulder with her nose.

"Am not," he denies futilely. "And anyway, so are you." She nips at his sleeve in retaliation.

He looks back down at his problem set, deciding he should at least try to maintain the pretense of studying. He feels lit up with nervous excitement, a livewire of emotion crackling beneath his skin. Had the beautiful man been flirting with him? And did *he* actually flirt *back?*
*Get it together, Warren,* he thinks. *This guy probably flirts on reflex. It doesn't mean anything.* He wipes his sweaty palms on his jean-clad thighs before picking up his pencil and determinedly getting back to work.

He's halfway through solving an equation when a shadow falls over the page. He looks up. The man is there again, leaning against the counter and angling his head to try to get a better look at Warren's textbook.

He gives a low whistle. "Thermodynamics?" he says. "Impressive. You're a student?"

Warren nods. His hand clenches around the pencil. "At Kale University."

"Ah, good old KU."

"You go there too?"

The man waves a dismissive hand. "For about half a semester. Wasn't really my speed."

"Oh," Warren says, unsure how to respond. In his peripheral he sees the two girls and their daemons leave, laundry carts rolling along behind them out the door.

The man shrugs. "It all worked out," he says with a self-deprecating smile. "Now I'm an entrepreneur."

"What kind of business are you in?"

"I own a coffee shop. Well, fifteen percent of a coffee shop. My friends own the other eighty-five."

"Which shop?" Warren asks curiously.

The man points out the window to the building directly across the street, the same one the woman with the cat daemon opens the door to most mornings. "The Palm. Best coffee in the city."

"I haven't tried it, but I'm sure you have no bias whatsoever."

The man grins, unrepentant. "Of course not." He looks consideringly at Warren for a moment, before adding, "My name is Johnny, by the way. JohnnyFontaine. This is Lucinda."

"Lucinda," his daemon corrects in a voice like velvet.

Minnie twitches at the sound of it, just once.

Warren's heartbeat quickens. "I'm Warren," he replies. He points to his daemon. "She's Minnie. It's nice to meet you both."

Johnny gives Warren a slow once-over, his gaze travelling up Warren's chest to the top of his curls and then back down again to meet his eyes. "The feeling is very mutual, Warren."

Before Warren can even attempt a response to that, they are interrupted by a loud metallic clang that echoes through the room and the sound of someone cursing vehemently. It's the boy with the dog daemon. He's muttering angrily at one of the dryers, pushing aggressively at the buttons and rattling the coin slider.

Warren gives Johnny an apologetic look, and then quickly moves from behind the counter. Minnie remains behind, lying low on her belly with her paws tucked beneath her. Only the sudden stiffness of her body belies her tension.

"What's wrong?" Warren asks, approaching the boy cautiously. "Can I help?"

"This piece of crap stopped halfway through the cycle!" he shouts, kicking at the machine again.

"Well, kicking it isn't going to fix anything," Warren says levelly. "Let me just try to—"

"Piss off," the boy interrupts. His daemon is standing between them, growling lowly. "You think I want to sit in this shithole for another hour while you mess around with this thing?"

"Hey," Johnny interjects. He's straightened from his loose-limbed slouch and is frowning at the boy. Lucinda is standing too, teeth bared and ears flat against her head as she stares down the dog daemon. "Don't be a podge. He's trying to help you."

Warren holds up a hand to forestall them. He's used to dealing with this: the machines are ancient and regularly break down, which generally results in annoyance all around.

"It's fine," he says calmly, walking back to the till and pulling out a few dollars in coins. "That machine isn't the most reliable. Here," he offers the coins to the boy, "try a different one."

The boy snatches them from the palm of Warren's hand and shoves them into his pocket. The rest of them watch as he pulls his damp clothes from the dryer, tossing them haphazardly into a plastic laundry basket. Then, instead of trying another machine, he goes to the door and wrenches it open, and he and his daemon stalk off into the night.

Minnie is trembling, just a bit. Warren doesn't think anyone would notice but him. He places a comforting hand on her back. Angry daemons always make them think of Daphne, his father's wolverine daemon, who dislikes Warren as much as his father does. She'd growled constantly at Minnie, always disapproving no matter how hard his daemon tried to please her. It had only gotten worse once she'd finally settled into her forever shape— Minnie is a sable and Daphne sees her as prey, dim-witted and inferior. Much the same way Warren imagines his father sees him.

"Well," Johnny says dryly, breaking the tense silence that has settled over the Laundromat, "that was certainly dramatic. Is it always so lively here?"

Warren shakes his head, smiling ruefully. "No. Usually everyone is half-asleep and avoids making eye contact."

Johnny huffs a laugh. "That sounds familiar. You just described the early morning coffee crowd."

"Do you work the opening shift?" Warren asks, for something to say. For some reason, he can't picture Johnny as a morning person.

To Warren's surprise, it's Lucinda who answers.

"Johnny hasn't seen a sunrise in months," she says, chuffing an amused breath.

"Lies and slander!" Johnny says in mock outrage. "I saw one just the other day, on our way home from the Big Block. Anyway, to answer your question: no, not unless I absolutely have to. I enjoy the nightlife."

"I guess that explains why you're here doing laundry at," Warren checks the time, "one thirteen in the morning."

Johnny's grin turns sly. "Maybe I just enjoy the company."

Warren flushes, and Minnie hides her eyes in the crook of his elbow. Johnny keeps saying things like that and Warren has no idea whether or not he's supposed to take him seriously.

"John," Lucinda says, headbutting him gently in the thigh. "You're going to give the poor kid a heart attack."

"Okay, okay. I'll dial back the charm." Johnny leans back against the counter, resting on his elbows. "So, tell me about thermodynamics."

They pass the time like that, discussing Warren's coursework. Johnny has surprisingly strong opinions on the Second Law of Thermodynamics, and seems to have no trouble whatsoever keeping up with Warren's admittedly rambling explanation of the Carnot cycle.

Warren keeps expecting Johnny to walk away, to go sit in the waiting area and pull out his phone like everyone else who comes in here. He half-wishes that he would, because his mind is spinning from the first real conversation he's had in weeks. His cheeks hurt from smiling and he knows he's speaking way too quickly, but he's actually having *fun* talking to Johnny, a near stranger. Minnie keeps sending him these sidelong glances like she can't believe it either.

Eventually Johnny's laundry is done and he gathers it up, stuffing it carelessly back into his cloth bag.

"Well," he says, slinging the bag over his shoulder. Lucinda pads over to his side and they stand at the threshold of the door. "Good luck on your test tomorrow."

"Today, actually. In about six hours."

"You're going to ace it."

"Thanks," Warren replies. "I hope so." His fingers knot together in his lap, hidden beneath the counter. "Have a good day, Johnny. Try not to sleep through all of it."

"Sure. Maybe I'll even catch that sunrise," Johnny says with a grin. "See you around, Warren."

Warren gives him a small wave as he steps out the door with Lucinda. "See you."

------

"I like them," Minnie says later on their bus ride back to the apartment. Her voice is quiet, as if she's telling him a secret.

"Me too."

"Do you think we'll see them again?"

Warren shrugs, ignoring the twist in his stomach. "Possibly. But don't get your hopes up, Minnie. They've never come in before this. It was probably just a weird week for them... I'd be surprised if they showed up again."

Minnie hums and settles deeper into his lap. "It might be nice," she murmurs, "to be surprised."

# CHAPTER 2

Warren is, in fact, surprised: Johnny and Lucinda do return to the Blue Wave Laundromat.

They come in once or twice a week to do laundry, but irregularly, and at seemingly random hours of the night. There is no pattern to their patronage that Warren can discern, and it keeps him on edge, his body thrumming with an undercurrent of anticipation that makes it difficult to concentrate on anything else. He spends his shifts alternating between watching the door, the window, and the old analog clock on the wall.

When they do come in, Johnny and Lucinda always hang out at the service counter chatting with him and Minnie. One night, Johnny drags over a chair to sit on, complaining good-naturedly about his aching feet, and from then on Warren keeps it waiting beside the counter for him.

At first Warren finds their presence overwhelming, so used to passing the time in silence with only his daemon for company. But Johnny is funny, and interesting, and kind beneath his bluster, and Warren finds that he genuinely enjoys spending time with him.

It doesn't hurt that he remains breathtakingly attractive.

The only problem is the flirting. Well, 'problem' implies that Warren doesn't like it— he *does* like it. He likes it too much. But after some observation, he's decided that it's meaningless. Johnny is the most extroverted person he has ever met, and Warren has mostly chalked their conversations up to him needing to stave off boredom while he waits for his laundry. Yet even though Warren doesn't think the flirtation is serious, he can't help but be charmed by Johnny. Maybe it's the way everything he says seems to be layered with good-natured self-deprecation— even his bragging seems like a joke that everyone else is in on. He is inherently likeable.

It takes a bit longer for Minnie, shy as she is, to warm up to their new companions. She spends the first few nights quiet and withdrawn, staying out of reach up on the countertop. But Johnny is friendly, and Lucinda is patient and unexpectedly astute, careful to keep her movements slow and nonthreatening. It doesn't take many visits before Minnie is down on the floor with the coyote daemon, whispering in her ear and making sly comments, mostly at Warren's expense.

They talk about anything and everything. Warren learns a whole slew of random facts about Johnny: that he is twenty-two years old, and that his favoritecolor is purple; that he speaks three languages, but can only write in two of them; that he loves apple syrup, but won't touch maple; and that for almost the entirety of his teenage years he and Lucinda were convinced she'd settle as a bird because of how much they both wanted to fly. Warren also learns that Johnny lives with his friend Zoe in the apartment above the coffee shop where they both work, and which Zoe apparently owns exactly fifty-one percent of because, as Johnny puts it, *He's such a control freak, Warren, you have no idea.*
Johnny and Zoe's other friend, Yolande, owns the remaining thirty-four percent of The Palm. Johnny tells him that the three of them met at university, and remained close friends even after Johnny dropped out mid-way through their first year. It doesn't seem to bother Johnny to tell Warren this, but he also doesn't offer up any details as to why he dropped out, and Warren is careful not to ask. Apparently, it had been Zoe's idea to buy the coffee shop, but Johnny had done most of the renovations and helped get the place operational while Zoe and Yolande were finishing up their degrees. That's how he'd earned his fifteen percent stake in the business despite being, in his words, *broke as fuck.* In turn, Warren tells Johnny the bare minimum about his situation with his father, just enough so that Johnny understands why he works thirty-two hours a week despite also being a full-time student.

Most of the time they are together he lets Johnny carry the conversation, content to follow his lead. Warren usually has coursework to complete, and Johnny seems interested enough to listen to him talk through it— sometimes he even helps Warren study, quizzing him on fluid mechanics or heat transfer equations. Their time together often feels surreal, like Warren tripped and fell into someone else's life for a few hours. He looks forward to it every week.

Just now, Johnny is tipping his chair back precariously, feet propped up on the counter ledge. He looks one wrong movement away from falling over, but when Warren points this out he only grins, and says, "I like to live on the edge," and it's so corny, but Warren snorts embarrassingly with laughter anyway.

It's that time of night where nothing feels quite real, that moment between the end of one day and the start of the next, when it seems as if the world is holding its breath in anticipation of dawn. On the floor, Lucinda is resting on her side, eyes closed but ears pricked to attention, legs stretched out in front of her. Minnie lies with most of her body draped across Lucinda's back, eyes half-lidded, looking like she could fall asleep at any moment. Her small form rises up and down in time with Lucinda's steady breathing, and it makes Warren drowsy just looking at them. He covers his mouth with the back of his hand as he stifles a yawn, thinking about how he'd love to cuddle up and snooze with someone the way his daemon is doing.

"Oh," Johnny says suddenly, letting his feet fall back to the floor with a thud. "I've been meaning to say: we should exchange numbers." When Warren just blinks at Johnny, thrown by the unexpected request, he adds wryly, "You know, in case I have any pressing laundry-related questions that just can't wait until I see you in person."

Warren knows he's joking, making light of his request in the face of Warren's peculiar reaction. Because, really, it's nothing special: people exchange phone numbers all the time, it's not a big deal. But for Warren, it kind of is. His stomach clenches.

"Here," Johnny is saying, "just add yourself to my contacts." He's smiling as he holds out his phone, but when Warren doesn't reach to take it, his expression falters "Or not," he says, drawing his hand back.

There's an awkward moment of silence. On the floor, Lucinda is watching them intently through slitted eyes, and Minnie is wide-awake, openly staring. When Warren meets her eyes she gives him a small nod.

"It's not that I don't..." Warren trails off nervously. He hates having this conversation with people. It always feels like such a risk, because once he reveals this part of himself their perception of him, for better or worse, will be forever altered. He looks down at his hands where they are twisting the hem of his sweater so he doesn't have to meet Johnny's gaze. Best to do this fast, like ripping off a bandage.

"I'm dyslexic," he says all in a rush. "I can't read. Well, I can a bit, but not easily, and it needs to be in a special font for me to even do that much, which I doubt you have on your phone— I mean, why would you?" He's rambling, he knows it, and he forces himself to stop, biting down hard on his lower lip. He looks up at Johnny.

Johnny is looking back at him, his expression indecipherable. "Oh. Okay," he says slowly, and it's the first time Warren can recall him sounding uncertain about something. "So…"

Warren takes a fortifying breath. "So," he says, unlocking his phone and offering it to Johnny, "this will be a lot easier if you just put your number in my phone instead."

A slow grin spreads across Johnny's face, lighting him up like a sunrise. "Yeah," he says. "I can do that." He takes Warren's phone, their fingertips brushing lightly in a way that makes Warren's heart flutter in his chest.

Warren watches as Johnny types in his information, then he takes his phone back and accesses WhatsApp from the newly created contact page. He has a dyslexic-friendly keyboard and font installed on his phone, of course, but it's still difficult to use unless he's really concentrating— which he's definitely not now, with Johnny's curious gaze fixed on him. He activates the dictation feature.

"Hello, Johnny," he says self-consciously into the phone, and hits send. A moment later, the screen on Johnny's phone lights up.

Johnny beams at it. "Excellent," he says, fingers flying as he taps at the screen. "I've added you to my contacts. Expect gorgeous selfies and terrible memes."

Warren laughs softly, breathless with relief. "I can hardly wait."

Johnny's expression turns serious and he leans forward to place his hand on Warren's shoulder, gripping gently. "Thanks for telling me," he says. "That was really brave."

There isn't a trace of pity in his voice, and Warren is achingly grateful for that. He swallows past the sudden lump in his throat. "No problem. It was kind of unavoidable."

"Still," Johnny insists, "thanks for trusting me."

Warren smiles at him. He feels buoyant, freer, the way he always does when he tells someone new and they react well. "You're welcome."

Johnny smiles back. He squeezes Warren's shoulder before settling back in his chair.

On the floor, Minnie is whispering something in Lucinda's ear, and Lucinda is grinning that open-mouthed canine grin of hers, tail swishing back and forth across the linoleum. Johnny has started telling a story about a nightmare customer he dealt with at the coffee shop recently, his hands gesticulating wildly as he speaks, and everything feels safe and good and normal.

*We're friends,* Warren suddenly realizes. *Johnny is my friend.*

And he's had a lot of new and strange experiences in the past six months, but this might be the strangest of them all.

------

When Warren arrives back at the apartment later that morning he still feels a bit like he's walking on air.

He enters their tiny kitchen, grabbing an apple from the bowl on the counter and a handful of trail mix from the reusable container in the cupboard. When he goes to open the refrigerator to get a drink, he sees that Karl has left him a note.

Karl, to his credit, has always been completely unphased by Warren's dyslexia. There is a whiteboard stuck magnetically to the fridge that Karl and his previous roommate used to write notes to each other, and when Warren moved in, Karl started using pictures instead of words, an accommodation that Warren didn't ask for, but for which he feels intensely grateful. Karl didn't make a big deal of it, just left Warren a doodle of a takeout container and a set of chopsticks with a question mark beside it one day. Since then, the two of them have been caught in a bizarre and oddly competitive game of Pictionary as they try to communicate across their vastly different schedules.

They rarely cross paths in person, with Warren working nights and the chaotic sleep schedule he adheres to when he's not in class. And Karl isn't often at the apartment— when he's not on campus, he has a whole group of friends he hangs out with, usually at the Castle Rock, a nearby cyber cafe the international students tend to frequent. He's never invited Warren to join them, but Warren is pretty sure he would decline anyway, so it works out.

They orbit around each other, peacefully sharing space, and Warren thinks Karl isn't actually a bad roommate. The only truly annoying thing about him is the way he manages to set the microwave on fire at least once a week.

Today, Karl has drawn what Warren is almost positive is supposed to be a pineapple, a carton of almond milk, and something that could either be an eggplant or a banana, he's not certain— Karl is kind of a crappy artist— so he assumes they need to go grocery shopping soon. He grabs the dry erase marker and quickly sketches a loaf of bread beneath the eggplant and/or banana.

"Strawberries too, please," Minnie pipes up, and Warren dutifully draws a strawberry. Daemons don't technically need to eat, the bond between human and daemon being usually enough to sustain them, but some daemons enjoy it. Minnie is one of those.

Warren finishes the apple and heads to his bedroom, setting the trail mix on the desk for Minnie to pick at. He pulls his phone from his pocket and activates the Voiceover function, then navigates to his contacts and double taps on Johnny's listing, the one Johnny entered himself only hours before.

"Handsome Johnny purple heart," intones the mechanical voice from his phone, and Warren's heart thumps in his chest. He sinks backward onto his mattress, feeling warm all over, and smiles stupidly up at the ceiling.

Minnie leaps onto the bed and presses herself along his side. "I'm really proud of you, Warren," she says, rubbing their cheeks together.

Warren scritches her ears. He's pretty proud of himself too.


------

It's nearing five o'clock on a dreary Thursday morning and Warren is in his usual spot behind the counter at the empty Laundromat, trying his best to stay awake, when his phone chimes. He opens WhatsApp and selects the text-to-speech function.

>>*Hey, Warren*
>>*I have to wash some stuff for work so I'm coming over to the BPL*

Warren grins down at his phone.

*Hello, Johnny,* he messages back. *Why are you awake?*
>>*I was working on a project, got sidetracked*
*Do you ever sleep?*
>>*do you?*
*Fair enough. We can both be sleep deprived idiots.*
>>*speak for yourself*
>>*I've embraced my nocturnal habits*
>>*mow*

Minnie sidles up to him. "Is that Johnny?" she asks eagerly. "Are he and Lucinda coming over?"

"Yes," says Warren, still smiling. "They're on their way now."

Minnie dashes to the window, planting her paws on the sill and leaning forward to press her face against the glass. "I see them!"

Warren tries to get his expression under control as Johnny opens the door to the Laundromat, a small wicker laundry basket tucked under his arm.

"Hello, sunshine," Johnny calls cheerily, ushering Lucinda into the room. She immediately lopes over to Minnie and begins snuffling at her fur as Minnie winds herself excitedly through her legs.

Warren's heart flips at the nickname. "Hi," he says. "This is a surprise... weren't you just in here two days ago?"

"Ah, aren't you glad to see me?" Johnny places a hand over his heart. "I'm hurt, Warren."

Warren can feel his cheeks heating. "I didn't say that," he mumbles, and Johnny laughs. The line of his throat when he tips his head back makes Warren's mouth go dry.

"Good," Johnny tells him, "Because I've got to get this stuff clean before opening or Zoe will beat me with his cane."

Johnny shrugs off his winter coat and tosses it carelessly onto a chair in the waiting area. He looks perfectly put together, even without sleep, in his usual skinny jeans and combat boots, this time paired with a light pink Henley that makes his dark skin look like it's glowing. Warren has to tear his gaze away, tugging self-consciously at his rumpled t-shirt.

"What stuff?" he asks.

Johnny holds up the wicker basket. "Aprons and dish towels for The Palm. I was supposed to wash them after closing yesterday, but I forgot."

Lucinda glances at him sidelong. "'Chose not to remember' might be more accurate."

"Quiet, you," Johnny grumbles good-naturedly, emptying the basket into the closest washing machine. He eyes his container of liquid detergent speculatively. "How much do you think I should use?"

Before Warren can respond, Minnie leaps up onto the rim of the washer and peers into the drum, head tilted. "Half a cap," she tells Johnny authoritatively.

"Thanks, darlin'," Johnny says, smiling at her. He pours in the detergent as instructed, then pulls some coins from his pocket and starts the machine.

Warren raises his eyebrows at his daemon behind Johnny's back. She sticks her tongue out at him in response before bounding over to join Lucinda, who is already sprawled out on the floor in front of the counter. Minnie plops herself right into the coyote daemon's space with no care for propriety, and Lucinda greets her with a friendly lick on the nose.

Johnny ambles over to the counter and pulls out his phone. "You have to see this TikTok," he says. "It will change your life."

The time passes quickly as it always does, the hours drifting away with the comfortable ebb and flow of their conversation, and before Warren knows it Johnny is pulling his laundry from the dryer. He hums thoughtfully, eyeing the pile of cloth in his basket.

"What is it?" asks Warren.

"Do you think these will get all wrinkled if I don't fold them?"

Warren rolls his eyes. "Bring them here," he says. "I'll help you."

Johnny beams at him. "You're a Saint."

They spend a while companionably folding aprons and towels together. Warren runs his fingertips over the logo on one of the black cotton aprons as he folds it. It's a stylized coffee mug with steam coming off the top, embroidered in white and silver thread.

"Huh," says Johnny. Warren looks up. Johnny is frowning at the clock on the wall. "It's almost six thirty. Aren't you supposed to be off at six?"

Warren nods, mouth twisting. "Yes, but I can't leave until Evana shows up."

"This happen a lot?"

"A couple times a week."

Johnny's frown deepens. "That's rude of her. You going to call Giles?"

Warren shrugs helplessly. "I mean, she's his girlfriend— I'm pretty sure he's going to give her a pass."

"Wow, corrupt," says Johnny, brows raised. "Isn't that like nepotism or something?"

"No idea," replies Warren. "Whatever it is, it means I've missed my bus."

"That sucks."

"Especially since I have class at nine today. Even if I catch the next one it means I'll have to turn around and come straight back here basically as soon as I get back to my apartment."

"You're in West Stave, right?" Johnny asks. "You really go all that way and then come back to the university district?"

"On Tuesdays and Thursdays when I have morning lectures, yes." Warren is starting to feel awkward about complaining. "But it's fine, I'll just go to campus early and study in the library or something."

Johnny shakes his head. "No, unacceptable," he says firmly. "Come over to the coffee shop with me. You can hang out there until your class starts."

Warren blinks at him. "I thought it didn't open until seven?"

"Sure, but I know the boss," Johnny responds with a wink.

Warren hesitates. Whatever is between him and Johnny feels delicate, almost dreamlike, sheltered as it is from outside influence by the relative isolation of the Laundromat. He's afraid that once exposed to the waking world it will shatter, and he'll lose this quiet intimacy he's come to enjoy so much.

"I don't know…" he starts.

Minnie interrupts him, her eyes wide and pleading. "Please, Warren?" she asks. "Please can we go? Lucinda says the biscuits are really good."

Warren is defenseless against her beseeching gaze. "I suppose," he answers slowly. "I mean if we really won't be in the way."

"Shane and Yolande won't mind," reassures Lucinda.

Johnny pats her head. "Lucinda is right," he says. "It'll be fine."

Warren, feeling distinctly outnumbered, nods his acquiescence.

By the time Evana finally arrives at twenty to seven, tapping away at her phone, they are packed up and ready to go. She stops in her tracks when she sees Johnny, but Warren doesn't pause to introduce them, just pulls on his coat and helps

Minnie settle on his shoulder, muttering a quick, "Bye, Evana," as he follows Johnny toward the exit.

Johnny nods to Evana on his way past. "Ma'am," he says, affording her the briefest courtesy. He holds the door for Lucinda and Warren, and then they're outside.

Warren huddles into his coat as the early morning air folds in around him, pulling his hands into his sleeves to keep them out of the wind. The sky is just starting to lighten as they cross the still mostly deserted street, treading carefully around the slushy puddles that litter the pavement like tiny, icy lakes. They step onto the sidewalk on the other side and approach a storefront with a sign above the door featuring all white letters in a bold, narrow typeface set against a black background.

"Here we are," Johnny says, and Warren can hear the pride in his voice. "The Palm."

He bends slightly to fit a key in the lock, and Warren glances curiously at the large window that takes up most of the exterior wall. The shades are drawn so he can't see inside, but he recognizes the coffee cup logo etched on the glass from the embroidery on the apron he folded earlier.

"Look," whispers Minnie near his ear. She is staring at the pride flag sticker affixed to the bottom left corner of the windowpane.

Warren smiles. "I see it," he whispers back.

The door unlocks with a click, and Johnny flashes Warren a quick grin over his shoulder as he pushes it open.

The smell hits him first, an inviting aroma of freshly ground coffee beans, earthy and rich, underlaid by something sweet, like caramelized sugar. It activates some kind of sense memory in his brain and his whole body perks up a bit at the promise of caffeine. Then he follows Johnny over the threshold and gets a good look at the interior of The Palm.

The space is warm and brightly lit, with natural wood floors and polished white surfaces embellished by gleaming copper accents. The back wall directly across from the door is exposed red brick from top to bottom; the rest of the walls are painted off-white, though they can hardly be seen beneath the veritable sea of framed art in a variety of colors and media that adorns them. Half a dozen small, round tables with chairs are arranged around the room, along with a comfortable-looking black velvet couch and two armchairs upholstered in a violet and cream pinstripe fabric. Perches and small animal beds are scattered throughout the room for daemons, which is a courtesy that not all establishments offer. Above all of it, strings of single filament light bulbs crisscross the ceiling like strewn stars. The whole effect is incredibly welcoming, as if he'd just stepped into someone's home instead of a business.

A familiar woman with a long black braid and piercings lining each ear is standing behind the service counter pouring beans into the hopper on one of the espresso machines. She looks up in surprise as Warren and Johnny enter the shop.

"Johnny," she says, her voice soft and sweetly lilting. "You're here early." She turns her gaze to Warren. "I recognize you. You work at the Laundromat across the street, right?"

Warren nods, but before he can introduce himself, Johnny jumps in .

"Yolande," he says, placing a hand on Warren's back and guiding him gently forward, "this is Warren. He's just been tragically inconvenienced by a fellow employee, so I thought we'd help him out by giving him a place to stay until his class starts later this morning. Warren," he continues, "this Yolande, the platonic love of my life and an all-around spectacular person. I have an inkling that you two will get along *splendidly.*"

Yolande rolls her eyes a bit at Johnny's theatrics. Then she smiles at Warren, a real one that meets her eyes. "Nice to officially meet you."

"You too," Warren tells her, and means it.

Lucinda has made her way to the couch where a small black cat daemon— presumably the aforementioned Shane— lounges with watchful amber eyes. Warren hadn't even noticed him at first glance, camouflaged as he is against the black upholstery, silent and still as a statue. Lucinda greets him with a gentle whiff, and the cat daemon rubs his cheek against hers in affectionate response. Minnie watches them avidly from her perch on Warren's shoulder.

Johnny hangs his coat on a rack near the door and motions for Warren to pass his over. Warren hastens to comply, dislodging Minnie as he sheds his navy pea coat.

She leaps to the floor and lingers shyly near his feet with her tail wrapped around his ankle.

"Is Zoe here?" Johnny asks, hanging Warren's coat over his own on the rack.

Yolande shakes her head. "He's gone to the bakery."

Johnny hums in acknowledgment. He goes around the counter and starts unloading the wicker laundry basket into a drawer beneath the counter. "Since I'm here I may as well help with opening today," he says, slightly muffled. "Zoe can catch up on planning for world domination or whatever it is he does in his office all day."

"That'd be great," she replies. "Thanks, John."

Warren is still standing awkwardly by the door, hand gripping the shoulder strap of his messenger bag. He's not sure what he's supposed to do now that he's here.

Yolande comes to his rescue, focusing her gaze on him as she stacks paper takeaway cups near the cash register. "So you're a student?" she asks him.

"Warren is an engineering major," Johnny says brightly, pulling an apron over his head and reaching back to tie it in one swift movement. "He's very smart," he adds, grinning at Warren over Yolande's shoulder.

Warren blushes, his fingers tightening around the shoulder strap.

Yolande looks at Warren with interest. "My mother is an environmental engineer," she says.

"Really?" Warren replies, nerves momentarily forgotten. "I considered that field. There are a ton of amazing real-world applications."

Yolande nods. "It's true, there's lots of work to do everywhere— especially back home, where my mother lives," she says. "Which discipline are you in?"

"Mechanical," he answers. "I'm also doing a minor in music."

"What?" Johnny gasps dramatically. "You never told me that! I thought we were friends, Warren." He sets his elbows on the counter and leans forward, grey eyes gleaming. "So what instrument do you play?"

"The flute."

Johnny's grin is shark-like. "Oh, that is too perfect."

Warren is saved from responding by the jingle of the bells above the door as someone opens it.

A man enters, his shoulder braced against the door as he pushes it wide. He's handsome, Warren can't help but notice, with an angular jaw and cheekbones so sharp they could cut glass. His dark undercut hair is styled meticulously, and he's wearing a long black trench coat that accentuates the lean lines of his body. In one hand he carries a silver-topped cane; in the other is a large white bakery box, held securely against his chest. His crow daemon is perched like a grim sentinel on his shoulder, black eyes glinting as she regards them all with a keen gaze. The man seems unphased by the eyes on him, his expression stoic as walks to the counter with an almost imperceptible limp.

Yolande smiles as he approaches. "Hello, Zoe," she says, reaching out to help slide the box onto the counter. Warren can't read the cursive label on its side, but he does note the stylized sun embossed in gold on the top flap.

Zoe nods in greeting. "Yolande." He turns to look at Johnny, raising one brow in silent query.

"Zoe," Johnny says hastily, "this is Warren. He works at the Blue Wave."

"Terrific," Zoe responds, dry as bone. "Any reason he's in my shop before opening?"

Johnny rolls his eyes. "Relax, it's like five minutes until opening. I invited him."

Zoe gives Warren an appraising look. It almost feels like he's passing judgment, and Warren shifts on his feet, uncomfortably reminded of his father. The crow daemon opens her beak just slightly, her dark gaze intent on Minnie, who shrinks back against Warren's leg, pressing her body low to the ground.

"Hi," Warren says, with a meek little wave that he immediately hates himself for. "Nice to meet you. This is Minnie," he adds, gesturing to her.

"A pleasure," rasps Zoe, inflectionless. He doesn't offer his daemon's name in return. He turns back to Johnny. "Since you're here, you may as well stock the display case."

Johnny gives him a mock salute. "Sure thing, boss."

Without another word, Zoe walks away toward the back of the store and disappears through an unmarked door. Warren breathes out a sigh of relief as he shuts it behind him.

Lucinda and Shane wander over to join the rest of them, Shane leaping gracefully to a perch mounted on the wall behind the counter. Lucinda settles on the floor beneath it, her limbs tucked close to her body, safely out of treading range.

Johnny lifts the bakery box to the top of the tall glass display case and opens the lid. Inside, the box is two-tiered and absolutely filled to the brim with baked goods— muffins, danishes, biscuits, and even cupcakes, delicately iced with red and pink hearts. Minnie comes out from behind Warren and stands up on her hind legs, sniffing the air curiously as Johnny begins to transfer the pastries to the display case. He tosses her a rogue raisin, which she catches midair before scampering away to burrow herself into Lucinda's side.

"So that was Zoe," Johnny says, lining up an array of muffins on the top shelf. He fixes Warren with a knowing look. "He's something, right?"

Warren bites his lip. "He seems... intense."

"That's one word for it," Johnny chuckled. "Don't worry: he's actually a big softie once you get to know him."

Lucinda snorts. "Don't let Zoe hear you say that."

"The crow knows all," Shane intones in a silky voice.

Minnie shudders, squirming closer to Lucinda. "She was so scary! I thought she was going to fly down and peck me."

"No," responds Shane. "She's just cautious, and for good reason. She wouldn't hurt you."

"No one will hurt you here," Lucinda adds, nuzzling at the spot between Minnie's ears.

Yolande shakes her head at the lot of them and walks around the counter to start raising the window shades, letting in the weak winter light. Outside, Warren can see a line of customers already queuing up on the sidewalk in front of The Palm, most of them with a reusable travel mug in hand. When Yolande flips the sign on the door, they begin shuffling forward, eager to escape the cold.

"So, Warren," Yolande says, making her way back to the till, "you're first in line: what can I get you?"

"Um…" Warren says stupidly. He hadn't actually considered ordering anything. The blackboard menu hanging on the wall behind the service counter is of no use to him, the handwritten chalk characters merging together in an unreadable jumble of white text. But it feels like it would be strange not to get something, so he tells her, "Just a black coffee, please."

He slips a hand into his pocket and pulls out some coins, handing them over to Yolande. It's his bus fare for today but he figures he can walk back to the apartment after school, which he generally tries to do anyway to save money.

"You're staying here for a while, right?" Yolande says, passing him back his change. Warren pours it into the tip jar without counting it. "I can put your coffee in a mug for you."

"Yolande is really passionate about sustainability," stage whispers Johnny. "Every time she fills a takeaway cup, she dies a little inside."

Yolande pokes him in the side with her elbow, but doesn't deny it.

"A mug would be great, thanks," replies Warren.

He moves aside to wait for his drink as the next person in line steps forward. Johnny has finished stocking the display case, and he takes Yolande's place behind the cash register as she begins filling drink orders. They dance around each other with practiced ease in the small space, Yolande's every movement graceful and deliberate, Johnny gesticulating charmingly as he greets customers.

Warren's eyes drift to the curve of Johnny's mouth, and he is surprised by how easy it is to spot the difference between the performative smile he dons now and the one he gives Warren in the privacy of the Laundromat. Warren misses the crinkles around his eyes, the mischievous tilt to the corners of lips, but at the same time he is ardently glad that there is a part of Johnny he gets to see that these people don't.

He makes himself look away before anyone notices him staring. His gaze is drawn to the hanging art piece that takes up most of the exposed brick wall at the back of the shop. It is rectangular in shape, composed of latticed strips of dark metal arranged in a gridlike pattern. Small, somewhat abstract triangular shapes made of a lighter, shinier metal are scattered across it, starting bunched together in the bottom corner and spreading farther apart as they reach the opposite corner at the top. The way they are spaced gives the impression of motion, and it brings to Warren's mind the image of a flock of birds taking flight.

Yolande catches him studying the metalwork as she hands him his coffee. "Do you like it?"

Warren nods. "I've never seen anything like it," he answers honestly.

Yolande's expression turns sly. "Johnny made it."

"Really?"

"Oi, Yolande!" Johnny interjects. "Come on— don't give away all my secrets at once."

"I didn't know you were an artist," says Warren.

"I'm not," Johnny protests, looking away. He scrubs his hand over the back of his neck. "It's nothing, really. Just a hobby I picked up."

"Bullshit," sing-songs Yolande, passing behind him to the sink.

Johnny sticks his tongue out at her before pointedly turning his attention back to the line of customers.

Warren is eminently curious, but decides to broach the subject again later when he's alone with Johnny. Instead, he leaves Johnny and Yolande to their work and goes to sit at a table near the window. Minnie rises from her spot by Lucinda and follows him. She leaps onto the tabletop and settles close to the ceramic mug Warren sets down, soaking in the secondhand warmth radiating from the steaming beverage.

Warren takes a sip of his coffee— it's good, not as bitter as some he's had before, smooth and easy to drink. Perhaps Johnny's boast about it being the 'best coffee in the city' has some merit after all, not that Warren is all that qualified to judge. He pulls out his phone and queues up an audiobook. He's about to slip his headphones on when the door jingles, and a flash of color makes him raise his eyes.

A tall woman in a striking red wool coat enters the coffee shop. She is objectively beautiful, her makeup perfect, her glossy brown hair tied back in a high ponytail with a few curled tendrils left loose to artfully frame her face. Her bird daemon— some kind of parrot, maybe, Warren thinks— is perched on her shoulder imperiously, his brightly colored feathers almost a perfect match to the bold shade of her coat. The woman walks confidently toward the service counter, heeled boots clicking noisily as she crosses the floor, heedless of the heads turning in her direction.

"Ooh," she says, stopping in front of the glass display case. "Are these the Valentine's Day cupcakes? I saw them on Instagram. Alina's really outdone herself."

Johnny is beaming at her from behind the counter. "Nadia!" he exclaims. "Can I tempt you?"

Jealousy flares in Warren's gut as the woman— Nadia— flashes Johnny a flirty smile. "Always," she purrs. "I'll take a red velvet one."

"That's it?" Johnny asks doubtfully, nodding distractedly at a customer as he passes them their change. "Come on, I know you love Alina's shortbread."

"Of course I do, it's delicious," Nadia says dismissively, "but I have a seminar to get to this morning. I'll get Jonas to pick me up some later. There'll be more, right? Valentine's Day isn't until Monday."

Before Johnny can respond, Zoe appears. "Back of the line, Nadia," he orders gruffly.

"Zoe!" Nadia greets him in a voice gone saccharine. Her daemon shifts slightly on her shoulder, feathers ruffling. "So nice to see you out of the crypt."

Zoe scowls at her. "Don't forget who controls your caffeine supply."

"You're delusional if you think Yolande and Johnny wouldn't smuggle it out for me, Barlow," Nadia replies sweetly, but she moves to the back of the line, exchanging a long-suffering glance with Johnny as she goes.

Warren looks away from the scene, feeling a bit like an intruder. A glance at his phone shows him that he has almost an hour before he needs to start heading to campus, and exhaustion settles over him like a heavy blanket as he remembers he still has a full day of school ahead of him. Minnie yawns widely and slinks beneath the table, kneading at his thighs as she curls herself onto his lap.

"Don't fall asleep," Warren warns, stroking her head.

"Never," she replies drowsily. "I'm just resting my eyes."

"You do that," he says indulgently, putting on his headphones. He folds his arms on top of the table and rests his head on them, thinking he'll just close his eyes for a moment...

"Hey, Warren," someone is saying. There is a hand on his shoulder, shaking him gently.

Warren scrunches up his face and shifts away from whomever is trying to wake him. He wants to sleep just a little longer.

"Warren. You're going to be late."

"Hmm?" He opens his eyes, blinking blearily at his surroundings, and for a moment he has no idea where he is. *The Palm,* his fuzzy brain supplies. When he looks up, Johnny is standing over him, an amused expression on his face. "What time is it?" Warren asks sleepily.

"Eight forty-five," says Johnny.

That snaps him back to consciousness. "Crap." He stands and scrambles for his belongings, holding his messenger bag open so Minnie can jump inside. Johnny has Warren's coat draped over one arm, and Warren takes it from him, donning it hurriedly with a murmured, "Thank you."

Johnny hands him a takeaway cup. "Refill, on the house." He holds out a paper bag. "And a muffin from me. It's chocolate," he adds with a grin.

"You're the best," Warren tells him gratefully, taking the bag. "Thanks for everything this morning." He hesitates, then says, "I'll talk to you later?"

"Yeah, for sure," Johnny replies. Warren starts for the door, but Johnny stops him with a palm to his chest. "Wait," he says. "Let me just…"

Then he reaches up and slides his long fingers into Warren's hair. Warren stops breathing, heart clenching in his chest. Johnny seems oblivious as he combs carefully through the messy curls, his fingernails scratching lightly against Warren's scalp as he works.

It's absolutely devastating.

When Johnny finishes ordering Warren's hair to his satisfaction, he drops his hand. "There," he says, smiling softly. "Much better."

Warren's head is still tingling, little sparks of pleasure shooting up and down his spine like firecrackers. He can't speak. All he can do is nod dumbly at him, and hope the expression on his face is something approaching normal as he turns to leave the coffee shop.

The phantom touch of Johnny's fingers in his hair haunts him all the way to campus.

# CHAPTER 3

Warren spends the weekend in an academic haze as he prepares for his upcoming midterms. He practices equations until the numbers blur together before his eyes, then listens to his audio textbooks for hours, trying to commit them to memory.

By the time Monday rolls around he is completely fed up with studying, and halfway convinced he should just drop out of school and go live in a forest somewhere like some kind of crazy, flute-playing hermit. He just wants things to be easy for once.

"Life isn't supposed to be easy, you know that," Minnie says in her gentle way.

Warren sighs. "I just feel stuck. Like I don't know where I'm going, or what I should do next."

"Well, running away won't help anything," she reasons. "Besides, why would living *by ourselves in a forest* make anything easier? What would we *eat,* Warren?"

And, well, it's hard to argue with the manifestation of your soul.

Classes are difficult that day, as Warren's tired mind struggles to keep up. Everything he'd memorized over the weekend seems to be locked away in his brain, just out of reach. He flubs his Mechanical Design presentation that afternoon, and while the DSA allows him extra time on exams, he just barely gets through the one for his Fluid Mechanics class. He leaves the exam room with a sinking feeling in his stomach, unsure whether or not he passed despite the hours of study he'd put in over the weekend. It leaves him feeling so frustrated he could cry.

He arrives late to orchestra practice and has to do the awkward shuffle of shame to his chair in the middle of the already-seated second row, while the conductor looks on disapprovingly. It's mortifying, and he's so unnerved by the experience that he loses his place partway through the fourth movement of Dvořák's Symphony No. 9 and never quite recovers for the rest of rehearsal.

By the time he boards the bus back to his apartment at the end of the day, he's in such a foul mood that even Minnie doesn't want to talk to him anymore. It doesn't help that the bus is crowded with the usual mass of evening commuters, only today everyone seems to be carrying red and pink bouquets, giant helium balloons, or cutesy stuffed animals holding hearts, reminding Warren that on top of everything else it's also Valentine's Day. He'd barely even noticed the date until now, but suddenly it feels like the holiday is being shoved down his throat. He spends the rest of the commute staring sullenly out the window.

When he goes to work later that night he finds the Laundromat populated by people who look just as miserable as he feels, and is immediately accosted by a rude woman who claims that one of the dryers put holes in her favorite blouse. She wants to be financially compensated for the price of a replacement, and Warren spends half an hour trying to explain the laundromat's liability policy to her.

After that he spills laundry detergent all over the front of his sweater while filling the small bottles for in-store sale, and has to rifle through the lost and found for something else to wear. He finds a baby blue t-shirt with a glittery pink cursive slogan across the chest. From the fit, it's very obviously a woman's shirt, but it's the only thing he can find that's even remotely wearable and he honestly just doesn't care anymore: it's a shirt, it'll do.

"Gender is just a social construct anyway," Minnie helpfully reminds him.

By three o'clock in the morning he's slumped defeatedly in his chair, listlessly scrolling through his phone.

Then Johnny enters the Laundromat, carrying his usual cloth laundry bag and a small bakery box balanced on the palm of one hand— and Warren sits up with a start. In his misery, he'd completely forgotten that Johnny had messaged earlier to let him know he would be stopping by.

As soon as he catches sight of Warren, Johnny bursts into surprised laughter. "What are you *wearing?*"

Warren crosses his arms over his chest defensively. "Hello to you too," he says. "There may have been an, uh... unfortunate, detergent-based catastrophe."

Johnny's brow furrows. "And this shirt was the solution?" he asks skeptically.

"Warren looks good in blue," says Minnie, ever loyal.

"Oh, I agree," Johnny assures her with a grin. "That's not the part that's funny."

Dread pools in Warren's stomach. "Oh, no. What does it say?"

"I'm not sure I should tell you."

"Johnny."

"Do you really want to know?"

Warren braces himself. "Just tell me."

"It says…" Johnny pauses for effect. " *'Daddy's Girl'*."

Warren's face feels like it's on fire. "You're lying."

"I'm not!"

"Lucinda, please tell me he's lying," says Warren, looking pleadingly at her.

She shakes her head. "Sorry, Warren. It's true."

"No," he moans, covering his face with his hands. "I've been wearing this for hours!"

"Oh, dear," says Minnie, but he can tell she's trying not to laugh.

"Traitor," Warren accuses, halfheartedly.

Johnny pats his shoulder. "There, there. It could be worse."

*"How?"*

"I'll get back to you on that one."

Warren sighs. "What a perfect ending to this terrible day."

Johnny places the bakery box on the counter and slides it toward him. "Maybe this will make you feel better."

"What is it?" Warren asks, peeking through his fingers.

"Leftovers," he answers, opening the box. Inside is a small assortment of baked goods, all of them decorated in various combinations of red, pink, and white, some featuring expertly piped hearts or roses. "It's the last of the Valentine's Day stock from The Palm."

Warren lowers his hands. "You brought these for me?"

"Yep," says Johnny, drumming his fingers against the sides of the box.

Lucinda nudges the side of Johnny's leg. "Give Minnie hers," she says, "before she starts drooling all over the counter."

Minnie's tail trembles with restrained elation. She fixes entreating eyes on Johnny. "I can have one?"

*Absolutely shameless,* Warren thinks. He doesn't know whether to be impressed or concerned.

Johnny smiles knowingly at her. "Of course, beautiful. I brought something special just for you." He reaches into the bottom of the box and pulls out a biscuit, one that appears to consist mostly of nuts and seeds, with a heart drawn on it in pink icing. Minnie's eyes widen at the sight of it.

Johnny holds it out for her to take, glancing briefly at Warren as he does so. He's more still than Warren has ever seen him, his hand perfectly motionless so that he doesn't accidentally touch Minnie as she reaches for the biscuit.

It's one of the most ingrained rules of society: daemons can touch other daemons, but a human touching someone else's daemon without explicit consent is the worst kind of violation. Warren knows Johnny wouldn't touch Minnie without permission— he *knows* that— but he still finds himself holding his breath as his daemon leans forward, her muzzle stretching toward Johnny's hand.

Then Minnie's clever teeth snatch the biscuit from Johnny's grasp, narrowly avoiding grazing his fingertips, and the moment ends, all of them left unchanged.

Warren exhales, feeling strangely disappointed. He thinks he senses Johnny's eyes on him again, but when he glances over to check, Johnny is watching Minnie instead.

"So good," she enthuses, either oblivious to the tension or purposefully ignoring it. Crumbs cling to her whiskers.

Johnny nods once. "Good," he says, seemingly unaffected. "Warren, you better start on those cupcakes before your daemon gets designs on them. I've got to get this stuff in the washer." He goes to start his laundry, leaving Warren to consider his cupcake options.

Warren stares blankly into the box as he attempts to compose himself, his thoughts a maelstrom of confusion and longing. *Do I want Johnny to touch Minnie?* he wonders. *Does* she *want that?*
The last person to touch Minnie other than himself had been his mother, a long time ago now. He knows it's a common thing that people do in close relationships, but it's just so... *intimate.*
He's been attracted to other people before— as few and far between as those instances may have been— has fantasized about having someone he belonged with, someone to hold and kiss, someone to touch and be touched by in return. But he's never imagined anyone touching *Minnie.* It had never felt right, not even in his imagination. He doesn't know what it is about this relationship that's different, that's making him wonder *what if?*

Not that he and Johnny are in a relationship. He's not even sure if Johnny is interested in men.

*So stop thinking about it,* Warren tells himself firmly. *It's not up to you anyway.*

Eventually he decides on a chocolate cupcake delicately iced with pink and while swirls. He lifts it from the box, then takes out a red velvet cupcake for Minnie, who is almost finished with her biscuit, and sets it on the counter for her. He looks questioningly at Lucinda, tilting the box toward her in silent offer.

Lucinda declines with a slight shake of her head. "I'm not big on sweets. I leave that for John," she says, wry.

It's a familiar tone from Johnny's daemon, who seems to be perpetually amused by some joke to which only she is privy. Warren is used to Minnie, who rarely hesitates to speak her mind, but as much as he appreciates his daemon's straightforwardness, he can admit to being intrigued by Lucinda's more enigmatic nature.

Warren shrugs, carefully peeling off the paper liner on his cupcake before biting into it— even after a day of sitting in a glass display case, it tastes heavenly. *Johnny brought these for me,* he remembers, and feels lighter at the thought.

"You are seriously missing out," he tells Lucinda, who only lolls her tongue at him in response.

"I'll have hers," Minnie mumbles around a mouthful of cake.

Warren gently pinches her side. "Don't be greedy."

Johnny returns to the counters and settles in his usual chair. He leans back and stretches his long legs out in front of him, ankles crossed. "So what's the verdict?"

"They're delicious," Warren says, sucking some stray icing off the tip of his thumb.

Johnny clears his throat a bit and looks away. "Glad to hear it."

"How was your Valentine's Day?" asks Warren, when the silence stretches just a little too long.

"Well, I was working for most of it," says Johnny. "Yolande and I got to critique all the awkward dates happening in the shop. We even came up with a rating system."

"That actually sounds kind of fun."

"Viciously mocking strangers with your friends is always a good time. Oh!" Johnny exclaims, his eyes lit with sudden glee. "I forgot that I have gossip to share! So get this: a *mysterious someone* left Yolande a bouquet of wild geraniums in the back room… but it was Zoe— *everyone* knows it was Zoe. He's been pining over her for *four years,*" he grouses. "I hope this means he's finally got his shit together."

"Wow," says Warren. "I never would have guessed. It kind of seems like he hates everyone."

Lucinda huffs in amusement. "Look closer and you'll notice that he hates Yolande just marginally less."

"True love," Johnny sighs mockingly.

Warren laughs. He's not sure if it's the sugar or the company, but he's starting to feel a lot better about life. He's even mostly forgotten about the damned shirt.

"So," Johnny smirks mischievously at him, "you're a flautist."

Warren has been waiting for this. "And you're an artist," he counters.

Johnny straightens, uncrossing his ankles and setting his feet flat on the floor. "Like I said, it's just a hobby."

Warren raises an eyebrow. "Pretty amazing for a hobby."

Johnny picks up Warren's discarded cupcake liner and starts folding it into squares. "I know some people in the industry and I… I just kind of picked it up. My friend Alisha is a glassblower and she lets me borrow her studio when she's not using it— which is usually at night, so..."

Something clicks into place in Warren's memory. "Ah. The drop cloths. Those were from the studio?"

"Yeah."

"And that's why you're up so late at night."

"Sometimes, yes."

Warren considers this. "But metal sculpting… come on, it's so cool that you do that."

"Really, it's nothing," protests Johnny. Lucinda makes a soft noise of disagreement, but Johnny quickly speaks over her, adding, "Alisha, though— now *she's* an artist. You should see some of her stuff, it's incredible."

Warren thinks this may be the first time he's heard true modesty from him, real and unmasked. It makes something tighten in his chest. He feels oddly protective, like he wants to shield Johnny from his own self-doubt, the way Warren wishes he could do for himself.

But before he can comment, Johnny leans forward and slaps his palms down on the counter. "Okay, your turn: tell me about the flute."

"There's not much to tell," Warren says with a shrug. "I've been playing since I was little, and I like it. It's probably the only thing I'm naturally good at," he confesses.

"He's *very* good at it," amends Minnie, who has been quietly listening to them talk while she cleans cake from her paws.

Warren blushes. "I've had a lot of practice."

Johnny hums thoughtfully, tipping his chair back. "And you have no problem with, you know…" He trails off, seeming unsure of how to continue.

"Reading the music?" finishes Warren, to spare him. "No, I've always been able to read it. Notes don't get mixed up the way words do." For once it doesn't hurt to admit that.

Minnie butts her head against his chest affectionately and Warren wraps an arm around her, squeezing briefly before she wriggles away from him to join Lucinda on the floor.

After that their conversation naturally progresses to music and musical tastes, and they begin a meandering discussion of their favorite artists and genres. Johnny claims to like old punk rock and modern hip hop, and not much in between—though Lucinda slyly cuts in to tease him about his secret love of country pop, which Johnny vehemently denies. Warren's tastes are more eclectic: he's drawn to anything he feels a connection with, regardless of genre. They spend some time taking turns sharing songs on their phones before they are interrupted by the ding of the washing machine, and Johnny leaves to move his clothes to the dryer.

Warren yawns, slouching down in his seat as a wave of exhaustion breaks over him. It's easy to forget when he's with Johnny, but it's almost four thirty in the morning and it's been over twenty hours since he last slept. When he glances out the window he can see by the reflection of streetlights on wet pavement that it's started raining again. He shivers at the thought of having to wait at the bus stop in this weather, rubbing his hands over his bare upper arms to ward off the sudden chill.

"Hey, are you cold?" Johnny asks, frowning as he returns to the counter.

"A bit," Warren admits. "I think I might just wear my coat."

Johnny starts unzipping his hoodie. "Naw, just take this. Much comfier."

"But… won't *you* be cold?"

He waves a dismissive hand. "I've got more drying as we speak. I'll just grab one of those later." He holds out the hoodie, shaking it enticingly. It's mostly black, emblazoned with a purple chevron across the chest, and has the faded look of a well-worn favorite. "Take it."

Warren does.

"Thanks," he murmurs, slipping it on over his shoulders. It's soft, and warm from Johnny's residual body heat— and also far too big on him, the cuffs of the sleeves dangling over his hands. He feels a bit ridiculous in it, but then he looks up and sees Johnny staring at him and the expression on his face is… well, Warren isn't sure exactly *what* it is, but he doesn't think it's bad.

It makes him feel a little giddy, actually, heat rushing to his cheeks. He curls into himself a bit, sniffing subtly at the hoodie's collar, inhaling the familiar aroma of Johnny's soap and deodorant, a heady combination of citrus and spice and skin, and of course the faint scent of coffee that underlies everything. It smells like concentrated Johnny, equal parts thrilling and comforting, and Warren wants to stay wrapped in it forever.

*I am never returning this hoodie,* he decides, and zips it closed with conviction, concealing the wretched lost and found t-shirt from view.

"Better?" Johnny asks.

Warren nods. "Much."

Johnny smiles at him, and Warren suddenly realizes that he is in nothing but a fitted white t-shirt. His eyes travel helplessly across Johnny's lightly muscled chest and arms, getting caught on the tattoos peeking out from beneath the bottom of his left sleeve.

"Like what you see?" says Johnny, distinctly smug.

"Um…"

"It's okay, you don't have to say it— I know I look good." Johnny tracks Warren's gaze to his arm. "Ah. You want to see them?"

Warren swallows, and tries to sound as casual as possible when he says, "Sure."

Johnny angles in closer to him and pulls his shirt up above his shoulder.

Warren's breath catches as he gets a better look at the tattoos, arranged in a half sleeve that covers Johnny's shoulder and continues wrapping down his arm to the top of his elbow. They're intricate, inked in bold, sweeping lines and swirls of vibrant color, not a bare patch of skin to be found. Some of the tattoos are abstract in shape, but most are not: Warren notes a pair of crossed revolvers, a king of hearts, and a set of cracked dice skewered on a dagger. The designs blend into each other, newer tattoos overlapping older ones like patchwork, and he wishes he had hours to study it all. Central to everything is a rabbit inked in brown and grey and white, depicted with long, black-tipped ears, and wreathed in sprigs of pink cherry blossoms.

"It's a jackrabbit," Johnny tells him quietly, tapping one finger against the tattoo. "My mother's daemon. She died when I was young."

"Mine too," Warren murmurs. "Her daemon was a nightingale." Impulsively, he reaches out and touches one of the jackrabbit's ears, brushing gently from base to tip.

Johnny inhales sharply.

Warren hastily draws his fingers back. "Sorry, I'm so sorry. I didn't—"

"No," Johnny says, grasping Warren's retreating hand. "It's okay. You can touch. I just wasn't expecting it."

He places Warren's hand back on his arm, his gaze intent. Warren has to look away from whatever emotion is shining in those moon-grey eyes. Instead, he starts to move his fingers lightly over Johnny's arm, continuing where he left off delicately tracing the curves of the jackrabbit's ears. On the floor nearby, their daemons are absolutely silent, pressed so tightly together that their fur blends in places, dark and tawny brown, like they are one creature instead of two.

Warren's heart beats like a hummingbird trapped in his chest. When he reaches the apex of the tattoo he changes the direction of his movement, skimming his fingers slowly downwards across the jackrabbit's back.

Johnny makes a small noise. Warren bites his lip, feeling flushed from head to toe. He thinks he might be trembling, but he can't focus on anything beyond the sensation of warm skin beneath his fingertips.

When he's mapped every line of the tattoo, Warren reluctantly draws away. He tucks his hands into the pockets of the hoodie, feeling bereft.

"Your tattoos are... really beautiful," he says softly, and it comes out hoarser than he'd like. He still can't quite meet Johnny's eyes.

Johnny's voice is soft too, when he says, "I'm glad you think so." Then he clears his throat and leans away, letting his sleeve fall back into place. "So, uh— it's Tuesday. You have class this morning right? Are you coming to The Palm to kill time before?"

"Yes," says Warren, nerves still thrumming with repressed desire. "Yes, I think I will."


------


It becomes routine on the days when Warren has a morning class for him to go to The Palm after he finishes his shift at the Laundromat. Sometimes Johnny walks over with him, but it doesn't take long for Warren to start going on his own.

The first time he'd done so he'd been extremely hesitant, even though Johnny had assured him that he'd talked it over with Yolande and she was fine with having Warren in the shop before opening. Warren had knocked timidly on the door upon arrival, but Yolande had unlocked it and waved him inside without any apparent concern.

"Warren, you know you're welcome here, right?" she'd told him. "Johnny's vouched for you and that's more than enough for me."

Touched by her kindness and wanting to be useful, Warren had helped her set up the dining area and prepare the self-serve milks and sugars, even though she'd insisted it wasn't necessary. They'd chatted for a bit, easy as anything, until it was seven and Yolande had needed to open the shop.

After that he's more comfortable. There is something inherently welcoming about The Palm— the variety of clientele he witnesses attests to that: university students, of course; some of the corporate crowd in the mornings; stay-at-home parents in need of an afternoon caffeine fix; and a whole slew of locals from every walk of life, many of them artists. It's also very obviously a queer-friendly space, practically a community hotspot, and Warren feels safe in a way he's not sure he's ever experienced in a public place before.

He develops a rapport with Yolande, and more often than not she has a drink waiting for him when he arrives. Warren enjoys talking to her, appreciative of her open-minded way of looking at the world. She is soft-spoken, but not shy, and has strong sociopolitical opinions that she upholds with conviction.

Minnie becomes friendlier with Shane too, put at ease by the cat daemon's calm and steady demeanor. It helps that Lucinda— whom Minnie has come to trust implicitly in these matters— is so obviously close with Shane. When Johnny and Lucinda are there, the three daemons usually forgo conversing with their humans to sit side by side on the couch, talking amongst themselves. While Shane isn't as physically affectionate as Lucinda, he accepts Minnie's affinity for touch without complaint, and Minnie tells Warren that Shane has many interesting stories from all the travelling he and Yolande have done. She is eager to hear them all.

On this particular morning, Johnny and Lucinda aren't at the coffee shop with them. Warren hopes that they're sleeping. They'd been at the Laundromat with him and Minnie two nights ago, and then Johnny had worked a double shift the following morning. At this point Warren isn't sure whose sleep schedule is worse: his or Johnny's.

Minnie is chatting with Shane at his cat perch behind the service counter where Yolande is working, while Warren sits at a table in the corner of the room out of everyone's way, nursing his coffee.

Zoe is there, as he always seems to be, mostly confined to his office, but occasionally wandering out to ask Yolande a question or do something in the back room where they keep the roasting machines. He is perfectly cordial to Warren, but seems uninterested in conversation beyond basic pleasantries, which suits Warren— who remains slightly intimidated by Zoe and his crow daemon— just fine.

Zoe joins Yolande behind the counter when The Palm starts to get busy. As soon as the crow daemon appears, Minnie makes her way back to Warren and climbs up the back of his chair to settle on his shoulders.

Warren tugs lightly on her tail. "Shy?"

Minnie sighs. "She still doesn't speak much to me. It's awkward."

"Hmm." He doesn't know what to make of that. Daemon relationships can be as tricky as human ones. "Well, I'm sure it's nothing to do with you," he tells Minnie. "You're lovely."

She fondly nuzzles his cheek in response.

Now that Johnny's pointed it out to him, Warren can sort of see something between Zoe and Yolande— if he squints. Zoe's daemon is settled on the edge of Shane's cat perch, just shy of touching, but more relaxed than Warren has ever seen her. Then there's the way Zoe keeps stealing glances at Yolande whenever she's turned away from him, or how he *almost* smiles once when she laughs at something he says.

When the morning rush has died down, Yolande places a careful hand on Zoe's elbow and murmurs something that has him nodding in agreement. He makes his way back to his office, leaning heavily on his cane, and takes a seat. Through the still open door, Warren can see him wincing slightly as he stretches his bad leg out in front of him.

Uncomfortably, Warren realizes that it must bother him more than he lets on, especially after standing at the counter for so long. He looks away before Zoe can catch him staring.

In his ear, Minnie whispers, "Lucinda says Zoe injured his leg jumping off the roof of a bank after robbing it with a crew of misfits. Apparently he was quite the delinquent as a teenager." She sounds positively gleeful about it.

Warren's mouth twists as he tries to contain his smile. "I think Lucinda is messing with you, Minnie."

Minnie pouts. "Well, there must be some kind of story behind it."

"Why don't you just ask his daemon?" teases Warren. "Since gossiping is your new favorite hobby."

"Warren! As if I would ever be so rude," she sniffs. "She wouldn't answer anyway. Maybe I'll ask Shane instead…"

Warren lets her contemplate that while he pulls a Rankine cycle problem set for Thermodynamics out of his messenger bag. He slips on his headphones, intent on tuning out the world around him and getting some studying done. It works for a while.

When he regains awareness of his surroundings, the sun has properly risen outside The Palm, light streaming in from the uncovered windows, and his coffee mug sits empty on the table before him. A glance at his phone shows him he has time for another cup, so he stands, careful not to jostle the half-dozing daemon on his shoulders, and heads back over to the counter.

Yolande refills his mug for him, and then holds out a tall milkshake glass. The beverage it contains is cold, pink, and topped by a mountain of whipped cream with chocolate shavings sprinkled over the top. A red paper straw is sticking out of the side, having barely escaped burial by toppings.

"Would you mind running this over to Nadia for me?" Yolande asks. "She's over there on the couch, in the green cardigan."

The familiar name stirs his memory. "Um… sure," Warren says, taking the drink.

Yolande smiles gratefully at him. "Thanks, Warren."

He turns toward the couch as directed and finds the woman with the red bird daemon that he remembers seeing in the shop a week or two before. She's curled into the corner of the couch with her legs folded sideways on the cushion, pouring over the textbook she holds open on her lap. Her daemon is perched on the backrest, reading over her shoulder.

As Warren approaches, the daemon looks up at him sharply and raises his wings a bit, startled. A beat later, Nadia looks up as well. She starts grinning as soon as she sees Warren, a glimmer of mischief in her green eyes.

Warily, he offers her the drink. "Hi. Yolande asked me to bring this to you."

"Well, aren't you sweet," Nadia says, smile growing. She's wearing thin-rimmed glasses in a tortoise shell frame, which she shoves up onto the top of her head before taking the glass from him. "Thank you."

"You're welcome," Warren mumbles. He makes to leave, but Nadia stops him.

"Sit with me," she says, waving toward the empty space next to her on the couch. It doesn't sound like a question.

Warren sits, setting his mug down on the low table provided for just that purpose. Minnie jumps off his shoulders onto the back of the couch a few feet away from the bird daemon.

Nadia turns her body to face Warren. "You're Johnny's friend. Warren, right?"

His heart beats a little harder at the mention of Johnny. "Yes. How did you— he talks about me?"

"Let's just say you've come up in conversation," she replies cryptically. "I'm Nadia, by the way. Yolande and I are roommates." Her daemon coughs pointedly, and Nadia fondly rolls her eyes. "And this is Vic."

Vic bows, wings unfurling gracefully at his sides. "Pleased to make your acquaintance."

"Likewise," Warren says, biting back a smile at the formality. "This is Minnie."

"Hello," Minnie says, ears perked as she edges closer to Vic. "I've never seen a daemon like you before. I like your feathers."

Vic puffs up a little at the compliment. "I am quite singular, it's true."

"Also very modest," Nadia quips. When Vic squawks in affront, she pets two fingers down his back in silent apology. "So you're a student at KU?"

"That's right," confirms Warren. "I'm in my third year. Are you a student too?"

She nods, tapping one manicured finger against the cover of her textbook. "I'm in medical school. And before you ask," she says, ticking off points on her fingers as she speaks, "yes, it's a lot of work; but yes, I still have a social life; no, I won't help you diagnose your friend's mystery illness; and *no,* I definitely won't look at any weird moles you may have."
"I wasn't going to ask *any* of that," Warren says, bemused.

"Then you have better manners than most people."

"That's disheartening to hear."

Nadia laughs. It's a nice sound, ringing bright and clear like bells. "I like you, Warren." She gives him a brief once-over, as she sips at her drink. "You're not my type, but I can definitely see the appeal."

"Uh… thank you?"

"I'm guessing I'm not your type either."

"Nope."

Nadia beams at him. "Good to know."

Warren smiles back. It may be the least painful coming out conversation he's ever had.

"Warren," Minnie suddenly says, "the time."

He looks at his phone and cringes. "Ah, sorry— I've got to get to class."

"No problem," Nadia says. "I've actually got to get going soon myself. It was good to properly meet you, Warren."

"You too," he says, standing.

Before he turns away, Nadia places a friendly hand on his arm. "Don't be a stranger, okay? We could use a fresh face around here."

Warmth blossoms in Warren's chest. "I won't," he says, and hopes it may even be true.


------


When he's at the apartment, Warren usually eats in his bedroom, but tonight he's sitting cross-legged on the shabby living room couch, balancing a bowl on one knee as he picks at his dinner.

It's nothing fancy, just rice and lentils and frozen kale that he'd thrown into a pot and boiled together with a bit of salt. The result is rather bland— possibly Warren needs to experiment with more seasoning.

On the other end of the couch, Karl is eating a bowl of the same, only he's dumped about half a bottle of hot sauce over his portion. Neither of them are particularly diligent about cooking for themselves, and even less so for other people, so it's exceedingly rare for them to be sharing a meal together. Warren, forever traumatized by the fraught silence of his father's dining room, has been filling the quiet by telling Karl about the open mic night— and, by extension, Johnny.

It's probably a terrible idea.

"So," Karl says, gesturing at Warren with his spoon, "to summarize: you had a meet-cute with a guy at the Laundromat and now he wants you to perform— for *free*— at his business?"

Make that *definitely* a terrible idea. "That's the gist of it, yes," Warren says warily.

Karl makes a face. "This sort of sounds like the plot to a bad YA novel. Is he at least hot?"

"Um…"

"So that's a yes," says Karl, sounding entirely too gleeful about it.

"Warren!" exclaims Daya, Karl's fruit bat daemon. "Tell us more! You never talk about boys." She's hanging upside-down from the bottom of the shade on the end table lamp, and her body sways as she speaks, like a candle flame dancing in a breeze.

Minnie, perched on the arm of the couch next to the end table, edges away from her. "There's a reason for that," she mutters.

Warren shovels a bite of food into his mouth. "Just forget it. I don't even know why I brought it up."

Typically, Karl ignores him. "So what are you going to play?"

"What?"

"For the open mic night. I assume you're going to do it."

"I'm not sure what I'm going to play," Warren says, scrubbing a hand through his curls. "I haven't figured it out yet."

"Do a pop cover," suggests Karl. "Carly Rae Jepson, or Dua Lipa or something."

"Ooh, play Yiruma!" Daya chimes in. "Crowd pleaser."

Karl points at her. "*Yes.* Everyone loves Yiruma."

Warren drags his hands over his face. "I don't know. Maybe I just won't do it."

"Pathetic," chirps Daya, then she lets out a squeak as Minnie smacks her with the end of her tail.

Daya drops from the lampshade and flies over to Karl, clinging onto the front of his shirt. Karl flicks a piece of rice at Warren in retaliation. It misses and lands somewhere in between the couch cushions.

"Why is this so important, anyway?" he asks. "Do you have a crush on this guy or something?"

Warren's cheeks heat. "No! I just… I want it to be good."

"Uh-huh," Karl replies doubtfully.

Warren regrets everything.

------

Warren actually does consider Yiruma: Karl and Daya have a point about the popularity of instrumental covers of songs like "River Flows in You" or "Kiss the Rain". But in the end he decides they suffer without piano accompaniment and instead settles on a classical piece, one he'd played during his audition for the university orchestra.

It's a Paganini composition, one of the caprices, fast-paced and technically difficult enough to be interesting even to an untrained ear. He's practiced it hundreds of times and performed it in front of an audience half a dozen more— he practically has it memorized, and he knows from experience that playing something familiar will help lessen his inevitable performance anxiety.

And, he admits privately, he's not opposed to showing off, just a bit.

He feels good about his choice all the way up to the Friday before the open mic night, when he starts second-guessing himself. He ends up spending the afternoon in a practice room in the music building, playing through the piece repeatedly until his arms ache from holding his flute in position for so long. Minnie takes on her customary role of calling out corrections for his intonation and posture, as invested in the perfection of this performance as Warren.

It's not until he's getting ready to leave for The Palm on Saturday evening that Warren realizes he has no idea what the dress code is for this event. Certainly not the all black formal wear he dons for performances with the orchestra, and his everyday fare of t-shirts and oversized sweaters doesn't feel like *enough,* not with all the eyes that will be on him.

He agonizes in front of his closet for close to an hour, before settling on his nicest pair of dark wash jeans and a white and grey striped button-down shirt layered beneath his favorite sky-blue cardigan— which he definitely doesn't pick because Johnny implied he looks good in blue, not at all. He adds a bowtie to complete the ensemble, but then discards it at the last minute, when Karl passes him in the hallway and nearly doubles over in laughter.

------

When Warren and Minnie enter The Palm a little after seven o'clock that night, they find it already buzzing with activity.

The coffee shop looks different than usual, with the furniture rearranged to make room for a temporary wooden stage placed against the brick wall. There's a microphone stand already on the stage and Warren can see Yolande and Zoe setting up the rest of the PA system, which seems to consist of a few speakers and an audio mixer. There are perhaps four dozen people milling about, most with beverages already in hand, chatting excitedly amongst themselves in small groups with their daemons. It's busier than Warren had been expecting, and he feels a spike of anxiety as he hovers near the entranceway.

Johnny spots him immediately.

"Warren!" he calls out from behind the service counter. "You made it!"

Warren starts making his way over to him, heart fluttering. "Hi, Johnny."

Lucinda comes out from behind the counter and trots over to Minnie, greeting her with an affectionate headbutt that almost sends her toppling. Minnie pounces on her back in return, and the two of them begin tussling playfully on the floor.

"Did you bring your flute?" Johnny asks as Warren approaches. Under his work apron, he's wearing a brightly colored shirt with the sleeves rolled up. Warren's eyes catch on his bare forearms, remembering the feeling of warm skin beneath his fingertips.

He pushes the thought aside and holds up his instrument case. "Yes."

"Good. I hear you really kill it on that thing."

"Please try to keep your expectations low," says Warren. "I really haven't done a solo performance since high school."

"Too late," Johnny grins. "But don't worry: even if you're terrible, we'll at least all get the pleasure of watching Zoe try to hide how annoyed he is by it."

Warren crosses his arms in front of his chest. "Gee, thanks," he replies. "No pressure."

"Hey," says Johnny, his expression gentling. He reaches across the counter to touch Warren's elbow. "Seriously, don't worry. Everyone here is really supportive, and if they're not, we'll throw them out."

"Really? You'd throw out customers, just like that?"

Johnny shrugs. "Perk of being in charge." He takes his hand back. "Anyway, you're just in time to order something before the show starts. What can I get you?"

"Just a black coffee, please," says Warren, dropping his arms back to his sides.

Johnny makes a face. "So boring," he complains. "That's what you always get. Let me make you a latte— I promise you won't regret it."

Warren nods. "Yes, okay. That would be nice."

"Great! Do you have a flavor preference?"

"What are my options?"

Johnny waves a hand at the menu. "They're all listed—" he starts, then catches himself, wincing. "I'm sorry, I forgot..."

Warren reddens. "It's fine, don't worry about it," he says hurriedly. "What do *you* like?"

Johnny's face brightens. "My favorite is the cinnamon vanilla latte. It's really good with coconut milk, if you don't mind swapping out the dairy. I like things sweet," he adds with a wink.

Warren knows he must be bright red by now. "Um, me too. That sounds good, I'll have that one."

He tries to pay but Johnny waves him off, saying, "I promised, remember?"

As Johnny moves over to the drink station, Warren takes a quick glance around, feeling eyes on him. He sees Zoe watching him with a thoughtful expression, his eyes narrowed and his mouth pressed in a straight line. His daemon is perched on his shoulder with her beak close to his ear, whispering something.

Warren turns away uneasily. He clears his throat and asks Johnny, "Are you performing too?"

Johnny shakes his head, focused on measuring out the coconut milk. "No, I'm hosting. Sadly, the best of my many talents aren't for public consumption." He glances up at Warren as he says it, smirking.

"That's— I mean..." Warren sputters. "That's good to know?"

Johnny laughs, eyes crinkling. "Isn't it? You can go sit, if you want," he tells Warren. "I'll bring your drink over when it's finished."

Warren nods, and turns to survey the room. It's crowded, every chair occupied, and most of the available wall space as well. Yolande and a woman Warren doesn't recognize with a crop of yellow hair and ring-tailed lemur daemon balanced on her shoulder are busy handing out milk crates to people without seats.

He spies Nadia, who's staked out a prime position on the couch, which has been set directly in front of the stage along with the two armchairs, arranged in a shallow u-shape. She's looking back at him over her shoulder. When their eyes meet, she waves him over.

Warren heads toward her, relieved he won't have to vie for a spot elsewhere. Minnie, her fur in disarray from wrestling Lucinda, joins him, leaping from the floor up into his arms.

Nadia greets them with a smile as they approach. "Warren! Come sit with us."

A man is seated next to her, impossible to miss, tall and broad-shouldered with long blond hair secured in a loose bun at the back of his head. Even more noticeable is his wolf daemon, who Warren sees sprawled out on the floor as he rounds the couch. She's huge, easily spanning two thirds of the length of the couch, and her fur is completely white. Vic is nestled contentedly on her head like a little red crown. Both the man and his daemon have ice blue eyes, and they track Warren synchronously as he seats himself in one of the armchairs that Nadia has evidently been holding in reserve.

"Warren," Nadia says, "meet Jonas, my boyfriend. And this beautiful creature is Huff," she adds, reaching down to pat the wolf daemon with easy affection. "Jonas, this is Warren. He's the one I was telling you about— Johnny's stray."

Warren's heart trips in his chest at being referred to as *Johnny's*.

"Hello, Warren," Jonas says. His voice is deep and lightly accented. "It's good to meet you." He leans across the space between the couch and Warren's chair, holding out his hand.

Warren shifts Minnie to his lap and takes it. "You too," he replies, slightly taken aback by the flex of Jonas' biceps as they shake hands.

"I know, right?" grins Nadia, too observant for her own good. "Jonas is a personal trainer."

"A fact which we all greatly appreciate," Johnny cuts in, approaching them with two steaming mugs in hand and Lucinda at his heels.

He's removed his apron, revealing the entirety of his outfit. Warren thinks he looks very handsome in a button-down shirt with a very Johnny-like graffiti print in bright shades of purple, pink, and yellow. It's paired with black jeans and suspenders, and Johnny's regular combat boots have been exchanged for a pair of black and white high top sneakers. He looks effortlessly fashionable in a way that makes Warren feel both over and underdressed at the same time, and he tugs self-consciously at the bottom of his cardigan, relieved that he decided to ditch the bowtie.

Johnny holds out one of the mugs to Warren, who accepts it with a murmured, "Thank you."

He hands the other mug off to Nadia, before folding his lanky frame into the remaining armchair with a sigh. Lucinda seats herself on the floor in front of him, leaning heavily against his legs.

Nadia frowns. "I was saving that seat for Yolande."

"Yolande is resourceful," says Johnny. "She'll find a spot. Maybe she can sit on Zoe's lap."

Nadia rolls her eyes. "And maybe hell will freeze over."

Warren takes a sip of his drink. It's delicious— rich and flavorful, with just the right amount of sweetness. "This is really good," he tells Johnny.

Johnny grins crookedly at him. "Told you so."

"Did you get me anything?" Minnie asks, poking at Warren's thigh with one unsheathed claw.

"Not unless you want to try a latte," answers Warren.

"No way," she says, sticking out her tongue in disgust. "Oh— no offense, Johnny."

"None taken," Johnny replies, amused.

Nadia has ripped open a packet of sugar and is in the process of adding it to her drink. Huff eyes her warily.

"Take it easy, Nadia," she admonishes. "Jonas says that stuff will kill you."

Nadia laughs airily. "Huff, dear, if there is one thing I've learned as a medical student thus far it's that *everything* will kill you."

Johnny snorts and Jonas shakes his head. Warren takes another sip of his drink to hide his smile. He feels warm all over, and not just from the latte. It's been a long time since he's been included in a group like this— he'd forgotten how much fun it could be.

Yolande appears suddenly, gracefully collapsing next to Nadia on the couch. Shane jumps soundlessly onto the backrest behind her.

"Hello, everyone," she says, tucking back the stray hairs that have come loose from the braided coil at the nape of her neck. "I'm glad you're all here. I think we're almost ready to start."

"Oh, good," Nadia says, bumping her shoulder companionably against Yolande's. "I was starting to wonder if you'd decided to turn this into one of your 'rallies for change' instead."

Yolande elbows Nadia's side. "I'm saving that for next time."

"Yolande," Johnny demands, sitting forward in his seat, "where did all these people come from? I swear there was only half this number last month. The Palm's Instagram page does *not* get this much traffic."

She nods in agreement, but it's Shane who answers. "Zoe put up a flyer at the Big Block."

"Ah. Yeah, that would do it."

"Jonas," Yolande says, leaning over Nadia to look at him. "I saw your name on the sign up sheet. You're performing?"

Jonas rubs a hand over his eyes. "Please, don't remind me."

"He lost a bet," Nadia informs them, green eyes glinting.

"To whom?" asks Johnny.

Nadia grins unabashedly. "To me," she replies. "Now he has to recite a poem dedicated to yours truly."

Jonas groans. "She made me write it myself."

Yolande smiles reassuringly at him. "Don't worry, I'm sure Nadia will love whatever you've written."

"Yolande, don't say that!" Nadia says. "I mean, it's true, obviously— but I want to keep him a little on edge. He performs well under pressure," she confides, winking lasciviously.

"*Nadia.*" Jonas' cheeks redden, and Warren feels a surge of sympathetic kinship for him. He knows what it's like to be on the receiving end of a wink like that.

"What? It's not like it's a mystery that we have sex."

"Don't be crass, Nadia," says Vic.

"But that's what we like best about her," Lucinda interjects, her tone all mischief.

"Thank you, Lucinda," Nadia says graciously.

Vic ruffles his feathers. "Don't encourage her."

Jonas pulls a slightly battered cracker from the pocket of his wool cardigan and offers it to Vic. "Don't worry, little bird. We all like Nadia just as she is."

Vic huffs, but takes the cracker.

"You're performing too, aren't you, Warren?" Yolande asks, turning to face him.

"Yes," Warren says, clenching his fingers around his flute case. Butterflies take flight in his stomach at the reminder of the reason he's been invited here tonight.

Johnny stretches his long arms overhead and grins. "We're finally going to get to hear an instrument other than a guitar."

"Are you nervous?" Yolande asks Warren kindly.

"A bit," he replies.

"I have just the thing," Nadia says. She reaches inside her white denim jacket and pulls out a small flask. "Liquid courage, anyone?" she asks, offering it first to Yolande.

Yolande refuses with a slight shake of her head. "I'm still on the clock."

Johnny also declines. "No need— I'm naturally charismatic."

Nadia passes the flask to Jonas instead, saying, "It's vodka, darling" when he raises a questioning brow. Jonas takes a long swig before offering it to Warren.

"Grimm, *yes,* " says Warren. He takes a gulp and immediately starts coughing as the alcohol burns its way down his throat.

Nadia laughs and Jonas starts chuckling at him. When Warren meets Johnny's eyes he sees they are sparkling with mirth. His mouth is tilting up at the corners and he's caught his lower lip in his teeth, like he's trying to bite back a smile.

Warren looks away, wiping his mouth with the back of his hand. He passes the flask back to Nadia, and she immediately begins pouring it into her coffee.

"That had better not be an outside beverage," says a gruff voice. They all look up as Zoe approaches.

"Of course not, Zoe," Nadia replies, capping the flask and shoving it back inside her jacket. "I would never."

To Warren's surprise, Zoe doesn't press the issue, only shakes his head at her and says, "The list of things you'd never do is too short for that to be believable." He stops in front of Johnny's chair and taps him on the shin with his cane. "Time to start. You're up."

"Duty calls," Johnny says cheerfully, springing to his feet.

Zoe takes his spot, lowering himself slowly into the armchair. His crow daemon leaves his shoulder and flies over behind Yolande, settling next to Shane on the backrest.

Lucinda moves to sit near Huff and Vic in front of the couch, ears pricked as she watches Johnny step onto the stage. He claps his hands a few times to get everyone's attention. Immediately, the excited chatter of the crowd starts to die down as people turn toward him.

"Hello, all you beautiful people! Thank you for coming out to our open mic night. We're excited to have everyone here." Johnny pauses to allow for the obligatory applause. "Now before we begin, just a reminder that if anyone wants to order anything during the show, Anika over there will be happy to help you out." He gestures to the service counter, and the yellow-haired woman Warren noticed earlier gives a wave. "Now let's get started. First up is Marie. Come on up here, Marie!"

There's another round of applause as a woman with chin-length brown hair makes her way to the stage. Johnny helps her adjust the microphone stand, then he hops down from the platform and comes to sit on the arm of Warren's chair. His leg— his lean, denim-clad thigh— is right next to Warren's arm.

Marie begins a jazzy vocal cover of... something. It doesn't matter. Warren can hardly hear her over the buzzing in his head as Johnny's leg *ever so lightly* presses against him. He can feel the heat of it through his shirt.

When Marie finishes her performance, Johnny stands to introduce the next performer and Warren can breathe properly again.

The acts blur together after that. Some people are new to the scene while others are obviously well-initiated, and there is a wide range in level of ability, though almost everyone is at least entertaining. The talents are varied but it's mostly singers, some accompanied by guitar or keyboard. A few people read poems or excerpts from novels, and one misguided soul even attempts stand up.

Through it all, Johnny works the room with ease, as interesting to watch as any of the acts— sometimes more so— a performer in his own right. He seems to be on a first-name basis with almost everyone and his introductions are peppered with inside jokes and references to past appearances. He continues returning to Warren's side between acts, and Warren isn't quite sure what to make of that, other than the convenient proximity of his seat to the stage. But it might mean more. He hopes it means more.

A woman with box braids finishes up her keyboard cover of an Adele song and bows, her dragonfly daemon flitting excitedly around her head. Her short-haired, tattooed girlfriend embraces her as she steps off the platform.

"Thank you, Nadia," Johnny says into the microphone. "Up next we have Jonas!"

Jonas stands abruptly, pulling a crumpled paper from his back pocket. He walks stiffly toward the stage, like a soldier marching into battle.

"Good luck!" Nadia calls after him.

Johnny slaps Jonas' back encouragingly as they trade places. "Go get 'em, big guy." He sits back down next to Warren and leans in close to his ear. "You're up after Jonas," he whispers, and the warmth of his breath makes Warren shiver.

Jonas spends a moment fiddling with the microphone, then he straightens and faces the audience.

"This is for Nadia," he prefaces simply, before launching into his recital with barely a pause for breath. *"My, love,"* he starts, *"you aren't a flower, you are every blossom in the wood blooming at once. You are a tidal wave. You are a stampede…"*
It continues like that, a love poem, full of sentimental prose and florid declarations of devotion. It should be cheesy— it *is* cheesy— but something about his earnest delivery makes the words land more on the side of touching.

Warren alternates between watching Jonas' performance and Nadia's face. She starts out smirking, but the longer Jonas speaks, the more sincere her expression becomes. By the end of the poem her eyes are shining, and she has both hands raised to cover her wide grin.

Johnny leans across Warren to speak to Nadia over the sound of applause. "What an absolute treasure that man is!" he shouts. "And to think, I remember when Jonas was weird and boring. What's your secret?"

"Not telling," says Nadia. "Get your own, Fontaine."

She stands to meet Jonas as he returns to his seat. He shrugs at her, red-faced and smiling sheepishly. When he draws near, Nadia cups his face and kisses him passionately, much to the delight of nearby onlookers. Jonas grabs her by the waist and pulls her close, sliding one hand around her back before he dips her, while Vic flies in enthusiastic circles overhead.

Johnny sticks two fingers in his mouth and whistles loudly at them. Yolande is giggling uncontrollably, sliding down into her seat, while Zoe looks on with an indecipherable expression.

Warren smiles and looks away from them as the butterflies return to his stomach. He opens his instrument case and begins to slot the pieces of his flute together with practiced motions, taking comfort in the familiar task.

Minnie stands up in his lap, resting her front paws on his collarbone. "You've got this, Warren," she says, her black eyes earnest.

"Thanks, Minnie," he says, stroking a hand over her head. She butts up into it, before leaping down to join the pile of daemons on the floor in front of the couch.

Johnny has made his way back to the stage. "All right everyone, settle down. I know he's is hot shit, but focus up. Warren is our last performer of the evening so let's all give him a warm welcome, okay?"

Warren takes the stage to a smattering of polite applause. Johnny briefly clasps his shoulder as they pass each other but Warren hardly feels it, too focused on the task ahead of him. A music stand has been set up already and he moves it in front of the microphone before he fans his sheet music out across it, arranging the pages just so.

He takes his place at the center of the stage and finally looks out at the sea of faces in front of him. It's far more intimate than performing with the orchestra, without the glare of spotlights to hide the audience from view. Warren closes his eyes and breathes deeply, lifting his flute to his mouth. The room goes quiet with anticipation.

He begins to play. The first few notes are wobbly, the pitch just shy of correct, but then Warren steadies his breath and takes control of the music.

He loses himself in it, chasing the caprice from note to note. It's easy to do in this piece, which requires a great deal of concentration in order for him to maintain control of his breath as he plays through a veritable catalogue of extended techniques. The quick-paced tempo drives the melody ever onwards, and before he knows it, he's reached the end of the piece. His fingers flicker across the keys of his flute as he plays one last flurry of notes, ending on an ascending flourish.

He stills, panting.

There is silence as the last note hangs in the air; then the room erupts in applause.

Johnny, Yolande, Nadia, and Jonas are all on their feet, cheering loudly. Most of the daemons are, too— Warren can see Minnie up on her hind legs— and even Zoe is applauding in his seat. Warren lowers his flute and grins at them, still trying to catch his breath. Then he steps out from behind the music stand and gives a quick bow, feeling high on the performance.

Minnie runs over and launches herself at him. Warren catches her one-handed and holds her against his chest.

"You did it, you did it, you did it!" she chants into his ear, and he laughs, feeling light as air.

Johnny is waiting for him when he steps off the stage. He grasps Warren's upper arms, holding him in place.

"You," he says, "are *such a con artist!* I honestly think you could give Zoe a run for his money." He's grinning broadly, teeth white against his dark skin. "Saints, you really had me worried for a minute there with all your talk of 'keeping my expectations low'." He leans in closer. His eyes are so bright. "Warren, you were *brilliant.*"

And Warren has spent a lot of his life trying not to be noticed, but he thinks he wouldn't mind being seen if it meant Johnny would just keep looking at him the way he is right now, always.

------

It's late when Warren finally returns to the apartment that night. He and Nadia and Jonas had stayed to help the others close up The Palm after the open mic crowd departed. It had been a nice way to decompress, rehashing the performances while collecting empty cups and reordering the furniture.

Warren manages to wait until after he's brushed his teeth and changed into his pajamas before messaging Johnny. Minnie leans drowsily against his hip as he sits cross-legged on the bed and activates the dictation function on his phone.

*I'm back at the apartment. Thanks for waiting at the bus stop with me.*

He doesn't have to wait long for a reply.

*>>no problem*
*>>got to say, I think you really impressed everyone tonight*
*>>some of those girls were definitely swooning*
Warren bites his lip. Johnny must know— he has to have at least *guessed*. But Warren needs to make sure.
*You know I'm gay, right?*

There is a brief pause. Warren's stomach twists.

*>>I mean sort of, but I didn't want to assume anything*
*Assume away.*
*>>and anyway being talented enough to make someone swoon is its own reward,*
*regardless of whether or not you're into the person*
*>>maybe I should take up an instrument to impress girls*
*>>alas, I am sorely lacking musical aptitude*
*>>guess I can't be good at everything*

Warren frowns at his phone. Is Johnny actually rambling over WhatsApp? For some reason that makes his heart beat faster.

He collects his courage and— quickly, before he can second-guess himself— sends,

*Just girls?*

Johnny starts typing, and then he stops. Warren holds his breath as he watches the little dots at the top of the screen appear and disappear, over and over. Then:

*>>no. not just girls*

Warren exhales. He tosses his phone aside and falls backwards onto the mattress, accidentally startling Minnie.

He doesn't stop grinning for the rest of the night.

# CHAPTER 4

March comes in like a lion, all roaring winds and ferocious rains as winter takes its last gasping breath before the arrival of spring.

Warren watches the temperamental weather through the windows of the Blue Wave, where he spends much of his weeklong mid-term break. Giles and Evana have jetted off to vacation in warmer climes, leaving Warren and the swing shift employee, Earl, to cover for their absence. Warren agrees to the extra shifts without fully thinking it through, the promise of cash wages too alluring to pass up in the face of his dwindling funds. He and Earl work alternating double shifts, and for seven days Warren and Minnie barely see the sun.

Confined to the Laundromat, he attempts to make some headway on his coursework, but mostly spends the time on his phone, listening to podcasts or watching videos— or messaging with Johnny on WhatsApp.

Something has shifted between them in the past few weeks. He can't pinpoint it exactly, couldn't explain what or why or how, but there is a slowly coiling tension that wasn't there before.

Never shy with physical contact, Johnny has become even less restrained, bestowing small, frequent touches that linger on Warren's skin long after Johnny's moved away. They've been talking more often too. They message every day— not about anything in particular, just random comments or check ins or little stories about their days— but it's amazing to Warren how quickly talking to Johnny has become such a normal and necessary part of his life.

He doesn't think twice about messaging *good morning* to Johnny when he starts his day, and it never fails to bring a smile to his face when Johnny replies. Just seeing the purple heart in Johnny's contact name pop up on his screen is enough to make Warren start grinning like an idiot. Maybe it's foolish, deriving this much joy from something so nebulous and prone to misinterpretation, but Warren couldn't stop himself if he tried.

Neither of them have mentioned the revelatory conversation that followed the open mic night, but Warren can feel it there between them, rife with possibility. Or maybe that's just his own wishful thinking. It's so hard to tell with Johnny, who is friendly with everyone and flirtatious by nature. The more Warren gets to know him, the less he feels like he understands him. It feels like he's missing something, some integral piece that would allow Warren to finally see the whole picture of Johnny's personality.

When Johnny comes to do his laundry that week at the tail end of one of Warren's double shifts, he takes one look at the dark circles beneath Warren's eyes and frowns.

"Saints, Warren. You look like crap."

"Thanks," Warren replies flatly.

Lucinda pads over to him and peers up at his face. "Have you eaten anything today?" she asks.

Has he? "I… don't remember."

"*No,* he has *not,*" says Minnie emphatically from where she is sprawled across Warren's lap.

"I can tell," says Lucinda. She closes her teeth gently around Minnie's dangling tail and tugs at it teasingly. Minnie makes an indignant noise and bats at Lucinda's nose with one sheathed paw.

Warren pushes the heels of his hands into his eyes. He's exhausted, and— yes, now that Lucinda has brought it up— also very hungry. "I guess I forgot."

"Warren, Warren, Warren," Johnny sighs, shaking his head in mock disappointment. "What am I going to do with you?" He plops his laundry bag down on one of the waiting area chairs. "Stay here. I'll be right back."

"Where else would I go?" Warren asks grumpily.

Johnny raises his eyebrows. "Wow. You're snarky when you're hungry, huh?"

Warren crosses his arms over his chest, unable to disguise the sulky look he knows must be on his face. Johnny walks over and bops him in the nose with one long finger. Warren goes cross-eyed trying to look at it, and they both crack up.

"That's better," Johnny says with a grin. "Now hang tight. I'll just be a minute."

He strides purposely out of the Laundromat, Lucinda jogging along at his heels. Confused, Warren watches them leave. Did Johnny forget something?

Johnny is actually gone for forty minutes, not that Warren is counting. He starts Johnny's laundry for him when Minnie suggests it— even though it feels like a strangely intimate thing to do— and then queues up a podcast he's been meaning to listen to about plasma waste converters.

He pulls off his headphones when Johnny and Lucinda finally return. Johnny is carrying a pizza box in one hand and a bag with the logo for a nearby convenience store in the other. Warren can see the outlines of drink containers through the plastic.

"Sorry it took so long," Johnny says. "I forgot that hardly anything is open at this time of night." He holds up the pizza. "I hope you like pineapple."

Warren feels a sudden pressure gathering in his throat and under his eyes. *I am not going to cry over pizza,* he thinks. He swallows against the press of tears and manages, "Pineapple is fine."

"Good. That would've been a dealbreaker for me."

"Thank you, Johnny," says Warren, as Johnny sets the food down on the counter in front of him. It feels inadequate, but he is so tired, and the food smells so good.

Johnny smiles at him. "What are friends for?"

And that— that sentence right there— is the crux of Warren's confusion. "Right," he replies faintly. "Friends."

------

The extra cash is a nice addition to his bank account, but Warren is relieved when the break is over and classes start back up again, eager to return to normalcy.

Before he knows it, it's the middle of the month, and his professors are urging them to begin preparations for end of term projects and exams.

Warren still goes to The Palm on Tuesdays and Thursdays before his morning classes, but he's started hanging out there on days when he has afternoon classes as well, before his evening shift at the Laundromat. He can reliably be found at the table in the back corner, which has become his spot when he's in the coffee shop. He likes it: it's quiet and out of the way, and he can sit with his back to the wall with his headphones on and not worry about being interrupted. It also has a direct line of sight to the service counter, a feature that is especially advantageous in the afternoons, which is when Johnny typically works his shifts.

It's late Friday afternoon, and Warren is finishing up an assignment before he goes back to his apartment for the night. He's found that it's easier to complete coursework here than at the campus library— perhaps because he doesn't have the best relationship with books, or because the caffeine provides a huge boost to his productivity, or maybe it's just something about the relaxed atmosphere here that helps relieve the stress of studying. Regardless, Warren has been alternating between sketching out a rough project design for his Control Systems final and stealing glances across the room at Johnny for about an hour, when Nadia suddenly drops into the seat across from him.

Warren looks up at her in surprise.

Nadia is always there on the same mornings as he is, and they have taken to sitting together and lamenting about their busy schedules. Nadia is both straightforward and totally shameless. She asks Warren all sorts of questions with little regard for propriety, but once he gets used to it, he finds her free way of speaking refreshing. It helps that he never feels any judgment from her; Nadia takes everything he says in stride and answers his questions easily in return. Warren has come to look forward to their conversations… but he rarely sees her at The Palm in the afternoon.

"Hello," he says. "I wasn't expecting to see you here today."

"I've just come from lecture," Nadia says, setting a travel mug down on the table. Her light brown hair is tied up in a messy top knot and she's wearing her glasses. "Yolande is volunteering this afternoon and I didn't feel like going home to an empty apartment."

Minnie ducks out from under the table where she's been lounging in one of the courtesy beds for daemons. "Hi!" she says, leaping to the tabletop.

Vic dips his body in greeting. "Good afternoon, Minnie." He hops from Nadia's shoulder to the back of her chair as she begins to shrug off her jacket.

"Are you really doing homework on a Friday?" Nadia asks Warren, nodding to his open notebook.

"Just a bit," Warren replies. "Finals are coming and I'm trying to get ahead."

"You're always studying."

"There's a lot to learn."

Nadia sighs. "Must you insist on being so earnest about everything?" She stands and picks up her travel mug. "I'm going to grab a refill. Do you want anything?"

"No, thank you."

"Suit yourself," she says, and goes. Vic stays on the back of her chair, conversing quietly with Minnie as he preens his feathers.

It's curious. A person and their daemon normally stay close to each other, not only out of desire, but also out of necessity. Everyone knows that separation from your daemon causes pain and distress for both of you, and can even result in death if the distance between you is great enough. It's called 'pulling', and Warren and Minnie have fortunately only felt it only a few times in their lives: twice by accident, and once by their own experimental design. The discomfort was great enough each time that they've both done their utmost to avoid it since.

The Palm isn't large, but the distance from this back corner to the service counter would be enough to cause pulling in an ordinary bond. But both Nadia and Vic seem totally unaffected. He would never ask about it— it's shockingly bad etiquette to inquire about a person's relationship with their daemon— but Warren wants to know *why*.

Johnny is working the service counter with Anika today, handling the customers while she prepares beverages. Warren sees the moment when Johnny notices Nadia join the line in front of the cash register. He watches the wide smile bloom over his face and feels only fondness— he knows the shape of Johnny and Nadia's friendship now, and it's beautiful to witness.

Warren keeps watching Johnny as Nadia pays for her coffee and starts walking back to the table with her refill. Another woman is approaching the cash register and Warren can just hear Johnny's voice across the coffee shop as he says, "Hi, there. I've never seen you in here before— I would remember a face like yours. What can I get for you?"

Warren hears the woman stammer something in response and feels a wave of empathy for her. Johnny flirts like breathing. It's just part of who he is— Warren *knows* that— but hearing him flirt with someone else still makes his insides twist unpleasantly, even though he knows he has no right to be upset.

Nadia approaches the table. She turns her head to follow Warren's gaze, and then rolls her eyes. "Johnny would flirt with the wall if he thought it would flirt back."

Vic scoffs at her. "That's rich, coming from you."

Nadia scrubs two knuckles against the back of his downy head. "Don't pretend like you don't enjoy it as much as I do."

"Johnny can flirt with whomever he likes," Warren says, willing himself not to blush. "It's none of my business."

"Uh-huh," says Nadia, raising one perfect eyebrow at him. But apparently she's chosen mercy this day, because she doesn't say anything more.

Instead she seats herself back at the table and pulls a packet of digestive biscuits from her bag. She opens it and offers one to Warren, who accepts, then breaks another biscuit in half and gives a piece to Vic. She gives the other half to Minnie when Warren's daemon looks pleadingly at her, before taking out a biscuit for herself and biting into it with relish.

Nadia eyes Warren's notebook of sketches and equations as she chews. "You know," she says thoughtfully, "Yolande and I have a standing study date every Sunday afternoon to help keep us on track. You should come."

"Yolande is a student?" Warren asks, brushing crumbs from his fingers.

"No, not technically. She's studying to take her law school entrance exams."

Warren furrows his brow. "How did I not know that?"

Nadia breaks another biscuit in half and feeds it to their daemons. "I don't know if you've noticed this, Warren, but Yolande is *extremely* good at getting information from people while revealing very little about herself in return. She's sneaky like that."

"It still feels weird that I didn't know that she wants to go to law school."

"Really, don't feel weird: she's a conversational acrobat, she'll leap right over to the next topic before you even realize she hasn't answered your question. Anyway," Nadia continues, "you should join us. I mean, I need to be held accountable, and we could help you with your textbooks. Speed things up a bit for you."

His dyslexia is an open secret between them at this point, and Warren is strangely unbothered by that.

"Maybe," he says noncommittally. He normally reserves Sundays for flute practice.

"Well, think about it. We'd love to have you." Nadia looks down at her phone. "Saints, is that the time? I'm supposed to meet Jonas for dinner. I'll message you later about Sunday, okay? I'm going to convince you."

Warren doesn't doubt it. They say their goodbyes, and then he goes back to his work.

A little while later, Minnie sits up and pricks her ears toward the front of the shop. She plants one paw on Warren's notebook to get his attention. "What's going on over there?"

Warren lifts his gaze.

There is a long line in front of the cash register and a crowd of people waiting near the drink station. Johnny and Anika have switched places, and Johnny is hurriedly making drinks, hands moving briskly as he seemingly struggles to fill orders. It's odd to see him so rushed— he usually makes working here look easy.

Warren hesitates, then stands and heads over with Minnie.

"What's going on?" he asks Johnny. Behind the counter he can see Lucinda pacing from one end of the small workspace to the other.

Johnny glances up at him. His mouth is set in a tense line. "One of the espresso machines isn't working. Normally we can pull four espresso shots at a time, but right now we can only do two. It's slowing everything down."

Warren exchanges a look with Minnie. "Let me try to fix it."

"You know how to fix it?" Johnny asks doubtfully.

"I can at least try."

"Zoe has a maintenance guy coming," says Johnny, handing a takeaway cup to a customer and quickly starting another beverage.

"But that doesn't help you now."

Johnny looks up at him again and Warren stubbornly holds his gaze. "All right," he drawls, "sure. I guess it's worth a try. Come on back here."

"Do you have a toolkit?" asks Warren as he rounds the counter.

Johnny nods. "In that corner cabinet."

"Here," Lucinda says, going to the cabinet in question and pulling it open with her teeth around the handle.

Warren does his best to stay out of the way as he carefully takes the machine apart. He occasionally feels Johnny's eyes on him but stays focused on the task at hand, checking over each component as he removes it from the machine. When he unscrews the water filter and examines it, he finds that it's covered by a layer of chalky residue. Beside him, Minnie is peering into the intake pipes.

"Limescale?" Warren asks, and she nods.

"What is that?" asks Johnny.

"Mineral deposit. Probably calcium carbonate, from the water supply… it can build up in pipes when water evaporates and cause blockages," explains Warren. "Do you have any white vinegar?"

"Yes, actually," Johnny says. "We use it for cleaning sometimes. Yolande insists it's better than chemical cleaners."

"Perfect. I'll need that and a kettle."

"I'll show you where they are, Warren," says Lucinda, leading him into the back room. He follows with Minnie riding on his shoulders.

Lucinda shows Warren where the vinegar is kept under the wash station sink. Warren finds an electric tea kettle on the counter nearby. He fills the kettle with vinegar and turns it on, and then goes back to the espresso machine and collects the intake pipes, steam wand, portafilter, dispenser screen, and anything else he can find that's removable. He takes all the parts back to the wash station and lays them in the sink.

Johnny ducks into the back room to grab a new stack of takeaway cups. "You're going to try to dissolve it?" he asks, wrinkling his nose against the sharp sting of concentrated vinegar.

Warren nods. "Vinegar contains acetic acid. It'll react with the calcium carbonate."

Zoe suddenly enters, crow daemon balanced on his shoulder. "What are you doing? Why is one of the espresso machines in pieces?"

"Warren is seeing if he can fix it for us," Johnny tells him on his way back out to the service area.

Zoe gives Warren an assessing look. "And can you?"

"I think I'm about to," says Warren, putting the drain stopper into the sink. The kettle has finished heating and he lifts it, slowly pouring the boiling vinegar over the parts in the sink.

"What was wrong with it?" asks Zoe.

"There was mineral deposit from the hard water and it choked the machine. You should invest in a water softener to prevent buildup… I think it will save you a lot of grief. It'll be cheaper than replacing the espresso machines, at any rate."

Zoe and his daemon watch silently as the chalky residue starts to bubble and dissolve.

"Um," says Warren, a little unnerved, "you should probably let these soak overnight. I can come back in the morning and help reassemble the machine, if you like."

Johnny comes to stand next to him, having apparently caught up on drink orders. "Well, would you look at that," he says, "it's working. Not just a pretty face, are you?"

Warren elbows him in the side. "Shut up."

Zoe turns to Warren and sticks out his hand. Warren takes it automatically.

"Thank you," says Zoe. "You just saved me hundreds of dollars in maintenance fees and who knows what else. I'd like to pay you for your work."

"Oh, no," says Warren, shaking his head. "Really, I couldn't possibly take money for this— and anyway, Johnny is always giving me free coffee, so…."

Zoe raises one eyebrow, shifting his gaze to Johnny.

Johnny chuckles nervously. "What? No, he's just joking, Zoe, don't listen to him. These are clearly the ravings of a lunatic— I would never give our stock away for free."

Zoe's mouth twitches. "I'm taking it out of your paycheck, Fontaine. Make sure that machine is back together and flushed out before the morning rush," he says over his shoulder as he heads back to his office. "And for Saints' sake don't forget to test the espresso before you serve it. I don't want to hear anyone complaining that it tastes of vinegar."

"Will he really take it out of your paycheck?" Minnie asks concernedly, once Zoe is gone.

Johnny shakes his head. "No, Zoe is all bark when it comes to stuff like that. He knows everything that goes on in here and if he cared that I was giving you freebies I'd have already gotten an earful about it."

There's a fond note in Johnny's voice when he speaks of Zoe, even when he's making fun of him. Warren doesn't understand their friendship, but he can see the strength of it. Just another piece of Johnny that he's been missing.

"If you say so," Warren says. "I find him difficult to read."

"It's an acquired skill, for sure," agrees Johnny. "But I think you really impressed him. Getting a handshake from Zoe is like finding water in the desert."

"So drink deeply," adds Lucinda, and Warren laughs.

------

Nadia does end up convincing Warren to come to her Sunday study session, not that it takes all that much effort.

It's a dull day, but the weather has been gentler lately, so he decides to take a chance and walk over to Yolande and Nadia's apartment. They reside in a neighborhood just outside the university district, about halfway between Warren's apartment building in West Stave and The Palm.

He's almost arrived when the clouds open up and release an unexpected rain shower. It falls heavily, making instant puddles on the pavement and sending people and their daemons sprinting for cover.

Warren picks up Minnie and does his best to tuck her under his jumper as he rushes along the sidewalk. He'd foolishly forgone a jacket, lured into false security by the milder temperatures, and it doesn't take long before he's soaked through.

The rain lets up quickly, but he's wet and shivering by the time he reaches the correct address. The apartment is located above a flower shop that has a white rose painted over the door. Warren studies it with mild interest as he messages Nadia to let her know he's arrived.

"Come in, come in," Nadia says, as she and Vic usher him inside. Her hair is up in two high buns on either side of her head, anime-style. "Saints, look at you—you're practically dripping!"

"We got caught in the rain," Warren says needlessly, brushing his sopping curls back from his forehead. Minnie jumps to the ground and shakes her fur, sending small droplets of water flying everywhere.

Yolande, looking relaxed in leggings and an oversized hooded sweatshirt, is watching them from the kitchenette where she is preparing tea. Her hair, Warren notices, is styled to match Nadia's.

"Let me get you some towels," she says. "Nadia, he'll probably need something to wear too."

"Right, yes, I'll find something. Stay here, Warren," says Nadia. She and Yolande both disappear down a hallway that presumably leads to the bath and bedrooms.

Warren toes off his shoes and lines them up neatly by the door, and then looks curiously around the apartment as he waits.

The main space is a living room, dining area, and kitchen all in one, open and relatively spacious, with a big window that looks out onto the street. It's cozy, with plush carpet and furniture that looks worn but comfortable. The living room is full of the mismatched decor that comes with cohabitation, framed photographs and books and random trinkets that litter the shelves like lost treasures. There is a purple yoga mat rolled up in one corner and a knitted blanket folded over the back of the couch, and the window sill is lined with small potted plants. A stick of incense is still smoldering in a metal holder on the end table, and the air smells faintly of sandalwood.

Shane is watching Warren from his tight curl on one of the couch cushions, slitted amber eyes peering over the top of his wound tail. Warren greets him with a nod and Shane yawns at him, pink mouth widening to show every tiny, pointed tooth, before he closes his eyes again.

Yolande returns with the promised towels. Warren takes one and bends to dry Minnie's fur, rubbing it until she deems herself dry enough and wriggles away from him. Her fur is sticking up in all directions, and she crouches down on the carpet to start reordering it with her paws.

Warren uses the other towel for his face and hair, before handing it back to Yolande with a grateful, "Thank you."

Nadia comes back into the living room with a small bundle of clothes in her arms and mischief in her eyes.

"Here," she says, passing the clothes to Warren. "You can change in the bathroom. It's just down the hall."

Warren finds it without any trouble and starts stripping off his damp jeans and jumper. He hangs them on the shower curtain rod to dry before unfolding the clothes Nadia gave him, a pair of black shorts and a pale green tank top that looks suspiciously small. He puts it on, and yes— it's a crop top.

Minnie tilts her head to the side. "Where's the rest of it?"

"I think you're looking at it."

He dons the shorts apprehensively, hoping for the best. The result is not ideal: they sit low on his hips and are only long enough to reach the tops of his thighs. They're made of some kind of stretchy fabric that clings to his body in a way he's not sure is entirely flattering, given his extreme lack of curves. When he looks in the mirror above the sink all he sees skin: pale and freckled and way too much of it. He feels ridiculous.

"At least there's no pink glitter?" offers Minnie.

Warren exits the bathroom and returns to the living room. Nadia is sitting on the couch with Vic and Shane, while Yolande is cross-legged on the floor in front of the coffee table, steaming teacup in hand. They all look up when he enters the room, and Nadia puts a hand to her mouth to hide her grin.

"Thanks for the clothes," says Warren, "but are you sure you don't have any, um, track pants or a sweater or something that I can borrow?" He tugs at the bottom of the shirt. It stubbornly refuses to hang lower than his belly button.

"Sorry, Warren," Nadia says with poorly hidden amusement. "You caught us right before laundry day, you know how it is."

Warren isn't sure he believes her, but it doesn't seem worth arguing. What's he going to do— demand to see her closet? Anyway, at least he's dry, if not exactly warm.

"You look cute," says Yolande, and Warren seriously contemplates returning to the bathroom to put his wet clothes back on.

"That's not actually as reassuring as you seem to think it is," he tells her.

Yolande's cheeks dimple slightly as she tries to repress a smile. "Are those my gym shorts?"

"Well, mine certainly weren't going to fit him," Nadia replies. "Come and sit, Warren. I grabbed your bag for you."

Warren sits next to Yolande on the floor and drags his messenger bag over by its strap. He crosses his legs, but it makes the shorts rise so high up his thighs that he decides to stick his legs straight out under the coffee table instead.

"Would you like some tea?" Yolande asks him. "It's chai."

"Sure, that would be great."

She rises gracefully and heads over to the kitchen to pour him a cup from a dark blue teapot with gold stars painted on it.

"Yolande makes the best tea," says Nadia. "It's probably one of the top five best parts about being her roommate. Which is saying a lot, because Yolande is a freaking awesome roommate."

"Love you too, Nadia."

"How long have you been roommates?" asks Warren, nodding in thanks as Yolande hands him his tea. She sinks silently back down next to him and starts organizing a stack of papers on the coffee table in front of her.

"Since second year of undergrad," says Nadia. "We were on the same intramural volleyball team, and during one of our matches there was a girl on the other team who would not stop trash-talking us— just the most vile, ironically misogynistic bullshit you've ever heard. Yolande ended up spiking a ball in the girl's face so hard that it made her nose bleed, and I thought to myself, *this is my forever friend.*"

"I still maintain that it was an accident," Yolande says, sipping delicately at her tea.

"Naturally," replies Nadia.

Warren grins. "So on top of everything else you do, you're also a secret volleyball assassin?"

"Allegedly," purrs Shane, and Yolande smiles into her cup.

"After I befriended Yolande," continues Nadia, "I convinced her to get a place off campus with me. And then of course then I met Johnny— and Zoe as well, unfortunately for all involved."

Yolande tosses a pen at her. "Zoe isn't that bad, give him a break."

Vic raises his wings in alarm as Nadia tries to dodge out of the way. The pen sails harmlessly over the back of the couch and lands with a soft thud on the carpet.

"Yolande," Nadia complains, righting herself, "whatever it is that you see in Zoe, please know that you are the only person he allows to see it."

"I know," says Yolande, and her smile goes soft and secretive.

Warren clears his throat. "Johnny told me that Zoe gave you flowers on Valentine's Day."

Nadia cackles. "Oh, Warren. Zoe has done so much more than that."

"Like what?"

"Don't—" Yolande starts, but Nadia talks over her.

"Okay, so, listen to this," she says, sliding to the edge of her seat. "Last year some guy was stalking Yolande at The Palm. He was always sitting in there just, like, *staring* at her. I thought Zoe was going to rip his eyes out. One day the guy tried to get Yolande to give him her phone number and just wouldn't take no for an answer— you know how some of these assholes are." Warren nods, because it seems like she's waiting for confirmation. "Anyway, I guess Zoe got fed up listening to him, because he grabbed the guy by the shirt and dragged him outside to the alleyway beside the shop. We couldn't see what happened in there, what Zoe said or did, but the guy never bothered Yolande again." She shrugs. "Maybe Zoe killed him. We just don't know."

"*Stop*," Yolande says, exasperated. "Saints, Nadia. Zoe didn't kill anyone."

"Besides," adds Shane, licking at his paw, "we had it handled."

"Well, obviously," replies Nadia, "and Zoe knew it too. That just makes it all the more interesting that he couldn't help but step in anyway."

"So are you together?" Minnie asks Yolande, and Warren is grateful to her for asking the question so he doesn't have to.

"Zoe and I have talked about it," Yolande responds. "We're taking it slow."

"Glacially slow," mutters Shane, and Nadia laughs.

Vic shuffles a bit on his perch. "Perhaps you all should do some studying at this studying session."

"He has a point," agrees Yolande.

Nadia is looking at her phone. "Actually… Yolande, can you help me with something?"

She stands, and tugs on Yolande's arm until she does the same. Warren watches, bewildered, as Nadia leads them back toward the bedrooms, Yolande following with a bemused expression on her face.

There is a knock at the door.

"Um," he says.

"Can you please answer that, Warren?" Nadia calls from somewhere down the hall.

"...Sure."

Warren stands, and suddenly remembers that all he's wearing is a crop top and shorts that barely skim his upper thighs. He winces, pulling at the legs of the shorts to try to get them lower, but his efforts are in vain.

The knock sounds again.

He sighs in resignation and crosses to the door. He undoes the latch and pulls it open.

Johnny is standing there, Lucinda by his side.

"Johnny," Warren says in surprise. He has the sudden realization that he's been set up— but to what purpose, he can only guess.

Johnny is silent, his mouth parted slightly, as if he'd started to speak and then abruptly stopped. He gives Warren a wide-eyed once-over, gaze catching and holding on the swathe of skin revealed between the bottom of the crop top and the waistband of Warren's shorts.

Sweat prickles on the nape of Warren's neck. The room feels over-warm, and his brain has gone fuzzy. He wants to hide but he is frozen in place, pinned by the weight of Johnny's stare.

The silence stretches.

After several long, excruciating seconds, Lucinda makes a noise like a cough, nudging her body against Johnny's legs— and the moment snaps.

"Hi," Johnny says belatedly, sounding strained. His eyes jerk up to Warren's face, and then compulsively drop back down to where the shorts cling to his hips, as if pulled by magnets.

Warren's hands fist at his sides. He's blushing so deeply it feels like he might combust.

"Johnny!" Nadia cries, reentering the room with Yolande in tow. "What a surprise."

As if released from a spell, Warren can suddenly move again. He steps backward away from the door and ducks his head to hide behind his curls.

Johnny shakes his head as if to clear it. "What are you talking about? You told me to come over ASAP."

"Did I?"

"I was at the studio," Johnny grits. "I was having an artistic moment."

Nadia's eyes light up. "Ooh, speaking of that— David wants to know when you're going to come by to see the gallery."

Johnny closes his eyes and pinches the bridge of his nose. He lets out a low noise of despair.

"Maybe not the best time, Nadia," suggests Lucinda.

Yolande rolls her eyes. "Come in, you two. We're supposed to be studying, but I guess this has turned into something else now."

Johnny and Lucinda follow the rest of them back to the living space. Warren returns to his spot on the carpet and starts pulling his books from his bag, trying to collect himself.

"Who's David?" asks Minnie, from where she has made herself at home on the couch next to Shane.

Lucinda glances at her sidelong. "Minnie…"

"David," chirps Vic.

"My friend," Nadia elaborates. "He and his partner, Ivan, own a gallery in East Stave. David saw some of Johnny's work and now he's *obsessed* with getting him to show there." She turns to look at Johnny. "But *someone* is being uncharacteristically shy about it."

"I'm not being *shy*," insists Johnny. "I don't have enough pieces for a show. And besides, has it occurred to you that maybe I want some things to be just for me?"

"Undercover artist," remarks Yolande, eyes on her notes as she flips a page.

"Don't you start too," sighs Johnny. He glances at Warren. "And do I even want to know the reason for… for all of *this?*" he asks, waving an encompassing hand at him.
"I don't know," quips Nadia. "*Do* you?"

Johnny narrows his eyes at her.

It feels as if maybe Warren's missed something important, like there's a layer to this conversation that's just out of reach— and he doesn't like it. He'd thought that the clothes were just some sort of benign prank on him, but the way Johnny is glaring at Nadia makes him wonder if perhaps Johnny was the target all along. Either way, Warren doesn't understand the joke.

"Minnie and I got caught in a rain shower on our way over," he explains, to dispel some of the tension. "Nadia and Yolande lent me some clothes."

"Poor you," Lucinda says to Minnie, sticking her muzzle into the soft fur at Minnie's throat. Minnie lifts her head obligingly as Lucinda starts grooming her with broad sweeps of her tongue.

"Just doing our part," says Nadia, examining her nails.

Johnny arches one eyebrow. "Mm-hmm."

Warren's blush has finally receded to manageable levels and he is beginning to feel the cool air of the apartment again. He wraps his hands around his teacup as a sudden draft causes goosebumps to rise on his arms. He shivers.

Johnny notices.

"For Saints' sake," he mutters. He yanks the blanket from the back of the couch and throws it over Warren's shoulders, before plunking himself down on the carpet next to him and pressing their sides together. "This okay?" he asks Warren.

"Yes," Warren croaks.

He holds the blanket closed in front of his chest with one hand and uses the other to pull one of his textbooks over and lay it across his lap. For no particular reason. He catches Yolande sneaking a glance at him, her mouth hooking up at the corners.

"This is ridiculous," says Johnny, wrapping one arm around Warren over the blanket. "Nadia, don't you own about a hundred of those wool cardigans Jonas likes so much?"

"Hmm? Oh, I think I left all of them at his place."

"You are a menace," Johnny tells her. "Yolande, I want you to know that I still love you, even though I suspect your role as an accomplice to this absolute travesty."

"Noted," Yolande says dryly.

Johnny huffs and slumps closer to Warren. His fingers begin rubbing absent, soothing circles on Warren's upper arm.

Heat curls in Warren's gut. He instinctively shifts nearer and their calves brush against each other, Johnny's jeans rasping along Warren's bare skin. It sends a jolt up his spine, and he has to bite back a gasp. Out of the corner of his eye, he sees Johnny lick his lips. Warren shivers again, not from the cold this time. Johnny's grip tightens on his arm.

"Johnny, please," Nadia is saying, "let's not allow paranoia and unfounded accusations to destroy our friendship."

Johnny says something in return, but Warren doesn't hear it, too focused on each and every place where their bodies are touching. Then Nadia is laughing, and Johnny is too, and Yolande is smiling widely at both of them.

And Warren— even wearing practically nothing— is warm to his very bones.

# CHAPTER 5

It's Tuesday morning, and Warren is killing time at The Palm again before his classes.

Johnny, he's learned, likes to sleep in when he gets the chance— understandable, given his late night habits— so he doesn't expect to see him today, but Yolande is there, in her typical place behind the cash register. Her current coworker is a young man who goes simply by 'Dodd'. He has big shoulders, shaggy brown hair, and a badger daemon who scuttles around his feet while he works.

Warren is sitting in his usual spot, enjoying a muffin and a latte— which is not as good as the one Johnny made for him— and minding his own business, when Zoe suddenly appears.

"I need your help."

Warren stares at him, muffin halfway to his mouth. "With what?"

Zoe takes the seat across from him. "I want to make our menu more accessible."

His crow daemon takes up a position on a perch fastened to the wall near the table, watching Warren from above. Minnie cranes her head to look up at her, then swivels back to Zoe.

Warren sets down his muffin. He isn't quite sure what to say. "Zoe, that's really… nice of you."

"'Nice' has nothing to do with it," Zoe says dismissively. He pointedly taps his cane on the floor. "Accessibility is important. Besides, more customers means more money in my pocket."

Zoe's daemon caws softly in agreement. Warren still doesn't know her name.

"Okay," he says, tugging at his hair. "Um… honestly, typed rather than handwritten, for starters."

"I advocated for typed," Zoe grumbles. "Yolande and Johnny wanted an *aesthetic*."

Warren smiles, relaxing a bit. "There are special fonts you can use, but really anything sans-serif and monospaced would be an improvement. I can send you a list if you'd like."

"That would be appreciated," says Zoe. "What else?"

"Make the menu larger. And you should increase the spacing between the lines and letters— not just for dyslexics, but for anyone with atypical vision or visual processing."

Zoe nods. "That all sounds reasonable. What do you think of our website?"

"Well…"


------


Warren hasn't seen Johnny since the failed study session at Yolande and Nadia's apartment, well over a week ago. That in itself wouldn't be especially unusual— except for the fact that Johnny hasn't replied to any of his text messages in five days.

Warren worries over it, and then feels stupid for worrying over it. Johnny has a busy life. He has lots of friends, and lots of things to do. And maybe he needs space, Warren reasons. Maybe he thinks Warren is being too needy. Or maybe Johnny has simply decided that this thing that's been building between them— whatever it may be— is just not worth the effort anymore. It would make a lot of sense.

But still, Warren worries.

He's worrying now, as he sits behind the counter at the Laundromat attempting the dual impossibilities of focusing on his coursework and resisting checking his phone every thirty seconds. He took the hint after the second day of being left on read and hasn't sent Johnny any new messages since. But it's hard not to reach out, and Warren just… misses him.

"Stop," says Minnie, placing her paws over his bouncing knee. "You're giving me a headache."

Warren forces his leg to still. "Sorry," he says, petting her head in apology.

She's been on edge too, taking the absence of Johnny and Lucinda like the rejection it may very well be. But they both agree that it doesn't seem like Johnny to cut and run. Warren likes to imagine that Johnny would at least talk to him about it first.

Which brings him back to worrying.

He wonders if he should message Yolande. Surely someone would have said something if Johnny was *actually* missing, right? But maybe he should check, just to make sure...

He's reaching for his phone, when there is a sudden scraping sound at the door.

Warren looks over— and his heart jumps in his chest. It's Lucinda. She has one paw raised, nails scrabbling at the doorframe, and her nose is pressed flush to the glass, her gaze imploring.

Minnie is off his lap and sprinting toward her before Warren can even think to move. He follows, hastily shoving his phone into his pocket.

"Open it, open it!" cries Minnie, skittering around Warren's feet as he reaches the door.

The instant he opens it wide enough for her to pass though, Minnie is outside and pushing her face up against Lucinda's, frantically touching her muzzle to her cheek, her ear, the side of her neck. "Where have you *been?*" she asks. "I missed you!"

"Sorry," Lucinda answers, and she sounds exhausted. "It's hard to explain…"

"Where's Johnny?" asks Warren.

He searches the darkened street behind her, looking for any sign of him. He can't be far— Lucinda wouldn't be able to function through the pain of separation. When he looks back at Johnny's daemon, he sees that she is panting shallowly with her tail tucked between her back legs. So not far, he revises, but perhaps far enough for pulling.

"Just needs your help," Lucinda says. "To get home."

Warren furrows his brow. The Palm is directly across from them. The windows of the shop are dark, but there is still a light on in the apartment above. "But where *is* he, Lucinda?"

"Not far. Come."

"Is he okay?"

She hesitates, and Warren's stomach clenches.

"Are *you* okay?" Minnie asks her.

"Yes," says Lucinda. "But we have to go."

Warren checks the time: three twenty-one. Damn it. Still two and a half hours left in his shift.

"What about Zoe or Yolande?" he asks.

Lucinda shakes her head. "Johnny doesn't want them to see him like this."

"Like what?" Warren asks with a sinking feeling.

She shakes her head again. "Warren, please. Help us."

"*Warren,*" hisses Minnie.

"Of course," he says hurriedly. "Of course, just let me—"

He rushes back inside and quickly locks the till, then runs back to the door, not even bothering with his jacket as he follows Lucinda out into the night.

They take up a swift pace along the sidewalk, Lucinda in front and Warren trailing close behind her. Minnie is beside Lucinda, keeping pace while shooting her anxious sidelong glances. She'd done a good job hiding it at the door, but Lucinda isn't moving quite right, drifting and swaying where she'd normally be steady, her footfalls interrupted by the occasional stumble over nothing. It makes Warren uneasy, afraid of what they'll find once they reach Johnny.

They don't travel far. Lucinda leads them past a few dark storefronts, then veers into an alleyway.

Johnny is there. Warren can just barely see him in the glow of the streetlights, sitting slumped against the brick wall near the entrance with his head in his hands. He looks up as they approach, the whites of his eyes shining moon-like in his dark face.

"Johnny," murmurs Lucinda, butting her head against his chest.

"Lucinda," Johnny says. His hands clutch unsteadily at her fur. "You're back. Where did you go?" His gaze shifts to Warren, a beat too slow. "Warren?"

"I'm here," Warren confirms distractedly. He's busy scanning Johnny over, looking for injuries. He seems unhurt, but he's shaky and a bit disheveled, like he's been sitting out here for a while.

Johnny starts to shake his head, then abruptly stops, as if it's hurting him. "You shouldn't be— I didn't… I don't *want* you to be here."

And that definitely stings, like a slap to the face.

Warren breathes through it. "Well, I am." He kneels in front of Johnny. The smell of alcohol is immediate and overwhelming, even from a few feet away. "You've been drinking?"

"I tried to stop him," says Lucinda mournfully.

"I fucked up," Johnny says, and his voice is all wrong, like it belongs to someone else. "Warren, I really fucked up."

"What happened? Are you all right?"

Johnny lets out a jagged laugh, head thumping back against the wall. "No, not really."

Warren feels helpless. He's never seen Johnny like this, vulnerable and so obviously in turmoil. "Are you hurt?"

"No."

"Okay," says Warren. "Okay, that's good. I'm going to take you home now."

"No," moans Johnny. "I can't go back there like… like this."

"Well, you can't stay out here. I won't let you."

"So stubborn," Johnny mutters, with just a trace of his regular humor. "I always forget."

"That's right, I am. Now give me your hand."

To Warren's relief, Johnny doesn't offer further protest. He helps Johnny to his feet, and then pulls one of his arms over his shoulders to keep him upright.

Now that Johnny is standing, his inebriation is more obvious. He sways heavily into Warren's side as they make their way slowly out of the alleyway, their daemons following close behind. Johnny is an uncoordinated tangle of limbs, his feet dragging and stumbling in a disturbing mirror of Lucinda's earlier movements. It makes Warren's chest ache to see it.

They are both staggering by the time they reach The Palm, Johnny from the drink and Warren from the effort of supporting the artless drape of Johnny's lanky frame across his shoulders. The entrance to Johnny and Zoe's apartment is at the corner of the building. Warren directs them to the door and helps Johnny with his keys when he fumbles with the lock. Inside, a narrow staircase leads to the top floor. Warren briefly wonders how Zoe manages it, before deciding he probably does it the same way Warren and Johnny are about to: carefully.

Minnie, too small to be of much help, bounds ahead and sits on the landing above, watching apprehensively as the rest of them tackle the ascent. Johnny braces himself with one hand on the railing while Warren supports his other side. Together they begin to take slow, shuffling steps up the stairs. Lucinda is in front of them, still moving in that odd, stilted way, and Warren realizes she must be experiencing the effects of the alcohol secondhand through her bond with Johnny.

About halfway up, Lucinda's hind legs suddenly slip out from under her, and Warren instinctively reaches out to stabilize her. She recovers before he makes contact and Warren quickly aborts the motion of his hand, his heart pounding.

When they finally reach the landing, they find that the door to the apartment is already unlocked. Johnny sags against Warren's side as he pushes it open.

Zoe is sitting on an armchair in the living room with his daemon, dressed more informally than Warren has ever seen him in pajama pants and a worn long-sleeved t-shirt. He watches them stumble through the door with his eyes narrowed and his lips pressed into a flat line.

"Zoe," Warren says in surprise. "You're awake."

"I heard you on the stairs," says Zoe. He inclines his head toward Johnny. "Is he all right?"

Warren shakes his head. "I don't know. I think physically, yes."

Johnny bends to hide his face in Warren's neck. "Tell Zoe I'm not here," he mumbles.

Warren meets Zoe's eyes and they share a look of mutual uncertainty. Warren shrugs a bit, trying not to jostle Johnny too much in the process.

"It's fine," Zoe says at length. His expression is troubled. "You've got him. I'll go." He stands, before adding, "Johnny's room is the last door on the left. There's ibuprofen in the bathroom."

He disappears down the nearby hallway and Warren hears the click of his bedroom door as it shuts behind him. Alone with Johnny once more, he takes a moment to collect himself while he considers the best way to cross the distance between the front door and the hallway.

Johnny still has his face hidden against the side of Warren's neck. Warren can feel him there, breathing. His lips graze lightly over Warren's skin, soft like butterfly wings. It sends a spark of pleasure zinging through Warren, and he fails to repress a shiver.

Johnny inhales sharply and shifts against him. The arm not wrapped around Warren's shoulders comes up to slide slowly across his chest, tugging gently at him to close the scant space between their bodies. His hand fists in the fabric of Warren's shirt, holding fast.

Warren can feel the warmth of Johnny's breath when he whispers, "You're wearing my hoodie."

Warren glances down. He is. He'd completely forgotten. "Yes. Should I—" His voice cracks a bit, and he has to stop to clear his throat. "Do you want it back?"

"Nope."

Johnny shifts again, moving behind Warren. His other arm slips from Warren's shoulders, hand skimming inexorably down Warren's side as he presses himself flush to his back. Warren's pulse quickens as Johnny's hand comes to rest just above his navel. Without thinking, he lifts his own to cover it. Johnny tilts his head to bury his nose in Warren's ruddy curls and breathes deeply. His mouth is hot on the nape of Warren's neck.

Warren's eyes fall shut of their own accord. He feels a rush of heat, as if all the blood in his body has been suddenly set aflame. He lifts his chin, just slightly, leaning into Johnny's touch. Johnny hums approvingly and begins pressing small, sucking kisses into Warren's skin.

Warren's brain goes hazy with desire.

He wants to melt back into Johnny's embrace— *Grimm,* does he want to. But he can smell the alcohol on Johnny's breath. Feel the unsteadiness of his movements. And he knows that he can't.

He opens his eyes.

"John," Warren whispers, and his voice is wrecked, even to his own ears. "We should get you to your room."

Johnny makes a noise of protest when Warren steps out of his arms, but lets him go.

Warren keeps his gaze lowered as he carefully props Johnny up against the wall. He bends to remove first Johnny's shoes, and then his own. His blood still burns in his veins.

"This is all wrong," he hears Johnny murmuring to himself, and Warren silently agrees.

"Come on," he says, standing and taking some of Johnny's weight back on his shoulders. "You need to go to bed."

They make it to Johnny's room without incident. Warren forgoes turning on the ceiling light, instead navigating by the distant glow of the lamp Zoe left on for them in the living room. Even in the dimness, he can make out the brightly patterned quilt on Johnny's double bed. He guides them over to it and tips Johnny sideways onto the mattress.

Johnny rolls to his back, hands resting on his stomach. With some effort, Lucinda climbs up onto the other side of the bed and lies down with the entire length of her body tucked close to Johnny's side. She rests her head on her paws and lets out a weary breath.

Minnie leaps onto the bedside table and crouches there as Warren starts maneuvering the blankets out from underneath Johnny's body. Johnny doesn't move to assist, just lies back and watches him with heavy eyes.

"You know," he says, slurring slightly, "this isn't how I imagined finally getting you into my bedroom."

Warren's hands stutter on the sheets. He swallows. "Me either, if we're being honest."

Johnny heaves a sigh. "What a waste."

And Warren doesn't know how he's supposed to respond to that.

"Take off your jeans, at least," he finally says. "They can't be comfortable."

Johnny snorts, amused by some private thought, and obligingly reaches for the button on his jeans.

Warren clears his throat and turns away. "I'm going to find you some water. Minnie?"

She shakes her head. "I'll stay."

Warren leaves. He takes a quick detour to the bathroom for the aforementioned ibuprofen, then makes his way to the kitchen.

It's a nice kitchen— small of course, but very modern, all dark wood and sleek, stainless-steel appliances. There's even a washing machine tucked beneath the long, black granite countertop that stretches across the back wall. Warren stares at it.

*Huh,* he thinks.

He doesn't have the mental capacity to process the implications of its presence, so he files the information away for later contemplation. Instead, he searches through the cupboards until he finds a glass, and then fills it using the water dispenser on the refrigerator door.

When he returns to the bedroom, Johnny has managed to get himself under the quilt, his jeans discarded on the floor. His eyes are closed. Next to him, Lucinda breathes steadily, asleep or close to it.

Minnie blinks at Warren from the bedside table, her eyes glittering in the half-light. Warren sets the water and ibuprofen down near her, and then gingerly sits on the edge of the bed. He studies Johnny's face, taking in the delicate skin of his lowered eyelids, the angles of his cheekbones, the shape of his lips— and oh, Warren *missed* him.

Johnny opens his eyes and their gazes lock.

"Warren," he breathes, "I'm so *tired.*"
Warren starts to reach for him and then stops, his hands clenching. His heart aches. He wants *so badly* to comfort Johnny. But now that the situation doesn't explicitly require it, he's not certain how to touch him, or understand the limits of what would be welcome. Despite what happened in the living room, the fact remains

that Johnny didn't contact him. He has to remember that. Johnny was hurting, and he didn't call for Warren— not for *five days*.

"You disappeared." The words just fall out of him.

Johnny swallows a few times. Warren tries not to watch his throat, the length of it, working.

"I'm sorry. I didn't… mean to."

Warren bites back the questions that crowd his tongue. "It's okay," he says, even though it's really not. "Go to sleep, Johnny."

"I don't know if I can," whispers Johnny, and his voice breaks over the last word.

Warren wants nothing more in that moment than to lie down next to him and stroke his hair. It would be so easy— Johnny is *right there*. But instead he just sits, frozen in mute indecision, cursing every tangled thought inside his head.

Minnie acts for him.

She leaps onto the bed and pads around the top of Johnny's head to his other side, near Lucinda. Then she nudges Johnny's temple with her nose before lying down in one swift motion, settling her head on his chest, directly over his heart.

Johnny gasps, sharp and tight. It's as loud as a gunshot in the quiet room. He freezes where he lies, his grey eyes gone wide with shock.

Warren is in shock, too. He trembles with it. He feels fragile suddenly, as if someone has reached a hand inside of him and grasped at something deep and precious.

"Hush," Minnie tells Johnny kindly. "Everything will be all right."

Johnny raises a hand as if to touch her— and Warren stops breathing. The world stills, suspended in the space between Johnny's fingers and the tips of Minnie's ears.

But Johnny doesn't touch her. His hands hovers there, just out of range, before he lets it fall limply back onto the bed beside him.

The rejection hits Warren like a blow, and he flinches. His mind reels, blood roaring in his ears as he struggles to contain his emotions. He meets Minnie's eyes over Johnny's chest. They both know what this means.

Minnie rallies, as she always seems to. She burrows deeper into Johnny's chest and continues to hush him, making small, wordless sounds of comfort until the tension starts to bleed back out of his body. Warren watches them, willing his pulse to slow.

For what seems like a long time, Johnny lies silent, blinking up at the ceiling. Eventually, his eyes slip shut.

Warren and Minnie wait until Johnny's breathing has evened out before taking their leave, two shadows vanishing back into the night.

------

"You're angry with me," Minnie says later, when they've returned to the Laundromat to finish what remains of Warren's shift.

"No," denies Warren. "Maybe. A little." He drags his hands over his face, rubbing tiredly at his eyes. "You shouldn't have done that, Minnie."

"*You* wanted to do that."

He shakes his head. "It wasn't the right time."

Minnie makes a frustrated noise. "*Never* would be the right time for you. Johnny likes you, Warren. He really does."

"He didn't touch you back."

She looks away. "He wasn't in his right mind. He probably wanted to make certain he had your consent."

"But it was okay for *you* to touch *him?*"

Minnie looks back at him, her gaze defiant. "Yes."

A daemon initiating contact with a human other than their own isn't quite as taboo as a human touching another person's daemon, but it's still definitely considered an act of impropriety outside of an intimate relationship. Some people are looser with this social convention, but Warren doesn't think that Johnny is one of them: Johnny freely touches other humans, and Lucinda isn't shy about interacting with other daemons, but Warren's never seen Lucinda touch another human, not even Yolande or Zoe. He isn't sure where the line is, or whether or not Minnie— and by association, Warren— has crossed it.

Warren sighs, placing his palms flat on the counter and leaning over them. He and Minnie are rarely in disagreement over anything but he doesn't know how to explain it to her, this bone-deep fear of pushing too far, too fast— and losing everything as a result.

Minnie touches her paw to the back of his hand. "It will be okay, Warren. You'll see."

"Just… be careful," says Warren. "Please."

"I promise."

------

Yolande messages Warren right before the end of his shift and asks him to join her at The Palm when he's finished working. Warren had already been planning on going to see her, but he's grateful for the invitation nonetheless.

When he arrives, still feeling strung out and emotionally compromised, Yolande is waiting for him with coffee and a hug.

"Zoe told me a bit of what happened," she says into Warren's shoulder, her slender arms wound gently around his waist. "It must have been a shock to see Johnny like that."

Warren nods. He tentatively puts his hands on Yolande's back, returning the embrace. It's the first real hug he's had in a long, long time. He'd forgotten how comforting it is to be held this way, without expectation, and he can feel a tiny bit of the tension he's been carrying start to dissipate.

On the ground nearby, their daemons touch their noses together in greeting. Warren can hear the soft rumble of Shane's purr as he rubs his cheek against the side of Minnie's face.

After a moment, Yolande pulls back to look at him. "Are you okay?"

"I'm fine," Warren tells her, swiping a hand over his eyes. He hesitates, then asks, "Did you know? That he was like that?"

She shrugs one shoulder, stepping away to put some space between them. "I noticed him spiraling a bit, but I didn't realize that it had gotten that bad. He's really good at hiding his feelings when he wants to be."

"He always seems so… happy. I didn't even know there was anything wrong until he stopped talking to me."

Yolande smiles sadly. "Johnny puts on a good show. He loves to talk— I'm sure you've noticed." Warren nods in agreement. "But not about the things that are actually important. He doesn't take the mask off, not for just anyone."

"I guess I knew that," Warren says slowly, because he's seen the cracks in the mask too— when Johnny speaks of his mother, or when someone brings up his art.

"I thought you might," says Yolande. "You two seem close."

"Maybe not as close as I thought we were."

"Just give him some time. The last couple years have been really difficult for him."

"What happened?"

Yolande shakes her head. "You should hear it from Johnny, I think."

Warren sighs. "I figured you would say that."

"Some secrets are meant to be kept."

"You're a good friend, Yolande."

Yolande smiles at him. "So are you, Warren."


------


Warren checks in with Johnny that evening, after giving him the day to recover.

*Hi. How are you feeling?*

He purposefully keeps his expectations low, mentally preparing himself to be left on read again. But Johnny replies almost instantly.

*>>ugh. Like absolute piss*
*>>this is why I don't usually drink anymore*
*>>Zoe forced me out of bed and made me eat a disgustingly greasy dinner though, so that helped*
*I'm sure you needed it. It's good that he's there with you.*
*>>yeah, he's a real one*

There is a brief pause. Then,

*>>I'm sorry about last night*

Warren bites his lip. He wants to ask what happened, but he doesn't want to pressure Johnny, too afraid of being shut out again. Instead he sends,

*Don't be sorry. I'm just glad that you're safe.*

This time the pause is much longer. Warren is about to put his phone away, disappointed, when another message pops up.

*>>are you busy tomorrow?*
*>>let me buy you breakfast. as an apology*

*You really don't have to do that.*
*>>I want to*
*>>please? I know a great bakery*
*All right. What time?*
*>>10?*
*>>we can meet there. I'll send you the address*

A location link appears in their chat window.

*>>does that work for you?*
*>>and also do you like waffles??*
*Yes and also yes. See you then.*


------


The bakery is called Sol.

Warren recognizes the stylized golden sun etched on the glass storefront. It's the same as the one on the bakery boxes they use at The Palm, and he realizes that this must be the source of the coffee shop's baked goods.

When he pushes open the door, he's immediately met by the scent of freshly-baked bread. It's incredible, a sweet and slightly yeasty aroma that somehow smells warm. He can hear Minnie sniffing greedily at the air from her place upon his shoulders.

It's busy inside, the tables all full in the small dining area. There is a brown-haired man with a bloodhound daemon taking orders at the service counter, and the line of people waiting there reaches almost to the entrance. Warren has to squeeze past them to make his way into the bakery proper.

He spots Johnny and Lucinda at a table by the window, near the back of the shop. Johnny is already looking back at him, and he waves Warren over. As he gets closer, Warren can see that Lucinda is sitting upright next to Johnny's leg, her chin resting on his thigh. She's tracking Warren and Minnie's approach with a wary expression.

"Hi," says Johnny, as Warren takes the seat across from him.

"Hello," he replies, and it feels awkward between them. Minnie slinks from Warren's shoulders into his lap, hiding shyly beneath the table like she hasn't done for months.

He and Johnny stare at each other for a moment, before Warren drops his gaze. There is a laminated menu on the table and he glances at it automatically, but it's completely unreadable.

Johnny clears his throat. "The waffles here are amazing. I already ordered for us. I hope you don't mind."

Warren shakes his head. "No, that's a lot easier. Thank you."

"No problem."

There is silence again. Johnny starts shredding the edges of a paper napkin, and Warren is momentarily transfixed by the movement of his hands.

"How are you?" he asks at length.

Johnny shrugs. "I still have a headache but it's nothing that some painkillers and rehydration can't fix."

"Good."

"Yeah. Do you—" Johnny starts, but he is interrupted by the brown-haired man from the front counter.

"Johnny," the man says. He's carrying two plates, both of which are stacked high with waffles. "It's good to see you."

"You too, Mal. It's busy in here today," remarks Johnny.

Mal slides their plates onto the table. "What else do you expect on a Saturday morning?"

Johnny grins. "I suppose you do have a shining reputation amongst the local brunch crowd. This is Warren, by the way."

"Hi," Warren says, and Mal nods politely at him before taking his leave.

"Mal runs this place with his partner, Alina," Johnny tells Warren. "She's the mastermind behind these waffles. And all other things delicious."

The waffles in question are golden brown and absolutely smothered in syrup. Piles of whipped cream and red berries line the edges of the plate, and everything's been sprinkled liberally with powdered sugar. Warren's stomach gurgles, helpfully reminding him that he hasn't eaten since dinner the night before, and he eagerly picks up his fork.

Minnie pops her head up over the edge of the table, drawn out of hiding by the scent of food. Johnny notices, and cuts off a piece of waffle from the stack on his plate. He holds it out to her like a peace offering. A look passes between them. Then Minnie leans across the table and plucks the waffle from Johnny's fingers with her teeth.

Warren lets out a breath he hadn't known he'd been holding. He takes his own bite of waffle and chews thoughtfully.

"Okay, you were right about these waffles: they're amazing."

"Trust and believe," Johnny says, smiling lopsidedly at him.

Warren can't help but smile back, and it diffuses some of the tension between them.

They eat in companionable silence for a while, before Johnny says, "I appreciate you helping me get back to the apartment the other night." He uses his fork to push the food around on his plate. "I was kind of a mess, huh?"

"I was worried about you," Warren tells him. "I just wanted you to be okay."

Johnny's mouth quirks. "I guess I owe you an explanation though."

Warren waits.

"Yeah, all right," sighs Johnny, setting down his fork. "*Saints*. Where to start?"

"At the beginning," suggests Lucinda.

"Yes, thank you, Lucinda. Astute as always," Johnny says distractedly, scritching the top of her head with his fingertips. He seems to be steeling himself against something. "Hell, this really isn't how I wanted to… to start telling you about this."

Warren caves in the face of Johnny's discomfort. "It's all right," he says. "You don't have to—"

"I do," Johnny interrupts him. "I really do. So here it goes." He takes a fortifying breath. "I grew up on a farm with my dad. You know that part already." He waits for Warren's nod of affirmation, before continuing. "When I came here for university I was eighteen and just the dumbest, most naive kid you can imagine. I'd never been to a city like this one before. I wanted to try everything... and I did. I partied almost every night, and slept through most of my classes as a result. Zoe was my roommate that semester—"

"And Johnny drove him absolutely crazy," Lucinda interjects wryly.

"Yeah," Johnny confirms with a fleeting grin. "I think he was pretty close to switching rooms. We were both business majors— I know," he says to whatever look he sees on Warren's face, "doesn't really seem like my thing. And it wasn't. I only chose it because my dad wants me to take over the farm someday."

"So you dropped out?" asks Warren, because he knows at least that much.

Johnny cringes. "Not right away. I got caught up with a bad crowd. They were really into gambling, and not in a fun, casual way, but like in an all day, every day kind of way. I got really into it too. I liked it. I liked the excitement, liked the feeling of beating the odds. For me, winning was the best high imaginable." And Warren can see it on his face, a gleam in his eyes at just the memory of it. Then Johnny sighs, and it flickers out. "But like I said, I was eighteen, and very stupid. Before I knew it, I had gambled away my tuition. So I dropped out of school, thinking I could just win back the money and start over again next term. I didn't tell my father— I lied, acted like I was doing great. Top of my class. He sent me tuition for the next year and I gambled that away too. I felt bad about it, but I did it anyway. I couldn't help myself."

Warren's heart twists. "Grimm, Johnny," he says. "I'm so sorry."

"Why?" Johnny asks darkly. "It was my fault. I lost myself in gambling and drinking... and people. Girls, boys— anyone who could distract me from the guilt. I owed so much money, and I did a lot of awful things to pay it back. I fell so far down that if it hadn't been for Zoe and Yolande, I don't know that I ever would have gotten back up. I owe them my life."

"Is that why you didn't want Zoe to see you when you were... to see you at your apartment?"

"He and Yolande have done so much to help me. They believe in me. I didn't want to let them down." Johnny shrugs helplessly. "So now you know my tragic backstory."

"Thank you for telling me," says Warren. It hurts to hear and it has to hurt more to be the one saying it, but he needs to see this conversation through to the end. He takes a deep breath before asking, "So what happened the other night?"

Johnny fidgets in his seat. "I've been going to these meetings," he says. "Um, addiction support group meetings."

"That's great," says Warren encouragingly.

"Yeah, it is," agrees Johnny. He rubs a hand over the back of his neck. "But I've been doing really well lately, so I... I skipped the last couple."

Lucinda lets out a low growl. "Against my advice."

Warren bites his lip, holding back his own comment.

"I know," Johnny says to both of them. "It was idiotic. And then one of my old friends invited me out and there was this poker game, and I just... I thought, what harm could one hand do?" He scrunches his shoulders unhappily. "But then we started drinking and one hand turned into two, into three— you get the picture. And before I knew it, I'd lost my rent money."

Warren's heart wrenches in his chest. "Shit."

Johnny barks a short, humorless laugh. "Exactly. Times were, I might have borrowed from the till at The Palm."

"But you didn't," says Minnie, her nails digging into Warren's thighs.

"No, I didn't. I haven't fallen that far off the wagon."

"Why are you telling me all of this?" asks Warren.

Johnny looks down, drumming his fingers on the tabletop. "Because I want you to know."

Warren shakes his head. "But *why?*"

"Because it's important," says Lucinda. "And we trust you."

Minnie looks at her solemnly. "Thank you."

"Thank you," echoes Warren. "But... if you trust us, then why the radio silence?"

Johnny huffs in fond resignation. "You're not going to let me get away with that, are you? I was embarrassed, Warren. I didn't want you to see me like that."

"Like what? Drunk?"

"Yeah, that— but also like… like how I used to be," Johnny says, scrubbing a hand through his short hair. "After I lost at poker that night I just felt so *angry* at myself, at everything. I was scared that things would go back to the way they were before. And then I missed another meeting and I felt bad about that too, so I went to a bar. And I guess I overdid it a bit."

"A bit," says Lucinda flatly.

Warren's fingers grip at Minnie's fur. "If you didn't want me to see you, then why send Lucinda to come get me?"

"I didn't," says Johnny. "That was all her."

Lucinda is shaking her head at him. "You did. You just don't remember."

Warren exchanges a look with Minnie. He thinks of the hot press of Johnny's mouth on the nape of his neck and wonders what else Johnny doesn't remember.

"Look," Johnny is saying. "I'm sorry for disappearing on you. That was unfair of me."

"No, please— don't apologize," says Warren. "I get it now. I'm sorry you didn't feel like you could talk to me about it. I wish I could have been there for you."

"You didn't do anything wrong," Johnny says, rushed. "I just— before, when I was... I couldn't let anyone in, not for real. I... I slept around, I partied, I lost way too much money— and I did it all with a smile on my face. But I don't want to be that person with you. I want to be real. Better."

Warren swallows around the lump in his throat. "You're real," he says, meeting Johnny's eyes. "You're real to me. And it's not like that anymore. I... I've seen you. And it's not like that."

"No, it's not," says Johnny. "Yolande helped me find the right kind of support groups. Zoe got me on track to pay off my debts. And they both kept me honest. They made me face my father."

Warren thinks of his own father and winces on Johnny's behalf. "Was he angry?"

Johnny shakes his head. "Not really. More like disappointed. You know how parents are."

Warren, who knows intimately what it's like to disappoint a parent, nods. He starts to reach for Johnny, then changes his mind and drops his hand to the table instead. "What did he say?"

"Once I finally came clean about everything he was more upset that I hadn't told him. He said he didn't care about the money or about school. He was just glad that I was getting help."

"He sounds like a good man."

Johnny's mouth ticks up. "Yeah, he is. Da just wants me to be happy."

"And are you?" asks Warren. "Happy?"

Johnny looks at him. "You know, I think I really am. Most of the time. When I'm not relapsing like an idiot," he adds self-deprecatingly.

"You're not an idiot, John. Everyone makes mistakes."

"Yeah, well. This was a pretty big one." Johnny holds Warren's gaze. "What about you?"

Warren's brow furrows. "What about me?"

"Are you happy?"

Warren swallows thickly. "Sometimes." Then, like a confession, "Most of the time, now."

Johnny's eyes crinkle as he smiles, soft and slow and real. "I'm glad." He reaches across the table and covers Warren's hand with his own.

Warren watches as Johnny carefully slides their fingers together, closing the spaces between them, like a puzzle piece slotting into place.

# CHAPTER 6

Warren wakes in increments, still chasing the remnants of some pleasant dream. It's like trying to catch the wind— the dream slips quickly from the grasp of his reaching mind, leaving only the impression of bright eyes and clever hands behind.

He extends his limbs out the sides of his narrow bed, stretching languidly as he blinks to awareness. The light creeping in from the curtains is warm and yellow, diffused, but bright enough to tell him that it's well past dawn.

Since the end of winter term classes the previous week, Warren has been drifting in pre-examination limbo with the rest of his classmates. He's primarily been using the extra time to work on his final projects, but an added bonus of the break has been catching up on sleep, now that he's free to laze the mornings away. For the first time in months, he almost feels well-rested.

From her place at the top of the pillow, Minnie yawns hugely. Warren reaches above his head to pat idly at her side, and then— as has become habit— he picks his phone up off the bedside table.

He has a new message from Johnny, and he's smiling before he even taps to open it.

>>*good morning, sunshine*

Warren's stomach flips as he turns to hide his grin in his pillow.

"That must be Johnny," Minnie says drowsily. Her tail flicks teasingly over his eyes.

"Maybe not," says Warren, batting it away. "You know I blush easily."

"Yes, but only one person has ever put *that* particular expression on your face."

And, well. It's true, isn't it? No point in arguing with the being that knows him best.

"Hush, you," Warren tells her, already sending his reply.

*Good morning!*

Blinking dots appear instantly at the top of the chat screen; wherever Johnny is, he must be on his phone. Warren checks the time: eleven forty-four.

*>>well, well. look who it is*
*>>did you really just wake up? I'm so proud*
*I did. Must be your bad influence.*

Warren regrets the words the moment he sends them. With what he knows now of Johnny's past, it could perhaps be seen as insensitive on his part. He's debating whether or not to attempt to backtrack, when Johnny sends a response.

*>>I prefer to think of it as good inspiration*

It's difficult to parse tone over WhatsApp, but Warren doesn't detect any hint of insult or unease, only Johnny's usual brand of wry self-mockery. So maybe he's overthinking this. It wouldn't be the first time. He bites his lip, and impulsively sends,

*Is that so? And in what other ways might you inspire me?*
*>>oh, I'm sure I could come up with something...*
And now Warren is *really* blushing.

He's still thinking of a reply when his bedroom door bangs open. He startles, then lets out a pained grunt as he drops his phone directly on his face.

"Hey!"

It's Karl, sounding uncharacteristically chipper. He has his hands on either side of the doorframe, bracing himself as he leans his upper body forward into Warren's room. Daya is hovering in the air over his shoulder, wings beating frantically as she works to stay aloft.

Minnie is a puffed up ball of fur on the edge of the mattress. "Don't you knock?" she grumbles.

Karl ignores her. "I'm going out for boba. Do you want any?"

Warren is half awake and fully suspicious. "Did you set the microwave on fire again?"

"No!" says Karl. He looks shiftily to the side. "But I *was* hoping you could look over the equations for my final organic chemistry lab."

"Sure, I can do that," Warren says. His nose throbs, and he swipes a finger under it to check whether or not it's bleeding. It's not.

Karl beams at him. "Thanks, Warren!" He disappears from Warren's doorway as suddenly as he appeared, Daya flitting along behind him down the hallway.

"Hey, what about my—" Warren starts to call after him, but Karl is long gone. "Never mind, then."

Minnie huffs. "That boy is trouble."

Warren chuckles at her prickliness on his behalf. Karl sometimes rubs Minnie the wrong way, but lately he's been having the opposite effect on Warren.

With classes over and exams looming, Warren and Karl have been at the apartment at the same time more often, studying separately and, amazingly, together on occasion as well. It's not something that they did at the end of their fall term, and Warren doesn't know what's changed since then, but he finds himself reluctantly grateful for it. Studying with Karl is a double-edged sword: on the one hand, it's comforting to be near someone who is going through the same hell he is; on the other, Karl's increasing level of anxiety has the effect of inciting Warren's own worries. But mostly, it's been good.

"It's fine," Warren says to Minnie. "Don't be too hard on him."

He glances back at his phone, where Johnny has apparently moved the conversation along after Warren's delayed response.

*>>btw, I'm coming over to the BPL tonight*

Warren frowns.

*Are you?*
*I thought you had GA group meetings on Thursdays?*

*>>I do*
*>>I'll come over AFTER, so stop worrying*
*Who's worrying? I know you're going to be just fine.*
*>>nice try, but I can hear that big brain of yours from here*
*>>you're as bad as Yolande*
*>>anyway, we need to catch up on drag race. I'll bring my laptop*

Warren smiles at the reminder of their most recent late-night activity.

*Yes, I'd like that.*
*Also I hope you know that comparing me to Yolande is actually a huge compliment.*
*>>just calling it like I see it*
*>>got to get ready for work*
*>>ttyl, Warren*
*Have a good day, John.*

Warren puts his phone away, not even bothering to hide the happiness in his expression. Minnie gives him a knowing look, and he pulls her into an unresisting cuddle. His heart is a balloon in his chest, buoyant and light.

It feels like hope.

------

On Thursday night, Warren waits until the Laundromat is empty and the two of them have completed their requisite viewing of *RuPaul's Drag Race* before asking Johnny the question that's been on his mind all evening.

"So how did it go at your meeting earlier?"

He's careful to keep his attention on the bolt at the top of the dryer door hinge, the one that he is currently attempting to remove using an Allen wrench.

Ever since Giles discovered Warren knows his way around a toolset, he's been leaving him lists of odd jobs to do in the lulls between customers. Tonight he's asked him to replace the rubber gasket on the door of dryer number eight. Warren doesn't mind so much— or he wouldn't if it weren't exam season, anyway. He's mostly just grateful Giles left him the necessary parts to complete the task this time.

Johnny is sitting on top of the machine next to the one Warren is working on, his long legs dangling down the front of it. He rhythmically taps the heels of his boots against the metal siding as he answers, "Oh, you know. The usual. I confessed my sins to my fellow sinners and tried my best not to notice the majority of them disassociating whenever I said anything that hit a little too close to home."

"That's... good," says Warren, panting slightly as the bolt, stuck fast by time and neglect, resists his attempts to loosen it.

"John did great," Lucinda says with obvious pride in her voice. "He was very honest."

Johnny lays a hand over his heart. "Aw, shucks, Lucinda."

She playfully closes her teeth around his ankle and Johnny yelps in mock offense, before gently shoving her off, tousling her fur a bit as he does so.

Warren smiles at their antics, then asks, "But it's helping? Things have been better?"

Warren half-expects him to dodge the question, but Johnny meets his eyes and says seriously, "Yes, it's helping. And it helps to come here afterwards too."

He's holding Warren's gaze, so Warren sees the moment when his grey eyes soften— Johnny *let's* him see it— and it makes something unfurl beneath his ribs, expanding outward like the petals of a flower stretching toward the sun.
Since that night back in March it's as if Warren has unlocked something, some faucet of Johnny that had hitherto been closed off to him. Johnny is still bold and flirtatious and funny in turns, but now he's also... open. Warren can see some of the places where Johnny is vulnerable, the soft underbelly of his personality. It's like an optical illusion: now that he's seen it, he can't unsee it— and it's honestly better this way. His friendship with Johnny had seemed too perfect, almost dreamlike. This feels *real*, like waking up and finding something better was waiting for you all along.

Warren looks away first, swallowing back the rising tide of his emotions. "I'm glad."

The bolt finally releases, and he carefully lowers the dryer door to the floor before kneeling down next to it. Minnie nudges a utility knife toward him, and Warren picks it up and begins cutting away the worn gasket from the inside of the door ring.

Lucinda comes around to sit on her haunches beside him, so close to Warren's arm that if he leaned just a little to the side he'd be touching her. The thought of accidentally doing so is dangerous and desirable in equal measure, and his skin prickles with awareness of her presence. He wonders whether or not it was a purposeful move on her part.

Lucinda tilts her head curiously as she watches Warren work. "What are you doing, exactly?"

"Replacing the seal," Warren explains. He edges away from her to create some space between them, and then applies downward pressure to the circular glass window until it pops out of the door. "It's worn out, so the machine is venting a lot of the heat that it needs to dry the clothes."

"Can I help?" Lucinda asks.

Warren casts a quick glance toward Johnny, who is watching them silently, then looks back at Lucinda. Her expression is earnest, her tail half-raised, and Warren feels a burst of affection for her.

"Of course," he says. "Will you help remove the old gasket, please?"

"It's here," says Minnie helpfully, using her nose to indicate the correct part on the now empty door ring.

Lucinda braces one paw on the metal frame, and then uses her teeth to peel off the rest of the rubber seal, before discarding it to the side, out of the way.

"Thank you," Warren tells her. He has the strangest urge to pet her, like he would do for Minnie. "You did a good job."

"You're welcome, Warren," Lucinda replies in her velvet voice, tail swishing behind her. She goes to Johnny, who leans down to ruffle the fur between her ears, murmuring something to her in a voice too low for Warren to hear.

He focuses on unpackaging the replacement part instead, mind drifting to the question of how Lucinda's thick fur would feel beneath his fingers. Would it be soft like Minnie's, or coarser?

*Stop,* he admonishes himself. *Just stop. Don't be weird.*

"So," Johnny says, watching as Warren begins pressing the new gasket into place, "have you always been this handy? I'm not going to lie: it's hot as hell."

Warren's mind blanks. He fumbles the part, his cheeks pinking. Minnie, as is her wont, comes to his rescue.

"Warren has always had a knack for taking things apart and putting them back together," she says. "But it never really had any practical application until we were… until we left home."

"Hmm," Johnny acknowledges absently. Then he abruptly straightens. "Wait. Important question: you *do* get paid extra for this, right?"

"No," says Warren, glancing up at him as he determinedly finishes installing the gasket. His cheeks still feel overwarm. "Why? Do you think I should ask for a raise?"

"Well, let's see," Johnny says as he begins ticking off points on his fingers. "You're doing work outside of your job description— work that your boss would have had to *pay someone else* to do— and you're doing it without any additional training?" He waits for Warren's nod of confirmation before concluding, "*Yes,* Warren, I think you should ask for a raise."

Warren hums in consideration as he concentrates on reinserting the glass into the propped up door. It's the trickiest part of this whole operation. Minnie has her paws raised to the opposite side of the glass, applying counterpressure to hold it in place.

"I suppose it couldn't hurt to ask Giles."

"I mean, if he says no we can always get Zoe in here to berate some sense into him," says Johnny.

Warren huffs a laugh. "Oh, I don't know if we need to go that far."

"You know he would though."

"I wouldn't bother him with it."

Johnny sighs. "You don't know your own damn worth, Warren," he mutters.

With a loud click, the glass finally slots into place beneath Warren's hands. "Yes, got it!" he grins triumphantly, and strokes an appreciative hand over Minnie's back when she returns to his side. "Nice work, Minnie."

She licks his cheek in response.

Warren looks up at Johnny. "Will you come here and help me hold this?"

Johnny hops down from the dryer. "As you wish."

He holds the dryer door in line with the hinge as Warren slides the bolt back into place and begins to tighten it with the Allen wrench, his arm straining with the effort.

"There. That should hold," he says, when the door has been successfully reattached.

"Impressive," drawls Johnny. "Who knew a scrawny thing like you had so much hidden muscle?" He runs a teasing finger down the bare skin of Warren's forearm.

Warren fights to hide the hitch in his breathing as the touch sears through him. "*Scrawny?*" he repeats, aiming for mock indignation but landing closer to real. "Is that supposed to be a compliment?"

Johnny laughs. "I suppose that depends on who's saying it."

"*You* said it."

"Warren, you should know better by now than to take anything I say seriously."

Warren blows out a frustrated breath and bends to collect his tools. This is the problem— this has *always* been the problem. Johnny flirts, and Johnny laughs, and Warren has no idea if he's meant to take it seriously or not.

"Hold up, are you *mad* at me?" Johnny asks in disbelief. "I'm sorry I called you scrawny, Warren. I didn't realize it was such a sensitive subject."

"That's not what I—" Warren pauses to compose himself. "I'm not mad. Anyway, you're right. I should know better."

"Don't start doing that."

"What?"

"Agreeing with me," says Johnny. "Sure path to destruction."

Warren turns his head to hide his expression, which he knows must be damning. He is upset, and it makes him feel foolish. He *hates* feeling foolish. "At least it would lead *somewhere*," he mutters under his breath.

"What was that?"

"Nothing. I think your laundry is done."

"No," Johnny starts. "What did—"

Lucinda halts his words with a headbutt to the thigh. "You'll have to excuse him, Warren," she says. "John has never known when to quit."

"Betrayal!" cries Johnny, pretending to stagger. "Way to hit me where it hurts, Lucinda."

Warren's lips turn up despite himself, his aggravation lessening in the face of their levity. "I hate to agree, but that was a little on the nose, Lucinda."

"Right? So uncalled for," Johnny adds.

Minnie gives him a shrewd look. "But at least you and Warren have stopped sniping at each other."

"Yeah, yeah. Daemons are smarter than humans, we get it," Johnny says flippantly. "I'm going to grab my clothes." He turns back to the dryer atop which he had previously been sitting and opens the door.

Warren watches him pull his clothes from the drum and thinks about the washing machine in Johnny and Zoe's apartment.

The question sits heavy on the tip of his tongue, but Warren hasn't asked it. He can think of several reasons why Johnny wouldn't use the machine at his apartment, but he knows which one he *wants* to be true. He's afraid that if he asks Johnny about it and Johnny doesn't give the answer Warren is hoping to hear, then his disappointment will be written all over his face. His feelings would be obvious. Warren would take Johnny's friendship— he *wants* Johnny's friendship— but if Johnny reads it on him, this hopeless crush that Warren has been harboring, and he *doesn't* return Warren's feelings, then it might get awkward. Maybe Johnny would stop hanging out alone with him, even as friends. And that isn't something Warren is ready to risk quite yet.

"Hey, did Nadia tell you about Jonas' birthday yet?" Johnny asks, interrupting Warren's spiraling introspection. He's looking over at him as he tosses his clean clothes into his laundry bag.

"No?" replies Warren, shaking his head to clear it. "I mean, I haven't seen her since last week— but, no. When is his birthday?"

"It's not for another two weeks but we're all going out for it," says Johnny. "It's sort of a tradition we have, dinner and then clubbing. The birthday person picks the restaurant, but we always go to the Big Block after. Zoe had the last birthday, back in January. Yolande actually found a place that serves *hotspot* for him, can you believe that?"

Warren smiles. "Well, if anyone could…"

Johnny snorts. "True enough."

"The Big Block… that's the one you were talking about before. In the Barrel district, right?"

"Yeah," confirms Johnny. "We used to go to the Emerald Palace, but one time the owner overcharged Zoe on his drink order and now Zoe has a blood feud with him or something. But the Big Block is great: loud music, bright lights, interesting people— my kind of place."

Warren considers it. He still has money from the extra shifts he worked during March break. He could afford a night out. But...

"I don't have a gift for Jonas."

Johnny rolls his eyes. "Nobody expects you to bring a gift, Warren. *I'm* not bringing a gift. That's not really part of it."

Still, Warren hesitates, thinking of the inevitable social hangover he'll experience the next day. He's an introvert who knows his own limits.

"Come on," wheedles Johnny. "It'll be fun. Just the six of us, dinner, dancing— what more could you ask for?"

Warren can think of one or two things. But Johnny is looking at him imploringly, and Warren is a weak, weak man. "All right, I'm in."

Johnny's answering grin is dazzling. "Excellent."


------


In what has fast become a weekly routine, Warren goes to Yolande and Nadia's apartment to study on Sunday afternoon.

About half of Warren's classes have final group projects or laboratory reports rather than a written exam, which is a source of both relief and frustration to him. It mainly means that he's spent most of his spare time over the last couple weeks meeting with his groupmates or in the lab gathering data. He hasn't been able to go to the coffee shop very often, and it's honestly been a little strange after almost three months of regularly hanging out there. So it's nice to still have a standing appointment with Yolande and Nadia. He'll almost be sad when exams are over and he no longer has an excuse to visit them on a regular basis.

Just now, Warren is sitting on the couch with Nadia, a spread of papers between them. He has his notebook open on his lap, slowly working his way through a practice problem set for his thermodynamics exam, while Minnie looks on and offers the occasional correction.

Nadia is flipping through a sheaf of handwritten flashcards as she quizzes herself on terminology for her anatomy final. Warren wishes he could help her, but if he's being honest with himself he probably couldn't read her handwriting even if he *wasn't* dyslexic, so they're mostly just keeping each other company. It's companionable in the way that shared stress can sometimes be, venting their frustrations and encouraging each other to keep working in turn.

They both look up when the front door opens and Yolande and Shane enter the apartment.

"Hi," Yolande says, closing and locking the door behind her. "Sorry I'm late. My Eco Justice group ran long." She pulls two identical travel mugs with The Palm's logo on them from her backpack's side pockets and holds them up enticingly. "But I brought coffee to make up for it."

"All praise Yolande!" cheers Nadia. She stands and skips over to collect the drinks from Yolande. "We've been suffering here without caffeine. I was *this close* to DoorDash-ing it."

Vic flies over to greet Shane, landing on the floor and hopping close enough to him to skim a wing over the cat daemon's arched spine. Shane purrs loudly in response, bumping Vic gently with his cheek.

Warren takes one of the travel mugs from Nadia when she returns to the couch. "Is that the group that's planning a protest next month?" he asks Yolande. He's learned that she's involved with multiple environmental action groups, several of which she leads. This particular one, if he remembers correctly, focuses on industrial pollution.

"Yes," says Yolande, coming to sit cross-legged atop the coffee table. Shane settles on his side on the carpet nearby, while Vic flies back to his perch on the backrest of the couch, near Nadia's shoulder. "This afternoon we were reviewing our mission statement and putting together some media scripts in case any of us get interviewed by reporters."

"Are you expecting to?" asks Warren.

"It could go either way, but at an event like this it's definitely one of our goals. Getting on the news is still one of the quickest ways to spread awareness."

"Will you be conscripting the rest of us to fill out the ranks?" Nadia asks, sipping her coffee.

Yolande smiles. "I'll let you know once I have the final head count."

To Warren, Nadia says, "Yolande sometimes asks us to come help with her events. What usually ends up happening is that we all get way more into it than the actual group members. Last time we were protesting a new development that would wipe out a— what was it, Yolande?"

"An ecologically significant forest corridor."

"Right, that. And then the next thing I knew Jonas was up in a tree, shouting at a bulldozer and refusing to come down until they 'stopped the build'."

Warren tries to picture reserved, dignified, six-foot-four Jonas shouting from a tree and utterly fails. "Does that actually work?"

Yolande shrugs. "We do our best. Most of the time the impact is small, but it's more about drawing attention to the issues than anything else."

"Jonas' stunt was very helpful in that regard," adds Shane.

"But at what cost?" Nadia jokes. "He had to cut off some of his lovely hair because he got sap in it."

"Huff was devastated," laments Vic. "So was I."

"A tragedy, to be sure," Shane says dryly.

From her backpack, Yolande pulls out a binder and a bound study guide that Warren has come to recognize as her law school entrance exam prep material. From what he can tell, she knows it inside and out.

"Have you scheduled your test?" Warren asks her, taking a careful gulp from his mug. The coffee is still steaming hot. Yolande must have come directly from The Palm.

Yolande nods, tucking a lock of hair behind one of her metal-studded ears. "I'm taking it on Wednesday."

"You're going to do great," Warren says, reaching across to give her ankle an awkward little pat.

"I hope so. I'd really like to start school in the fall."

"Oh, please," says Nadia, shuffling through her flashcards. "You're going to get in and you know it. You already have your specialization picked out and everything."

Minnie leaps over to the coffee table and peers inquisitively at Yolande's notes. "What do you want to specialize in?"

"Social justice," replies Yolande.

Minnie looks up at her, her expression sincere. "That's perfect for you."

Yolande smiles at her. "Thank you." She turns to Warren and Nadia. "How goes studying?"

"Ugh," complains Nadia. "I just want to get this anatomy exam done and over with. It's all multiple choice and everyone knows I do *much* better on practicals."

"How many exams do you have, Warren?" asks Yolande.

"Only two."

"And then you're done?"

Warren nods. "Except for the final concert with the orchestra in May. It's a performance requirement for my music minor."

"Is your family going to be in town for that?"

"Oh," says Warren, caught off guard. He resists the urge to bite down hard on the side of his thumb as a wave of panic sweeps over him at the thought of seeing his father. "Um, no. I don't really… have anyone."

Minnie returns to his side and lies down with her chin resting on his knee, while Yolande and Nadia exchange a look.

"You know," Nadia starts slowly, "most of us don't have relationships with our families. I mean, Zoe is an orphan. Jonas— thank the Saints— broke away from a family so ultra-conservative they may as well be a cult. And I was raised by boarding schools. I haven't seen my parents in *years*." Warren stares at her. He hadn't known any of this. Nadia sees his stunned expression and continues with a wry grin. "Admittedly, we're not all so tragic. Johnny's father is a real-life angel, and Yolande— actually, Yolande gets on really well with her parents. What's your deal?"

"Just lucky I guess," Yolande says with a half-smile. "But they're really far away. A whole continent, even."

"That's right," says Nadia. "Which brings me back to my original point: it's just us here. We take care of each other."

Warren is speechless. He doesn't know how to articulate the intense gratitude he feels flooding through him. These are his *friends*. He knew that already, but... he's had friends before, and it wasn't like this. He'd never realized how superficial those friendships were, until he had these people in his life.

Warren is dismayed to find his eyes filling with tears. He blinks them back. "Thank you," he manages. "That… that means a lot."

Yolande reaches out her hand, and Warren takes it. "Nadia is right. We're here for you." She squeezes his fingers, her smile turning mischievous. "Regardless of what happens with Johnny."

Warren shifts his gaze to the side. "I'm not sure what you mean."

Yolande and Nadia regard him with twin expressions of incredulity, Vic squawks, and even Shane looks askance at him.

Warren squirms under their collective regard, his cheeks pinking. "I don't—"

"No," Nadia interrupts, waving a forestalling hand at him. "Please spare us the attempt. You're not fooling anyone."

Warren winces. "Am I that obvious?"

"Warren, sweetie, you light up like a freaking *sunbeam* whenever he's around. It's disgusting. And cute."

"Disgustingly cute," offers Vic, and Nadia points at him in agreement.

"What's the deal with you two, anyway?" she asks. "Johnny is being uncharacteristically tight-lipped about it. At least to me," Nadia adds, glancing sidelong at Yolande, who only shrugs in response.

Warren crosses his arms over his chest and sinks deeper into the couch cushions. "There's no 'deal'. We're friends."

"But you want more," Shane says, his tail twitching.

Vic shuffles sideways along the backrest until he's near enough to peer down at Minnie. "I've watched you with Lucinda. It's quite telling."

Minnie scrunches herself closer to Warren's hip. "I really like her," she concedes. "And Warren really likes Johnny."

"So what's the issue?" Nadia asks, puzzled. "Ask him out. If he says yes, great; if he says no, then nothing changes. Hell, you could probably hook up with him and go back to being friends afterwards. You don't need to worry: I've known Johnny for a while now, and he doesn't get hung up on stuff like this. It's not a big deal."

"That's the whole problem!" Warren blurts. "I *want* it to be a big deal. I want it to matter. I'm not interested in a hook up…" He trails off, then quietly admits, "I want more than that."

Yolande lifts a hand to hide her smile. Nadia doesn't even bother, just grins unabashedly at him.

"Aww," she coos. "That's really sweet, Warren! Tell him that, he'll love it."

"But what if he doesn't," says Warren, tugging at his hair. "What if I tell him and it ruins everything? I just wish I knew what he wanted. Sometimes I think he wants more, but other times he backs off and I just… I don't know."

Warren considers telling them about Minnie touching Johnny. About Johnny *not touching her back.* But it feels… private. Like something he wants to hold close and keep safe. He can tell with a glance that Minnie feels the same way.

"Have you tried talking to Johnny about it?" Yolande asks.

"Not… directly," Warren says, thinking of his daemon's head on Johnny's chest.

She gives him a look. "Maybe you should."

"Maybe."

"*Okay,*" Nadia says, tossing down her flashcards. "Enough about Warren's boy problems. Let's talk about *my* boy problems instead." She presses her palms together and regards them with a serious expression. "What in the name of every Saint who suffered am I supposed to get Jonas for his birthday?"


------


Warren finishes his final exam on the last Friday in April, and it's like a weight has been lifted off his shoulders. He's free from coursework for the next four months and feels positively *ecstatic* about it.

He exits the lecture hall with a spring in his step, Minnie sprinting joyfully out ahead of him, and pulls his phone from his bag. With exams complete he's able to think of other things, such as Jonas' birthday outing tonight.

He swipes over to WhatsApp and messages Johnny.

*Guess what? I just finished my last exam!*
*>>CONGRATULATIONS!!!*
*>>knew you could do it*

*Thank you! I'm ready to celebrate.*
*Can you send me the address for where we're all meeting tonight?*
*>>I'll just swing by and pick you up, it's easier*

Warren blinks at his phone. Johnny wants to pick him up from his apartment? He turns the thought over in his mind, wavering between uncertainty and elation.

*Are you sure? It's not out of your way?*
*>>yeah, it's not a problem. the restaurant is near your place anyway*
*>>see you at 7*

Warren settles on elation.

# CHAPTER 7

When he gets back to his apartment that afternoon, Warren immediately starts trying to figure out what to wear. He's never actually been to a club before, so this is not an easy task. He does a cursory online search that does nothing but reiterate to him how insufficient and unsexy his wardrobe truly is, before resigning himself to wearing his usual brand of boring-but-comfortable apparel.

Halfway through his deliberations, Nadia messages everyone to remind them that the restaurant Jonas chose has a *smart casual dress code*, adding, *that means NO SEE-THROUGH CLOTHING— I'm looking at you, Johnny!*

Which is… intriguing, but ultimately unhelpful, and Warren has to perform another search to figure out what "smart casual" entails.

In the end he decides to wear his white oxford shirt layered under an oatmeal colored crew-neck pullover, paired with light wash jeans and his cleanest white canvas sneakers. It's definitely not sexy, but it's *him*.

"You look very handsome, Warren," Minnie says, impatient, when he spends too long staring critically at himself in the mirror for her liking. "Will you brush my fur now, please?"

With his outfit sorted and Minnie brushed, Warren moves onto his hair. A glance at the time tells him he only has another ten minutes before Johnny is meant to arrive, so he hurries to the bathroom.

Twenty minutes later, Warren is still fussing with his perpetually messy curls, trying to order them into something approximating a style, when he hears a knock at the apartment door. He looks helplessly at his product-covered hands, and then to Minnie.

"Don't look at me," she says. "I can't even reach the doorknob."

Karl appears from who knows where to lean in the bathroom doorway. "I think your date is here."

"He's not my date."

"Are you sure about that?" Karl asks skeptically. "I've never seen you spend so much time on your hair before."

"Or any time at all," Daya chimes in.

Warren scowls at them in the mirror. "It's not a date, it's— you know what? Never mind. Will you please just let him in for me? I need another minute or two."

"Gotcha," says Karl, and leaves.

Warren gives up on styling, and washes the product from his hands. He uses his damp fingers to scrunch water through his curls in one last, desperate attempt to tame them, and then exits the bathroom.

He can hear Karl and Johnny from down the hall and the rich, warm tone of Johnny's voice makes his stomach flutter in anticipation. When he reaches the living room, he sees them talking together in the front entrance.

Karl is standing very close to Johnny, beaming up at him. Warren watches in horror as he giggles at something Johnny says, and then leans even closer, resting the tips of his fingers lightly on Johnny's forearm.

The spike of jealousy Warren feels is instantaneous. It propels him forward, toward them. Minnie is already ahead of him, making a beeline for Lucinda.

Johnny sees them coming over Karl's shoulder. He smiles widely. "Warren!"

As soon as Warren is within range, Johnny grabs his wrist and pulls him near, forcing Karl to take a step backwards.

"Oh," says Warren, startled by their sudden proximity. "Hi."

Johnny gives him an attentive once-over. He whistles lowly. "My, my. Don't you look nice. Very geek chic."

Warren blushes. "Uh, thanks. You look good too. I like your coat."

Johnny is wearing a light grey sport coat with the sleeves rolled up over a white v-neck t-shirt, paired with dark grey chinos and his black and white high tops. He's wearing jewelry too, rings adorning almost every finger, and a black leather cuff around his left wrist. The short, tightly twisted coils of hair on the top of his head shine, and his fade has been freshly trimmed. He's so gorgeous that it makes Warren's chest ache. It's unbelievable that he's even *met* a person who looks like this, let alone is friends with him.

Johnny grins knowingly at Warren. He runs his thumbs down the lapels of his sport coat, and says, "What, this old thing? Gee, golly! Thanks, mister!"

Warren rolls his eyes. "Never mind. I take it back."

"Nope. You've said it, can't take it back now. You think I look *good.*"

"You own a mirror, John. I know you know this already."

"Sure, but it never hurts to hear it."

Karl is observing their back-and-forth with a sullen expression. "Aren't you going to introduce us, Warren?"

"Did you not do that part already?" Warren asks coolly.

"We didn't get the chance, no."

"All right," Warren sighs, long-suffering. "Johnny, this is my roommate, Karl. Karl, this is my— uh, Johnny. This is Johnny."

If Johnny notices Warren's stumbling introduction, he doesn't show it. "Good to officially meet you, Karl. It's nice to be able to put a face to the name."

"Same to you, Johnny," replies Karl, with a simpering smile that kind of makes Warren want to smack him.

Johnny winks at Karl, then looks back to Warren. "Warren, we got to go. I need to make a quick stop before we head to the restaurant."

"Okay," Warren nods. "I'm ready." He grabs his keys and wallet, and then they're out the door.

"I won't wait up!" Karl calls after them as they start down the stairs.

Lucinda chuffs. "Oh, he's *funny.*"

"Hardly," Minnie sniffs disdainfully.

The sun is setting as they make their way out onto the street. It's a perfect spring evening, cool and clear, and Warren is feeling good as he and Johnny walk along the sidewalk in the direction of midtown. It's hard not to, with this man by his side. He wonders what the people they pass think of them, if they're thinking, *those two belong together.* Warren pretends, at least to himself, that it's true. He holds the thought close for a moment like a warming ember to his heart, then releases it, a wish sent to the sky.

Warren raises his face toward the waning light. "So where are we going?" he asks.

"Alisha's studio. I left my wallet there last night," Johnny says, sheepish.

That gets Warren's attention. "Really? You're taking me to the studio?"

"Don't get too excited. We're just making a quick stop, in and out."

Lucinda is walking ahead of them with Minnie. Over her shoulder, she says, "We probably have time for a short tour though. John can show you what he's been working on."

"I'd love that," Warren says eagerly. Johnny has been so secretive about his art.

Johnny grumbles something under his breath, and then sighs. "If you want a tour then we'd better pick up the pace."

The studio turns out to be a utility room located at the back of a cooperative art gallery.

They take a side entrance into what seems to have been a series of small rooms that have since been converted into one open space. A row of windows high on the exterior wall lets in natural light, and metal support beams crisscross the ceiling where the second story floor has been removed. There is a forge against one wall, and workbenches placed throughout the room. The walls are stripped to cinder blocks that have been painted and sketched upon so many times over that it's impossible to tell what their original appearance may have been. The room smells like a workshop, slightly smoky from the forge, and a bit like charred wood and the astringent scent of chemical cleaning solvents. Underlying everything is the tang of burnt metal— Warren can almost taste it on his tongue, coppery and sharp.

He turns in a slow circle, taking everything in. Tools and art supplies are scattered haphazardly throughout the studio, like a child's play area left in disarray, and artwork in various states of completion clutters every surface, including the floor. The room is an unstated gallery of half-finished masterpieces. Most of them are blown glass, which must be Alisha's work, but there, in the far corner, Warren can see metal.

Johnny strides directly to one of the workbenches and picks up his forgotten wallet. He slips it into his back pocket. "Got it. Let's go."

"What about the tour?" asks Minnie. She's standing on her hind legs, head swiveling and ears pricked as she surveys the room curiously.

Warren has already made his way to the far corner. There are two workbenches there. One is covered in piles of metal, obviously the raw materials of creation. He notes bike chains, mattress springs, aluminum siding, copper pipes— and a dozen other types of scrap metal, most of it worn or rusted. A pair of battered work gloves lay on a folding chair nearby. Both of them are stained and scorched, and one has a deep tear along its seam.

The other workbench is littered with tools, only some of which Warren recognizes, including an arc welder. But his eyes skip over them and go straight to the large, partially completed sculpture on the center of the worktop.

It's a tree, formed by tightly woven strands of metal that have been twisted and shaped into roots, and trunk, and outstretched branches. The branches taper into twigs, off of which hang tiny, perfect cherry blossoms.

The piece is stunning, a deft facsimile of nature. The tree looks as if it's dripping in blossoms, the branches shaped in such a way as to appear weighed down, even as they reach ever outward, yearning toward some invisible sun.

Warren is in awe.

"This is yours," he says quietly, when Johnny comes to stand beside him, Lucinda at his heels.

"Yeah," Johnny answers, matching Warren's tone. "Alisha's collaborating with me on it."

Sure enough, Warren can see that the blossoms are made of pink and white tinted glass. He's impressed that such a brittle material can be made to imitate something as soft as flower petals.

"It's incredible," he murmurs. He reaches out to touch the twisting trunk, looking first to Johnny, who nods his permission. Warren traces his fingers up the woven metal strands. "It's made of… electrical wires?"

"That's right. I try to use scrap where I can."

Minnie leaps to the top of the workbench, nails clicking on the metal surface as she circles the base of the sculpture. "Johnny, why don't you want to show your work? It's so good!"

"Ah," Johnny says, rubbing one hand across the back of his neck. "Thanks, darlin'."

"What made you choose this type of tree?" asks Warren, still fascinated by the curving metal branches.

"My mother's grave," says Johnny, without inflection. At his side, Lucinda makes a wounded sound, low and involuntary. "We buried her at the farm under a big old cherry blossom tree in the springtime."

He raises a hand to his left bicep, directly over the place where Warren knows his tattoos are concealed beneath his clothing. Warren thinks of a jackrabbit daemon wreathed in cherry blossoms, and mentally kicks himself for not making the connection sooner.

"I'm sorry, I didn't mean to—"

Johnny cuts him off. "No, it's fine. You didn't know."

"How old were you when she...?"

"Seven."

So young. Warren's chest swells with emotion. "What was she like?" he asks, and then cringes at his own words. "You don't have to answer that."

Johnny shakes his head. "I don't mind." He smiles, small and wistful. "She was… joyful. Energetic. She'd take me out to the fields while Da was working and teach me how to start a fire, shoot a gun— all kinds of things I probably had no business learning at that age. Most of the time it was just us and a thousand acres of land. She was my whole world." His smile thins. "Then she got sick. And she didn't get better."

"I'm sorry," whispers Warren.

"It was a long time ago. I don't remember her being sick. I mostly remember Da, how devastated he was by it," says Johnny, his gaze turned inward. "After Ma passed, it was just the two of us for a really long time. He didn't want me to come here for university. He was worried something might happen to me." His expression clouds. "Rightly so, as it turned out."

Warren's throat feels tight. He swallows, and asks, "Have you shown this to him?"

"No."

"John, I know you don't want to hear it, but…" Warren trails off, wary of overstepping.

"Go ahead," Johnny says. "Whatever you're thinking, just say it."

Warren meets his eyes. "I just don't get it. Why hide this amazing thing that you can do? Why not share it with him?"

Johnny gives an irritated shrug and looks away from him. "Maybe I don't want it to turn into another thing I fail at."

"I don't think you can fail at making art."

"I just don't want to disappoint anyone again. If it's private, if it's just for me, then I can make as many mistakes as I want and no one needs to know about it. What's so wrong about that?" demands Johnny.

Warren holds up his hands. "Nothing. There is nothing wrong with that."

Johnny sighs heavily. He has one hand fisted in Lucinda's fur where she is pressed against the side of his leg. Minnie is at the very edge of the workbench, as close to them as she can get without leaping off. She looks seconds away from launching herself at Johnny, propriety be damned.

Warren bites his lip. This time, he wants to be the brave one.

"Can I hug you?" he asks Johnny.

Johnny looks at him in surprise. "Yeah. Of course."

It takes them a moment to figure out how they fit together. Johnny has a good seven or eight inches of height on Warren, and they have to bend and stretch to accommodate each other. Warren has the startling realization that they've never actually done this before. Why has he never hugged Johnny? What was he *waiting* for?

They settle into an embrace. Warren wraps his arms around Johnny's waist and pulls him close, while Johnny folds his arms over Warren's shoulders, curving into him. He leans down to hook his chin over the crook of Warren's neck, surrounding and surrendering in equal measure.

Warren's skin hums with the nearness of him, the heat. He rests his cheek on Johnny's chest, inhaling the familiar smell of his body— soap and light sweat, and the comforting spice-and-citrus scent of his deodorant. It feels good to hold him like this, with their chests pressed together and Johnny's heart beating steadily against his own. It feels right.

Beside them, Lucinda lowers herself to the concrete floor as Minnie descends from the workbench to bury herself in her side. Warren watches Lucinda turn to nuzzle affectionately at Minnie, her snout pressed to the top of his daemon's furry head, and feels a rush of tenderness for them both.

Johnny exhales shakily, tucking his face into Warren's neck. "Thanks," he murmurs. "It's weird talking about this stuff."

Warren tightens his arms around him. "I know."

There is a long, contented pause. The only sounds are that of their shared breathing and the low rustle of their daemons' fur. It's peaceful like this. Safe. Warren thinks he could stay here forever, just like this, and be happy.

Then Johnny says, "Do you ever talk about it?"

"About what?" Warren asks, absently rubbing his cheek against the fabric of Johnny's shirt.

"Your mother."

"Oh." He is taken aback by Johnny's words, though he supposes he should have been expecting them. "No, not really."

"Do you remember her?" asks Johnny, pulling back to look at him.

Warren straightens to meet his gaze. "A little."

"What do you remember?"

"She was…" Warren closes his eyes, searching his mind for the few, precious memories of his mother he's stashed away like hoarded treasure. It's been a long time since he's purposefully thought about her, and he finds it doesn't hurt as much as he was expecting it to. He doesn't remember much— red-gold hair, a soft voice, a gentle touch. Comfort.

"She was kind," Minnie says, soft as snow.

"Yes," agrees Warren, opening his eyes. "And she was musical. She had a beautiful voice. She played the piano and we'd duet together sometimes." He smiles faintly up at Johnny. "She was an artist too, like you. She loved to paint."

"She sounds lovely, Warren," Johnny says, hushed. His eyes gleam in the semi-darkness.

"She was."

"How did your father take it when she passed?"

"I don't... I didn't see him much," Warren says, struggling to keep the bitterness from his voice. "He was away a lot, on business."

Johnny steps back from their embrace. He keeps his hands on Warren's upper arms, holding gently. "You know, you haven't told me very much about him."

"Trust me, you're better off for it."

Johnny raises a brow. "Warren's mysterious past," he says, with a hint of teasing.

Warren shakes his head. "Not mysterious. Just not worth talking about."

"If you say so."

"We should leave," Lucinda interrupts quietly. "It's getting late."

Johnny checks his phone. "Aw, hell. Yeah, we need to go."

They take a moment to gather themselves before heading for the door. As they leave the studio, Warren casts one last, fleeting glance at Johnny's sculpture and sees it for what it truly is: a reminder of things lost, but not forgotten.


------


By the time they arrive at the upscale restaurant located just outside the Barrel district, Warren has mostly managed to shake off the melancholy that had fallen over him at the studio and he hopes it's the same for Johnny.

It helped to walk the streets and see the city coming awake around them with its second life, the one that starts when the sun sets and the artificial lights come on. There is a thrum of excitement in the air, of possibility. Warren had forgotten how it feels to be part of it, rather than just watching through the window of the Blue Wave.

The hostess leads them to a large, round table where they are welcomed by a chorus of greetings from their friends. They are the last to arrive. Two adjacent chairs sandwiched between Yolande and Nadia's seats have been left open for them. Johnny goes to the one beside Nadia so Warren takes the spot next to Yolande, who smiles warmly at him as he sits.

She has a septum ring in tonight that coordinates with the stack of silver rings lining the outside of each of her ears. She's wearing purple eyeliner that makes her brown eyes pop, and her long hair falls in waves down the back of her black, sleeveless jumpsuit. Warren— despite being the least qualified person at this table to judge— thinks she looks very pretty.

"Nice of you two to join us," Nadia says, giving Warren and Johnny a sly look over the top of her wine glass. "Get caught up in something?"

Warren coughs, but Johnny only grins at her.

"What Warren and I get up to in our spare time is none of your business," he says with a wink, pulling out his chair so that Lucinda can slink under the table.

Larger daemons are relatively rare, and many establishments aren't set up to accommodate them. So while Zoe and Nadia's bird daemons are easily able to find perches, and Minnie and Shane fit comfortably on their human's laps, Lucinda and Huff are relegated to the space beneath the table. Neither appear especially bothered by it. Lucinda, at least, would probably be out of the way enough lying beside Johnny's chair, but Huff is just too big. Warren suspects Lucinda's true intent is to keep her friend company and he is fairly confident that Minnie will be joining them presently as well.

"Sushi, Jonas?" Johnny remarks as he takes his seat. "Didn't see that one coming."

Across the table, Jonas dips his head in admission. "We ate fish all the time back home. It's one of the things I miss most."

"Saints know why," Nadia mutters, not quite under her breath, and Yolande and Johnny laugh.

"My love," Jonas says, "you'll need to be more open-minded if we are to travel there together."

"What's this?" asks Johnny. "Going on a trip, are we?"

Nadia nods, draining the last of her wine. "Jonas, for some godforsaken reason, wants to return to the cold and generally inhospitable land of his birth, for a visit."

Jonas raises his eyes heavenward. "It's not so cold in the summer."

"But you agree that it's inhospitable."

"I think that you'll enjoy it more than you believe you will," Jonas insists. Their words have the cadence of a well-worn argument, no bite in them, and Warren exchanges an amused glance with Yolande.

"Well, of course," Nadia replies. "I'll be with you, won't I?"

Jonas leans over to kiss her on the cheek. Johnny coos mockingly at them and Nadia casually flips him off in response, before she remembers where she is and quickly drops her hand.

"How did you two meet?" Warren asks. "I don't think I've heard that story yet."

Nadia and Jonas both start speaking at the same time, and then stop.

"Go ahead," Jonas tells her.

Nadia smiles at him. "Thank you, darling." To Warren, she says, "Jonas and I met in Biomedical Ethics in second year. We had dissenting opinions on… well, pretty much everything. But mostly about paternalism in public health practices. It resulted in many, shall we say, *passionate* discussions. Eventually we arrived at some common ground, and we've been together ever since." She smirks. "Classic enemies to lovers romance."
Jonas shakes his head. "It wasn't *that* dramatic."

"It really was though," Huff says, her voice muffled from under the table. "There was so much yelling."

"Don't forget the name calling," adds Vic. "They still do that. But the names are nicer now."

"*Much* nicer," Nadia agrees, refreshing her wine from the open bottle of white on the table. She lifts her glass. "A toast!" she declares, grinning. "To Jonas, my darling, my stud muffin, babycakes, the syrup to my waffles, he of the long—"

"*Stop,*" Jonas groans, covering his face with his hands. "Nadia, please."

Nadia's grin softens with sincerity. "To Jonas, on the occasion of his twenty-fourth birthday."

Warren's glass had been filled before he sat down. He raises it, and the others do the same, Johnny and Yolande holding up their water glasses in lieu of wine. They toast to Jonas' birthday, and then twice more to congratulate Yolande on her completed entrance exams, and to celebrate the end of the school term for both Warren and Nadia.

The wine is dry and crisp, light on Warren's tongue and almost too easy to drink. The last time he'd had wine had been at his father and Janis' wedding, a few years ago now. He suppresses the memory of that day before it can fully form, focusing instead on the conversation around him as his friends banter back and forth across the table.

A waiter with a chameleon daemon stops by to take their orders and Warren subtly nudges Johnny, tapping his finger on the front of his menu card in a wordless request. Johnny understands immediately and— without drawing any attention to it— begins quietly reading to him. If anyone else at the table notices, they don't remark upon it. It might be the best restaurant experience Warren has had up to this point.

"So what are everyone else's plans for the summer?" Nadia asks, once they've all finished ordering. "Zoe?"

"Working on my tan," Zoe says, deadpan.

Johnny lets out a loud guffaw, and Warren bites the inside of his cheek to keep from doing the same. Yolande is giggling into her hand, and he sees Zoe shoot a pleased sidelong glance in her direction.

"Unlikely," quips Nadia. "I know how committed you are to the vampire aesthetic. My guess is that you'll probably just sit around The Palm all summer, plotting."

"How well you know me," Zoe replies dryly.

Nadia makes a face at him, and turns to Johnny. "What about you, Johnny?"

"No specific plans for the summer as of yet... other than working, of course," he responds. "But I am going to visit Da at the end of May."

"Boring," says Nadia dismissively. "Though do give my best to the esteemed Mr. Fontaine."

Johnny raises a brow. "*Boring?*" he repeats in mock affront. "How dare you! What a terrible thing to say to the most interesting person you know."

Nadia scoffs. "Speaking of the most interesting person I know... Yolande?"

"I'm going to visit my family too," Yolande volunteers. "And I'm picking up some more hours at Legal Aid in preparation for law school interviews."

"So diligent, love that for you," Nadia says. "Warren? What about you? Please tell me something exciting."

Warren pauses with his wine glass halfway to his mouth. He hasn't really let himself think about summer. Last year he'd spent it with Janis at his mother's family's lakehouse, hiding from his father and doing his best to ignore the implications of Janis' recently-announced pregnancy. For all the good that had done him, in the end.

"Um," he says, setting down his glass. "I'll probably just be working, I guess? I might try to get a head start on my coursework for next term."

"You're not going to keep working at the Laundromat during your final year of school, are you?" Yolande asks, concerned. Warren shrugs helplessly at her. "Warren, that's crazy. You're always so tired."

On the other side of Yolande, Zoe is frowning at him.

Warren squirms in his chair. "I mean... it's a job, and I need one. Plus it's never busy when I'm there so I get a lot of studying done." *And where else would have me?* he adds to himself.

"But the night shift," Yolande insists. "There has to be something else out there that at least lets you get some proper sleep."

"What about the coffee shop?" suggests Nadia. "Aren't you guys always looking for more part-time employees?"

"Perhaps," says Zoe, exchanging a glance with Yolande.

"Really," Warren says, feeling unspeakably awkward, "please don't worry about it. I'm fine."

On his lap, Minnie is nervously chewing her tail. Warren reaches down to gently pull it from her mouth, stroking her back soothingly with his fingers. From the corner of his eye he sees Johnny watching them both with a thoughtful expression, but when Warren looks up at him, he turns back to the table.

"Jonas," says Johnny, in an obvious attempt to change the subject. "Is your impending vacation the reason behind this captivating new facial hair?" He gestures to Jonas' short blond beard. "Is this an attempt to get back in touch with your rugged side?"

The conversation devolves from there, with Nadia suggesting other, more intimate reasons for Jonas' new look.

Under the table, Warren bumps his ankle against Johnny's in silent gratitude. Johnny bumps back, and then proceeds to leave the side of his leg pressed to Warren's. It's just the smallest bit of casual contact, but it makes Warren's pulse flutter wildly all the same.

When the waiter comes by to deliver their food, Warren let's him refill his wine glass. He doesn't move his leg for the rest of the meal. Neither does Johnny.

------

Warren is buzzing from the wine by the time they leave the restaurant. The cool nighttime air keeps him steady on his feet, but the world around him still wavers in his vision, as if he's walking through a moving train car.

They make their way down the sidewalk in pairs, with Nadia and Jonas holding hands out in front. Nadia is wearing a long-sleeved red dress with a high neckline that cuts across her collarbones. It hits mid-thigh, and Warren had been under the impression that, aside from the length, it was surprisingly modest— until he'd followed her out of the restaurant and realized it had absolutely no back.

*No wonder Jonas hasn't been able to take his eyes off of her all night,* he thinks. The birthday boy himself is in a navy button-down that makes his pale blue eyes look almost electric. Beside him, Huff walks with her head held high, while Vic stretches his wings in the air above.

At the back of the pack, Zoe is dressed in a slim cut three-piece suit. He's coordinated with his daemon, wearing black from head to toe, except for the silver watch clipped to the pocket of his waistcoat and his usual silver-topped cane. Walking next to him in his oatmeal colored pullover, Warren feels a bit like the ugly cygnet in a line of glamorous ducklings. But he finds he doesn't mind so much, the alcohol doing its job of softening the sharpest edges of his self-doubt.

In the middle of their little group, Johnny and Yolande are walking arm in arm, talking lowly. Their height difference might border on comical, if it weren't for Yolande's deadly-looking heels. In them, she's almost of a height with Warren, though still nowhere close to matching Johnny. Shane is trailing her in the shadows of the storefronts, his amber gaze alert as always.

Warren's eyes, as they are prone to do, are drawn to Johnny. He is lovely in the half-light cast by the streetlights and illuminated signs they pass along the way, his dark skin glowing, his stride relaxed and confident. Beside him, Lucinda matches his gait with ease, as lean and long-limbed as her human.

They suit each other. Warren has always thought so, and so has Minnie— the two of them have discussed it at length. Looking at Johnny and Lucinda now, Warren is filled by affection so strong it feels as if he's radiating with it, as if everyone around him should be able to see it, pouring out of his body. From her precarious perch on his shoulder, Minnie is watching them too, and Warren reaches up to give her a commiserating pat when she sighs longingly into his hair.

"Warren," Zoe says suddenly. "I want to talk to you about your work situation."

Minnie loses her balance and Warren quickly uses his hand to steady her. "Oh," he says, stomach clenching. "You do?"

Zoe continues, heedless of Warren's reluctant tone. "You *could* work at The Palm, we'd make a spot for you. But that would be almost as pointless as working at the Laundromat in terms of your resume."

"My resume?" Warren repeats, flustered by the intense gaze of Zoe's daemon as she regards him from her human's shoulder.

"Yes," says Zoe. "If you don't have some relevant job experience you'll never get hired after graduation. Have you looked into engineering internships at all?"

"Not… really."

"Why not?"

Warren, who has been avoiding thinking about his future beyond graduation for so long that it's become second nature for his mind to recoil from any mention of it, mumbles something about job searching being overly difficult and time-consuming.

Zoe nods, as if this is completely understandable. "I may be able to help with that. I know a guy who owns an engineering tech company. I could send him your resume."

"I couldn't ask you to do that," says Warren. Ahead of them, the rest of the group has gone quiet, obviously listening in.

"You didn't ask," Zoe says firmly. "I offered. And it's not like I can guarantee you a job. If Josef doesn't think you're a good fit he won't hire you, simple as that."

"All right," Warren responds, mostly just to put an end to the conversation.

"Good," says Zoe, sounding satisfied. "Email me your resume later this weekend."

And that's that. Warren's head hurts and, for a moment, all he wants to do is go home. Then Johnny looks back at him with a wide grin, and Warren remembers why he should stay.

"Zoe," Nadia calls over her shoulder. "Who's DJ-ing tonight? Please say Tamar."

"Yes, Tamar. As you requested, several times," Zoe says, and Nadia cheers.

Yolande falls back to walk next to Zoe. "Zoe owns shares in the Big Block," she explains to Warren's confused expression. "He has partial say in operational matters."

"Haskell basically lets him do whatever he wants, as long as it turns a profit," Johnny says, walking backwards to face them.

Yolande gently bumps Zoe's shoulder with her own, smiling up at him. "He's really turned it into something good."

"And made it queer-friendly," adds Nadia.

"It was already halfway there," says Johnny. "Zoe just fixed some, let's say, *atmospheric* issues."

"It doesn't make economical sense to be exclusionary," Zoe says gruffly.

Johnny barks a laugh, and Nadia turns to roll her eyes at Zoe.

"Yeah, sure," she says. "Purely business."

"And here we are," Yolande says cheerfully. "The Big Block."

They are approaching a large, windowless building with a black brick facade. Warren sees a simple sign above the door with no text, only the graphic of a crow drinking from a near empty goblet against an illuminated blood red background. The distant sound of a thumping bass line can be heard reverberating through the walls out onto the street.

There is a long line outside the club, but they bypass it and go straight to the entrance, where a big man and his equally big mastiff daemon are monitoring the door.

Zoe nods at the bouncer. "Benedict."

Benedict nods back, and steps aside to allow them entry.

Zoe and Yolande head inside with their daemons, but Jonas and Huff stop in front of the door, blocking it.

"Wait," Jonas says. "How old are you, Warren? You're legal, right?"

"I'm twenty," Warren says defensively.

"Hmm," Nadia says. She tilts her head and squints at him, mockingly skeptical. "Can anyone verify this? Show us your ID, the most embarrassing one you have."

Warren flushes. "Nadia," he grits out. "I *know* you know how old I am."

Lucinda huffs, and moves to stand in front of Warren. "Leave him alone, Nadia."

Johnny wraps an arm around Warren's waist. "Yeah," he says. "It's not Warren's fault that he has such a babyface."

Warren elbows his side. "I'm not a baby."

Johnny bends to murmur in his ear, careful not to brush against Minnie. "Believe me. I'm *well* aware."

Warren's brain short-circuits.

Jonas, seemingly satisfied, enters the Big Block with Huff at his heels. Nadia follows with Vic, tossing a cheeky grin back at Warren and Johnny as she goes.

Johnny slides his arm from around Warren's waist and takes his hand instead, lacing their fingers together. "Come on. Let's go have some fun."

He leads the way inside, pulling Warren along behind him. They walk down a narrow passageway that has a coat check area and several doors leading to washrooms. The music becomes progressively louder as they travel toward a heavy-looking black steel door at the end of the hall.

Johnny pauses just in front of it. "Ready?" he asks, squeezing Warren's hand. He waits for Warren's nod of assent, then pushes open the door.

Immediately, they are hit by a wall of *sound.*
The music inside the club is percussive and loud— Warren knew that it would be, but he isn't just hearing it, he's feeling it as well, a resonant wave that pulsates through his body. It might be similar to playing in the midst of an orchestra, except that it's not just instruments, it's *people* too, shouts and whoops and the thud of

moving feet. Minnie's nails are digging sharply into his shoulder and Warren would have stopped in his tracks if it weren't for Johnny's hand, tugging him over the threshold and into the club proper.

They enter a wide, busy room, clearly a converted warehouse, with a high ceiling and metal support posts that have been left bare to preserve an industrial aesthetic. The floors are black laminate and the decor is minimal, mostly black and red, with wrought iron accents. Three walls of the rectangular room are lined with booths, and the fourth is taken up by a long, brightly lit bar. The large space left open in the center of the room is obviously the dance floor, already packed with writhing bodies. The seating areas are dim, but the dance area is lit up by multicolored beams and pulsing strobe lights.

Warren's eyes catch there as Johnny guides him around the perimeter of the room. People don't touch other people's daemons without permission— that's a fact— but Warren hadn't considered how unavoidable that might be in the crush of bodies on a dance floor. He experiences a brief moment of panic, before he realizes the purpose of the low, cushioned benches that line the area on two sides. They are courtesy spots, designated places for daemons to go to avoid being touched while their humans dance. And they are certainly being utilized, by dozens of daemons in a variety of forms and sizes, though Warren still spies others in the midst of the dancers, either taking their chances or among trusted friends.

"I don't think I want to do that," Minnie says into his ear. She is watching the dancers with wide, darting eyes.

Warren reaches up with his free hand and loosely grasps her tail. "Then we won't."

Johnny leads them to a roped-off booth near the bar. The booth consists of a round table encircled by a high-backed black leather bench. Zoe and Jonas are already seated there, on either side of the red-topped table. Even though Nadia is nowhere in sight, Vic is perched on Jonas' shoulder, preening himself. Huff is lying on the floor in front of the booth, ears pricked and head swiveling, as if she's a sentry keeping watch.

Johnny takes a seat next to Jonas, forcing him to shift further into the booth, and pulls Warren down next to him before releasing his hand. Lucinda lowers herself next to Huff, looking relaxed and interested in her surroundings, obviously at ease in this place.

Warren flexes his slightly sweaty fingers as Minnie drops down to his lap. The relative sanctuary provided by the booth is already doing much to soothe his overwhelmed senses, and his mind begins to shift from stunned to inquisitive as he adjusts to the atmosphere of the club.

"Where are the girls?" Johnny asks, shrugging out of his grey sport coat and letting it fall haphazardly onto the bench behind him. He has to speak loudly to be heard over the music.

Zoe nods toward the bar, and sure enough, Warren can see them there, Nadia leaning over the bartop to converse with the bartender with Yolande standing close by.

As he's watching them, Warren sees a man approach Yolande from behind and say something into her ear. She shakes her head, but he moves closer— then hurriedly backs away, hopping on one leg.

Johnny bursts into laughter. Across the table, Zoe's mouth has turned up at the corners.

"Did she just stomp on that guy's foot?" Warren asks, bemused.

"That's our Yolande," Johnny says, grinning proudly. "Tiny and ferocious."

Nadia and Yolande make their way back to the booth, shot glasses in hand. Yolande slides the three she's carrying onto the table, and then sits next to Zoe in the space he makes for her. Shane leaps to the top of the backrest behind her, and Zoe's daemon stretches up to momentarily touch her beak to his cheek.

Minnie watches the brief exchange with rapt attention, and Warren knows it's because she's never seen Zoe's daemon touch anyone other than Zoe before, not even Shane.

"Birthday shots!" Nadia shouts, passing them around. She sits down next to Warren, who has to press himself tightly to Johnny's side to accommodate her. Not that he minds terribly much.

"None for me," says Johnny. His eyes cut once to Warren, then away. "The birthday boy can have mine."

Jonas thanks him and slides Johnny's shot glass over to himself.

Warren picks his up, eyeing the blue-tinged liquid inside suspiciously.

"It's called a sex bomb," Nadia says, nudging him with her elbow, "because Jonas—"

"Happy Birthday, Jonas!" Yolande cuts in, raising her shot glass and tossing back the contents in one quick motion.

Zoe, Nadia, and Jonas follow suit— Jonas taking his two shots in quick succession— while Johnny cheers them on.

Warren takes a tentative sip from his glass, bracing himself for the bitter burning sensation he associates with liquor. He is pleasantly surprised when the drink instead tastes sweet and fruity, almost like juice. He finishes it in two gulps, managing not to spill any.

"That was really good," he says.

Nadia grins at him. "Let's do another."

They do. Zoe buys this round, bringing back something clear and carbonated for Johnny to drink as well. This time Warren finishes his shot in one gulp.

"Time to dance!" exclaims Nadia. She rises, pulling Warren up with her.

He stands awkwardly to the side as Johnny and Jonas slide out of the booth after him. Jonas immediately grabs Nadia's hand, and the two of them and their daemons head toward the dance floor.

"Yolande?" Johnny asks, raising his brow at her.

She shakes her head. "Not yet."

"Okay," he shrugs. "Let's go, Warren."

Warren wants to, or at least he's pretty sure that he does. He's feeling warm and happy from the shots, and going anywhere with Johnny seems like a really good idea right now. But Minnie is a stiff ball of tension in his arms, so he hesitates.

Johnny must see it on his face, because he reaches out to tug at Warren's sleeve. "Dance with us!"

"Maybe later," Warren says.

"Come on," pouts Johnny. "I promise it'll be fun."

"John," Lucinda says warningly. She's looking at Minnie.

Johnny follows her gaze, his expression softening. "You don't want to go?" he says to Minnie.

She squirms a bit, avoiding his eyes. "Too many people."

"Minnie and I will watch for a while first," decides Warren.

Johnny nods reluctantly. "All right, fair enough. Do you want us to stay?"

Warren shakes his head. It's a kind offer, but he can see Johnny fidgeting where he stands, eyes flickering to the dance floor. "No. You two go have fun."

Johnny puts his hand on Warren's shoulder and squeezes briefly, before trailing his fingers down his arm, lingering. "See you soon, I hope," he says, and then he and Lucinda lope off into the crowd.

Warren and Minnie watch them go.

"Sorry, Warren," murmurs Minnie.

"It's fine," he tells her, scritching her ears. "I'm not ready yet either."

He turns back to the booth and has the slightly horrifying realization that Yolande and Zoe have been sitting within earshot for the entirety of his and Johnny's exchange.

"Sit with us," Yolande says.

Warren does, blushing faintly. He mentally prepares himself for some good-natured teasing, but it never comes: instead, Yolande asks him about his upcoming orchestra performance. Warren latches onto the subject with relief.

The air is thumping with sound so they have to shout to be heard, but for a while they manage to hold a semblance of a conversation over the table. Yolande is shouldering most of it with occasional input from Zoe, because Warren keeps getting distracted searching for Johnny in the throng of dancers. He finally spots him near the edge of the dance floor, sandwiched between two people.

Johnny's eyes are half-closed, his body swaying as he rides the rhythm like he and the music are one. He has his hands on the hips of the person in front of him and someone else has slotted themselves against his back, their arms wrapped around his waist from behind. Even from across the room, Warren can make out Johnny's joyful expression, his grin wide and white as he raises his face to the flashing lights overhead.

Warren's chest feels brittle. His heart is glass, prone to shatter.

The look on his face must give him away, because Yolande breaks off speaking to track his gaze. She looks back at him with sympathetic eyes.

"It's only dancing, Warren," she says, reading his thoughts with devastating precision. She leans across the table so she can speak quietly, keeping the words just between them. "Johnny hasn't taken anyone home in a long time."

"I'm not... it isn't—" Warren's head swims. He forces himself to take a calming breath. "Thanks, Yolande."

Yolande pats his hand. "Have some faith."

He gives her his best attempt at a smile. He misses the happy feeling from before, and looks mournfully at his empty shot glass.

When his eyes move back to the dance floor, he sees that Johnny has abandoned his previous partners and is dancing with Nadia and Jonas instead. The music has changed to something fast and upbeat, and the three of them are bouncing and bopping wildly to it, laughingly shouting lyrics at each other.

He watches them for a while before he loses them in the shifting crowd. On the other side of the table, Yolande and Zoe are talking and Warren tries halfheartedly to pick up the thread of their conversation. The music changes again, this time to a song that Warren vaguely recognizes.

Yolande grins.

"That's my cue," she says, standing. Shane rises too, spine curving as he arches his back. "Nadia and I always dance together when Robyn comes on, no exceptions."

Like a prophecy made real, Nadia comes running up to the booth, shouting, "Yolande, Yolande! It's our song!"

Yolande takes her hand, and they hurry back to the dance floor, Shane darting after them.

Immediately after they leave, a grey-haired man in a plaid jacket approaches the booth, almost as if he'd been waiting for an opportunity. He goes directly to Zoe and says a few words that Warren can't quite pick up over the din. Then Zoe stands, and the two of them disappear together into a room off to the side of the bar, leaving Warren sitting alone.

He's not alone for long. Jonas drops heavily onto the bench across from him, in Zoe's abandoned spot. He is loose-limbing and smiling wider than Warren has ever seen, holding a drink in each hand, and wearing a glittery silver sash that he hadn't been before. Huff collapses onto the floor nearby, laying her big head on her paws.

"Hi!" Warren says, glad to see a friend.

"Hey, Warren!" Jonas grins back. "Are you having fun? I'm having fun. So many people are buying me drinks!" He slides a martini glass filled with pink liquid over to Warren. "Here, take one!"

Warren picks it up and takes a sip. It's delicious. He takes a bigger sip. "Weren't you dancing?"

"Johnny sent me over," says Jonas. He scratches the side of his head. "I forget why though. Do you remember, Huff?"

Huff makes a noise into her paws that could mean anything.

Jonas pats her on the head. "It's okay, buddy," he tells her.

"I like your sash," Warren says, because it's true and he wants Jonas to know it.

"Thanks! Nadia gave it to me. And now people keep buying me drinks, which is really nice of them!"

"What does it say?" Minnie asks. She's half-standing in Warren's lap, her chin resting on the edge of the table.

"'Birthday Bitch'," Jonas proclaims proudly.

Warren chokes on his drink, and then bumps his glass when he doubles over, coughing. The glass tips, spilling its contents across the tabletop. Minnie makes a dismayed noise as she scrambles away from the dripping liquid.

"Oops," giggles Warren. Normally spilling something would be mortifying, but right now it just seems funny.

Jonas comes over to thump him on the back, even though Warren isn't coughing anymore. *Jonas is a good person,* he thinks.

"Hmm," says Jonas, surveying the remains of Warren's drink spread across the table. "I think you need a new one. Let's go to the bar."

They go to the bar.

They sit on two high-backed stools near the end of the long counter. Jonas orders drinks for them, two more shots, which Warren pays for.

"You're the Birthday Bitch!" he insists, when Jonas tries to stop him. "You can't buy your own drink."

Jonas nods seriously. "You are very wise."

They clink glasses and take their shots. This time the alcohol is brown and only mildly sweet, with a nutty aftertaste that Warren isn't sure that he cares for. He smacks his lips together, and then does it twice more because it makes an interesting sound.

Jonas orders beers for them next. Warren forgets to pay, but Jonas doesn't seem to notice. This is fun. Warren is having fun. And Jonas is *so nice!* He'd known as much, but never really interacted with him one-on-one before.

Jonas pulls his phone out of his pocket. It's buzzing, and the screen is lit up. "It's Nadia!" he says happily. "She wants me to come back and dance. Are you coming?"

Warren starts to shake his head but it makes everything around him spin, so he stops. "No."

"Okay," says Jonas agreeably. He wobbles slightly as he stands up, taking his beer bottle with him. "See you later!"

Warren is sad to see him go. He takes a sip of his beer and makes a face. *Not good.* He pushes it off to the side.

Time blurs for Warren. He feels pleasantly wavy inside, and imagines his blood rolling back and forth inside of him, like the tide on a beach. Minnie is a puddle of fur on his lap, boneless. Beneath his feet, Warren can feel the floor vibrating with bass notes, and he gets lost for a while counting the beats that rattle up through his bones.

Minnie stirs, and Warren looks up absently when he senses a presence beside him.

It's a man.

He's tall, and has golden eyes and long, dark hair that's been pulled into a low ponytail at the base of his neck. He's wearing an olive green tank top that shows off his heavily muscled arms, but Warren is more interested in the leather harness strapped across his chest. The harness is supporting a shoulder guard where the largest owl daemon Warren has ever seen is perched, watching him imperiously with round, yellow eyes.

*No wonder this guy needs so many muscles,* Warren thinks.

"Is this seat taken?" the man asks in a deep voice.

Warren shakes his head, because no, it's not. Then he has to brace his palms on the bartop to steady himself when the spinning sensation returns.

The man sits next to him, his daemon lifting her brown and white spotted wings for balance as he does so.

"Have you been here before?" he asks, and then winces at himself for no reason that Warren can discern.

"No," Warren tells him. "I haven't. This is my first time."

"Mine too," the man says. "I'll be honest— it's not really my type of place. My sister and her wife dragged me out tonight. She's the DJ."

In Warren's lap, Minnie mutters something incoherent.

"Oh," says Warren. "DJs are neat."

"Apparently so," the man says, wry. "Can I buy you a drink?"

More alcohol sounds like a great idea to Warren. "Can it be pink?" he asks, remembering the delicious drink he'd accidentally knocked over earlier.

The man laughs, and it's a good sound. "Sure, I think we can manage that."

They order drinks, and the man starts asking Warren questions about himself. When Warren tells him he's a student at KU, the man's eyes light up. It turns out he's a graduate student in the linguistics department, and he eagerly starts telling Warren about his thesis topic, something to do with epic poetry in the modern era. Warren thinks he would probably find it very interesting, if only he had more experience with poetry— or literature in general, and the reading thereof.

As it is, he's having a hard time following the conversation. Mostly he's just sipping at his drink and listening to the low rumble of the man's voice, which is nice enough. Warren nods, and smiles, and hopes he's doing those things in the correct places. He must be, because the man is smiling back at him. Warren looks into his gold eyes and thinks, *aurum, atomic number seventy-nine,* which leads him to *silver, argentum, atomic number forty-seven,* and then he thinks of Johnny's eyes. He misses Johnny. Maybe he should go find him.

The man abruptly stops talking, and for a moment Warren isn't sure why.

Then two hands come to rest on his shoulders, big and warm. Minnie makes a happy noise, and Warren knows who's behind him before he even tips his head back to look.

"Hi, Johnny!" He grins, automatic, at the sight of Johnny's beloved, upside-down face regarding him from above.

Johnny smiles back. "Hey, Warren. I've been looking for you."

Lucinda comes to stand beside Warren's stool, just shy of brushing his leg. She raises her muzzle as Minnie leans over the side of Warren's lap to give her a welcoming lick.

"I've been here," Warren says. He leans back further in his seat to butt the top of his head into Johnny's sturdy chest. Then, because he's thinking it and it's true, he adds, "You have my favorite smile. Did you know?"

Something flickers across Johnny's face, an emotion passing too quickly for Warren to track. His fingers curl tighter over Warren's shoulders.

"Ah, thank you," he says. He clears his throat. "I'm just checking in— we're almost ready to leave. Are you doing okay?"

"I'm great!" Warren tells him. "I'm having a nice conversation with, um…"

"Peytr," the man supplies. His daemon's ear tufts twitch.

"Right, Peytr," says Warren, nodding, because he was definitely told that at some point.

"How's it going, mate?" Johnny says to Peytr. His voice is pleasant enough, but there is an edge to it that Warren can't quite place.

"Oh, just fine," replies Peytr, sounding amused.

"Cool." Johnny bends nearer to Warren. "Warren, we're just over at our booth," he says. He's close enough that his lips brush Warren's ear, the sibilance of his words almost physical. "Come join us when you're done here."

"Okay," Warren manages, dazed.

Johnny pats Warren's shoulders, then nods once at Peytr and leaves.

Warren instantly misses his hands. He looks at Peytr. "I guess I'd better go back to my friends."

Peytr's smile is resigned. "It seems so. It was nice talking with you, Warren."

"You too," Warren tells him. "Good luck with the, um… the poetry… thing."

He stands, lifting Minnie and holding her to his chest. The floor wavers beneath his feet as he makes his way back to the booth where his friends are waiting for him.

------

"Are we leaving already?" Warren complains later, as he stumbles down the sidewalk leading away from the Big Block. "I didn't even get to dance."

"Don't worry," Yolande assures him. "We'll be back here again next month for Johnny's birthday."

She's got an arm around his waist, and Johnny is on his other side with one of his arms wrapped around Warren's shoulders. They're guiding him down the street, and Warren loves them *so much*. They are the best friends he's ever had. The best! But wait, Yolande said something… oh!

He turns wide eyes on Johnny. "You have a birthday!"

"I've been known to, yes," Johnny says wryly.

Zoe, leading their little group, turns back to regard Warren with one brow arched in disbelief. Warren grins at him. Zoe is *really* funny sometimes.

Nadia would agree with him. He looks around for her, before remembering that she and Jonas disappeared somewhere together— possibly back to Jonas' apartment, Warren wasn't paying that much attention— and so the rest of them are walking to Yolande and Nadia's apartment without them.

Well, Warren is doing his best to walk there. His feet refuse to cooperate with him, dragging and stumbling across the concrete. He stares down and watches them, one foot in front of the other in front of the other— then he starts to feel dizzy and swings his head back up.

Have his feet always moved so quickly? He isn't sure. Minnie will know. He should ask her. But where did she go? Warren doesn't want to be separated from her. Panic rises up inside of him. *Where is she?*

He stops dead, forcing Johnny and Yolande to stop with him. "Wait!" he exclaims. "Where's Minnie?"

"You're holding her, Warren," Johnny says patiently.

"Oh." Warren looks down. Sure enough, Minnie is there, cradled in his arms like an infant. "Hi, Minnie."

She blinks up at him. "Hello."

"*Saints,*" Yolande laughs. "How much did he have?"

"He's a lightweight," says Zoe, unimpressed.

"At least he hasn't puked," Lucinda says cheerfully.

"Yet," mutters Shane.

"He's going to be just fine," says Johnny. "Aren't you, sunshine?"

"Absolutely," Warren nods, right before he trips over nothing. He reaches out to steady himself, grasping Johnny's t-shirt. His *damp* t-shirt. "Why is your shirt wet?" he asks. He can see Johnny's belly button through the front of it and the sight of it flusters him.

"Ugh," Johnny groans. "Drunky McDrunk Jonas spilled his disgusting lager on me. Going to take forever to get the smell out of my clothes. Who let him have so many drinks, anyway?"

"It was the sash," Warren says, nodding sagely. He keeps on nodding even after he's finished speaking.

Johnny snorts, bumping their hips together affectionately. "You are *so* wasted."

Something niggles at the back of Warren's mind, something he's been meaning to ask. Now seems like the perfect time.

"You have a washing machine," he says to Johnny, looking up at him. "I saw it, that night when… that night. You have a washing machine."

Johnny stares back at him, uncomprehending. "Yes?"

"So then…" Warren's mouth works, struggling for the correct phrasing. "So why do you do your laundry at the Laundromat?"

The silence is palpable. No one speaks, or even utters a sound.

Then Johnny says, "Ah. Yeah, we do have one. It, uh. Doesn't work. Our washing machine is broken."

Zoe's daemon makes a choked noise, like a caw got stuck halfway down her throat. Lucinda shushes her.

"Oh." For some reason, Warren is disappointed.

"Why don't you get a new one?" Minnie wants to know, flipping around in Warren's arms to look at Johnny.

"Ah, you know…" Johnny says, his eyes flickering to the side, "money."

"Right, money," Warren agrees, because yes, that's totally reasonable. "Of course."

"Should get Zoe to rob another bank," Minnie mutters nonsensically.

"*What* did she just say?" Yolande asks, slightly strangled.

The corner of Zoe's mouth twitches. "Bank robbery? That's a new one, Lucinda."

Lucinda flashes her teeth. "I thought we needed to spice up your reputation a bit."

Johnny lets out a burst of laughter, and turns his face into Warren's hair to muffle it.

Warren giggles, happy. He likes being here, tucked under Johnny's lean, strong arm, feeling his laughter resonate through his body. It's a good place.

The next thing he knows, they're inside Yolande and Nadia's apartment. He doesn't remember getting there, but he's standing with his shoes off in the living room, and Yolande is placing a glass of water in his hands.

"Drink this," she says.

Warren does as he's told.

Johnny is on the couch, slumped comfortably into the cushions. Warren sits down next to him, because he wants to be near him, simple as that.

And it is simple, right now. All of it. He feels like he could do anything, and it would be okay, the line between desire and action thin and easy to cross. He eyes Johnny's thigh consideringly, and then just sort of tips himself sideways to lay his head there, face turned toward Johnny's stomach. Above him, Johnny makes a low noise of surprise, but doesn't protest.

Warren settles into a comfortable position on his side, and Minnie tucks herself into the space between his chest and cushioned backrest. The colors of the knitted blanket draped there are too vibrant and it hurts to look at them, so he closes his eyes.

Suddenly there are long fingers in his hair, petting through his curls. It's the best thing Warren has ever felt. His scalp tingles and his spine goes liquid. He tilts his head into the touch, humming.

Distantly, he can hear the sounds of his friends talking to each other, Johnny's soothing baritone, Yolande's sweet soprano, Zoe's soft rasp. He doesn't know what they're saying. It doesn't matter. Warren's head is a cloud and he is floating on a current of euphoria, content.

Time passes. Warren keeps drifting. The fingers keep stroking through his hair.

"Is he asleep?" someone asks.

"I'm not sure," comes the response, and that's Johnny, Warren knows that for sure. He should say something, so that Johnny knows he's still awake.

"You have really nice fingers," he says.

The fingers pause.

"No," Warren whines. "Don't stop." The stroking resumes, and he sighs contentedly. From somewhere far away he can hear Yolande giggling.

Johnny bends his head close to Warren's ear. "The look on your face right now is kind of driving me crazy," he whispers, and Warren's stomach dips pleasantly at the rough cadence of his voice. "You look totally blissed out, Warren."

"Mm-hmm," Warren hums in agreement, because yes, he is.

"You sound that way too."

Warren nods. Johnny is bent almost double, curled over him, and it makes him feel safe, sheltered. He squirms nearer just to be closer to the warmth of him, the scent. Johnny always smells *so good*. He pushes his nose into Johnny's abdomen, nuzzling a little.

Johnny's hand clenches where it's buried in Warren's curls, gripping tightly. Warren lets out an involuntary whimper at the sudden pull.

"Okay!" Johnny says. He stands abruptly, forcing Warren from his lap. "It's time to get you home."

Warren sits up, blinking and confused. Johnny's hands are fisted and his eyes are wild, and Warren's not sure what just happened, but he's pretty sure it was his fault.

"Are you okay?" he asks, his voice small. "Did I do something wrong?" In his peripheral he can see Yolande and Zoe in the kitchenette, watching them.

Johnny's eyes soften. "No. But I think you need to sleep this off." He reaches out his hand, and Warren takes it, letting Johnny pull him up from the couch. "Come on. I'll walk you back to your apartment."

------

Whether it's the walk, the fresh air, or the second glass of water Yolande made him drink before they left— or all three combined— by the time they make it back to Warren's apartment, his head is a lot clearer. He's lost all of his previous euphoria. Now he just feels tired.

"All right," says Johnny, as soon as they're inside. "Time for bed, you two."

"Yes, please," Minnie says groggily.

Warren yawns. "Too tired for bed." He lets Minnie loose from his arms. "You go on without me. I'll sleep here."

"The couch is right there," Johnny says dryly. "Let's at least try for that."

"Will you carry me there?" Minnie asks him.

Before Johnny can speak, Lucinda says, "I'll do it." She picks Minnie up gently by the scruff of her neck and carries her into the living room.

Johnny crouches down by Warren's feet to remove his shoes, and Warren is reminded of the time when he'd done the same for Johnny. He thinks of that, and then of everything that followed: the moment in the entranceway. Johnny's bedroom. Minnie's choice.

"You didn't touch her," he says quietly.

Johnny makes an inquisitive noise. "Hmm?"

"Minnie. You didn't touch her back. Do you remember?"

Johnny stills. "I remember."

"Why didn't you?" Warren asks. "She wanted you to."

Johnny stands. He meets Warren's eyes and says, "I wasn't sure if… if that was something that *you* wanted."

"I wanted it."

Johnny swallows compulsively. He looks sort of stunned, as if what Warren's said is unexpected, rather than obvious.

It makes Warren bold. He reaches out to catch Johnny's sleeve, pivoting nearer to him. "I wanted it," he repeats, firmer.

Johnny's breath hitches, and Warren's eyes fall to the curve of his slightly parted lips. He lifts his other hand and fits it to Johnny's waist beneath his sport coat, fingers curling in the fabric of his t-shirt. He doesn't know what he's doing— he just knows he needs to do *something*. He steps closer, narrowing the space between them, until their chests are flush together. It feels like he's standing on a precipice, poised to fall.
Slowly— *slowly*— Johnny reaches up to cup his hand around the nape of Warren's neck. He holds him in place as he leans down and touches their foreheads together. They're so close that the only thing between them is their breath. Warren can feel Johnny panting, just slightly, hot against his cheek.

From the living room, one of their daemons lets out a low whine. Warren's eyes flutter shut.

Johnny brushes the sides of their noses together, the slide of skin intimate, expectant. Their lips are so close. It would take nothing for Johnny to close the scant centimeter between them— Warren is *aching* for it. But Johnny doesn't. He seems to be waiting for Warren to make that last, critical movement. And Warren wants to make it. He *will*.

He leans in, heart pounding, and—

The lights blink on.

Warren and Johnny spring apart as if they've been burned.

Karl is standing in the entrance to the living room, backlit by the hall light, staring at them. "Oh," he says. "Sorry."

Warren can't respond. He feels as if he's had the wind knocked out of him, his chest tight with shock and disappointment. He looks over at Johnny to gauge his reaction.

Johnny won't meet his eyes. "I should go," he says. "I'll talk to you tomorrow, okay? Drink some more water before you go to sleep."

The bottom drops out of Warren's stomach. "You're leaving?"

"Yeah," Johnny says. His fingers fidget with the buttons of his coat. "I got to— yeah. See you later, Warren. Karl."

He's out the door before Warren can mount a proper protest. Lucinda tosses him a sympathetic glance over her shoulder as she follows.

The moment the door shuts behind them, Karl points an accusing finger at Warren and says, "I *knew* it was a date!"

Warren groans, and turns to press his burning face against the cool plaster wall.

*If only.*

# CHAPTER 8

It takes Warren the rest of the weekend to physically and mentally recover from Jones' birthday.

Regaining consciousness on Saturday morning— cotton-mouthed and heavy-limbed, still dressed in his jeans and pullover— is like entering a waking nightmare. His mind immediately begins replaying the events of the night before, and he is hit by a flood of anxiety-inducing memories before he even makes it out of bed.

Every word he can remember saying, every reaction he showed, every single stupid comment or unsolicited touch he'd given— it's all there, small, sharp-edged moments that tear the fragile joy, the hard-earned confidence he'd garnered, to shreds. His mind is running in circles trying to analyze the others' responses to him.

*What do they think of me now?*

His memory of the latter half of the evening is hazy, but there are some parts that he remembers with vivid, merciless clarity: spilling his drink across the table; being so drunk that Johnny and Yolande were obliged to carry him through the streets; questioning Johnny about the washing machine in front of everyone; and— of course, because his brain hates him— the aborted kiss at the end of the night, and how eager Johnny had been to get away from him afterwards.

It makes Warren want to scream.

Instead, he clamps his hands over his ears and squeezes his eyes shut, as if that will block out the scenes playing through his head on loop, each one more disastrous than the last.

He doesn't realize that he is making any noise at all, until Minnie closes her teeth around his wrist to make him drop his hand, and he becomes uncomfortably aware that the distressed, high-pitched whine he'd been distantly cognizant of is actually coming from him.

"Think of something else," Minnie says firmly. "*Anything* else."

Warren turns his face into the pillow and recites the first hundred decimal places of pi in his head, and then keeps on going for another fifty, until the panic begins to subside. It's an old strategy, honed to perfection in his private school days, while sitting in a row of desks and hoping with everything inside of him not to be called upon to read aloud. He breathes into the pillowcase, keeping a firm hold of his thoughts so they don't stray back into the past.

"That's right," says Minnie, gentler now, "be here, with me." She wriggles her way under his arm, until Warren has no choice but roll over and hold her properly.

He imagines all of his memories of last night being shoved into a box inside his mind, sealed away to be examined at some nebulous point in the future, when they've been dulled enough by time and distance to safely handle. Then he thinks about other things: the sounds outside his window, the play of sunlight across the wall, the setlist for the upcoming end of term concert. In time, he feels calm enough to start his morning routine.

Ultimately, he thinks while he brushes his teeth, the problem is that he's exposed too much of himself, more than anyone would or should ever want to see.

Abashed and ashamed, he resolves to avoid his friends as much as possible, giving clipped, one-word replies to anyone who reaches out over WhatsApp— and only doing that much so they don't worry over him. Eventually, everyone gets the message and stops trying, even Johnny. It adds a heaping pile of guilt on top of everything else Warren is feeling, which isn't helped by the disapproval he can sense from Minnie.

Warren avoids Karl too, even after he creeps into the kitchen to get something to eat and finds that Karl has left him a bottled sports drink and a drawing of a curly-haired stick figure drinking from a glass with the equation "$H_2O + C_6H_{12}O_6 + NaCl + KCl = $ :)" written beneath it in clear, evenly spaced characters.
*Water, sugar, sodium chloride, and potassium chloride,* he translates in his head— hydration and electrolytes. It almost makes him smile. But Karl saw him with Johnny, and the thought of that is enough to send Warrenspiraling right back into a vicious cycle of embarrassment and self-recrimination.

He retreats from everyone, spending two days holed up in his room with his laptop, some juice boxes, and a box of crackers, until he's forced to head to campus on

Monday afternoon for orchestra rehearsal. It's difficult to leave the apartment, but his sense of responsibility outweighs his lingering anxiety, and he forces himself out the door in time to avoid being late.

Being outside helps. Being with people who don't know him well helps. But playing music helps the most. He's feeling better about himself by the end of rehearsal, enough so that he decides to go to his shift at the Laundromat, instead of following through on his original plan, which had been to call in sick.

He works his shift, goes back to the apartment, and then sleeps until the early afternoon the next day. When he wakes up, everything seems brighter, more manageable.

He makes some food and decides to eat it in the living room where Karl is sprawled out on the couch with Daya on his chest watching some reality TV show Warren's never seen before. He has no idea who these people are or what they are all so upset about, but as soon as he sits down Karl starts up a running commentary interspersed by bouts of slightly maniacal laughter that makes Warren grin despite himself, even as Minnie rolls her eyes at them both.

Not once does Karl attempt to talk to him about anything other than the television show. It reminds Warren that being with other people can be good sometimes, and he has a sudden and overwhelming urge to hear Johnny's voice. He runs his thumb over the screen of his phone and thinks about calling him— somehow, he knows that Johnny would pick up.

*Later,* he thinks to himself. *Soon.*

------

The final show for the music department is set for Friday afternoon, and the orchestra is scheduled to rehearse every day until then in preparation.

When Warren arrives at the auditorium for practice on Wednesday, the conductor corners him right away. She tells him that that principal flautist has broken her wrist, and then asks him to take over the solo in the finale piece, a Mozart concerto they've been drilling for months.

Warren is the second chair in the flute section so he knows the solo passably well, but it's notoriously difficult, and with his self-confidence still in tatters, his first instinct is to refuse and hand it over to the third flautist instead. But he also doesn't want to disappoint anyone, and that part of him wins out. He reluctantly acquiesces.

Any tentative plans he'd been forming to reconnect with his friends are shelved in favor of mastering the solo. He spends hours practicing, memorizing every note and musical direction on the score, determined not to miss a beat. He needs this to be perfect.

Between work and practice, the rest of the week blurs by.

On Friday morning, Yolande messages him to ask if he wants to go out for lunch with her and Nadia. Warren feels true regret when he has to turn her down, sending an apologetic explanation in reply. Yolande simply wishes him luck, and tells him that they will do lunch another time. The relief Warren experiences is so strong that even he knows it's disproportionate to her response.

When he arrives at the campus auditorium for the concert that afternoon, he finds it already buzzing with the usual pre-show excitement as his fellow music students go about making the final preparations for their performances. In addition to the orchestra, there will be performances by various instrumental ensembles as well as from composition students presenting their final works. Warren doesn't need to worry about any of that tonight: fortunately, his music minor only requires one performance credit, and he's filled it with the orchestra.

The orchestra is set to perform last. Warren sits with Minnie at the back of the auditorium in his concert blacks— the same trousers, shirt, and tie combination he's worn to every performance since his senior year of high school— and watches the audience filter in. It's mostly friends and family of the performers, and a few faculty members that he recognizes from the department. There won't be anyone here for him, Warren knows that. It's an old ache, dull, like a bone that was broken long ago. He barely feels it anymore.

He watches the ensembles perform, but once the composition students start their presentations he goes to the rehearsal room off the side of the stage. It's crowded with humans and daemons, but he makes a spot for himself and Minnie in a corner and runs through his solo a few more times before the conductor calls for the orchestra members to assemble themselves.

While the music program director gives a short introductory speech— and thinly veiled plea for funding— Warren takes his place with the rest of the orchestra, seated in the first chair of the flute section, right at the edge of the stage. It's a spot he's never performed from before: normally, he's seated in the middle of the section.

Beyond the stage the audience is rustling in anticipatory silence. Warren casts a tentative glance toward the rows of people he knows are watching, but he can't make out individual faces past the glare of the stage lights. He turns away and concentrates on organizing his sheet music on the stand. Minnie whispers a few encouraging words in his ear before dropping to the floor beneath his seat, as close as she can be to him without inhibiting his ability to play.

The performance begins. The opening song is a Dvořák symphony, a standard showcase piece meant to highlight the brass and woodwind sections. It's followed by a Ghibli film medley that the orchestra members had voted on for this year's popular music selection. It's easily Warren's favorite piece of the set, and Minnie's too. She crouches under his chair humming softly to herself, so low that even Warren can't hear her, but he knows instinctively that she's doing it.

The medley ends, and the conductor pauses for applause before she motions for the string section to play the opening notes of the Mozart concerto. Warren sits with his fellow flute section members, counting rests on the side of his leg, waiting. When the time comes for his solo, he stands. He doesn't need his sheet music for this so he closes his eyes, listening for his entrance point in the measure. He isn't nervous as he lifts his flute to his mouth— this is what he excels at, the one thing he knows he won't screw up. He's not good with words, or feelings, or *people*— but music he understands. Music he gets *right*.

Everything around him falls away. He's practiced so many times that it doesn't feel like performing at all, more like he's a conduit for the music that is flowing out of him. Minnie taps her paw against the top of his shoe, keeping time like a second heartbeat, in sync with him as always. Warren breathes and sways with the melody, getting lost in the rhythm of the music until he's followed the notes to their inevitable conclusion.

Solo complete, he opens his eyes and retakes his seat as the stage comes back into focus around him. Distantly he hears a short burst of appreciative applause, but he barely registers it as he rejoins the orchestra for the final movement of the piece.

The concerto ends triumphantly on a crescendo of strings. The quiet holds for a moment, and then the audience breaks into applause. Warren stands with the rest of the orchestra and takes a bow. When he rises, he lifts his face toward the spotlights and breathes deeply, riding out the combined highs of relief and success: his third year is officially over.

"Warren!" Minnie says excitedly over the din. She's standing on her hind legs peering out into the audience. "Warren, look!"

Warren looks. The house lights have come on and he can see the sea of faces in front of him. A piercing whistle has him whipping his head to the side of the auditorium.

There, standing in the aisle and cheering loudly, are Johnny and Yolande.

Warren is so unprepared to see them there, grinning at him, that he completely misses his cue to leave the stage. He hasn't seen Johnny or Yolande in days, and he hadn't realized how much he'd truly missed them until this very moment. His eyes well, and he blinks rapidly to clear the sudden blurring of his vision.

He continues to stand there, staring at his friends, until Minnie bats his ankle with her paw to refocus his attention. He belatedly follows after the rest of his section, casting one more disbelieving glance in their direction as he goes.

------

When Warren exits the music building, he finds Johnny and Yolande waiting for him.

Minnie sprints ahead and takes a running leap at Lucinda, practically tackling her as she faceplants into her chest. Lucinda gives a happy chuff and tucks her nose into the fur at Minnie's neck. Shane watches them from a safe distance, the end of his tail twitching mildly.

Warren approaches Johnny and Yolande sheepishly, unsure of what to say after a week of minimal contact. Yolande pulls him into a hug as soon as he's within range, and his reflexive apology dies in his throat. Being held by her calms something inside of him. He exhales, feeling some of the tension he's been carrying leave his body.

Johnny is watching them, grinning crookedly. He looks so good standing there in his patterned shirt and purple suspenders, with his sleeves rolled up over his leanly muscled forearms, and the rings on his fingers glinting in the late afternoon light. Warren really wants to take a page out of his daemon's book and just pounce on him.

"You did so well!" Yolande enthuses, squeezing Warren once before releasing him

Johnny steps forward. He pulls a bouquet of yellow flowers from behind his back and presents it to Warren with a flourish. "Congratulations! You were brilliant up there."

Warren accepts the bouquet gingerly, his heart flipping over in his chest. No one has ever given him flowers before. He runs the pad of his finger over one of the brightly colored petals.

"Sunflowers?"

Johnny shrugs one shoulder. "They remind me of you."

Warren blushes. "Thank you." He clears his throat a bit. "How did you… I mean, I didn't know that you would be here."

"Warren," Yolande says. "Of course we're here. Nadia wanted to come too, but she had to help Jonas with a last-minute event at the gym."

"Oh," Warren replies awkwardly. "Well, thanks. You really didn't have to come."

"Pretty sure we did," says Johnny. "And by the way— why did I have to hear about this momentous occasion from Yolande? Didn't feel like sharing with the rest of the class?"

Warren shifts on his feet. "It's not a big deal. It's just an end of term concert, so the music students can earn performance credits."

"And we know you don't like sitting still for long periods of time," adds Minnie from where she's perched atop Lucinda's back.

"Hey!" Johnny protests. "I can sit still. Sometimes. For a good cause."

"I guess I just didn't think you'd be interested," Warren says honestly.

Johnny rolls his eyes. He takes Warren's flute case from him, and then grasps his newly freed hand, linking their fingers together. "If it involves you? Assume that I'm interested."

Warren swallows. "Noted."

"You two, I swear," Yolande says, shaking her head at them. "Okay, come on. We're going to get celebratory ice cream."

Warren wants to object that he's not a child in need of a reward for a job well done, but ice cream actually sounds pretty great, so he keeps his comment to himself.

It ends up being gelato, purchased from a food truck at a park just off campus. They sit on a bench to eat it, Warren sandwiched between Johnny and Yolande, with his bouquet laying carefully in the space between his and Johnny's thighs.

Their daemons are in a furry pile on the grass nearby— that is, Minnie and Lucinda are in a pile, while Shane reclines facing away from them with his back against Lucinda's. Minnie hasn't stopped touching Lucinda since they exited the music hall, and Warren might find that embarrassing if Lucinda weren't so obviously enjoying it.

He's still a bit tense, waiting to be called out for his anti-social behavior, but the longer they go without mentioning the night of Jonas' birthday or its aftermath, the more he relaxes. Yolande talks about her exam scores and which schools she's applying to, while Johnny regales him with the recent goings on at The Palm. Warren listens, taking small, savoring bites of his mango chocolate chip gelato and feeling lighter than he has in days.

"Speaking of applications," Johnny says to Warren, "Zoe said to tell you that you should send him your resume, ASAP."

"Ah," says Warren. He hesitates, then asks, "Is it weird that he's doing this for me? It kind of feels like I'm taking advantage."

It's been bothering Warren since Zoe brought it up that night. The last thing he wants is to be a burden to anyone, least of all his friends.

"No way," says Johnny. "Zoe has connections all over the city, and he's not shy about using them. You're doing *him* the favor by letting him flex a bit."

"It just seems like something I should figure out for myself."

Yolande turns sideways and draws her legs up to sit cross-legged on the bench, facing him. "Zoe did the same thing for me when I told him I was thinking about law school. Apparently I needed to *strengthen my credentials*," she says in a passable imitation of Zoe's rasp. "He helped me get a volunteer position at Legal Aid— which, I have to admit, looks a lot better on my resume than 'Junior Instructor at Auntie's Modern Dance Academy'."

Johnny shudders. "That woman was terrifying."

Yolande makes a face. "You don't have to tell me. The point is, there's no shame in accepting help, Warren. Especially not from a friend."

"I suppose," Warren says, tugging at a loose thread on the end of his tie.

Johnny pops the last bite of his cone into his mouth, and then throws a casual arm along the top of the bench behind Warren. It takes all of Warren's willpower not to just lean back into it and tuck himself into the newly open space at Johnny's side.

"Face it, Warren," Johnny is saying, oblivious to Warren's internal struggle, "you're one of us now. Once Zoe decides to take you under his wing, that's it."

"I'll send it to him," Warren says distractedly. "I don't think I stand a chance at getting the job, but I'll send it."

"That's the spirit."

Yolande's phone starts buzzing. She takes it out of her pocket and looks at the screen. "Hm. Sorry, I have to take this." She stands and starts walking away from the bench, Shane rising to follow her. Over her shoulder she calls, "John, tell Warren your news!"

Johnny makes an annoyed sound.

Warren looks at him questioningly. "What news?"

"Yolande exaggerates— it's not really *news*. More like… an opportunity."

"Oh?" prompts Warren.

Johnny sighs in resignation. He stretches out his legs and crosses one ankle over the other. "Remember David, Nadia's friend with the gallery?"

"I remember. You met with him?"

"Yeah. He came to see me, actually. Ambushed me at the studio. I blame Alisha, honestly— she must have told him when I was in."

"What did he want?"

Johnny crosses his arms over his chest. "He, uh... he wants to take me on as an apprentice."

Warren straightens, his eyes widening. "Are you serious?"

"Hold on, don't get excited," Johnny says, raising a forestalling hand. "It's contingent on me taking a few classes at the Art and Design College. Um, a metal fabrication course. And one for sculpture and installation."

Warren grins at him. "That's amazing! You're going to do it, right?" When Johnny doesn't speak, his grin falters. "Right?"

"I'm considering it."

Warren looks toward the copse of trees where Yolande is standing with her back to them. She's still on the phone and she seems tense, her spine straight and one hand fisted at her side. Shane is pressed against her with his tail wrapped around the back of her leg.

Minnie hops onto Warren's lap. Out of the corner of his eye, he sees Lucinda come over and rest her muzzle on Johnny's thigh. She lets out a long sigh, and Johnny uncrosses his arms to place a palm on the top of her head.

Warren remembers what Johnny told him in the studio, about how he didn't want to disappoint anyone again. Cautiously, quietly, he asks, "You're worried you'll fail?"

"Let's just say I wouldn't bet against it," replies Johnny.

"Why?"

Johnny gives him an irritated glance. "School isn't my strong suit— you know that. I'm not great with assignment constraints, or deadlines… or rules in general, really. I like to do my own thing."

Warren thinks about that for a moment. It's true that school isn't for everyone— Grimm knows he's had his own problems with standardized learning— but this isn't just any class: this is something Johnny *enjoys*. Who knows where it could lead him?

"I could help you," Warren says. "Maybe I could hang out in the studio with you while you're working on your assignments, like you've done for me at the Laundromat. Help keep you on track."

"You really want that kind of responsibility on your shoulders?"

"Sure. If it's for you."

Lucinda makes a soft noise of surprise. Johnny just stares at him, something vulnerable in his expression.

Warren nudges Johnny's ankle with the toe of his sneaker. "You should do it, John. You'd probably be the best in the class."

Johnny scoffs, but his mouth turns up at the edges. "Maybe." He tilts his head, looking at Warren consideringly. "Hey— we're good, right? I just want to make sure after... you know."

Warren *does* know. He can sense the specter of their almost-kiss, hovering there between them. "Yes? I mean, I am if you are."

"Yeah. I just didn't hear much from you this week. It seemed like you might be upset with me."

Warren frowns. That makes zero sense. Why would *he* be upset with *Johnny?*

"Not with you."

"Okay. Good." Johnny's brow furrows. "Wait, does that mean that you're upset with *yourself?*"

Warren gazes down at his lap, at the familiar contrast of his pale hands resting on top of Minnie's dark fur. "I acted like an idiot."

"Warren, you were drunk. *Everyone* acts like an idiot when they're drunk." Lucinda coughs pointedly. "I mean," Johnny adds hastily, "you weren't an idiot. You were actually very sweet."

Warren looks up at him in confusion.

Johnny opens his mouth like he's about to say more, but both of their attention shifts to Yolande as she strides determinedly toward the bench, her mouth a tight line.

She stops directly in front of them and says, "I need your help."


------


It's a short walk from the park over to Johnny and Zoe's apartment.

Zoe comes out of The Palm when they arrive. On his shoulder, his crow daemon spreads her wings wide and drums them up and down without taking flight. Warren isn't sure whether it's meant to be a greeting, or if she's just stretching.

"Nadia and Jonas?" Zoe asks.

"On their way," replies Yolande, and he nods.

"You know," Johnny says, as he unlocks the apartment door and holds it open for the rest of them to shuffle through, "as much as I enjoy a spot of intrigue in the evening, I wouldn't object to enlightenment in this particular case."

Yolande tosses him a wry look over her shoulder as she starts climbing the staircase. "Aren't you the one who's always saying that things are more interesting in the dark?"

Warren can't quite disguise the flustered noise he makes at that.

Johnny smirks. "In the *literal dark*, Yolande, not the metaphorical one. As you well know."

"Patience, John. I don't want to have to explain all over again once the others get here."

They troop into the apartment. Yolande stays standing, but Johnny goes to sit in one corner of the couch, and Zoe takes the armchair.

Warren trails after Johnny and settles cross-legged on the carpet near his feet, leaving the rest of the couch free for Nadia and Jonas. Minnie climbs up onto his shoulders, and Lucinda drops down next to him, almost close enough to touch. Warren is careful to keep his hands on his knees.

Johnny, Yolande, and Zoe start up a discussion about the coffee shop's shift schedule while they wait. Warren tunes them out. In the light of day, he gets his first good look at the living room. It's modern and austere, with black leather furniture and a large flatscreen television mounted on the wall. The only decor he can see is a lamp on the end table and a framed painting hanging above the couch. The atmosphere of the painting is dark and moody, almost lonely. It depicts a ship at sea in the middle of a storm, white-capped waves rolling menacingly all around it, a doomed vessel unable to escape its fate.

Warren doesn't linger on it. He shifts his gaze, absently wondering if Johnny spends much time here. It seems unlikely— there is nothing of the color and warmth he'd glimpsed in his bedroom.

Without his permission, his mind flashes back to the image of Johnny lying on his bed, his hand hovering above Minnie's head, so close to touching her that Warren could almost feel it. He forcibly suppresses the memory when Minnie makes a distressed noise into the side of his neck, and reaches up to stroke her ears in apology.

The sounds of thumping feet in the stairwell announce Nadia and Jonas' arrival.

"We came right from the gym," Nadia says as they enter the apartment. "What's going on, Yolande?"

She sits in the open spot in the middle of the couch, and Vic flies to perch on the backrest behind her. Jonas takes the other end of the couch, Huff lowering herself to the floor by his feet.

"Thanks for coming so quickly," Yolande says. "I really appreciate it."

"It's not a problem," Jonas assures her. He's slightly sweaty, dressed in shorts and a tank top with what must be his gym's logo on it. "The class I was covering just finished."

Nadia leans forward, clasping her hands together attentively. "So?" she prods. "Don't keep us in suspense. What happened with the Eco Justice thing?"

Yolande puts her hands on her hips. Warren has only the vaguest idea of what she's about to say— something about a rally at the Exchange building tomorrow. She'd barely spoken to him and Johnny on their way over, too busy sending out a flurry of messages from her phone.

"As some of you know, I've been helping organize a protest against a big-name drug manufacturing company," Yolande starts. "They're notorious for skirting environmental laws, but their latest transgression has the potential to cause a lot more damage than usual, and no one has stepped up to hold them accountable for it yet."

"Why not?" asks Jonas.

"Money," Zoe replies. "Nothing shuts up detractors like cold hard cash."

"Typical," Johnny mutters disdainfully.

"Unfortunately, yes," says Yolande with a sigh. "The company is holding a press conference tomorrow afternoon at the Exchange to introduce their latest product, a stimulant they're calling *jilefa*."

Warren's blood runs cold. On his shoulder, Minnie's body stiffens.

"The manufacturing process produces some really nasty byproducts," Yolande continues. Warren can barely hear her over the white noise in his head. "So nasty that it can't be produced here without the company paying some hefty disposal fees and environmental damage fines. They've gotten around that by operating out of manufacturing facilities in other countries where the environmental laws are more… lax."

"Or nonexistent," grumbles Shane, his tail thrashing back and forth across the carpet.

Johnny gives a low whistle. "Shady."

Yolande nods. "Which is why Eco Justice planned to protest outside the main entrance during the press conference to raise awareness. If more people knew what the company was up to, then maybe they'd hold them accountable for it." She grimaces, and Warren forces himself to pay attention. "But we've run into a problem. We don't know who, or how, but someone leaked the details of our rally to the company. They've tightened security on the building, and asked the city to temporarily close off access to the side street in front of the Exchange."

"Lovely," Nadia says in disgust. "And what is the name of this dastardly organization?"

Yolande opens her mouth, and Warren already knows what she is going to say. It almost feels like an out-of-body experience, like watching a conversation he's seen played out before.

"Dalton Pharmaceuticals."

Even prepared, hearing those words is enough to make Warren flinch. Lucinda shoots him a concerned sidelong glance.

"I don't think I understand the problem," says Nadia, Vic ruffling his feathers behind her. "It's not illegal to protest, right? They can't stop you from doing that."

"Right," agrees Yolande. "But the effectiveness of our rally will be severely diminished— a few dozen people protesting behind barriers a block away isn't going to make the evening news."

"So what are you going to do?" asks Johnny. "I assume you have a plan."

He sits to attention, spreading his legs slightly in the process, and his knee comes to rest against Warren's shoulder. Warren doesn't even feel it, too preoccupied with the sour apprehension rising up from his stomach.

Yolande exchanges a glance with Zoe. "Half of a plan," she says. "Most of my group is going to remain protesting on the main street, but some of us want to try to do a sit-in in the lobby of the Exchange. I was hoping you would all join me."

"I'm always up for some anti-corporate activism," Johnny grins. He bumps Warren's shoulder with his knee. "Warren?"

"Sure," Warren replies faintly. Minnie's nails are digging into the skin above his collarbone.

Yolande smiles at them. "Thank you."

"I'm in too," Nadia says. "And so is Jonas."

"Of course," says Jonas, then furrows his brow. "But the Exchange is privately owned. Won't they just kick us out?"

"It's true that they can call the police to remove us— in fact, they probably will," Yolande answers. "But if we time this right, we can make it so that every stakeholder and member of the press that enters the building sees us and hears our message before that happens."

"Sounds like a party," Johnny says. "How are we getting inside?"

Yolande crosses her arms over her chest. "That's the part I haven't figured out yet. I'm open to suggestions."

"We could pose as reporters," offers Nadia. "I could sweet-talk Ivan into letting me borrow some of her fancy cameras."

"We'd need credentials," Jonas points out.

"I might be able to drum something up. I know a guy who specializes in fake IDs," says Johnny.

Nadia begins to question Johnny about the authenticity of his source, but Warren stops listening to them. An idea has taken root in his mind. He gnaws on the side of his thumb as he thinks it though.

"Whatever you're thinking right now, stop," Minnie whispers in his ear. "It's not worth it, Warren."

Warren disagrees. This is for Yolande, his *friend,* who has always been kind to him, even when he'd done nothing to earn it. This is his chance to give something back. To stop being useless.

He takes a steeling breath, and says, "I could get us in."

Everyone stops talking at once. Warren's fingers tighten on his knees as their eyes turn to him.

Zoe raises a brow. "How?"

"Through the main door."

"*How?*" Zoe repeats. His crow daemon is watching Warren intently.

"JosephDalton is the CEO of Dalton Pharmaceuticals," says Warren. "He's also my father."

There is a painful silence. Minnie leaves his shoulder and curls up in a tight ball on the floor near Lucinda.

"Wait," Johnny says slowly. "I thought your last name was Hanson?"

"It's my mother's maiden name. I've been using it since... since my father kicked me out."

"Why didn't you tell me— us?"

Warren tugs at his hair. "It never seemed... relevant."

"Relevant?" Johnny repeats. He rises and moves to stand in front of the couch facing Warren. "He's your family. Seems pretty relevant to me."

Warren scrunches his shoulders. "He disowned me. I'm *not* part of his family anymore. I don't have any of his money, or his influence. And I... I don't like thinking about him."

Zoe's tone is all business when he asks, "If he disowned you, how will you get us in?"

"Not many people know about it. He never made it public knowledge. I think he was hoping I would just... disappear."

"Which you did."

"Yes," agrees Warren. Minnie is anxiously chewing on her tail, and he lays a tentative hand on her back. "But if I gave my name to security, I think they'd let us in."

"What if your father sees you?" Johnny asks, his eyes flickering to Minnie. "Will he be upset?"

"My father doesn't usually go to press conferences," Warren tells him. "He prefers to let his PR people handle them. He doesn't care about fame, only profit."

Nadia rolls her eyes. "So noble of him."

"It's worth a shot," Yolande says. Her expression is cautiously hopeful. "If you're really okay with lying to security for us, Warren."

He nods. "I can handle it." *Probably,* he adds to himself.

"WarrenDalton," drawls Johnny. He shrugs when Warren looks up at him. "Just trying it out."

"I can't believe your dad is the evil corporate antagonist in Yolande's heroic fight against environmental injustice," Nadia says, sounding awed. "Did not see that one coming."

Warren winces. "I know he's terrible. I'm sorry."

"Don't apologize for him," says Yolande. She crouches in front of him, laying a hand on his forearm. "We are not our fathers."

Warren's throat feels tight. He ducks his head to hide his eyes behind his hair.

Zoe taps his cane on the floor. "All right. Everyone put your *Poor Warren* hankies away— we've got a protest to plan."


------


When Warren gets back to his apartment later that evening, the first thing he does is search for a vase for the bouquet from Johnny. It quickly becomes apparent that neither he nor Karl owns one, so he pulls an empty almond milk carton from the recycling bin and cuts the top off, filling it with a small amount of water before placing the flowers inside.

That done, he goes to his room and shuts the door. He deposits the makeshift vase on his desk, and then sags onto the edge of his bed, letting out a long sigh. He rubs at his eyes, exhausted from the emotional toll of this day. All he wants to do is sleep.

Knowing that he won't want to get back up again once he lies down, Warren makes himself change out of his concert clothes before he climbs into bed. He zips Johnny's hoodie over his pajamas as an afterthought. It doesn't smell very much like him anymore, but somehow just knowing that it belongs to Johnny is comforting enough.

"I don't like it," Minnie says quietly from her spot at the foot of the bed. It's the first thing she's said to him since his revelation in Johnny and Zoe's living room. "It's not a good idea, Warren."

"It's for Yolande," he replies grimly.

"She would understand if you changed your mind."

"It'll be fine. He won't be there."

The bedspread rustles as Minnie shifts uneasily. "You don't know that."

It's true: he doesn't. But he knows he wants to help Yolande, and he isn't going to let his fear of his father get in the way of that.

He sets his jaw. "We're doing this."

Minnie doesn't respond.

Warren rolls over to face the wall, his chest tight. Some people are always at odds with their daemon, but it's rare for Warren and Minnie to argue. It's jarring, like hearing a dissonant note in a familiar song

His phone pings with a message notification, and then twice more in rapid succession. When he checks, he sees by the purple heart in his contact name that all the messages are from Johnny.

Too tired to attempt to read them, Warren activates the text-to-speech function—and then wishes he hadn't when the mechanical voice intones,

>>*I googled him, you know*
>>*JosephDalton*
>>*what a piece of work*

Warren's heart drops to his stomach.

*I know.*
*He's not a part of my life. I told you that.*
>>*I knew he disowned you*
>>*I didn't know you were some rich kid whose father owns a quarter of the city*

*Does that matter? None of its mine.*
*>>I don't know. It mattered enough for you not to tell me*

Warren swallows against the sudden lump in his throat. He looks at the sunflowers on his desk, thinking about what he wants to say. Eventually he sends,

*Remember what you said before, when we were at Sol?*
*About not wanting me to see you how you used to be?*
*That's how I feel too.*

When Johnny doesn't respond right away, Warren adds,

*I didn't want you to see me like that, as some useless kid who's never had to work for anything in his life.*

Three dots appear at the top of the screen as Johnny types. Warren chews on the sleeve of his hoodie, waiting.

*>>that's not how I see you*
*>>Warren, you KNOW that*
*>>I guess I just don't understand why you didn't tell me who your father was in the first place*

It feels like they're talking in circles and Warren is too weary to continue. He gives up, quickly sending,

*Going to bed. See you tomorrow.*

He doesn't check to see if Johnny's sent a reply before shoving his phone under his pillow. He feels like a coward.


------


The next afternoon the six of them, along with five Eco Justice members, meet outside of a cafe near the Exchange building.

As planned, everyone is dressed formally in dark clothing, and there's not a piercing, tattoo, or provocative slogan in sight. There's barely even color, aside from a few people with dyed hair, and those who are wearing makeup.

"Do I seriously have to wear a suit?" Johnny had complained the evening before, when Zoe and Yolande were outlining their plan. "I can't remember the last time I wore a tie."

"You like theatre, right?" Zoe had replied. "Think of it as a costume. We need to look like we belong in the realm of the wealthy."

And, Warren has to admit, they do. It's honestly eerie to see the individualism and personality stripped away from them all. They could be any group of young professionals meeting for a late lunch in the financial district— except that all of them have poster boards hidden under their clothing.

Yolande handed them out once they assembled, a series of incendiary battle cries written in big, bold, black and red lettering. Warren doesn't know precisely what they say, but he gets the general gist, and he trusts Yolande enough to tuck one into the back of his shirt beneath his suit jacket without question.

They review the plan once more, and then head down the street to the Exchange. Warren tries to keep his nerves in check, but the closer they get to the building, the harder it is to ignore his growing sense of dread.

Minnie is a tense presence at his side. She's still upset with him, and he doesn't blame her for it— he's actually beginning to agree with her about the stupidity of his choices. But it's too late to back out now: this plan hinges on him being able to get them through the front door, and he's not going to disappoint his friends.

As they approach the main entrance of the building, Warren can see the security guard sitting inside the little glass booth from which entry into the Exchange is controlled. There are several other uniformed guards milling about the exterior, and a few of them eye their advancing group with suspicion.

Warren takes a breath, collects his courage, and strides toward the entrance.

He doesn't get far. A hand closes around his wrist, halting him.

"Wait," says Johnny.

Warren turns to him, surprised. They haven't spoken directly to each other since their aborted conversation that night before. "What is it?"

Johnny looks at him, his grey eyes stormy. "Are you sure you're all right with this?"

"Yes. I'm sure." Warren tries to sound like he means it.

Johnny watches him for a moment longer, his gaze assessing. Then he nods once, and drops his hold on Warren's wrist.

"Okay, then," he mutters, just loud enough to be heard by their group. "Let's go piss off some rich people."

Warren narrows his eyes and straightens his shoulders as he approaches the seated security guard. He gathers every ounce of bravado he has within him, every imperious word he's heard from his father, and every look of condescension he's ever had directed his way, and channels it all into his outward expression, hoping against hope that it will be enough.

He doesn't remember exactly what he says. The lies roll off his tongue, as does the indignant tone he adopts when he is asked to verify his claims. His nervous flush must be mistaken for aggravation as he presents his identification, because it works: the guard buzzes them inside.

"Nice work," Yolande murmurs, patting his shoulder briefly as she slips past him.

She takes the lead, gathering her small army of activists around her as they enter the lobby of the Exchange. There are already groups of reporters with camera crews there waiting for the press conference to begin, as well as several well-dressed members of the public, a few of whom Warren recognizes as his father's associates. He ducks his head, leaning a bit behind Jonas' bulk as he attempts not to be noticed by them in return.

*What am I doing here?* he thinks, as Minnie slips inside his jacket, out of view.

Yolande directs them to sit in a line blocking the hallway that leads to the event room where the conference is meant to take place, so that anyone seeking access has to go through them first. Only Zoe remains standing, taking up a vigilant position by the main entrance. On Yolande's command, they pull out their hidden posters, and then the Eco Justice members start up a chant.

The guard from the door becomes aware of what's happening, and Warren tries not to feel guilty about the panicked expression on her face as she comes over to demand they vacate the premises. Her Rottweiler daemon makes an effort to growl at them, but he sounds more anxious than menacing and backs off as soon as Huff bares her teeth.

Yolande and her group are in their element, and Johnny, Nadia, and Jonas have taken up the cause as well, enthusiastically joining in with Yolande's call-and-response. Warren tries his best to match their conviction, but his nerves are thoroughly rattled and the noise and steadily increasing tension in the room are not helping with that. The best he can do is hold up his sign in the direction of the members of the media as they start to take notice.

As the cameras start rolling, Yolande stands. Shane sits proudly at her feet as she begins to speak, her words factual and emotionally charged, meant to inform and incite in equal measure. When she reaches the end of her recitation, she starts over again from the beginning.

*It's not really about the words,* Warren remembers her saying during their planning session. *The people at the Exchange aren't going to be interested in what I have to say. It's just about making a scene long enough to get noticed.*

They have definitely been noticed, but Warren knows they don't have much time left. Zoe had estimated twenty minutes maximum in the lobby, just enough time to make an impact before the authorities were called. Yolande is in the midst of an interview, speaking passionately into a microphone with a camera directed at her, when they hear the first siren.

"Scatter!" Zoe yells.

They scatter. Warren and Minnie scramble to their feet and follow the rest of the group out the door and back out onto the street.

Outside, it's chaos. As planned, the rest of the Eco Justice members have left the designated protest area and have congregated outside the main entrance to provide support and cover for the sit-in group's exit. The handful of police officers who had been monitoring the street and the hired security guards from the Exchange are working together to try to wrangle the disorderly crowd. Above the shouting coming from all around him, Warren hears the wail of sirens getting closer, and feels a spike of panic: the plan was to be gone before police backup arrived.

He has Johnny and Lucinda in his sights as they make a break for the main street, but a security guard steps between them, stopping Warren in his tracks. The guard moves toward him. Acting purely on instinct, Warren spins on his heel and runs in the opposite direction, away from his friends, Minnie dashing along at his heels.

Warren keeps running until he rounds the corner of the Exchange building. When it becomes evident that no one's given chase, he stops, holding onto a nearby concrete pillar for support as he tries to catch his breath. Panting, still shaking with adrenaline, he takes in his surroundings. He's on a side street, near the entrance to the building's parking garage.

"Warren!" someone calls.

Warren turns, his stomach sinking.

It's Janis. Pretty, perfect, second-wife Janis. She's wearing a flowing floral print sundress, and smiling widely as she pushes a baby carriage down the sidewalk toward him. Her terrier daemon sits in the basket underneath, looking as sweet and docile as Warren remembers, a small bow on his head in the same fabric as Janis' dress.

"Janis," Warren says weakly. He is rooted in place, every muscle locked in incipient fear. If Janis is here, then his father won't be far away.

"Oh, Warren— it *is* you!" Janis says happily as she draws nearer. "I haven't seen you in so long! Joseph said you were away at school, but you haven't been home in months, not even for holidays."

So his father hadn't told her about his disinheritance then.

"I have been at school, yes," replies Warren. He's unsure of what to tell her, of how much to explain. "It's been… difficult to get away."

"Didn't you want to meet your new brother?" Janis asks, oblivious to Warren's turmoil. "His name is—"

"Janis."

Warren's heart stutters at the sound of his father's voice. He isn't ready for this.

JosephDalton walks out of the parking garage entrance and comes into view. It's been over half a year since he's seen him, but he looks exactly the way Warren remembers, stern and self-possessed, dressed in an expensive-looking black suit, his light hair slicked back from his forehead.

When he catches sight of Warren he makes a reflexive movement of surprise, barely perceptible, before his blue eyes harden.

"*You.*"

The look his father gives him is so cold that it sends chills up Warren's spine. Daphne, his father's wolverine daemon, starts up a low growl, her hackles rising. On the sidewalk in front of Warren, Minnie is frozen, caught in her predatory gaze.

"Janis," his father says, without looking at her, "go to the car. I will be right with you."

She goes, shooting an apologetic glance at Warren as she pushes the baby carriage down the ramp and deeper into the parking garage.

"Father," Warren starts, "I—"

"Stop. I don't want to hear a single bumbling word from your fool mouth."

Warren's mouth snaps shut, and he hates himself for it. High above his father's head, he catches a glimpse of red feathers, there and then gone again before he can properly track their source.

"You're here, so I have to assume you had a hand in the absolute debacle that occurred here this afternoon," his father says flatly, almost disinterested. "I thought I had made myself clear when I told you to leave, but here you are again, embarrassing us both."

Warren looks away from him, his face burning with shame. He'd forgotten what it felt like to be made to feel small, to want to vanish.

Minnie rises to her hind legs, glaring up at Warren's father. "Warren is *not* embarrassing!" she declares, and Warren is instantly filled with love for her, his brave little daemon. "You don't know him at all and you never have!"

Without warning, Daphne charges, pinning Minnie to the ground with two sharp-clawed paws.

Minnie lets out a startled yelp as she hits the pavement, and Warren's chest constricts. It's as if someone has suddenly reached inside of him and closed their fist around his heart.

"Treacherous little weasel," Daphne hisses, teeth bared, and Minnie struggles desperately to get out of range of her snapping jaw.

Warren's whole body is stricken with tension. His father's disapproval has always been an icy thing, cruel but predictable, ever-present; Daphne's is like wildfire, volatile and quick to ignite. Her rage is both fearsome and familiar, and seeing Minnie once again at her mercy makes the feeling of powerlessness Warren had experienced every day in his father's house come flooding back.

He remembers now, what it's like to be vulnerable, the threat of someone's teeth at your throat. How could he have forgotten? Minnie certainly hadn't.

His father looks on impassively as Daphne presses down harder on Minnie's chest, shifting to crush Warren's daemon beneath her bulk. Warren can almost feel it, a heavy weight that steals the breath from his lungs.

In Daphne's hold, Minnie goes limp.

*Playing dead,* Warren thinks hysterically. He still can't make himself move.

Then Minnie gasps, sharp and pained. It strikes him like a bolt of lightning, shocking him into action.

"Stop!" he shouts. "Get away from her!"

"Oh?" his father says. "Look, Daphne— it seems the boy has finally grown a spine. Is that, I wonder, what led you to believe you could make some sort of difference here today?"

Warren grits his teeth, hands clenched at his sides.

"But nothing you do will ever truly matter in the long run," his father continues, still in that maddeningly indifferent tone. He sneers at Minnie. "Just look at your disgrace of a daemon. She's weak. Worthless. Just like you."

And Warren has told himself time and time again that he is done listening to this man, but it's impossible to ignore the doubt that rises up as his father stands before him, saying aloud the secret fear Warren holds deep inside of himself, the truth of his nature that he's tried so hard to deny.

*Weak. Worthless.*

There is motion in his peripheral vision, and suddenly Lucinda is there, with Johnny close behind her. They come up on either side of him, Lucinda baring her teeth at the sight of Minnie in Daphne's grasp.

The relief Warren feels is fierce and immediate. Bolstered by their presence, he says, "Let Minnie go. Right now."

Daphne growls, and raises her muzzle to snap her teeth at him.

Lucinda snarls at her. She takes one intimidating step toward the wolverine daemon, and then another, head low and fur bristling.

"You heard him," Johnny says, standing tall at Warren's side. "Let her up."

His father regards Johnny and Lucinda with disdain. "You know, Warren," he says conversationally, "every time I think you cannot disappoint me further, you prove me wrong."

"I'm not the disappointment, *you* are!" Warren snaps, his voice cracking with emotion. "You let *me* down, not the other way around."

His father narrows his eyes at him. "You are the greatest mistake of my life, and if you ever meddle in my affairs again, I will do much worse than disinherit you."

"Actually," Warren replies, with dawning realization, "disinheriting me was the kindest thing you've ever done. So you can take your threats, father, and kindly *fuck off.*"

Johnny releases a loud guffaw, then slaps a palm over his mouth.

JosephDalton gives a contemptuous shake of his head. "This is a waste of my time. Daphne!" he calls sharply, as he turns away. "Come."

As soon as Daphne releases her, Minnie scrambles to her feet and runs to Warren, leaping up into his arms.

"*Warren!*" she cries, as he catches her and clutches her tight to his chest.
"All the Saints and your Aunt Eva," Johnny mutters, his eyes still trained on the retreating figure of JosephDalton. "What the hell, Warren— that was your *father?*"

Warren barely hears him, too preoccupied with the trembling daemon in his arms. All of his tenuous bravery has abandoned him, swept away by a tide of terrible guilt.

"I'm sorry," he tells Minnie, burying his face in her fur. "Minnie, I am *so sorry*. I should have listened to you."

"It's not your fault," she whispers.

The noise he makes at that is wretched, a jagged laugh that turns into a sob halfway out of his throat. "It is though. All of it."

Minnie just tucks herself closer to him and doesn't speak another word.

------

The protest ends up making the evening news, which Yolande is understandably thrilled about.

They watch it at The Palm, where Eco Justice has gathered to celebrate. Anika and Dodd are working the service counter, but Johnny jumps onto one of the espresso machines to help them make drinks once they arrive. Everyone is talking and laughing around him, but Warren hears it all as if he's listening from underwater, the sounds muddled and indistinct.

He's numb, and has been ever since Johnny and Lucinda led him back to the coffee shop. They'd tried to talk to him, cajoling and consoling in turns, but Warren had found it difficult to speak, too emotionally fatigued to hold a conversation. He hasn't let Minnie out of his arms, and she's shown no interest in leaving them.

Warren hasn't told the others about the confrontation with his father, having no desire to dampen the celebratory mood with his personal drama. The only ones who know are Johnny and Lucinda… and Nadia and Vic.

Warren had found that out on their walk here, when he'd found the words to ask, "How did you find me?"

And Johnny had simply answered, "Vic."

Warren looks at Vic now, perched on Nadia's shoulder where she sits next to him on the black velvet couch, her legs curled up on the cushion. He remembers the flash of red wings he'd seen in the sky over his father's head and feels a spark of gratitude.

"Thank you," he says to Nadia and Vic, "for looking for us. And for sending help."

"You're welcome, Warren," Vic replies solemnly.

"How did you do it?" Warren asks, because everything is muted right now, even his sense of propriety, and he wants to know. He directs the question to Nadia. "How did he find me without you? You're not separated."

*They can't be,* he thinks. *It would be obvious… wouldn't it?*
Vic shudders, his feathers rippling. Nadia lifts a hand to soothe him, petting gently. "No, we're not separated," she says, keeping her voice low, and Warren exhales. "But we can *be* separate."

"What do you mean?"

"It was a punishment at one of the boarding schools my parents sent me to," Nadia explains. "If you broke the rules, the headmistress would lock you and your daemon in different rooms, to make it hurt— the pulling, you know?" she says, and Warren nods. "The rooms were further apart each time. It was meant to be a deterrent, but I've never been good at doing what I've been told. Vic and I found out that once you become accustomed to it, it stops hurting so much. And then we were free to do as we pleased."

"Accustomed to it?" Warren repeats warily. "How do you become accustomed to pulling your bond?"

"It takes time, and practice. Lots of practice. But it can be done."

Nadia sounds flippant, but Vic's wings are hunched and he's gripping her shoulder so tightly that his talons have pierced through the sleeve of her blouse.

Warren thinks about Daphne holding Minnie apart from him. He thinks about how wrong it felt, and then he thinks about stretching their bond *on purpose*, and feels revulsion so strong it's almost nauseating.

Something of his distress must show in his expression, because Nadia places a cautious hand on his arm. Warren has to force himself not to recoil from it.

"Warren. It's okay," Nadia says gently. "I don't regret it, and neither does Vic. It's actually been very useful, as you found out today. "

Minnie lets out a whimper, rubbing her head against Warren's chest, and everything is suddenly too much for him. His shield of apathy is crumbling, and he can sense his emotions crowding in, just waiting to overwhelm him. He doesn't want to be here when that happens. He stands, mumbling an apology to Nadia as he goes.

Johnny catches his shoulder as he's about to leave The Palm.

"Where are you going?"

"I need to leave," says Warren, without meeting his eyes.

"Are you all right?" Johnny asks, and then shakes his head in irritation. "Stupid question. Let me try again: I want to help. What can I do?"

Warren musters a smile, but even he can tell that it's wrong on his face. "Nothing. Everything is fine."

"Of course," Johnny replies, with the inflection of someone who does not agree even the slightest bit with what has just been said.

"Really, I'm okay," Warren says, shrugging off Johnny's hand. He backs away, turning toward the door. "I just need to be alone for a while."

"No."

Warren pauses with his hand on the door handle. He looks back at Johnny. "No?"

Johnny gives him a lopsided smile. "No."

Minnie sits up in his arms to stare at Johnny as Warren turns to face him. "Why not?" he asks.

"Because I want you to stay."

"Here?"

Johnny shrugs. "With me. Doesn't have to be here."

Warren shakes his head. "Not here."

"All right," Johnny replies mildly. "How about upstairs? We can watch a movie or something."

Warren can barely think. Upstairs is Johnny and Zoe's apartment. Is that where he wants to be when he inevitably crashes? And does he want *Johnny* there when that happens? The answer comes more easily than he expects.

"Yes."

"Great. Let me tell the others we're leaving."


------

They go upstairs.

The first thing Johnny does is shrug off his suit jacket. "I'm going to change," he says, fingers working at the knot of his tie. "Do you want something else to wear?"

Warren nods. "Yes, please."

"Okay. Don't go anywhere," Johnny says, as he heads to his bedroom.

Warren remains standing where he is in the living room. The painting with the doomed ship is on the wall directly across from him, and his eyes are drawn to the way the waves are depicted rising against its battered hull, one strong surge away from overwhelming it.

"Is Minnie all right?"

Warren startles. He looks over at Lucinda— he hadn't even realized she'd stayed behind with him. She's sitting back on her haunches with her ears pointed toward him, keen gaze flickering between Warren's eyes and the bundle of fur in his arms.

"She will be," replies Warren, and Minnie twitches. He strokes a hand along her back.

"You should sit down," Lucinda says softly. "You look tired, Warren."

He goes to the couch and sits. The leather is cold, and the creaking sound it makes as he shifts uncomfortably on the too-firm cushions makes him wince. Lucinda watches him squirming, her expression thoughtful.

Johnny returns wearing purple plaid pajama bottoms and a black t-shirt. He holds out a bundle of clothes to Warren.

"Here," he says. "Before you ask, the pajamas were a gag gift from Nadia. They're too short for me, but I think they'll suit you just fine."

Warren takes the clothes from him and goes to change in the bathroom. He closes the door in some relief, glad to have a moment alone.

He braces his hands on the edge of the sink and just breathes for a moment, leaning forward with his head between his arms. When he glances up he sees his reflection in the vanity mirror. He looks how he feels, exhausted and wan, his freckles stark on his too-pale face. There are circles so dark they look like bruises beneath his blue eyes. The same blue as his father's.

Warren turns away from the mirror.

He strips efficiently, and then kicks his clothes into a pile in the corner of the room, figuring he can collect them later. He puts on the pair of pale yellow pajama pants he'd been provided with and finds that Johnny was correct: they do fit him.

"Are those cowboy hats?" Minnie asks, her voice scratchy with disuse.

Warren looks down. There are indeed little red cowboy hats printed on the pajama pants, along with white clouds and green cactuses, all in a cutesy cartoon style.

"Apparently so," Warren says, bemused.

The white t-shirt he'd been given is too big in the shoulders and hangs almost to mid-thigh, but it's soft and smells like Johnny, which more than makes up for what it lacks in fit. He gathers up his daemon and exits the bathroom feeling more comfortable than he has all day.

He pauses when he catches sight of the living room.

"Is that… a blanket fort?"

It certainly appears to be. The furniture has been rearranged to hold aloft a large bedsheet that now spans the width of the room, creating a tented space in the middle of it.

At the sound of Warren's voice, Johnny rises from the floor where he'd been fussing with a nest of pillows and blankets.

"Uh, yeah," he says, one hand rubbing the back of his neck. "It was Lucinda's idea. Kind of silly, I know, but Da used to make them for me when I was having a hard time, and I just thought…" He shrugs. "I guess I thought you might like it."

"I like it," Warren confirms. He smiles, small but true. "I really like it."

Johnny smiles back at him. "Good. Hey, are you hungry? I could make us something to eat."

The thought of food makes Warren's stomach churn unpleasantly. He shakes his head. "I'm not hungry."

Johnny's smile slips sideways. "All right. Do you want to just…?" He gestures to the blanket fort.

Warren really does just want to crawl into the cozy-looking den Johnny has made and go to sleep, to distance himself from this day. But, he realizes, cringing at his own selfishness, it's still early in the evening, and Johnny probably wants dinner.

"If you want to eat I could—"

"No, it's fine," Johnny assures him. "I'll get Zoe to order something for us later. Go get comfy. I'm just going to grab my laptop and I'll be right with you."

Warren nods and ducks down to crawl inside the blanket fort. He feels a bit awkward doing it. He hasn't done this in… maybe ever. At least not that he can remember. On really bad days in his father's house, he would sometimes take the covers off of his bed and hide in his closet, but it wasn't like this, a space meant to be both whimsical and comforting at once.

The light is softer inside the fort, and it smells good, like clean laundry and Johnny. Warren recognizes the blanket spread out across the carpet as the quilt from Johnny's bed. It's a patchwork of colors and patterns, beautiful, but worn at the edges, like it's been used well and often.

He settles himself on one side of the quilt, lying on his back and resting his head on one of the pillows that have been laid out on the floor in front of the couch. Minnie curls herself into a ball on the center of his chest, and he wraps an arm around her middle to keep her close.

"Are the accommodations to your liking, my good sir?" Johnny jokes, as he ducks his head under the low roof.

"Mm," says Warren. "Four stars."

"Only four?" says Johnny. He sets his laptop on the floor, but doesn't move to open it.

"It's still too bright."

"Ah. We can fix that."

Johnny leaves the fort and a moment later the overhead lights blink off.

"Better?" he asks, as he crawls back inside and flops down onto his back next to Warren.

"Much."

They lie in silence for a few minutes. Johnny traces his fingers over the seams of the quilt, while Warren stares up at the roof, willing his body to relax. He thinks that if they can just stay here and be still together for a while, he might be able to hold his emotions a bay long enough to fall asleep.

Then Johnny breaches the quiet. "So… your dad is pretty shitty, huh?"

Warren tenses, and Minnie's ears go flat against her head.

"Very tactful, John," Lucinda murmurs from her spot on the floor near their feet.

Johnny nudges her in the side with his socked toes. "What? He *is.*"

"You knew that already," Warren says to Johnny.

"I did," Johnny admits. "I guess I just didn't realize the vast extent of his shittyness." When Warren doesn't respond, he cautiously adds, "We don't have to talk about it. But maybe we should?"

"Did you lure me into this blanket fort under false pretenses?" Warren asks, grasping for levity to counter the anxiety blooming in his stomach. "I thought we were going to watch a movie."

Johnny huffs an amused breath. "No, I 'lured' you here because I thought maybe you needed to talk about what happened, and this is a nice place to do it. We can still watch a movie if you want to."

"What makes you think I need to talk about it? I'm perfectly happy not talking about it," says Warren, keeping his eyes trained on the ceiling.

He can hear the eyeroll in Johnny's voice when he says, "Well, for one thing you haven't let go of your daemon since I found you, and— I don't know. You just seem… upset." He hastens to add, "And rightfully so, after *that*."

Warren worries his lower lip between his teeth. He meets Minnie's eyes, and she inclines her head slightly. He sighs in resignation.

"He hates me. My father. I'm sure you could tell."

Johnny winces. "Yeah." His fingers tap restlessly on his stomach. "Has it always been that bad?"

Warren shrugs against the pillow. "It got worse as I got older. As it became more obvious that I was… lacking."

"Because of your dyslexia?"

Warren hums in agreement.

Johnny makes an angry noise. "He's three kinds of fool for that." He goes silent for a moment, like he's thinking, and then carefully says, "I'm almost afraid to ask, but did he ever... hit you?"

"Not me," Warren says, hitching Minnie closer.

His father had never hit him: he hadn't needed to. He'd found other ways to hurt Warren. It had been distance mostly, a lack of attention, of interest: neglect, cold and— he recognizes now, with time— calculated to make Warren feel as bad as possible about himself. It had worked better than he would like to admit. Sometimes, Warren thinks he would have preferred Daphne's rage.

"*Saints,*" Johnny mutters.

"It's not completely his fault." Warren's always thought it, but he's never spoken it out loud. He doesn't know why he says it now, except that the concern he hears in Johnny's voice makes something in him want to confess. "I wasn't what he wanted, and it was... difficult for him to accept that."

Johnny turns his head on the pillow to fix Warren with an incredulous look.

"Are you serious? Warren, that's crazy. Normal people don't abuse their kids because they didn't get the one they wanted. Look at my Da— you think he wanted a mess like me? I've disappointed him in a dozen different ways, but I've never doubted that he loves me."

"Of course he does," Warren says. He can barely speak through the pressure that's gathered in his throat. "You're not worthless, like me."

Johnny rolls all the way over onto his side to face him. "You're *not* worthless," he says firmly. "I've seen you with your daemon, Warren. I've seen how much you love her. So I know you don't believe that."

Warren's eyes sting. He squeezes them shut, willing the tears away. He doesn't want to cry in front of Johnny, especially not about this.

The quilt rustles as Lucinda leaves her spot by their feet and comes to lie at Warren's side. He opens his eyes and tips his head to watch as she settles close to him on her belly, not quite touching, but radiating warmth in the scant space between them. She keeps her eyes trained on Warren as she curls her tail against her side and sets her head down on her front paws, going still.

Minnie makes a small noise and slips off of Warren's chest into the small space that separates him and Lucinda, shifting until she's wedged snugly between them.

"Hey," Johnny says softly, and Warren turns to look at him. His grey eyes are more serious than Warren has ever seen them. "Tell me you don't believe that."

Warren hesitates.

Minnie says, "He didn't want us."

Johnny exhales through his nose, frustrated. "Listen to me, both of you: you are *not worthless.*"

"But I'm not—"

"No," Johnny cuts in. "However you're about to end that sentence, it's wrong. You *are,* Warren. You're kind. You're smart. You're hardworking." He pauses to flash Warren a quick grin. "You're *extremely* cute. You're the whole damn package, sweetheart."

Warren shakes his head. If Johnny doesn't stop talking, the stinging at the corners of his eyes is going to worsen and spill.

But Johnny continues, unaware of how close Warren is to breaking apart. "So whatever you're thinking in that big brain of yours about not being good enough? About being *worthless?* It's bullshit. And I think you know that."

Warren inhales sharply and raises his hands to cover his eyes as they spill over. Minnie moans in distress, pushing her face into his ribs.

"Hey, *no,* don't—" he hears Johnny say, as if from far away. Then, closer and more urgently, "Warren, I want to touch you. Can I touch you?"

Aware that it might shatter him, but wanting it too much to say no, Warren nods, rolling toward him.

Johnny doesn't hesitate. He wraps his arm around Warren's shoulders and pulls him close, his hand sliding up to grip the back of Warren's head in a comforting hold.

Warren curls into him, tucking himself beneath Johnny's chin and pressing his forehead to his collarbone. He's crying in earnest now, but it doesn't feel overwhelming. Here, in the safe space Johnny's made for him, it feels more like release.

He doesn't know how long they stay like that, but after a while his ragged sobs turn to sniffles, and then he is just breathing into Johnny's shirt, as Johnny's fingers rub soothing circles into the skin at the nape of his neck. Warren feels empty, but in a good way. Unburdened.

He senses movement at his back, and suddenly Lucinda is hovering over him. His breath catches as she leans down to nose gently across his cheekbone.

"Warren," she murmurs in her velvet voice, and then begins to lick the remnants of tears from his skin.

Something races through Warren at her touch, a magnetic thrill that sets his whole body alight. He draws in a tight breath, his mind reeling. At his hip, Minnie lets out a small, high-pitched whine, but Warren is too stunned to really process it, caught in a current of sensation that feels like electricity beneath his skin.

After a moment that's somehow both endless and too short, Lucinda draws back, and Warren can suddenly think again. He can't believe what just happened.

*Is that how it was for Johnny, when Minnie touched him?* he thinks wonderingly. But his wonder is quickly morphing into uncertainty as Johnny stays silent beside him.

"John…" he says, tilting his head back to look at him. "John, I—"

"It's okay," Johnny says, hushed. He lifts his hand to brush the curls off Warren's face, his fingers coming to rest on his cheek, right where Lucinda had touched him. "I promise."

"It was me, I wanted to," Lucinda whispers near Warren's ear. She lowers herself again, but this time in a warm line flush against his back.

Warren feels it like the press of an electric coil, his spine tingling. He twists to look at her, reaching one hand out automatically.

Lucinda is looking back at him, her eyes half-lidded. She would be the picture of relaxation if her head weren't tilted to one side, her neck ruff so close to Warren's fingers that he can almost feel the phantom touch of fur. Still, he hesitates.

Johnny kisses the top of Warren's head. "Go on," he murmurs into his hair. "Touch her back."

Moving slowly, heart racing in his chest, Warren reaches out and brushes his fingers along the fur at the back of Lucinda's head. He feels it when Johnny gasps, shivering against him as if Warren has just caressed a bare nerve ending with his fingertips.

Minnie hums contentedly, and Warren closes his eyes. His blood is singing with euphoria— touching Lucinda feels the way music *sounds*. He sifts through her thick fur experimentally, and she pushes her head up into his touch when he curls his fingers, gripping.

Lucinda lets out a blissful sigh at the exact same moment Johnny does— and *oh,* it means... something.

It means something.

# CHAPTER 9

"You didn't come home last night."

It's the first thing Karl says to him the next morning, when Warren comes into the kitchen to get himself a snack after showering.

Warren shoots him a quick glance over the top of the refrigerator door. "You noticed?"

Karl rolls his eyes. Despite it being almost noon, he's still in his pajamas. He's sitting on the edge of the counter with his legs hanging over the side, eating a bowl of breakfast cereal. Daya is perched on the top of his head, her tiny limbs gripping his hair for balance as she peers down at Warren with interest.

"You're my fr— my roommate, Warren. Of course I notice if you don't come home."

"Oh." Startled by Karl's candidness, and feeling suddenly as if he owes him an explanation, Warren offers, "I was at Johnny's place."

Karl pouts. "Lucky you."

Warren's face heats. "It's not like that."

Minnie makes a skeptical noise, but quietly, so that only Warren hears her. He appreciates her discretion.

"So what *is* it like then?" asks Karl around a mouthful of Cinnamon Toast Crunch.

Warren purses his lips. It's a fair question, and one he's been asking himself since he woke up that morning in the blanket fort in Johnny and Zoe's living room.

Minnie had been awake already, blinking groggily at him from her spot on the pillow next to his, as Warren came slowly to awareness. Someone had covered him with a blanket, and the light around him was soft where it filtered in through the bedsheet; outside the fort, he could hear the sound of low voices coming from the direction of the kitchen. One of them was definitely Johnny, which meant the other was likely Zoe, but Warren couldn't make out what they were saying. The scent of cooking food had set his stomach gurgling in reminder that he'd missed dinner the night before, but he'd stayed put, snug and comfortably warm under the blanket. His eyes were still a bit swollen and his ribs ached from crying, but it was a good ache, like the pull of muscles after a deep stretch. He'd felt lighter— *free*— as if untethered from some weight he hadn't even realized had been holding him down.

He'd reached for Minnie, running the fingers of one hand over her ears, and she'd sighed in contentment, pushing up into his touch. Warren had been struck, then, by the visceral memory of Lucinda's fur beneath his fingertips, the dense softness of it, not the same as Minnie's silken coat, but still smooth and plush, like velvet.

The remembrance of it sent a wave of exhilaration rushing over him. He had touched Johnny's *soul*. Johnny had *wanted* him to. It was breathtaking. Sensing the turn his thoughts had taken, Minnie had whispered, "I felt it, you know, when you touched her. It felt like heat— *everywhere.* Inside every part of me."

"It was like that for me, too," Warren whispered back, though he'd known she knew it already. "Is that what it was like when you touched Johnny?"

"Not quite. It was… it was as if I was standing outside of a closed door, knowing there was a hearth waiting on the other side, but not being able to feel its warmth," she'd told him, her expression rueful. "But I could feel him, a little, through their bond, when you touched Lucinda."

As if summoned, Lucinda had appeared in the entrance to the blanket fort. Her gold eyes glinted when Warren met her gaze. A moment of recognition had passed between them, before she'd lowered her head, appearing almost bashful for the first time in their acquaintance.

"Come for breakfast, you two," she'd said quietly. "John made pancakes."

They'd followed her out of the fort and joined Johnny and Zoe in the kitchen for a breakfast of blueberry pancakes and fried potatoes. Warren had kept his eyes on his plate, eating steadily, his appetite returned in full force after the stress of the previous day. Minnie's had too— she'd stolen an entire pancake off of Warren's plate, and then hid on his lap beneath the table to devour it in quick, tidy bites. When she'd popped her head up again, looking for another, Johnny slid one over to her before she even had to ask for it. She'd made a happy noise at him, before taking the pancake in her teeth and disappearing back under the tabletop.

Johnny chuckled, and Warren had looked up at him reflexively, attuned to the sound of his laughter. Johnny had already been looking back at him. When their eyes met, the corner of his mouth lifted, just slightly, his smile soft and secretive.

A giddy thrill ran through Warren at the unspoken acknowledgement of the new intimacy they shared, and he'd had to look away, overcome. His eyes had fallen upon the washing machine beneath the granite countertop, and it occurred to him that he should offer to try to fix it.

He hadn't.

Johnny and Zoe had to meet with Yolande for a shareholders meeting at The Palm— "Which is generally eighty percent Yolande and I nodding and smiling while Zoe says numbers at us, fifteen percent Yolande talking about ethically-sourced coffee beans, and five percent the three of us coming up with increasingly ridiculous pun-based drink names," Johnny had told Warren with a wry smile— so Warren had taken his leave shortly after breakfast, regretfully changing back into his clothes from the protest. They'd felt wrong against his skin, ill-fitting after the comfort of Johnny's clothing. It had been the first reminder that the sense of rightness he'd experienced beneath a blanket fort in Johnny's living room was not his reality.

On the bus ride back to his apartment, Warren had done his best to hold onto the joy he'd felt, the certainty, but neither could withstand the doubt that crept insidious into his mind.

The connection he'd felt to Johnny and Lucinda had been real. When he'd touched Johnny's daemon, it had meant *everything*: belonging, acceptance— even love.

But what if it hadn't meant that to Johnny?

For most people, allowing someone else to touch your daemon was a serious act of trust, reserved for the most intimate of relationships. As far as Warren knew, Johnny abided by those social norms... but maybe he didn't. Warren wasn't certain what defined an intimate relationship for Johnny, but he knew how much he loved his friends, how loyal he was to them. What if Lucinda touching Warren was an act of comfort provided to a good friend, and nothing more?

Now, back at his own apartment, Warren stares blankly at the contents of the refrigerator and thinks about how best to answer Karl. What is it like between him and Johnny? Where do they stand now?

"Johnny is my friend," he finally says, closing the refrigerator without taking anything out of it. "But," he adds, before he fully thinks it through, "maybe not just my friend, anymore."

"Anymore?" Karl prompts, raising his spoon to his mouth. "What changed?"

"I touched his daemon."

The words just spill out of him, like water from a too-full cup. Warren regrets them instantly, acutely aware of the breach of privacy he has just committed, especially when Minnie gives a short bark of dismay and hides herself behind his legs.

Karl chokes on his cereal. "*What?*" he splutters, between coughs.

"Yeah, it… it happened."

"Warren, that's serious stuff," Karl says, wiping his mouth with the back of his hand. "I didn't realize you guys were that close."

Warren shrugs helplessly at him. He hadn't realized it either.

"So is he your boyfriend now?" Daya pipes up, wide-eyed.

"No."

"But you *will* be together."

"That's none of your business," Minnie snaps, at the same time Warren replies, "I don't know."

The look Karl gives him is half-incredulous, half-pitying. "You touched his daemon, and he was okay with that. How much more proof do you need?"

Warren looks away from him, scrubbing a hand through his damp curls in frustration. "People don't have to be romantically involved for that to happen."

"That's true. It's not as common as you may think, though," says Karl, and Daya chirps in agreement.

"I would *never* let one of Karl's friends touch me," she declares, before reluctantly adding, "Not unless he really, *really* wanted me to."
Karl makes a face. "Yeah, no— you don't have to worry about that. Daya's right though," he says to Warren. "It's not something people *or* daemons just do on a whim."
"I *know* that," Warren replies sharply, crossing his arms over his chest. "But it's... complicated. I'm not going to make any assumptions." *It's too important*, he adds to himself.

Daya tilts her head at him. "Seems pretty straightforward to me."

"Humans overthink *everything*," Minnie grumbles, for once in agreement with her.
"Maybe just *your* human," Daya says, nudging her nose into Karl's hair affectionately.

Karl jumps down from the counter and goes to the sink.

"Look," he says, setting his bowl inside with a clatter, "this conversation is giving me hives, so I'm going to say this once and be done with it: Johnny is insanely attractive and, much to my eternal disappointment, he seems really into you. I think it would be a mistake if you didn't at least make an *attempt* to get with him."

He departs without waiting for a response, leaving Warren standing in the kitchen, his mind a jumble of mixed emotions.

"I hate to say it," Minnie murmurs, coming out from behind Warren's legs to look up at him, "but he has a point."

"Which is?" he asks warily.

"That it would be a mistake not to try," she says. "Johnny *wants* you, Warren. If I felt it, then I know you did too."
"I felt it," Warren confirms. Because he *had* felt it, the thread of Johnny's desire woven through Lucinda's affection and loyalty. It had been hard to miss, the perfect echo of Warren's own yearning.

"But you don't believe it."

"I believe it. I just… don't believe it can last, and— I don't know, Minnie. Would it really be worth the risk? Everything is fine the way it is."

"But it could be *better*," Minnie insists, and Warren's heart twists.

Hope wars with reservation in his chest, with the instinct to deny that what she's said could possibly be true.

Because here is the root of Warren's hesitation, the reason he can't allow himself to just reach out and take what he thinks Johnny is offering to him: what if whatever Johnny feels for him is temporary? What if Warren is only a brief diversion for him until someone else comes along, a better match to Johnny's shining personality, to his bold wit and effortless charm?

He doesn't think Johnny would set out to hurt him on purpose. Warren has never seen even a hint of malice from him, and he believes that Johnny's feelings are genuine— he'd *felt* them, after all. But feelings change, and Warren isn't the type of person that people tend to keep around. He never has been. He's hovered at the edge of every social circle he's ever been part of, always on the outside, looking in. He isn't inherently likeable the way that Johnny is— it takes real effort for Warren to be personable, to be engaging enough for others to take interest in him. The thought of what will happen once Johnny inevitably sees through the cracks in the veneer of his personality hangs over him like a sword. Try as he might, he can't shake the notion that no matter the strength of Johnny's feelings, they'll never hold up to the truth of Warren's nature.

"What if we're not enough?" he whispers.

Minnie makes a distressed noise. She leaps up into Warren's arms when he holds them out for her, tucking her face into his neck. He holds her tightly, and for a long moment they just breathe together, taking solace in each other.

When Minnie speaks again, her voice is tremulous, but sure.

"Lucinda wouldn't have done it if they weren't certain— Warren, I *know* her. She wouldn't have let it happen."

Warren breathes out shakily. In the end, this is the truth he holds closest: Minnie is his daemon, and he trusts her implicitly.

"So what do we do?"

"We need to talk to them about it," she says decisively.

"All right," Warren agrees, heartened by her confidence. "We will."


------


But they don't talk about it.

Johnny ends up having to work a string of double shifts at the coffee shop when Anika and two other baristas all come down with bad colds in the same week. Johnny, Yolande, and Zoe are scrambling to cover the hours, and the situation is only exacerbated by the handful of new part-time employees they'd hired in anticipation of Yolande attending law school in the fall, all of whom are in need of training. With Warren working nights, and Johnny exhausted from long days at The Palm, they haven't managed to see each other in person since the weekend.

Minnie sulks over it, feeling their absence more keenly after the recent closeness they'd shared. Warren at least has the option of communicating with Johnny via text. He and Johnny message each other frequently, but by wordless agreement they keep the conversation at surface-level, avoiding anything deeper than complaining about work, gossiping about their mutual friends, or discussing Johnny's upcoming travel plans. It's fun talking with Johnny this way— it always has been. His flirty banter, while enjoyable, can be disarming, and Warren does best when he has time and space to think over his replies.

As the days pass, some of the earlier urgency he'd felt fades, and what happened in the blanket fort becomes just one more thing he and Johnny don't discuss. Warren can sense it lingering between them, a suspended chord waiting for resolution, but if he's honest with himself he doesn't mind the delay. After the events of the previous week he welcomes the simplicity of their interactions— and really, what would be so terrible about things staying the way they are? Johnny is a good friend, and Warren thinks he could be content with that.

On Thursday, Nadia invites him over to hang out at her and Yolande's apartment, claiming that as the only other person in their friend group without current daytime responsibilities, he is morally obliged to keep her company. Warren agrees, happily.

They end up on the apartment's tiny balcony, which is big enough to hold two plastic patio chairs and not much else. Warren sits in one of the chairs with his feet on the edge of the seat and his knees drawn up to his chest, arms loosely encircling them. Nadia reclines on the other, slouched low with her crossed legs stretched out in front of her.

The weather is warm for May, the sun a hot ball in the cloudless sky, so it isn't long before Warren shrugs off his hoodie. Nadia makes him put on sunscreen, citing her status as a medical student while ominously intoning, *I know too much.* She slathers it on herself too, and then the pair of them lounge with their eyes closed and their heads tipped back, basking in the sunlight like a pair of lazy house cats.

It's a little disconcerting, at first, for Warren to see Nadia and Vic with his new understanding of what they've done to their bond. He isn't sure whether to acknowledge it or not: on the one hand, he wants to apologize for leaving so abruptly after they'd confessed to him, wanting to be sure they both know that he doesn't judge them for their choices; but on the other, it seems completely inappropriate to bring it up, especially since Nadia does him the courtesy of not asking about his run-in with his father.

In the end, he decides the best thing to do is to let it lie. Neither Nadia or Vic are behaving any differently toward him and Minnie so Warren makes an effort to do the same. It's easy to do when Nadia is perfectly herself: clever, bold, and caring, with a tendency toward lewdness that he finds both amusing and slightly mortifying.

Minnie certainly doesn't seem to have any qualms about settling next to Vic on the balcony railing. The two of them are speaking quietly, while Warren and Nadia embrace the natural indolence that overtakes all students in the summertime by doing absolutely nothing.

It's nice. He hadn't realized how much he needed to just *be* with someone, and not have to worry about trying to interpret any underlying meaning from their words or body language. There is no agenda here, other than spending time with his friend, and it's relaxing.

"Don't take this the wrong way," Nadia says, breaking the comfortable lull in conversation the two of them have fallen into, "but you seem happier than usual."

"Do I?" asks Warren, keeping his gaze trained on the sky.

"Yes. You're more... mellow or something. Less stiff around the shoulders. It's a good look for you."

"I guess I have been feeling pretty good this week."

"Anything specific happen that you want to talk about?" Nadia asks, in the overly-casual tone of someone trying to sound nonchalant.

She's obviously hinting at something specific, and Warren is pretty sure he knows what. He decides to offer her something else instead.

"Hmm," he says, pretending to think about it. "Well, I had a job interview yesterday."

Nadia turns her head to the side to look at him over the top of her fashionably-large sunglasses. "Really? Warren, that's great news!"

"Thanks. It was a complete surprise."

Warren honestly hadn't been expecting much when he'd sent his updated resume to Zoe on Sunday evening. But two days later he'd received an invitation to a remote interview with one JosefSokolov from Waterfall Technologies.

He'd immediately gone to the company's website. Minnie sat on his lap with her ears perked as he'd browsed through it and discovered that Waterfall was a fledgling aerospace technology company specializing in satellite design and deployment. Despite Warren's natural disinclination toward optimism, it had been difficult to temper his excitement at the possibility of working there, especially after discovering that Waterfall built and tested many of their satellite components in an on-site laboratory.

He'd quickly confirmed the interview appointment and then, inspired, had gone on a job-searching spree. Seeing the application requirements of many of the posted positions had been overwhelming, and had made him realize that Zoe had probably been correct in his assertion that Warren should be looking for more engineering-based pre-graduation experience. He'd known it already, deep down, but he can admit that he'd needed the push to start searching in earnest.

"For Waterfall, right?" Nadia asks, still looking over at him. "I remember Barlow mentioning that. How'd it go?"

"I think it went okay," replies Warren. It had all happened so quickly that he hadn't even had time to get anxious about it beforehand. "I talked to Josef."

Mr. Sokolov— *call me Josef*— had not been what Warren had pictured when he'd imagined the CEO of Waterfall Technologies. After running through some standard questions with the company's stern-faced HR Manager— whose expression hadn't changed when he'd nervously brought up his dyslexia, though her komodo dragon daemon had flickered his tongue at him in a way that Warren had chosen to interpret as sympathetic— Josef had jumped onto the call.

He was younger than Warren had been expecting, and more handsome, too, with bright hazel eyes that had fixed on Warren with a palpable amount of focus. It had been an interesting conversation, veering in and out of professionalism. Josef had been enthusiastic, and his fox daemon had kept her ears pricked forward the whole time, her assessing gaze reminding Warren of Zoe's daemon. Warren had managed to keep up with Josef, somehow, even when the other man had gone off on a tangent about nozzle design. That had seemed to please him, and Warren left the call feeling cautiously hopeful.

"I know him through Ivan and David," Nadia says. "He can be a lot, but he's a good guy— one of those natural born leader-types, you know?"

Warren nods at her. "Yes, I got that impression."

"What position did you interview for?"

"It's just an engineering internship, but I'd really like to get it."

"Anything to get you out of that Laundromat," Nadia agrees. "Did you know that Zoe thinks it's actually just a front for Giles' other, less savoury businesses? I shudder to think what those might be."

"I'd believe it," Warren says grimly. "I've been wondering forever why he even *needs* a night shift employee— hardly anyone comes in after midnight." *Except for Johnny,* his mind supplies fondly. "The only reason I haven't brought it up with him is because I need the wages."

"I get it," says Nadia. "Got to make that scratch. Well, I hope you get the internship."

"Me too." Warren is at the point where he thinks that even if he doesn't get the Waterfall position, which is likely, he'll keep searching until he finds something else.

"What about your new job?" he asks, remembering that Nadia had told them all she'd picked up a summer job as a research assistant for an undergraduate professor that she'd kept in contact with. "When does that start?"

Nadia sighs and re-crosses her legs, smoothing her hands over her long skirt. "Officially? Not until next week. But Dr. Lewin already has me doing a bunch of safety and ethics training for the lab work." She wrinkles her nose. "Which is *extremely* boring, truth be told, but I'll do it if it means I get to help him with his cardiovascular research."

"That's… heart stuff, right?" Warren asks. He has very little knowledge about the medical field in general. Hospitals make him queasy.

"You got it," Nadia nods. "Vic and I are pretty certain we want to specialize in cardiology. I mean, we still have to do a bunch of clinical rotations, so who knows what will happen, but that's the goal for now."

Warren smiles at her. "No matter what you do you're going to be great at it. You're one of the smartest people I know, Nadia."

"Thanks, Warren," she says, smiling back. "Hey, you're coming out with us on Saturday, right? For Johnny's thing?"

She means Johnny's birthday. Technically, it isn't until the thirty-first, but he'll be visiting his father on the actual date so they're celebrating a week early.

"Of course I am," Warren says, a bit indignantly, because it's not as if he's going to miss Johnny's *birthday*.

"Of course you are," Nadia mocks. "Why did I even ask?"

"What's that supposed to mean?"

"Just that your crush is showing."

"You're the one who told me not to bother denying it!"

"And I stand by that," Nadia says. "It's impossible to miss anyway, at this point, especially when you're in the same room as him. You get this look on your face that's like…" she trails off. "Vic, help me out here."

"Gooey? Sort of like you're melting inside," Vic suggests, and Minnie hides her face in her paws.

Warren's cheeks pink. "I like being where he is," he mutters. "I can't help what my face does about it."

Nadia lifts her eyes heavenward. "Saints, between you and Johnny it's just constant heart-eyes emojis."

"Really?" Warren asks, momentarily forgetting his embarrassment. He leans over the space that separates their chairs. "What does he say about me?"

Nadia mimes zipping her lips. "Nope. I have been sworn to secrecy by my best girl. You're not getting anything more out of me."

Warren slumps back in his seat, definitely not sulking. He works his lower lip between his teeth, thinking.

There is a part of him that desperately wants to tell Nadia about what happened with Johnny's daemon. He's seen her interact with Huff, so he knows that she would understand his conflicted joy. But he's already told one person too many, and Nadia *knows* Johnny and Lucinda. It makes it so much more personal, and he's not sure he's prepared to hear her opinion— which she would *definitely* give— on this particular matter.

"Ugh, it's so hot out here," Nadia grumbles to herself. She gathers her brown curls into a messy bun on the top of her head, securing it with a hair tie that she pulls from around her wrist. "We should probably go inside for a water break soon," she adds to Warren.

He hums noncommittally, and Nadia shoots him a curious glance at the nonresponse.

"What's up, Warren?"

Warren releases his lip. He clasps his hands together in his lap as he comes to a decision. "Can I ask you something?"

Nadia raises a brow at him. "Does this have anything to do with that fact that I heard through the grapevine—"

"So, Yolande."

"—that you slept over at a certain-someone's apartment last weekend?" Nadia continues, without pausing.

Warren looks over at their daemons. Minnie has one ear flicked toward them while Vic grooms her fur with his beak. They are both suspiciously quiet, listening.

"It's related, yes," he finally says. "But not in the way that you're probably thinking."

"Do go on," Nadia prompts, leaning an elbow on her armrest and propping her chin on her hand, the picture of attentiveness. "I'm dying of suspense over here."

Warren turns in his chair to face her, bracing the soles of his sneakers against the armrest. He takes a breath and then, before he can change his mind, asks, "How did you and Jonas transition out of the 'just friends' phase?"

Vic makes a scoffing sound, and Nadia breaks into laughter.

"What?" Warren says defensively. "What did I say?"

"Oh, no, it's not you," Nadia assures him, grinning. "It's just— Jonas and I never really *had* a friendship phase in our relationship. We went from hating each other to sleeping with each other very, *very* quickly."

"Oh," says Warren, a little flustered. "That must have been..."

"Confusing," Nadia says. "The word you're looking for is confusing. But the sex was *really* good. *Is* really good," she corrects with a wink.

Warren scrunches up his face. "No offense to you or Jonas, but please, spare me the details."

Nadia smirks. "Sweet, innocent, Warren."

"I'm not!" he denies, even though he sort of is, when it comes to this. "I just have very little interest in hearing about my friends' sex lives."

"That's fair," Nadia concedes. Then her expression becomes serious. "Look, I know it can be hard to make that leap. Trust me, I've been there."

Warren looks at her skeptically. "You literally just said that you and Jonas weren't friends before you got together."

"Right, but here's the thing: the sex was amazing—"

"We've established that."

"—*but* I kind of thought that was it, that it was going to be a purely physical relationship and nothing more. I thought that was the way I wanted it, too." Nadia lifts her shoulders in a wry little shrug. "Then I got to know him better, and my feelings started to change."

"What did you do?" Minnie pipes up, her eyes fixed on Nadia.

"At first I ignored it," Nadia admits. "What we had was fine, and I didn't want to mess anything up by asking for more."

"What changed?" Warren asks, because something must have. "What convinced you that it would be worth asking?"

"Huff," she says without hesitation. "Huff convinced me. Well, she and Vic."

"I told Nadia right from the beginning that Jonas liked her," Vic says proudly.

Nadia nods. "He did. He's wiser than he looks."

Vic squawks, raising his wings to fly across the short distance between them. Nadia holds out her arm for him to land on without looking away from Warren.

"But really, it was the way they started to act around each other, like a pair of lovesick teenagers," she says. "It was so *easy* between them. I was almost jealous… and let me tell you, it's a very strange experience being jealous of your own daemon."
Warren and Minnie exchange a brief glance. He's never been *jealous* of her, exactly, but he thinks he can understand what Nadia means. Sometimes when he sees Minnie with Lucinda, he is filled with so much secondhand affection that he feels like he could burst from wanting Johnny.

"I thought if our daemons could become that close," Nadia continues, "then why couldn't Jonas and I? It made me wonder if he was holding back, and once the idea was in my head I couldn't shake it. So one day, Vic went and sat on Jonas' shoulder, and then, while Jonas just sat there with this adorably dumbfounded expression on his face, I flat out told him that I wanted more. And as it turned out, so did he."

"But what if you had been wrong?" Warren asks, as Minnie hops down from the balcony railing and comes to sit hunched on the ground in front of his chair. "What if he hadn't? I'm not as brave as you are, Nadia. I'm not sure I could take a risk like that." Just the thought of it makes his stomach clench with anxiety.

"Is it risky to put your heart in someone else's hands?" Nadia says. "Absolutely. But it's a risk worth taking, in my opinion."

"It's different for you," Warren says quietly. "I have more to lose."

Nine furrows her brow. "What do you mean?"

"If I lose Johnny, I lose the rest of you too. You were his friends first," explains Warren. He feels a twinge of shame as he says it. Nadia and Yolande and Zoe and Jonas have all been nothing but kind to him, but Warren knows deep in his heart that if they had to choose between him and Johnny, they would choose Johnny— and they would be right to.

Nadia's expression softens. "Warren, I can't speak for everyone else, but you're *my* friend. It doesn't matter that I've known Johnny longer. I am more than capable of being a friend to both of you."

Warren ducks his head, his throat constricting. Nadia graciously allows him time to compose himself.

"I know it's hard to believe," she tells him gently, "but sometimes trusting people works out. I was perfectly happy on my own, just me and Vic against the world." Vic chirps in agreement, and she strokes his feathers appreciatively. "I still would be, if someday Jonas stops finding me beguiling and starts finding me obnoxious instead."

"That would never happen," Vic interjects loyally. "He loves you."

"I know, dearest," Nadia soothes. "My point is that even if what we have with Jonas and Huff doesn't last forever, I still think it's worth having. Knowing someone on that level… there's nothing else quite like it."

Minnie sighs wistfully as Nadia's words settle around them. Warren reaches down to scoop her up into his arms, pulling her in close to his chest. The longing he feels is so intense it's almost physical.

Nadia is watching them carefully. "Was that too much?"

Warren shakes his head. "It wasn't too much. Thank you," he says, meeting her eyes. "For a lot of things, really, but especially for… for being my friend. I hope you know that you're my friend too."

Nadia smiles at him. "I know," she says, reaching out her hand. Warren takes it. "For what it's worth? I think once you and Johnny figure this thing out it's going to be *magic*."

Warren tips his head back again to look at the clear, blue sky, and— for the moment— allows himself to believe it.

------

He receives the job offer from Waterfall on Friday morning. It's a summer internship, temporary but well-paying, and comes with the possibility of extending his contract into a part-time position in the fall.

Warren has been working hard to manage his expectations, but apparently he's done too good of a job of it because the news takes him completely off guard. He has to close the lid of his laptop and just breathe as he processes it.

It's too good to be true.

Minnie doesn't share his disbelief. She is beside herself with excitement, yipping joyfully as she dashes in circles across his bedroom floor.

"We're going to learn so much! Think of it, Warren— real engineering work!"

"Minnie, calm down," Warren says, struggling to constrain the wide grin that is threatening to take over his face.

"No!" she shouts, leaping at him and making them both fall back onto his bed together. "This is a good thing, and we're allowed to be excited about it! Admit that you're excited!"

"Okay, okay!" he says, giggling uncontrollably as she kneads her paws into his ribs, exactly in the spot where he's most ticklish. "I'm excited!"

Later, he makes himself go over the contract in full, but he has so much trouble focusing that it takes him three attempts even with his text-to-speech program activated. He ends up sending the document to Zoe, just to be safe. As soon as Zoe gives him the all clear, Warren signs it and sends it back to Waterfall without delay.

After he sends it he immediately messages Johnny to tell him the good news. Johnny lets Warren know how thrilled he is on his behalf with a string of progressively overdramatic congratulatory gifs. Even anticipating it, Warren is still touched by his supportive response.

Early the next afternoon he heads over to The Palm, where Johnny is working his last shift before his two-week long vacation. Warren sends him a message before leaving to let him know that he and Minnie are on their way. When they arrive at the coffee shop, Lucinda is already waiting for them by the door.

Minnie goes to her immediately, lifting her face as Lucinda leans down to touch their foreheads together. When Lucinda licks her nose, Minnie purrs loudly enough that Warren can hear it over the low din of the coffee shop.

Neither of them has ever been shy about showing their fondness for the other— at least not since those first few meetings, a lifetime ago in January— but after what Nadia had told him about Vic and Huff, Warren sees their interaction in a new light. Their devotion to each other is so obvious. It's there in every touch, in every look that passes between them, a tenderness that can't be mistaken for anything other than pure adoration. Is that how it could be for him and Johnny? Could they share the same kind of easy affection that their daemons do?

Lucinda turns her head to look at Warren, her expression coy. She steps nearer to him, and then, in a stunning act of familiarity, she whiffs a soft breath of greeting on the back of his hand.

"Hello, Warren," she says quietly, the words hot on his skin.

"Hi," Warren ekes out.

He holds himself still as Lucinda sniffs a delicate path across his knuckles. She keeps her muzzle just shy of touching him, maintaining the smallest measure of propriety between them, but that doesn't stop the phantom tingles from running through his hands, a reminder of what it would feel like if he reached out and made contact.

His fingers flex, just slightly.

As if sensing his crumbling restraint, Lucinda moves away from him. She gives him a little wink, and then turns back to Minnie.

"Minnie, let's go find a place to cuddle," she says, leading the way toward the seating area.

Minnie nods, pausing only to whisper, "Johnny has been watching you the entire time," before quickly following after her. She shoots Warren a sly glance over her shoulder as she goes.

Warren looks to the service counter, and his heart skips in his chest.
Johnny *is* watching him, his expression rapt. When their eyes meet, a slow grin begins to spread across his face.
And, *oh*— Warren had almost forgotten what it's like to see him in person. They talk every day, but seeing Johnny's wide smile, the small crinkles that appear at the corners of his eyes, the way he bounces a bit on the balls of his feet as Warren starts walking toward him… there isn't anything else like it.

"Well, well, well," Johnny says as Warren approaches. "Look who's come to brighten my day. Couldn't wait until tonight to see my handsome face, hm?"

Warren shakes his head at him, but doesn't make any attempt to conceal his grin, as he says, "Maybe I just wanted a coffee. I hear it's the best in the city."

Johnny sticks out his lower lip in an exaggerated pout. Warren is struck by a sudden and insane urge to bite it.

"I'm devastated, of course," Johnny tells him, as Warren wrenches his gaze away from the jut of his lip. "But you're in luck." He slides an unlidded takeaway cup out from behind the espresso machine and pushes it toward Warren. "Congratulations on your new job, Warren."

"Thank you," Warren says, eyeing the cup with suspicion. He assumes it holds some kind of caffeinated beverage, but whatever it is can't be seen beneath the mound of whipped cream and rainbow sprinkles that sits atop it. "Why do you have confetti sprinkles?"

"Oh, you know," Johnny says blithely. "Special occasions— birthdays, and the like."

"It's *your* birthday. So maybe this one should be for you?" suggests Warren, poking at the side of the cup with his fingertip.

"You don't like it?" asks Johnny, sounding hurt. Warren can't tell if he's joking or not.

"No, no, I like it," he says hurriedly. To prove it, he picks up the whipped-cream monstrosity and takes a sip. It's not as sickly sweet as he was expecting. He takes another sip. On second thought, it's delicious.

Johnny is watching him with a knowing look. "It's good, right?"

"Yes, it's good," Warren admits, wiping his lips with the back of his hand.

Johnny slaps his palms on the counter. "I knew you'd like it! I've got you all figured out," he says, charmingly smug. "Anything else you want?"

"So much." The words leave his mouth without forethought, and Warren flushes at his own daring.

Johnny's eyes flash. He leans over the counter, and says, "Name it, and it's yours."

Warren has to look away from the intensity of his gaze. He clears his throat. "I was actually wondering if you had a minute? I have something for you."

Johnny straightens. Warren thinks he must be imagining the note of disappointment in his voice as he says, "For me? The suspense." Johnny begins untying the strings of his apron. "You okay if I take a quick break, Roeder?"

A man looks up from where he's been flipping through a stack of receipts at the cash register. Warren doesn't recognize him, so he must be one of the new hires. He has to fight off a wave of revulsion when he can't immediately spot the man's daemon, but then he catches sight of the tiny brown spider on the counter in front of the till, and the revulsion recedes.

The man—Roeder— nods at Johnny in reluctant agreement. "Don't go far. I'm still getting the hang of the espresso machine," he cautions.

"I'll be right over there," Johnny reassures him. "Come on, Warren."

Warren follows him over to the nearby couch. Johnny sits sideways, drawing one leg up onto the seat, and Warren sits down next to him. He places his drink on the low table in front of the couch, and then unloops his messenger bag from his shoulder and sets it on the floor by his feet.

Their daemons have already made a cozy spot for themselves, but when Warren and Johnny sit down, Minnie leaves Lucinda's side to hop up onto the backrest behind them. Johnny smiles at her and she sidles closer to him, before crouching low with her tail wrapped around her body. Lucinda stays where she is on the end of the couch beside Johnny, her body curved in comfortable repose.

Johnny looks at Warren expectantly. "So, what's this about a present for me?"

"It's not much," Warren warns him, reaching into his bag to take out a small package wrapped in newspaper. "But I know you have an early flight tomorrow morning, and I didn't want you to have to carry it around all night at the Big Block, so… here. Happy Birthday."

He thrusts the package toward Johnny, who takes it without hesitation.

"You didn't have to do this, you know," Johnny says, as he begins tugging at the seams of the paper.

"I know I didn't have to," says Warren. "I wanted to."

Johnny's mouth quirks. "Oh, well, if you *wanted* to, then I'm hardly going to be the one to deny you."

He finishes unwrapping the package, and then just... stares.

"What is it?" asks Lucinda, her ears pricked forward as she peers around Johnny's hip to get a better look.

Johnny lifts a pair of elbow-length gloves from the pile of newspaper and holds them in his hands. They're brown suede leather, reinforced with bright purple padding stitched onto the fingers, palms, and backs of the hands. Warren had been wanting to get Johnny new welding gloves since he'd seen the battered pair in the studio that day back in April, but couldn't justify the purchase until now, after accepting the job offer from Waterfall. He'd thought the gift clever, but now he is second-guessing himself. Are they too much? Not enough? The longer Johnny stays silent, the more anxious Warren becomes.

Johnny turns the gloves over in his hands, rubbing his fingertips over the surface of the leather. "These are—"

Warren interrupts him before he can finish speaking, too nervous to wait for the end of his sentence.

"I can return them if they're not the right kind, or if you don't want them. But I thought you could use them for the metal fabrication classes— you know, if you decide to take them. And whether or not you do, you still need new gloves." Warren knows he's rambling, but can't seem to stop. "I saw your old ones and they're a *disaster*, I don't know how you haven't burned your fingers off. These ones are heat-resistant, and they have extra protection at the hands, and—"
"*Stop.*"

Warren abruptly ceases talking when Johnny puts a hand over his mouth.

"They're perfect. Thank you," Johnny says, his words laden with sincerity.

Warren blinks at him. "You're welcome," he murmurs. His lips lightly graze the skin of Johnny's palm as he speaks.

Johnny inhales sharply.

He makes an aborted movement, like a shiver half-suppressed, and Warren can't help the small noise he makes at the momentary grip of Johnny's fingers around his mouth.

Johnny stills at the sound, his eyes going hot and focused. They stare at each other over the top of his hand. Warren is pinned in place by the weight of Johnny's attention. His heart is beating, beating, *beating*, picking up speed like a boulder rolling downhill.

Then Johnny exhales, slow but audible. He holds Warren's gaze as he moves his palm away from his mouth, sliding it over his cheek in a lingering caress. His hand comes to rest on the side of Warren's head, cupping his jaw.

Warren has to hold his breath, he feels *so much*.

He releases it, toes curling in his shoes, when Johnny's fingers sink into the hair behind his ear, sending sparks of pleasure shooting across his scalp. Distantly, he hears Minnie let out a low whine, but he is too caught up in the moment to be self-conscious about it. Instead he turns his face, deliberately leaning into Johnny's touch.

Johnny's eyes darken. Warren hears the click of his throat when he swallows. His thumb begins to brush a gentle line across the top of Warren's cheekbone, back and forth, back and forth.

Warren's pulse thuds loudly in his ears. With Johnny touching him like this, with so much tenderness, he can't *think*. He just wants to—

"Johnny."

Warren jolts in surprise, and Minnie lets out a squeak as she topples from the backrest onto the seat cushions.

Johnny quickly drops his hand from Warren's face, grumbling under his breath as he turns to face the intruder. "What is it, Zoe?"

Zoe is standing in the doorway of his office, looking at them with his eyebrows raised. Warren can't quite meet his gaze, still recovering from the interrupted moment.

"Didn't you already take your break?" Zoe asks Johnny.

"...Maybe."

Zoe levels him with an unimpressed look. "John."

"Zoe, it's my *birthday,*" Johnny complains. "Be nice to me."

"It's not your birthday," Zoe says flatly.

Johnny gives him a cheeky grin. "Close enough, isn't it?"

"You wish," replies Zoe. He turns to Warren. "Congratulations on the internship, by the way. I think you'll enjoy working with Josef."

"Ah— me too," says Warren, resting his hand on Minnie's head as she climbs into his lap. "Thanks again for getting me the job."

Zoe shakes his head. "I didn't get you the job. You did that on your own," he says. On his shoulder his crow daemon ruffles her feathers, her beak opening and closing once, soundless.

"You sent my resume to Josef," insists Warren. "And I never would have tried for it without your encouragement."

"Maybe I just didn't want you loitering around here all summer distracting my employees," Zoe says, his eyes sliding over to Johnny. He gives him a significant look. "Break's over, Johnny. The newbie is in the weeds." He nods toward the service counter, where Warren can see a long line has formed as Roeder struggles at the drink station.

Johnny whips his head around. "Aw, hell," he mutters.

Message delivered, Zoe disappears back into his office. Johnny stands and Lucinda rises with him, jumping down from the couch. She pushes her front paws forward and bows to the floor, her back curving in a deep stretch.

Johnny starts to move, and then stops, turning back to Warren. Their eyes lock and Warren senses it again, that suspended chord hanging between them, heavy with potential.

Warren yearns for resolution.

He doesn't know what Johnny sees in his expression, but whatever it is, it makes his grey eyes soften. "See you tonight, Warren," he says quietly.

It has the cadence of a promise.

"See you," Warren replies, matching his tone.

As he watches Johnny walk away Warren feels a tug in his stomach, like being caught on the wrong side of gravity. His hands clench. He wants to reach out, catch the sleeve of Johnny's henley. He wants to say, *wait. Stay.*

If things were different between them, he would.

It is an acute reminder of why he needs so badly to define their relationship. It feels like he and Johnny have been circling each other, both of them advancing and retreating, testing each other's limits, neither one of them quite sure where the other will land.

Warren is tired of spinning in circles. He *wants Johnny*.

The points of Minnie's nails are digging into his thighs. He forces himself to calm, rubbing the fur at the base of her ears in apology.

As the tension ebbs, clarity settles over him, and Warren's mind sharpens to sudden purpose: he's going to kiss JohnnyFontaine. Tonight.

# CHAPTER 10

"Bye!" Warren calls as he prepares to leave the apartment later that evening.

Karl sticks his head out of his bedroom. "Where are you going?"

"Out for Johnny's birthday. To dinner and the Big Block."

"In a *sweater vest?*" Karl asks incredulously.

Warren looks down at his clothing. He's in the same light wash jeans that he wore to the club the last time he went and a white t-shirt layered beneath a dark grey sweater vest. He hadn't thought he'd done too badly. He'd even managed to get his curls relatively under control tonight.

"Yes?" he tries.

"*No.* Wait here."

Warren exchanges a baffled glance with Minnie as Karl ducks back into his room. He returns moments later, marching toward Warren with a bundle of clothes in his arms. Daya flutters over to hang upside-down from a nearby wall sconce, as Karl holds out a pair of black trousers and a yellow plaid flannel shirt.

"Here," he says. "Wear these."

Warren eyes the clothes skeptically. "What's wrong with what I have on?"

"You want a list?"

Minnie's ears flatten. "Warren looks nice!"

Karl holds up his hands. "I'm not saying he looks *bad*, I just think his style could use a little more… edge to it. Especially if you're going to a club. With Johnny."

Warren wavers. "Are you sure?" he asks. "Yellow isn't really my—"

"Trust me," Karl cuts in. "Color is a good thing, especially if you want to stand out."

Warren gives him a flat look. "I don't."

Karl sighs, long-suffering. "Just put them on. You can thank me later."

"Fine." Warren takes the clothes from him and goes to his room to change.

"Leave the shirt unbuttoned!" Daya calls after him.

"I'll unbutton *you*," Minnie mutters, too low to be heard, and Warren breathes out in amusement.

When he reemerges from his room, Karl gives him a satisfied nod.

"Better," he says.

"I think the trousers are too small," Warren says, tugging at the skin-tight fabric. He had struggled to get into them.

"They're supposed to be like that," Karl tells him. "It's basically the entire point of wearing them."

"If you say so," Warren replies doubtfully.

But when he catches sight of his reflection in the mirrored closet doors by the front entrance, he doesn't hate what he sees. The trousers are distressed at the knees and upper thighs, showing just the tiniest amount of skin, and their tight fit gives definition to his legs and waist in a way that even Warren, critically examining himself in the mirror, can admit is appealing. His white v-neck t-shirt, a remnant from high school that he hadn't intended to be seen, is a bit too short and tight across his chest and shoulders, but it looks all right contrasted against Karl's oversized button-down. The shirt is loose-fitting and hangs to the top of Warren's thighs, which must be an intentional fashion choice, since he and Karl are close to the same height. When he runs his hands down the sides of it, its fabric is pleasantly soft beneath his fingertips.

"Roll up the sleeves," Karl suggests, when he sees Warren fidgeting with the shirt cuffs.

Warren shakes his head. He likes having a place to hide his hands. "They're fine."

Minnie cocks her head to the side. "I like it," she says. "I didn't think I would, but I do."

Warren likes the outfit too. He looks different, but not so much so that he isn't able to recognize himself beneath the borrowed clothes. It's a good change, he decides, as he kneels down to tie the laces of his shoes, and hopefully a harbinger of other good changes to come.

------

The restaurant Johnny has chosen for his birthday dinner— a trendy diner that specializes in plant-based comfort food— is located only two blocks from Warren's apartment, though he's never been there before.

Johnny has been raving about it all week, sending Warren admittedly mouth-watering photos from the restaurant's Instagram page. He'd provided his own descriptive captions for them, jokingly written from the perspective of an over-enthusiastic food blogger. Warren had chalked it up to excitement on Johnny's part, a bit of silliness meant to entertain them both while working.

It dawns on him now, as he picks up the diner's pictorial menu card, that it had more likely been Johnny's attempt to familiarize Warren with the food in a way that allows him to peruse his options independently. By matching the pictures he sees to his memories of listening to Johnny's captions, Warren is able to avoid asking for help deciphering the accompanying text.

A lump forms in his throat at the consideration shown for his comfort, and he has to swallow past it before placing his order. He catches Johnny's eyes across the table and mouths, *Thank you.*

Johnny winks at him, his lips curving into a pleased little smile. The affection Warren feels for him in that moment warms him to his core.

It's a balmy evening, so the six of them and their daemons are eating outside on the diner's sidewalk patio, a decision that is especially appreciated by Lucinda and Huff, who are able to stretch out their long limbs on the pavement. The conversation is upbeat: it seems as if everyone has a bit of good news to share. Warren tries to pay attention to Yolande— newly accepted into KU's faculty of law— as she tells them about the classes she will be taking in the fall, but he's finding it difficult.

Johnny is looking especially gorgeous tonight in a pair of brightly colored floral print trousers and a high-collared white button-down shirt. Yolande and Nadia have gifted him a crown of purple, pink, and white flowers, which he wears proudly atop his head. It should look ridiculous, but he's somehow arranged it so that the flowers are artfully nestled amongst his springy curls.

Warren is hard-pressed not to just openly stare at him over his plate of vegan mac and cheese. Despite his best efforts, his eyes keep straying to Johnny's perfectly shaped lips as he remembers his goal of kissing him.

Every time it happens, Minnie makes a little rumbling sound in the back of her throat, and Warren has to force his gaze away before anyone else notices. Based on the amused looks Nadia keeps casting in his direction, he's not exactly succeeding.

Minnie and Lucinda are huddled together on the ground near Warren's chair. Halfway through the meal, laughing at a story Jonas is telling about one of his clients, Warren catches Lucinda staring at him. His heart tumbles over at the fond look in her eyes. The urge to touch her is so strong that he has to clasp his hands together beneath the table to stop himself from reaching out.

Later, when they leave the restaurant, Johnny casually takes Warren's hand, like that's just what's supposed to happen. It sets off a familiar flutter in Warren's stomach as the butterflies take flight. The two of them walk side-by-side with their daemons ahead of them. Out of the corner of his eye, Warren sees Johnny watching Minnie as she weaves in and out of Lucinda's legs excitedly. The smile on his face is contagious— Warren can't help but smile too.


------

Entering the Big Block is easier this time— not *easy,* because places like this will never be easy for him — but still, it's easier now that he knows what to expect. Minnie stays close to him as they both adjust to the flashing lights, the swirling colors, the *noise.* The atmosphere is raucous, but the presence of his friends helps buffer it, and eventually Warren stops wanting to cover his ears with his hands.

They take the same roped-off booth as last time, apparently reserved specifically for their use, which he guesses must be Zoe's doing. Warren sits in the middle of the u-shaped bench, comfortably squashed between Johnny and Yolande.

Yolande bumps their shoulders together. "We match," she says, indicating his shirt with a nod of her head.

Indeed, Warren notices, her cropped halter top is the same shade of yellow as his plaid flannel. He smiles at her. "I'm glad I didn't miss the memo."

"You look really good tonight, by the way," Johnny says, reaching over to fiddle with one of the buttons on Warren's shirt. "I've never seen you in these clothes before."

"They're Karl's," admits Warren. "I'm just borrowing them."

"Hmm." Johnny gives him an appraising once-over, his eyes lingering on the bit of exposed skin at Warren's thighs. "Well, I think you should seriously consider forgetting to return the trousers."

Warren suddenly finds himself extremely grateful for Karl's fashion intervention. "Maybe I will," he replies.

Nadia and Jonas return to the booth from their run to the bar, each of them carrying a tray of drinks.

"The blue ones are alcoholic and delicious; the purple ones are just delicious," Nadia tells them, as she and Jonas slide into their seats.

"Excellent," Johnny says, taking a purple drink.

Warren does the same. Under the table, Johnny shifts his leg, the side of his knee coming to rest against Warren's. Neither of them withdraw.

"Happy Birthday, John," Yolande says, smiling at him.

"Thanks, love."

"How old are you again?" Nadia asks. "Twenty-three? Yikes."

Johnny squints at her. "Nadia, you're approximately two months younger than me."

"Age before beauty," she replies sweetly, and Vic inclines his head in agreement.

Zoe snorts. "You flatter yourself."

"What's that, Barlow? I couldn't hear you over the volume of your pompadour."

Warren chokes on air. Johnny thumps his back, laughing.

Zoe frowns. "It's not *that* high." He runs a self-conscious hand over the top of his head as his crow daemon glares at Nadia from his shoulder.

"Nadia, that was mean," Yolande admonishes, but Shane's tail is quivering.

"I'm just saying what we're all thinking," Nadia says defensively. "But anyway, back to how old Johnny is."

Johnny scoffs. "I may be old, but at least I'll never be as old as Jonas."

"Hey!" Jonas protests. "Respect your elders."

"You'll also never be as young as Warren," Yolande points out.

"Aw, little baby Warren," Nadia coos. "I always forget how young you are. A wee lad of twenty."

Warren wrinkles his nose. "You're just jealous of my youthful glow," he says.

"Would we call that glow?" Nadia wonders. "Or perpetual blush."

He sticks his tongue out at her.

"Very mature," Nadia sniffs.

"On that note," Jonas says, "Happy birthday, Johnny. Hopefully this is the year you finally start acting your age."

The rest of them echo his wishes, and Johnny beams.

"Thank you, thank you," he says, adopting an air of great importance. "Truly, you are all fabulous people whom I love dearly. But enough about that— this is *my* night, so I hope you'll all indulge me in a toast." He raises his glass and the rest of them follow suit. "To new things!"

"New things?" inquires Warren.

Johnny lifts one shoulder nonchalantly. "Yeah. New jobs, new paths, new… things." He holds Warren's gaze as he says it. The look in his eyes is anything but indifferent.

Minnie tightens her grip on his shoulder as Warren's gut curls warmly with a feeling he can't quite place. Anticipation, maybe.

All of them remain talking at the table for a while. Warren isn't quite able to keep up with the teasing and toasting. The din of the club is distracting enough that he keeps missing obvious places to jump in, always finding the right words just a beat too late. But he doesn't mind, content to sit and sip at his drink as the conversation flows around him.

He feels it when Johnny starts to get restless, the bouncing of his leg beneath the table giving him away. Over the tabletop, he sees Lucinda bobbing her head to the rhythm of the music from where she sits on the floor in front of the booth with Huff.

Warren isn't surprised when at the next break in conversation, Johnny takes the opportunity to declare, "Time to dance!"

"Yes!" Nadia cheers.

She leads the way out of the booth, Jonas and Johnny following after her. Even Zoe stands, his mouth set in a determined line as if he's mentally preparing himself for some monumental task.

Warren hesitates, his nerves catching up with him.

"Come on," Yolande says quietly, laying a hand on his arm. "I promise it'll be fun."

Minnie butts her head against the side of his neck. "Let's try," she whispers, and Warren nods.

"Okay," he says to Yolande, and the two of them stand to join the others.

Johnny whoops when he sees them coming, and Nadia grabs hold of Warren's wrist, towing him along behind her as they make their way over to the dance floor.

They manage to carve out a small space for themselves in the throng of dancers. Most of their daemons choose to stay out of the crowd to avoid being unintentionally touched, making use of the courtesy benches bordering the dance area that have been provided for just that purpose. Only Minnie and Zoe's daemon decide to risk staying with their humans. They aren't the only daemons on the dance floor, but they are certainly in the minority.

Warren can sense Minnie's unwillingness to be parted from him, and he knows it's mostly his fault. This is an uncharted social situation for him, and he doesn't want to make a fool of himself in front of his friends. Warren loves music, but he isn't an experienced dancer. His apprehension about that, combined with the loud noise and the proximity of the people around them, creates a feedback loop of anxiety between him and Minnie that makes her cling to him.

But his fears are allayed almost immediately: it turns out no one really cares whether or not he can dance.

The six of them arrange themselves in a loose semi-circle near the edge of the crowd. All of them are moving in some fashion, dancing to an upbeat song that Warren recognizes from one of Johnny's playlists. He judges Johnny, Yolande, and Nadia to be the best dancers in their group— or at the very least the most confident— but there's not a consistent style between them. Mostly, everyone just seems to be trying to make each other laugh. Once he realizes that no one is going to call him out for his lack of skill, Warren stops worrying and instead starts enjoying the spectacle his friends are making of themselves.

Zoe leaves after a few songs, making significant eye contact with Yolande before he goes. The rest of them stay. Nadia has Jonas in a mockingly-formal ballroom hold, as the two of them waltz together in a small circle. Johnny takes Yolande's hand and twirls her, spinning her out away from him and then back into his arms again, both of them laughing as she attempts to stay *en pointe*. Warren sways to the music, watching them.

Under the glow of the spotlights, Johnny looks otherworldly.

Everything about him is bright and beautiful, from the shine of his skin to the gleam of his eyes. The lights glint off of his mother-of-pearl inlaid belt, and his eyebrow piercing glitters. His white shirt is almost sheer, and Warren can see the colors of his tattoos beneath his sleeve. Johnny is dressed to attract attention, and he's getting it— it's not just Warren's eyes that are drawn to him like magnets.

But even without all the flash, Johnny would be impossible to miss. He rides the rhythm of the music with loose-limbed ease, moving with entrancing fluidity. Joy radiates from him as he dances, the smile on his face almost blissful. He's clearly in his element, surrounded by people but dancing as if he is alone, totally unselfconscious.

"You're staring," Minnie teases.

Warren shrugs, unashamed. How can he do otherwise? Johnny is the sun, and Warren is caught in his gravitational pull.

The song changes. The opening notes are only vaguely familiar to him, but Yolande and Nadia recognize them immediately. They begin jumping excitedly, holding hands and singing the lyrics at each other. After the first verse, they coax Warren into joining them. He can't stop grinning as Yolande and Nadia move wildly around him. And maybe it's just the fact that they are two of his favorite people, but Warren finds that he's actually enjoying dancing in a club.

"I'm going to join Lucinda and the others," Minnie says into his ear, once the song has ended.

Warren nods. Both of them are feeling more confident now and, honestly, having Minnie wrapped around his neck like a furry scarf is making him sweat.

"Good idea," he says. "Do you want me to take you to them?"

"I'll be fine," Minnie assures him, briefly nuzzling his temple. "Have fun," she adds, before leaping to the ground.

Warren turns to watch as she dashes off. The courtesy area is only a few meters away from where he's standing but he can't see it through the crowd, and he experiences a flash of panic when Minnie disappears from his sight. He relaxes again once she reaches Lucinda, the moment communicated to him by a burst of elation that echoes through their bond.

When he turns back to his friends, he finds that Yolande is gone and Nadia and Jonas are dancing together in a slow, dirty grind. Warren quickly looks away from them, cheeks heating, and searches the crowd for Johnny. The colors of the lights kaleidoscope around him in flares and halos, making it difficult to pick out individuals in the undulating sea of dancers. He's on the verge of giving up and returning to the booth, disappointed, when someone puts a hand on his shoulder.

Warren turns.

It's Johnny, bright-eyed and shining with sweat, his flower crown askew on his head.

"Hi," says Warren, slightly breathless at the sight of him.

"Hi," Johnny replies. His voice is low in spite of the noise, pitched so only Warren can hear him. "Looking for someone?"

"You," Warren confesses.

Johnny hums in approval, his fingers tightening unconsciously on Warren's shoulder. "It's my birthday," he says.

Warren tilts his head at the non sequitur. "I know."

"You know what would be the best birthday present? Even better than welding gloves?"

"What?"

Johnny leans in close. His lips brush the shell of Warren's ear, as he says, "Dance with me."

A pulse of desire thrums through Warren. "Okay," he replies, a bit unevenly.

Johnny grins, skimming his fingers down Warren's arm before taking his hand. "Follow me."

Warren follows. Johnny seems to know exactly where he wants to go, leading him through the crowd to the corner of the dance floor farthest from the speakers. At this distance, Warren feels just the slightest tug on his bond with Minnie, but no pulling.

Once satisfied with their location, Johnny turns to face him. He puts his arms around Warren's waist and pulls him close.

"Put your hands on my shoulders," he says.

Warren can hardly believe this is happening. He does as directed, stretching up to rest his hands lightly on Johnny's shoulders. He can feel the warmth of Johnny's skin against his palms even through the fabric of his shirt. It's incredibly distracting.

Johnny starts to move with the music, encouraging Warren to move with him.

"You're so stiff," he complains mildly. "Loosen up."

Warren huffs. "Thanks for the advice."

Johnny chuckles. "Just do what I do. Move your hips."

Warren tries. He really does. But he can't seem to unlock his muscles, his body tense with nerves. Every time he loses the rhythm it gets harder to find it again, and his tension increases. It frustrates him almost to tears: this moment is significant and he's *ruining it.*

"I'm sorry," Warren says, cringing as he treads on Johnny's toes yet again. "I'm so bad at this."

Johnny pulls away from him and Warren is flooded with disappointment, so sure that he is going to just give up and go find someone else to dance with, someone less awkward, who can match his grace.

But he doesn't. Instead, Johnny moves behind him, fitting his front to Warren's back.

"Relax," he says, putting his hands on Warren's hips. "I've got you."

"Oh," says Warren, stunned by the warm line of Johnny's body against his.

He flails, unsure of where to put his hands. He holds them awkwardly out in front of himself for a moment, before tentatively settling them over top of Johnny's on his hips. He feels it when Johnny's fingers flex beneath his, and it makes his pulse quicken.

Johnny begins moving in a rhythmic sway, using his grip on Warren's hips to hold their bodies in alignment. Warren moves with him as best he can, grateful for the simplicity of the motion. He concentrates on the music, counting the beats in his head the way he does when he plays his flute. Eventually, he feels himself start to catch the rhythm.

*Finally,* he thinks, relieved.

Johnny makes a pleased sound. "Yeah, there we go. You've got it, Warren."

"We're literally just swaying," Warren responds self-deprecatingly.

"Who needs more than that?" Johnny says, threading their fingers together. "This is nice. Isn't this nice?"

"Mm," agrees Warren, because it is, but he doesn't have the words to describe it right now.

They dance like that for a while. Warren isn't sure how much time passes. He gets lost in the movement of their bodies, in the hot puff of Johnny's breath on the back of his neck. Distantly, he registers the music change to something slower, more sensual, with a thumping bass line that he can feel vibrating through him. The lights dim with the change in music, and in the darkened ambience everything seems more intimate. Heat spreads through Warren as Johnny shifts, pressing somehow closer.

"This okay?" he murmurs, moving their joined hands to rest on Warren's lower abdomen.

Warren nods. He is acutely aware of his own heartbeat as it pounds in his chest. He takes a deep breath. The club smells as all such places do, of artificial fragrances, sweat, and alcohol from the mass of people around them, but Johnny smells like himself, familiar and desirable, and a little bit floral from the flower crown he's still wearing. Warren lets his head loll back and turns his cheek to Johnny's shoulder, eyes drifting half-closed as he breathes him in.

Johnny shifts again. His arms tighten around Warren's waist as he curls over him, his nose coming to rest in Warren's hair. He inhales deeply.

Warren swallows, his throat dry. He has been held this way by Johnny once before. He remembers how he'd felt standing in the entranceway to Johnny and Zoe's apartment with Johnny wrapped around him from behind, kissing his neck. He'd felt wanted. *Desired.* He feels that way now, and it makes him bold. Following some deeply-rooted instinct he didn't even know he possessed, Warren leans back into Johnny's hold, pressing his ass flush to his groin.
"*Fuck,*" Johnny exhales shakily.

He steps out of their embrace. Warren only has a moment to be confused, before Johnny's hands are on his shoulders, tugging at him.

"Turn around," he rumbles.

Warren does. With the lights dimmed he can't quite make out the expression on Johnny's face before he crowds in close again, bringing the front of their bodies together.

Johnny raises his hands to curve around the sides of Warren's neck, his long fingers curling into the hair at the back of his head. Warren has to brace his hands on Johnny's chest for balance, shivering at the sensation of nails scratching lightly against his scalp. Johnny resumes dancing, picking up the rhythm. He moves with new intent, his hips rolling, and Warren is helpless to do anything but follow.

He has never felt this way before, so caught up in desire for another person that he can't process anything else around him. The only thing in his head is *Johnny, Johnny, Johnny.* If he currently possessed the mental faculty to consider it, he would be terrified by how little he cares about anything else. He does manage to spare a fleeting thought for Minnie, who must be able to feel all of this through their bond. Is she as wrapped up in Lucinda as he is in Johnny? Almost certainly yes, but he is too inundated by emotions to sort out which are coming from her and which are his alone.

When Johnny's thumbs start to move in slow, maddening circles at the top of his spine, Warren loses what little remains of his self-control. He collapses forward, sliding his hands around Johnny's back to his shoulder blades, resting his forehead on his collarbone. The scent of Johnny's skin is overwhelming, and Warren is filled with the sudden need to taste it. He tilts his head up and presses his open mouth to Johnny's throat. Salt blossoms on his tongue. Johnny gasps, jerking against him. The fingers in Warren's hair tighten, pulling at the strands and sending a flash of heat straight through him.

Warren moans, his hands fisting in the back of Johnny's shirt. He's hardening in his trousers— there's no way Johnny doesn't notice, plastered together as they are. He can feel Johnny's pulse racing against his lips, matching the frantic beat of his own. They're barely even dancing now, mostly just holding each other, with Johnny panting shallow breaths against Warren's temple.

"Warren," Johnny says, hoarse in his ear. "I want… can we…"

He trails off, sounding as wrecked as Warren feels.

Warren needs to see his face. He raises his head, and Johnny's hands slide from Warren's neck to his upper arms. This close, facing each other, the difference in their heights has never been so obvious. Johnny has over half a foot on him, and Warren has to tilt his head back to meet his gaze.

Johnny's eyes are almost black, his pupils dilated. The way he's looking at Warren makes the scant space between them feel electric. Warren's body is buzzing like a wire stripped bare, throwing sparks. He wants to kiss Johnny. He's never wanted anything so much.

He doesn't know how.

"John—"

Warren's words are cut off as he is slammed into from behind. He stumbles, and Johnny catches him against his chest.

"Watch it!" Johnny snaps at someone over Warren's shoulder.

"Shit, sorry," mumbles a drunken voice, before it drifts away into the crowd.

Warren barely registers the exchange over the roaring in his head. His senses are flooded, his awareness of the world around him expanding, as if he's suddenly resurfaced after spending too long underwater. He hadn't realized how muted everything beyond the bubble of space he and Johnny occupied had become, until that bubble had been breached, and all of it came rushing back in. Everything is too much— the lights are too bright, the music is too loud, the people are too close. Warren needs to *get away*.

"Hey," Johnny says. He lifts a hand to Warren's cheek, but Warren steps back from him before he can make contact. Johnny frowns. "Are you okay?"

"I— I need some space. I'm sorry," Warren says. He feels like an idiot. No one else would be this upset by someone just bumping into them. Why can't he be normal?

Johnny raises his hands placatingly. "It's all right. Let's go back to the booth."

Their moment well and truly broken, Warren miserably trails Johnny as he clears a path off the dance floor. Minnie and Lucinda are waiting for them when they break through the crowd.

"Warren!" cries Minnie.

Warren picks her up and cradles her in his arms. Holding her is an immediate balm to his frazzled nerves.

"What happened?" Lucinda asks. "Minnie just about jumped out of her skin."

"Some drunk kid crashed into us while we were dancing," Johnny says, when Warren doesn't respond. "But it's fine. We're just going to take a break."

They make their way back to the booth, where they find Yolande and Zoe sitting close together on the bench with their daemons. Warren can sense them watching him as he takes a seat on the opposite side of the table, but he avoids their questioning eyes.

"I'll go get us some water. Be right back," Johnny tells him, gesturing toward the bar. Lucinda shoots Warren a concerned glance over her shoulder as they go.

Warren shrugs out of his flannel button-down, too hot with the mixture of shame and frustration burning inside of him. Yolande is trying to meet his gaze, but Warren doesn't feel like talking to anyone right now. He pulls out his phone and keeps his eyes downcast, aimlessly scrolling as he waits.

When a few minutes pass without Johnny's return, he chances a look at the bar. He sees Johnny there, leaning casually against the bartop. He's not alone. He's talking to another man, laughing at something he's just said. As Warren looks on, the stranger puts a hand on Johnny's chest and moves in close to speak directly into his ear. Johnny doesn't move away.

It's like being doused with ice water. There is a cold plummeting sensation in the pit of Warren's stomach as he watches Johnny smile and wrap his hand around the stranger's wrist, leading him away from the bar. They disappear into the crowd, headed in the direction of the dance floor.

Warren stands, reeling. Minnie scrambles up to his shoulder, clutching at him so tightly that her nails pierce skin.

*Of course,* he thinks as he stumbles away from the table. *Of course I'm not enough.*
How could he be, when Johnny— bright, beautiful, *brilliant* Johnny— could have any person he wanted? The realization feels like a loss, like the death of a possibility Warren has been nurturing for months, and he runs from it.

He should leave, go back to the privacy of his apartment to lick his wounds. But there is a part of him, small but insistent, that is unwilling to abandon this night entirely, that stubbornly wants to stay and see it out to its conclusion.

*Delusional,* he tells that part of himself.

The rest of him needs space to recover from the bitter sting of disappointment, so he ends up in the washroom, as far away from everyone as he can get without leaving the club. It's miraculously empty, but he doesn't think he would care if it wasn't. He stands with his hands braced on the edge of one of the sinks, head hanging between his straightened arms.

His chest aches.

"Warren," Minnie says, placing her small paw on top of his hand, "don't overthink this. You *know* how Johnny feels about you."

"It doesn't matter how he feels about me," Warren says. "It doesn't matter if he wants me. It'll be a mess, because I'm not..."

"Not what?" Minnie asks.

*Right for him,* his mind supplies.
Warren isn't fun. He can't dance. He gets overwhelmed by people and noise, and has emotional breakdowns in club washrooms. He is jealous and anxious and insecure. *Warren* wouldn't want himself. How can he expect Johnny to?
"It doesn't matter if he wants me," Warren repeats despondently, "because he'll never want to *keep* me."
"Of course he will! You're *wonderful,*" Minnie says fiercely, ever loyal.
Warren gives her a watery smile. His daemon has always been the best part of him: even when he hates himself, he never hates her. Minnie reminds him that there must be something worthwhile in him— there has to be, because *she* exists.

But right now that's not quite enough. Not when he's mourning the loss of something he never even had in the first place.

The washroom door opens.

Zoe enters. He crosses the room without acknowledging Warren.

Warren tracks his progress in the mirror as he comes to stand a few feet away, his back to the row of sinks. Zoe still doesn't speak. Warren's mouth works as he tries to think of something to say, some excuse for why he is hiding in the washroom like a child. When he can't come up with anything, he lowers his eyes.

The silence stretches.

Then, without looking at him, Zoe says, "The washing machine isn't broken."

Warren glances over at him. "What?"

"At our apartment," Zoe says, a little impatiently. "It works fine. It always has."

Warren stares. He hears the words, but he can't seem to make sense of them. At his elbow, Minnie has gone completely still.

"So," continues Zoe, tapping his fingers on the head of his cane. "Do with that information what you will."

Warren feels dizzy. He closes his eyes and tightens his fingers around the edge of the sink to steady himself, his mind spinning as he reexamines the last four months of his life from a different angle. If the washing machine was never broken, then that means—

Warren opens his eyes and turns to face Zoe.

"Zoe," he says, "*thank you.*"

Zoe shakes his head in denial. "It wasn't my idea. Ivory made me tell you."

Warren's eyes widen and Minnie makes a noise of surprise. It's the first time either of them has heard Zoe's daemon's name.

Minnie moves closer to Zoe, going up on her hind legs to speak directly to the crow daemon where she's perched on his shoulder.

"Thank you, Ivory," she says solemnly.

"You're welcome, Minnie," Ivory replies. Her voice is beautiful. She looks at Warren. "You should go find Johnny and Lucinda now."

Warren doesn't need to be told twice.


------


Warren exits the washroom quickly, Minnie at his heels. He scans the club as he makes his way back toward the booth, searching for any sign of Johnny and Lucinda.

Yolande is still there when he arrives, sitting at the table with Shane curled up on the seat beside her, his head resting in her lap.

"Warren!" she calls. She sounds loose and happy, and perhaps a bit tipsy. "There you are!"

Warren hurries over to her. "Yolande, have you seen Johnny anywhere?"

"Oh! Actually, he's been looking for *you*," says Yolande, absently tucking back a lock of hair that has come loose from her long braid. "He went to help some random guy find a ride home, but then he came back. He's like a magnet for helpless drunk people," she adds in a conspiratorial whisper. "It's the charm. And probably also the face."
*Definitely tipsy,* Warren amends.

"Where is he now?" he asks, his eyes still scanning the crowd.

"Mm… not sure. Maybe he's dancing?" Yolande's face lights up. "You should go dance with him! It's his *birthday*," she says earnestly. She reaches out and wraps her fingers around two of his, shaking his hand a little.

Warren looks over at her and smiles. Yolande smiles back at him, her eyes slightly hazy. He sees the moment when they change focus, flickering to someone behind him.

"Warren."

Warren's heart flips over at the sound of Johnny's voice. He turns, and Minnie gives a happy yip at the sight of Johnny approaching with Lucinda at his side.

"Johnny," Warren says. Yolande's fingers slip from his as he takes a step toward him.

"Hey," Johnny says, walking up to him. He sounds relieved. "Where'd you go?"

He leans in to be heard over the din, one of his hands coming to rest on the side of Warren's waist like it belongs there. Lucinda moves in closer as well, gently touching her nose to Minnie's cheek.

"Nowhere," says Warren. "It's not important. Can we talk?"

Johnny furrows his brow. "Sure. What's up?"

Warren shakes his head. "Not here. Somewhere quieter. Outside?"

"Oh," Johnny says, blinking at him. "*Oh.* Yeah, okay. Let me just—"
"No, *now,*" Warren says firmly. The thread of his patience is frayed, near snapping. It drives him to take Johnny's hand from his waist and start marching him toward the club's exit.

"What's the rush?" Johnny asks, without offering any resistance whatsoever to the insistent tug of Warren's hand.

Warren squeezes his fingers. "Just… come on."

They meet Zoe on their way, headed back in the direction of the booth. He gives Warren a curt nod as they pass by each other, and Ivory raises her wings approvingly.

Outside it's much quieter, the noise of the club replaced by the familiar sounds of the city. The night is warm and clear; if it weren't for the glow of the streetlights, they would be able to see the stars.

People line the sidewalk in front of the Big Block, most standing together in small clusters as they wait to be allowed entry. Warren leads Johnny past them and around the corner of the club, into the narrow alleyway that separates it from the building next-door. His goal of relative privacy achieved, he drops Johnny's hand and turns around to face him, crossing his arms over his chest.

"You lied to me." It's not what he meant to say, but the accusation bursts forth from him regardless.

"Huh?" Johnny starts. "What are you—"

"About the washing machine," Warren interrupts, committed now to the course of this conversation. "It's not broken. Zoe told me."

Johnny frowns. "He did?"

Minnie nods apologetically from where she sits with her tail wound around Warren's ankle. "Just now."

Lucinda sighs and slumps to the ground at Johnny's feet, her ears lowered.

Johnny sighs too. "No, it's not broken. I'm sorry I lied to you about that."

"Why did you?" Warren presses. He thinks he knows the answer— he *hopes* he does— but he needs to hear Johnny say it.
"I didn't do it on purpose. I just— *ugh.*" Johnny cuts himself off with a frustrated noise. He looks down, his hand going to the back of his neck. "It's kind of embarrassing, Warren, to admit that I wanted to spend time with you so badly that I resorted to doing laundry in the *middle of the night.*"

"Because we're friends?" Warren asks, his voice wavering with uncertainty.

Johnny looks up at him, his shimmering gaze landing dead-center. "Because I *like* you."

Minnie lets out a soft gasp. Lucinda raises her head from her paws at the sound. She makes a low, entreating noise, and Minnie goes to her.

Warren stays where he is. He swallows, trying desperately to tamp down the wild, reckless hope that's been simmering inside of him all evening. "Are you sure? Because when you flirt with me I can't tell if it's a joke or if..."

Johnny's face crumples a bit. "It's not a joke," he says. "It's *never* been a joke. Saints, I've been doing this all wrong, haven't I?"
"Doing *what?*" Warren says, clenching his fists. He feels like he's about to fly apart. "I can't figure it out, John. If you like me like that, why didn't you just *tell* me?"

"I wanted to!" Johnny replies, his voice rising. "But I didn't know how to without—" He stops. Purses his lips, breathes in. "I've never done this before, all right?" he says, quieter.

Warren narrows his eyes in confusion. "What are you talking about? Yes, you have. You've *told* me you have."
"No, not like..." Johnny scrubs a hand over his hair, knocking his flower crown sideways on his head. He shoves it irritably back into place. "Look— *yes,* I've been with a lot of people. And I've enjoyed it, no regrets. But I've never wanted *more* from any of them, you know? I've never wanted anything serious. Not until I met you."

It's too close to what Warren's been longing to hear for him to believe it. "Me? Really?"

"Yeah, you," Johnny says. "You popped up from behind that washing machine with your big blue eyes, curls everywhere, soaking wet in that frankly *terrible* shirt, and I just… *wanted* you." He half-shrugs, looking as chagrined as Warren has ever seen him. "I thought we'd flirt, and then maybe if I was lucky we'd do a bit more than that. But that was all. I wasn't looking for anything else. Then I got to know you and— I don't know, Warren." He spreads his hands, helpless. "I just really liked you."
Warren's heart is racing in his chest. "But what does that *mean,* Johnny?"

And then— and then Johnny destroys him with a sentence.

"It means that I'm yours."

The words ring in Warren's ears.

He knows there must be other sounds around him— muffled music, chattering voices, the hum of traffic— but all of them are far away, irrelevant. Nothing exists beyond this, beyond *them.* Warren can't hear anything else past the sound of Johnny's voice, and the incessant pounding of his own heart.
"I'm yours," Johnny repeats. He smiles, small and lopsided, at whatever dumbfounded expression he must see on Warren's face. "I've *been yours.* I've just been here waiting, hoping that you want to be mine too."

Warren stares at him. He can't speak. His mind is a discordant mess of thoughts and emotions, a cacophony of noise trying to resolve into something that makes sense.

"You really didn't know?" Johnny asks, his voice soft. "I felt like I was so obvious. Especially after you and Lucinda… Warren, you *touched Lucinda.*"

Warren's eyes stray reflexively to her. She's already looking back, her ears pointed toward him. Minnie is looking at him too, her whiskers twitching as she leans against Lucinda's side.

"I know I did," Warren begins slowly, the words sticking in his throat as he tries to order his thoughts through the chaos in his head. "But I wasn't sure if you meant it.

Sometimes I thought… and I felt... but then the night of Jonas' birthday, when you left—" He bites down hard on his lower lip.

Johnny steps toward him. "You should know," he says, his gaze fixed on Warren, "that I wanted to kiss you that night. I wanted it more than I've ever wanted anything in my *life*. But not while you were drunk."

Warren takes a measured breath, trying to slow his rabbit heartbeat. "I'm not drunk now."

Johnny licks his lips. "No. You're not."

Warmth swoops down through Warren's stomach. "I want to kiss you," he whispers.

Johnny smiles. It's Warren's favorite one, the one that makes his eyes crinkle at the corners. "So kiss me."

Warren doesn't hesitate. He closes the distance between them in one stride and reaches up to take Johnny's face in his hands, drawing him down.

At the touch of their lips, the discordant noise in his mind swells into a symphony.

Johnny's arms wind around his waist, his hands coming to rest on the dip of Warren's lower back. He angles his head, adjusting the fit of their mouths. It transforms the awkwardly determined press of Warren's lips into something softer, sweeter.

Warren's blood is singing in his veins, heat rushing to every part of him. *This* is what he wanted, for so long. This feeling, as if every chord between them has come together in perfect harmony.

His whole body is flushed with exhilaration as he moves closer, sliding his hands up into Johnny's hair. He accidentally dislodges the flower crown in the process. It slips forward this time, and Warren pulls back in surprise as it falls onto his brow and tickles his nose.

Johnny grunts in annoyance. He yanks the crown from his head and flings it off to the side, further into the darkened alleyway. Warren bursts into laughter at the disgruntled expression on his face. The corner of Johnny's mouth turns up at the sound. When their gazes meet, Warren can see a spark of shared amusement in his glimmering grey eyes.

"Let's try that again," Johnny murmurs. He places his hand on the fiery curve of Warren's cheek and draws him back in.

Warren's laughter dissolves into a breathy moan as Johnny kisses him deep and slow and careful. Somewhere nearby, one of their daemons whimpers. The other answers with a low groan, and Warren feels a wave of desire from Minnie, spreading outward across their bond like ripples on water.

Johnny must feel something too. He kisses Warren harder, and starts walking him backward until his back is flush against the brick wall. Warren's eyes fall shut, a giddy thrill running through him as Johnny crowds in close, slipping his hand beneath the hem of his t-shirt where it's ridden up at his waist. The edges of the bricks are digging into his spine, but Warren decidedly *does not care,* as Johnny's fingers caress over his bare skin. He shivers at the touch, a gasp catching in his throat. Johnny hums approvingly against his lips in response, chest-deep, and it sets Warren's nerves alight.

The kiss deepens further. Warren loses himself in it, in the taste and the sounds and the feel of their lips sliding together. Johnny is directing the movement of their mouths, guiding Warren with the hand he has on his cheek, encouraging him to open to him. In this, at least, he seems to know precisely what he wants, and Warren is more than willing to give it to him. When Johnny shifts to fit a thigh between both his, pressing slightly upwards, Warren goes hot all over. His knees wobble and he has to grip the front of Johnny's shirt to remain upright, twisting his fingers in the fabric as something flutters in his stomach, wild and alive. Johnny is *such* a good kisser. Warren can't believe he went so long without knowing that.

By the time they're forced to part for air, both of them are panting.

Warren opens his eyes, his chest heaving. Johnny is watching him, his expression soft and a little wondering. He slowly lowers his hand from Warren's cheek, caressing down his neck to cup the bend where it meets his shoulder, his thumb coming to rest on the top of Warren's collarbone.

Warren's gaze falls to the curve of his lips, dark and shining from their kissing. *I did that.* Desire kindles low in his belly at the thought, and he has to look away from Johnny's lips before he does something ill-advised, like bite them.

Behind Johnny he can see their daemons pressed together in a tangle of fur and limbs, mirroring their humans' embrace. As he watches, Minnie butts her head up against Lucinda's muzzle with a small, blissful sigh that Warren feels down to his very core.

He knows in that instant that there's no returning from this. Not for her. Not for him. He needs to know if it's the same for Johnny.

"Johnny..." he starts cautiously.

"Warren," Johnny sing-songs sweetly in reply. His thumb traces a teasing line across Warren's collarbone, brushing lightly over the exposed skin there.

It's distracting enough that Warren almost forgets what he's trying to ask. "Are you—" His voice falters and he has to clear his throat before he can continue. "Are you sure this is what you want?"

Johnny raises a confused brow. "What, making out with you in an alleyway?"

Warren shakes his head. "No. This." He gestures back and forth between them. "*Us.*"

Johnny's expression clears. "Yes," he says, soft but firm, "this is what I want." He tilts Warren's chin up with a gentle hand, and Warren doesn't stop himself from leaning into the touch. "But it's not all that I want."

Warren breathes out. "It's not?"

"Not even close."

The pitch of Johnny's voice is so low that Warren can *feel* it, a rumbling vibration in his chest. He bites his lip at the sensation, his eyes going half-lidded. Johnny leans forward and kisses him chastely, right on the spot where Warren's teeth are making white indentations in the flesh of his lower lip. When he retreats, Warren doesn't let him go far. He puts his hand on the back of Johnny's neck and reels him back in for a proper kiss.
It's good. It's *so* good. But It only lasts a moment before Johnny suddenly pulls away again. Warren is left disoriented at the abrupt parting, but when he follows Johnny's gaze he understands.

Minnie is sitting at their feet, her eyes trained on Johnny. Once she has his attention, she rests a tentative paw on the side of his shin. The expression on her face is cautious, but determined. Warren can feel it through their bond, now that he's not completely caught up in kissing Johnny, all of the hope and longing that she's putting into this single act.

Johnny sucks in a breath. In one swift motion he releases Warren and crouches down in front of Minnie, reaching his hand out toward her. His fingers hover over the tips of her ears, and Warren finds himself holding his breath at the familiar scene.

Minnie tilts her head beneath Johnny's hand, angling upwards. She stays there, not touching him, her gaze steady. Johnny's eyes flicker up to Warren. Then, his movement deliberate, he lowers his hand until it's cupping the back of Minnie's tiny head.

The effect of his touch is instantaneous. Minnie gasps in at the same time Warren exhales, all the air rushing out of his lungs as sparks shoot down his spine.

Johnny is wide-eyed, his fingers flexing in Minnie's fur as if he isn't sure whether to draw back or tighten his grip. Warren can see Lucinda standing behind him, watching intently, her body stiff with focus. Her eyes reflect the glow of the streetlights outside the alleyway, glinting gold in the dark.

Minnie makes the decision for Johnny. She moves until she's pressed right up against him, rising onto her hind legs so she can place her paws on his knees. She nudges her nose firmly into his sternum, her meaning clear. Johnny doesn't deny her. He picks her up without hesitation, cradling her close.

Warren's pulse stutters. He can't breathe through the shock of it. Johnny is literally holding Warren's soul in his hands. It's thrill and comfort and terror and awe all at once. The conflict within him is almost incapacitating— he doesn't know whether to tell Johnny to release her immediately or ask him to hold on to her forever.

Warren takes a gasping breath at the sudden, urgent press of a muzzle against his thigh. He knows it's Lucinda without looking. Unthinking, he drops his hand to her neck and curls his fingers into her fur. It's as galvanizing as he remembers only *more*, his nerves already lit up by the echo of Johnny's touch on Minnie.

Lucinda lets out a high-pitched whine at his touch, leaning heavily into him. At the same moment, Johnny stands, still holding Minnie. Warren reaches for him with the hand not tangled in Lucinda's fur, needing to be nearer to him. Johnny meets him halfway. When they touch, it's like a circuit closing.

"You feel that, right?" Johnny says. His voice cracks on the last word. "Please tell me you feel it."

"I feel *you,*" Warren manages. He tightens his fingers in Lucinda's fur. "Both of you."

"Me too," Johnny sighs, stroking his hand down the curve of Minnie's spine. She nuzzles closer to him, purring.

"Ah," Warren stutters, his skin sparking at the phantom touch. "And that. When you touch her, it feels like you're touching *me.*"
"Is that so?" Johnny says, and strokes his hand over Minnie again. When Warren shivers, he grins. "Oh, this is going to be fun."

Warren's eyes drop to Lucinda when she nudges him. They exchange a conspiratorial look. Then he purposefully runs his fingers up the back of her head, burrowing them deep into her fur.

"*Saints,*" moans Johnny.

"I can do it too, you know," Warren says wryly, and Lucinda chuffs her amusement. "It's good?"

"*Very* good," Johnny replies around a burst of slightly breathless laughter.

Joy wells in Warren at the sound. He can hardly contain it, his body overfull with emotion. "I didn't know it was like this," he confesses.

"I didn't either," says Johnny. He shifts nearer, touching his forehead to Warren's brow. "I can't believe I have to get on a plane tomorrow morning. Talk about bad timing."

Warren tightens his grip on Johnny's hand. "I know."

There is a loaded pause. Then Johnny says, "I could… *not* do that?"

Warren tips his head back to look at him. "John, no. You have to go. You've been looking forward to this trip all month."

"Sure," agrees Johnny. He lowers his voice. "But I've been looking forward to other things for longer."

They stare at each other as the words hang between them, charged with meaning.

*Stay,* Warren thinks desperately. *Stay with me.* It's what he wants, and this time he knows that he could ask for it.

Instead he takes a shuddering breath, and shakes his head. "Go home, Johnny," he says. "See your dad. I'll be here, and when you come back..."

He trails off as Johnny bends to kiss him, long and soft and thorough. It soothes something inside of Warren that he didn't even realize needed soothing, a trembling note at the end of a melody finally brought to rest. Minnie gives a contented sigh and cuddles closer to Johnny, as the tempo of Warren's heart slows to *adagio*.

The kiss breaks gently. When Johnny speaks, he's speaking his words almost directly into Warren's mouth.

"When I come back," he says, "I'm not letting you out of my arms for a week. At *least.*"

The joy inside of Warren rises up and overflows. He tips forward, his temple thudding against Johnny's collarbone as he settles his head on his chest, right next to Minnie's.

"Yes," he says, as Johnny's hand rises to cup the back of his neck. He can hear the happiness in his own voice. "That sounds good to me."

# CHAPTER 11

>>*WarrenI have a problem*

Warren frowns down at his phone as he settles cross-legged on the living room couch. He balances his plate on his knee and picks up his sandwich— an easy late dinner before he has to trek over to the Laundromat for his shift— in one hand, using the other to dash off a quick reply to Johnny's message.

*What's wrong?*

The response comes swiftly.

>>*I can't stop thinking about you*

Warren's heart jumps in his chest. He drops his sandwich back onto the plate and raises his hand to his mouth, pressing the heel of his palm to his lips as he tries to contain the wide grin that is threatening to overtake his face.

*You're so ridiculous.*
>>*ridiculously smitten, you mean*
*I mean that you're ridiculous. That was terrible.*
>>*you liked it*
*I'm not admitting to anything.*
>>*I bet Minnie has her paws over her eyes right now*

Warren glances over at his daemon. She doesn't, but it's a near thing. She's lying down by his hip, rubbing her face against the side of his thigh and purring gently.

*Come back and find out.*
>>*soon*

Warren exhales heavily, and sets his phone down on his lap. He picks up his sandwich again and takes a bite, chewing it sullenly.

Johnny has been gone for ten days. It feels like longer. They talk as often as they can, but the apparent remoteness of the Fontaine farm means that Johnny's internet access is spotty at best. The reception drops in and out, and though they've tried, video calls have been next to impossible.

Warren misses him.

He would have regardless, but he's finding it especially difficult now that he knows what it could be like between them. Now that he knows what it's like to touch Johnny, and to kiss him, and to *be kissed* by him; now that he knows what it feels like when Johnny holds Minnie, and the exact texture of Lucinda's fur beneath his fingertips. To have had all of that and then to have had it taken away, if only temporarily, leaves Warren aching.

Minnie rests her chin on the top of his thigh and sighs longingly.

"Four more days," he tells her, scritching her ears.

"They'd better bring back gifts," she mutters.

Warren exhales in amusement, and picks up his phone again.

>>*so what have you been up to?*
>>*I hope you slept in*
*I did. Then I had to fill out some forms for Waterfall.*
*Did you have a nice day?*
>>*it was all right. I helped Da repair some fences in the back pasture*
>>*I swear I'm doing more work on this so-called "vacation" than I ever do at the slat*
>>*do NOT repeat that to Zoe*
*I would never.*
*Did you tell your dad about the apprenticeship?*
>>*I did*
*And?*
>>*you were right. he said I should go for it*
*Of course I was.*
*Have you signed up for classes?*
>>*i'll work on it later*
>>*have I told you yet today that I miss you?*
*I could stand to hear it again.*
>>*I miss you*
>>*I miss how insufferable you can get when you're right about something*

*Hey!*
*>>I miss your eyes and your hair and your smile*
*>>I even miss that face you make when you're worried*
*>>you get this little divot right between your brows*
*>>it's so stupid*
*Gee, thanks.*
*>>stop that*
*Stop what?*
*>>you're doing that thing again where you're not focusing on the part that matters*
*Which is?*
*>>that I miss your stupid face!*

Warren grins helplessly. This is what talking to Johnny has become: heat in his veins and butterflies in his stomach, cheeks sore from smiling. The constant affection makes him feel like a shaken can of soda pop, effervescent and light, and so full of happiness he could burst.

*I miss you too.*
*All the time.*
*>>saints*
*>>I really want to kiss you right now*
*>>I want it so bad, warren. you have no idea*

The flare of heat in Warren's stomach is instantaneous. Next to him, Minnie gives a muffled moan and pushes her face against the side of his thigh.

*I have SOME idea*, he sends back. *I want that too.*

Warren isn't new to attraction. He's felt it before: for a boy in his high school calculus class who held his hand once beneath their desks; for a cellist in the orchestra who used to smile at him from across the stage; for an acquaintance in first year who made him laugh during their group study sessions in the library— but none of it compares to this.

What he feels for Johnny is all-consuming, like a chemical reaction that destroys all trace of its components. When he thinks of Johnny there isn't room for anything else in his head. His mind is filled by thoughts of Johnny's lips, his hands, his eyes; of the dance they'd shared at the Big Block, and of kissing him in the alleyway afterwards. Even just the memory of those things makes his blood run hot, his belly coil. Warren never really understood *desire,* not before Johnny. Now he does. Now he understands *exactly* what he wants.

And soon it will be back within his grasp.

"Ugh," groans a sudden voice. "Please stop looking at your phone like that. I'm embarrassed *for* you."

Warren's head snaps up in surprise. In his distraction he hadn't even heard Karl enter the apartment, but there he stands in the entranceway, holding two takeaway cups from the bubble tea shop down the street. He starts kicking off his shoes while Daya peers judgmentally at Warren from where she clings with her thumb claws hooked into the front of Karl's shirt.

Warren's cheeks, already flushed from Johnny's words, redden further. "Uh. Hi. I'm just—"

"I *know* what you're doing," Karl interrupts, coming into the living room. "You've been doing it for over a week now. It's bordering on unbearable." He holds out one of the cups. "Here. Don't worry, I got it at twenty-five percent for you."

Warren cautiously takes it from him, unsure of what's brought on this particular act of generosity. "Do you want some money?"

"Nah," Karl says, waving a dismissive hand at him. "I owed you anyway."

"Oh," Warren replies, a bit bewildered. "Okay... thanks."

"No problem." Karl makes to leave, then stops. He looks away from Warren, toeing at the carpet with one socked foot. "I'm happy for you, Warren," he mutters, almost too low to be heard.

Warren gives him a skeptical look. "Really?"

Karl rolls his eyes. "Yeah, of course. He seems good for you."

Warren is struck by a sudden and intense fondness for him. He sometimes forgets that Karl is the person who helped him when he'd had no one else in the world to turn to. They might not be close, but they're still *something*, and Warren is grateful for it.

The feeling only lasts a moment, before Daya impishly adds, "Just don't mess it up."

Minnie growls at her.

"I'm not planning to," Warren says flatly.

"Good," says Karl over his shoulder, as he heads down the hall toward his room. "And tell your boy to come home so I don't have to bear witness to your tragic gay pining anymore."

"You're just jealous!" Warren calls after him.

Karl pauses at the threshold and looks back at him. "I don't get jealous of my friends," he says, and then disappears into his room.

*Huh,* thinks Warren. He slumps back into the couch cushions, smiling around his straw as he sips at his bubble tea. *Friends. All right then.*

------

Yolande is behind the service counter when Warren and Minnie enter The Palm the next afternoon. She's speaking with a customer, but when she catches sight of Warren her polite, close-lipped smile transforms into a bright grin.

Warren grins back at her and goes to join the short line in front of the cash register. He can see the backs of Nadia and Jonas' heads where they're seated on the couch, and Vic's brightly colored tail feathers fanned out against the backrest. Zoe is with them, sitting in the armchair nearby with Ivory perched at his usual spot on his shoulder, scanning the coffee shop like a watchful sentry. When their eyes meet, she acknowledges Warren and Minnie with a slight raise of her wings. On Warren's shoulder, Minnie dips her head in reply.

"Hi," Yolande says, when he steps up to the counter. Shane is sitting next to the cash register, his tail curled neatly around his paws. "You received Nadia's summons, I see."

"It was hard to miss."

"The all caps were a little much," Yolande agrees. "What can I get you? Do you want to try a latte today? We have some new flavors."

Warren glances over to the drink station where Dodd is working. He shakes his head. "Just a black coffee, please."

Yolande gives him a shrewd look. "No one makes a latte quite like Johnny, huh?"

He half-smiles as he hands over some coins. "He knows what I like."

Shane huffs. "I'll bet he does," he murmurs, and Warren blushes.

Minnie bats a sheathed paw at Shane's tail in retaliation. The cat daemon only flicks it lazily at her response, purring amusedly.

Yolande completes the transaction and starts untying her apron. "I'm just about to go on break. Help me carry the drinks and we can join the others."

Warren nods and follows her to the drink station, where they collect an array of mugs from Dodd to take over to the couch area.

"Warren!" greets Nadia, patting the empty spot beside her. "Come sit."

Jonas is on her other side and Huff is on the floor in front of the couch, spread out across both their feet. She looks up as Warren approaches and flashes him a toothy canine grin.

Warren passes Nadia a mug of tea as he takes a seat on the couch beside her, careful to avoid trampling on Huff's tail.

"I recognize that hoodie. Missing Johnny today?" Nadia asks, not without sympathy.

Warren huddles into it a bit, and Minnie tucks herself inside the collar. "Always," he replies.

"That's very sweet," says Jonas. He sounds sincere.

"You are *so* besotted," Nadia coos, definitely not.

Warren shrugs and doesn't bother to deny it. There's no point, especially since she and Jonas had been the ones to find him and Johnny in the alleyway beside the Big Block two weekends ago, so wrapped up in each other that it had taken a shrill squawk from Vic to startle them apart.

"I believe the term is 'whipped'," Zoe says, his mouth twisting around the word in distaste.

"You would know," Nadia mutters lowly, and Jonas lets out a loud cough.

Warren raises his mug to hide his smile.

Zoe shows no reaction. He takes his drink from Yolande as she settles on the armrest of his chair, leaning her hip against his upper arm. Shane hops onto the armrest on Zoe's other side and stretches up to rub his cheek along Ivory's wing. When Ivory lowers her head to bury her beak in Shane's fur, Zoe places a hand on Yolande's thigh, just above her knee.

Nadia gasps, and throws a hand in front of Warren's eyes. "Zoe! This is public indecency!"

"*Nadia,*" Warren complains, pushing her hand away.

"Indecency?" Zoe repeats dryly, while Yolande raises her eyes heavenward. He very pointedly does not remove his hand from her leg. "Then what do you call what I caught you and Jonas doing in my office last year?"

Nadia laughs at him. "Please. Who gets scandalized by a little bit of—"

"No, no," Jonas cuts in, raising both hands in surrender. "You're right Zoe, she takes your point. We definitely don't need to bring that up again— right, Nadia?"

Nadia gives him a consoling pat on the knee, and mimes zipping her lips.

"What did you do in the office?" Minnie asks, poking her head out of Warren's collar. "I want to know."

"Trust me, you really don't," Huff tells her, while Vic nods his agreement in the background.

"Anyways… what were we talking about before this?" asks Jonas, still looking a bit flustered.

"Pride. The parade is next weekend," says Nadia. She looks at Warren. "You're coming with us, right?"

"I've never been," he replies.

Nadia looks shocked. "What, really?"

Warren shakes his head. "I've never had anyone to go with before."

Her face softens. "Okay, so now you have no choice. You're definitely coming."

"I wasn't going to say no."

"Good. But we'll have to find you something cute to wear…" Nadia taps her chin with one finger. "I'm picturing you in a rainbow crop top and denim cutoffs. Ooh, and suspenders! Maybe we can find matching pairs for you and Johnny! So adorable."

Warren wrinkles his nose. "No crop tops," he says. Then he reconsiders, recalling the stunned expression on Johnny's face when he saw Warren in Nadia's shirt. "No crop tops *this* time," he amends.

Nadia smirks knowingly at him. "Noted."

"Is tonight your last shift at the Laundromat?" Yolande asks, taking a sip of her coffee,

Warren nods. He'd given Giles his two-week resignation notice last Monday. "No more night shifts," he says happily. "I might cry."

Jonas reaches around Nadia and taps Warren's shoulder with his fist. "Congratulations, man!"

"Thanks," Warren says, rubbing at his shoulder. "I'm looking forward to sleeping seven nights a week."

"Maybe John will get some more sleep too," Yolande says slyly. "Since he won't have to stalk you at the Laundromat anymore."

"But where will they hang out now?" Nadia asks with faux concern. "Will they ever see each other again?"

Warren ducks his head. "Maybe we'll finally go on a date somewhere," he mumbles into his mug.

Yolande and Nadia look at each other, and then they both burst out laughing. Jonas grins, and even Zoe's lips turn up at the corners.

"What's so funny?" Warren demands.

"I don't know how to break this to you, Warren, but you and Johnny have already been on a lot of dates," Yolande says.

"No way," Warren says. "I'm not *that* clueless. I would know if he asked me on a date."

"Would you though?" Nadia wonders. "Would you really?"

Warren narrows his eyes at her. "I'm going to ask him. Just to prove you wrong."

He pulls out his phone and hurriedly sends a message to Johnny.

*Yolande says we've already been on dates.*
*Crazy, right?*

The little dots at the top of the screen appear as Johnny starts typing a reply. Warren wraps his fingers around Minnie's tail as he waits.

*>>I'm sure I don't want to know how the topic came up, but... honestly? she's not wrong*
*>>would it have killed you to take a hint?*

Warren purses his lips. When he looks up, Yolande is watching him expectantly.

"No," he says. "I refuse to accept this."

*Hanging out at my place of work does NOT count as a date.*
*I will not allow you to rewrite history like that!*
*>>it SO COUNTS!! I brought food, I provided entertainment*
*>>we watched an entire season of riper!*
*>>what more do you want from me??*
*For starters, for you to say, "Warren, go on a date with me."*
*>>I did! I asked you to Jonas' birthday thing*
*That was a group activity! And you did NOT say it like that.*
*How was I supposed to know that's what you meant?*

There is a long pause. Warren takes the opportunity to tune back into his friends. They seem to have lost interest in his current dilemma, and have moved the conversation along. Nadia is explaining something about cardiovascular imaging to Yolande, while Zoe looks on in faint discomfort.

Warren tunes them out again when his phone pings.

*>>damn it*
*>>Lucinda agrees with you*

Warren snorts, and Minnie snuffles her amusement into his neck.

*Tell her she is very wise.*
*>>I will not*
*>>I'm pretty sure she already likes you better than me, and we don't need to increase the margin*
*>>but anyway, let me try again*
*>>Warren, will you go on a date with me?*

Warren grins. He twists the cuff of his sleeve around his hand and brings it up to cover his mouth.

"Wow, the look on your face right now," Yolande giggles. "What did John say?"

"None of your business," Warren says, slightly muffled through the fabric of his hoodie.

"I told you," Nadia says with a wink, "*magic*."

Warren bumps his shoulder into hers. To Johnny, he sends:

*As long as you don't take me to a Laundromat.*
*>>I promise*
*>>it'll be a proper date*
*I've never actually been on one.*
*>>well that's going to change*

Warren grins wider, and Minnie lets out a soft, happy trill.

Nadia waves a hand in front of his face. "Still with us, Warren?"

Warren looks up guiltily. "Sorry. What did I miss?" he asks, pocketing his phone.

"Jonas has an announcement to make," Huff informs him.

Warren leans around Nadia to look at Jonas.

"It's great news," Jonas says. He pauses, seemingly for effect, while Huff beats her front paws on the floor like a drumroll, the uneven rhythm of it making Minnie wince. "I got us all tickets to see Sacred Ash!"

The rest of them— minus Nadia, whose face betrays no expression— stare at him in varying degrees of confusion.

"What's Sacred Ash?" asks Warren.

"A death metal band from Jonas' hometown," replies Nadia, slightly apologetically.

"They're playing a concert here in December," Jonas says, throwing his arm around her shoulders and squeezing excitedly. "They're very good, you're going to love them."

From his place on the backrest behind Jonas' shoulder, Vic subtly shakes his head.

"Oh," Yolande says slowly. "That sounds… fun. You got tickets for all of us, you said?" She exchanges a glance with Zoe.

Zoe frowns. He opens his mouth as if to speak, but closes it quickly when Nadia makes a throat slashing motion in his direction.

"Yep, six tickets— and you're *all* coming," Nadia says, still glaring at Zoe. Then she leans down to whisper in Warren's ear. "Bring earplugs."

Warren bites his lip to keep from laughing. He slides lower in his seat and leans into Nadia, resting his head companionably on her shoulder as Jonas begins enthusiastically telling them about Sacred Ash.

Warren listens, feeling warmed through by the thought of *six tickets*, by the fact that Jonas still expects him to be here, a part of this group, six months from now. Minnie leaves Warren's collar and moves to curl up on his lap, purring gently.

Six months ago, Warren was adrift. He remembers sitting in the Laundromat, staring out the window and feeling totally disconnected from the world outside, like everything was flowing around him but he wasn't a part of it. It felt as if he could vanish, and no one would even notice.

Now he has these people in his life. They know him, they *see* him, and they aren't going to let him disappear. With them, he belongs.

Warren isn't going anywhere, and he couldn't be happier about it.


------


It's closing in on five thirty in the morning, and Warren is crouched down behind one of the washing machines, replacing a broken drive belt on the tub spinner. It's not difficult work, but he's still sweating a bit in the persistently humid air of the Laundromat as he stretches the belt to fit over the motor pulley.

Minnie is watching with her head tilted to the side, her sharp eyes examining the belt for twists or tears.

"You know," she says thoughtfully, "as tedious as working here has been, at least now you have the option of appliance repair technician as a fallback career."

"Always looking on the bright side, aren't you, Minnie?" Warren says dryly.

She lifts her chin. "One of us has to."

He swipes half-heartedly at her and she dodges out of his reach, giggling.

"Too slow!" she teases.

Warren rolls his eyes. "As if you don't already know every move I'm going to make."

Minnie shakes her head. "Not always. Sometimes you surprise even me."

"Oh?"

Minnie only licks his hand in response, and then uses her nose to nudge the screwdriver in his direction. Warren shoots her a questioning look, but nevertheless takes the hint and sets about closing the rear panel of the machine.

He's just tightening the last screw when he hears the door buzz, signaling the arrival of a customer. Warren sighs. He'd been enjoying the quiet of the empty Laundromat, a peaceful end to his final shift.

"Hey," someone calls in a rich baritone. "Can I get some change?"

Warren's breath catches in his throat.

He stands up quickly, the screwdriver clattering unnoticed to the floor behind him. He can hardly believe his eyes.

Johnny is there, leaning casually against the wall near the entryway, with his hands tucked into the pockets of his black and gold bomber jacket and his gaze fixed on Warren. His posture is relaxed, almost careless, but Lucinda gives him away. She stands just in front of him, her body tense and her ears pricked forward, black-tipped tail swishing eagerly behind her. Both of them look a little worn around the edges, as if they haven't slept in a while. Judging by the canvas duffel bag on the floor near Johnny's feet, airline tags still attached to the straps, they probably haven't. Johnny's hair is slightly mussed, his grey eyes bright but sleepy, and—he's beautiful. So beautiful.

Warren has never seen a more beautiful sight in his entire life.

"Johnny," he breathes.

Johnny smiles, lopsided and perfect. "Hello, sunshine."

"Lucinda!" Minnie cries, streaking past Warren to get to her.

Lucinda meets her halfway, releasing a puppyish yip when Minnie barrels into her legs. She lowers her head to butt her muzzle into Minnie's side, snuffling excitedly at her. Minnie responds by sinking her teeth into the fur at Lucinda's ruff, biting playfully there until the coyote daemon decides she's had enough and pins Minnie to the ground with one big paw, so she can lick her face all over.

Their daemons' exuberant tussling is endearing, but Warren only has eyes for Johnny, who has left his place by the wall and is now striding resolutely in his direction.

"What are you doing here?" Warren manages, heart skipping in his chest, before Johnny is upon him.

He doesn't pause before he cups Warren's face in both hands and leans down to bring their mouths together, kissing him deeply.

Warren melts into it. He wraps his arms around Johnny, gripping the back of his jacket to steady himself as a dizzying mix of relief and desire surges through him. Johnny smells incredible, that familiar, heady combination of soap and skin and something uniquely *Johnny* that never fails to send heat rushing through his veins. He tastes good too, and feels even better, his hands warm and heavy on the sides of Warren's face. He is everything Warren has needed and longed for, and he's finally *here*.

Johnny breaks the kiss with a satisfied hum. "Been wanting to do that for two godforsaken weeks," he murmurs, nudging their noses together.

Warren laughs, soft and breathless. "How did you..." He shakes his head to clear it. "I thought your flight wasn't until Sunday?"

Johnny shrugs one shoulder. "Caught an earlier one."

"Missed the city?" Warren asks, smiling up at him.

Johnny's moths his hands down the sides of Warren's neck, bringing them to rest on his shoulders. "Something like that."

"John was insufferable," Lucinda says, coming over to them. "He practically packed his bag himself."

Warren raises an eyebrow. "Is that so?"

Johnny shifts his gaze to the side. "Maybe."

Curious, Warren places one hand on Johnny's cheek. It's hot beneath his palm. "Are you *blushing*?"

Johnny brushes his hand away. "Psh, 'course not." He taps a teasing finger on Warren's cheekbone. "I leave that to the experts."

Minnie hops up to Johnny's shoulder, wrapping her tail around the back of his neck for balance.

"Whoa!" she says, wobbling slightly as she finds her footing. "You're so tall!"

Johnny turns his head to grin at her. "Hello, darlin'," he says, and— easily, like there's nothing to it— reaches up to caress a hand over her side.

Warmth spreads through Warren at the contact. He'd forgotten how good that feels, how clearly he can feel Johnny's touch through his bond with Minnie. He'd never imagined anyone touching his daemon before he met Johnny, but *oh*— it feels *right* when it's him.

"Did you bring me anything?" Minnie wants to know, her eyes wide and entreating.

Johnny reaches into his jacket pocket and pulls out a small bag of airline pretzels. The plastic packaging crinkles as he shakes it enticingly at her. "You doubted?"

Minnie cheers as he tears it open. He offers one to her and she takes it, nipping teasingly at the tips of his fingers before she draws away. Beneath the startling hyperawareness of contact, Warren feels himself flushing a bit at the obvious affection his daemon is showing.

He looks down when Lucinda brushes against his knee. She looks back at him with a hopeful expression, and Warren doesn't hesitate to reach out and rub the fur at the base of her ears. His fingertips tingle as she tilts into his touch.

"Warren," she sighs happily.

Johnny wraps an arm around Warren's waist, keeping him close. "So how was your final shift?" he asks, as Minnie leaps from his shoulder to the floor, the bag of pretzels held covetously in her teeth. "Anything interesting happen?"

Warren gives him a wry look. "You mean other than my boyfriend unexpectedly returning from his sojourn to the countryside?"

Johnny's eyes flash. "Boyfriend, huh?"

Warren ducks his head. The word had come naturally to him in the moment, but he hadn't meant to say it— at least, not quite this soon.

"I mean, if you..." He trails off uncertainly.

Lucinda nudges his fingers with her nose. When Warren meets her gaze, something settles over him, a calmness borne of sudden surety. He's touching Johnny's *daemon*. There's no reason to hold back here, not when he and Johnny have already given the most precious parts of themselves to one another. The proof of that is right here, beneath his fingertips.

He looks back at Johnny. "Yes," he says, unwavering. "If that's what you want."

Johnny makes a pleased sound, and then uses his thumb and forefinger to raise Warren's chin, angling his head up as he bends down to kiss him softly.

"Yeah," he murmurs against Warren's lips when they part. "I'm your boyfriend."

Warren knows the smile on his face must be ridiculously soppy, but he can't help it. His chest swells with emotion, barely contained, and hearing those words in Johnny's voice does nothing to stem the giddiness that's rising up within him.

Distantly, Warren registers Lucinda lowering herself to the floor as he lifts his hand from her fur. He touches Johnny's face, tracing his fingers up the side of his jaw and across his brow, just marveling at his presence.

"I'm so happy you're here," he says softly.

Johnny's answering smile is blindingly bright. He moves his hand to cup Warren's cheek. "Yeah? Did you miss me?"

He's teasing. Warren knows this, but he isn't in the mood to tease back. He looks directly into Johnny's eyes and leans into his touch. "Yes. I missed you."

Johnny's expression changes instantly, his eyes going dark and heated. He curves into Warren so that his warm lips are just barely grazing the shell of his ear as he whispers, "I missed you too."

Warren shivers, full-body, at the sensation. "*Johnny*," he says, his voice cracking over the syllables.

Johnny makes a sound of wordless approval and sweeps Warren's hair back with a gentle hand, before he presses a kiss to the tender spot just below his ear, sucking lightly.

Warren gasps, his knees going weak as a wave of pleasure rolls through him. Johnny puts a steadying hand on his waist and begins kissing a path down the side of his neck, relentless in his apparent quest to drive him out of his mind. Somewhere in the distance, Minnie lets out a high-pitched sigh. Warren sighs too. He arches his head to the side, opening for Johnny, trying to give him more, give him everything— *anything*— so long as he keeps his perfect lips on Warren's skin.

Warren is so enthralled that he doesn't even realize he's being moved until his back bumps into the washing machine behind him. Johnny raises his head from the crook of his neck, and Warren doesn't even get the chance to protest, before hands are gripping the back of his thighs and he's suddenly being lifted upwards.

He grabs at Johnny's shoulders for balance, his stomach swooping with the abrupt change in gravity as Johnny boosts him— seemingly without effort— to sit on top of the washing machine.

"*Grimm,* John," Warren laughs, breathless and amazed.

He slides his hands down Johnny's arms, fingers curling around his biceps. Johnny flexes, just a bit, and Warren swallows, his throat going dry at the feel of hard muscle beneath his palms.

Johnny smirks at him. "All right up there?" he asks, stepping into the space between Warren's spread knees.

"A little warning would have been appreciated," he manages, his pulse fluttering as Johnny's hands settle heavily on his upper thighs.

"Where's the fun in that?" Johnny wonders.

Warren's gaze flickers to Lucinda, sprawled out on the checkered linoleum with her eyes closed as Minnie licks tenderly at the underside of her muzzle. If the rapid rise and fall of his daemon's chest is anything to go by, Johnny is not quite as unaffected as he seems.

"I've thought about this, you know," Warren admits quietly.

A slow grin spreads across Johnny's face. "Thought of me? Late at night? Do go on."

"Mm-hmm." Warren winds his arms around Johnny's neck, drawing him in until their chests are pressed flush together. "So many times. The Laundromat would be empty…"

"Like now."

Warren nods. "I'd be up here and you'd be…"

"Where?" Johnny murmurs, his eyes falling to Warren's mouth.

"Right… *here,*" Warren whispers, and kisses him.

This high up, he doesn't have to stretch for it. He hooks his ankles around the back of Johnny's legs to hold him in place, and then uses his teeth to tug at his lower lip, the way he's thought about doing every day since he met him.

Johnny moans, his fingers tightening on Warren's thighs. Heat sears through Warren at the sound, starting low in his belly and spreading outward like wildfire, igniting every part of him. His hands go to Johnny's hair, gripping tight to his short curls as Johnny slants his mouth to kiss him back, deep and hot and perfectly messy.

Warren doesn't know how long they stay that way, kissing frantically, but it's nowhere near long enough before the Laundromat door opens with a loud buzz.

He and Johnny jolt apart. Minnie and Lucinda do too, their nails scraping on the linoleum as they scramble to their feet.

Giles enters the building. He stops short when he sees them, his bulldog daemon grunting as she collides with his calves. For a moment they all just stare at each other, Warren and Johnny still panting slightly as they try to catch their breath. Then Giles lets out an annoyed sigh.

"Count yourself lucky this is your last shift," he grumbles at Warren.

"I do," Warren mutters, quietly enough that only Johnny hears him.

Johnny grins. He keeps his voice low when he says, "Come home with me?"

Warren gives him an incredulous look. "You have to ask?"

"Just checking," Johnny says, patting Warren's thighs once before he steps out of the vee of his legs. "I'll wait outside. Need to cool down a bit," he adds, louder.

"Get out," Giles says flatly.

Johnny presses a quick kiss to Warren's cheek, and then goes to pick up his duffel bag.

Warren blushes. He and Johnny have been making out in full view of the street outside the large glass window for the last ten minutes, but somehow that small peck on the cheek feels both more public and more intimate. A declaration of sorts.

He watches as Johnny slings his bag over his shoulder and heads for the door. Giles is watching too, glaring at Johnny with his arms crossed over his chest. Johnny seems impervious to it, grinning broadly as he holds the door open for Lucinda. She winks at Giles' daemon before she slinks outside, Johnny following cheerfully after her.

Warren makes an ungraceful descent from the washing machine and trails Giles into his office. Minnie winds herself impatiently around Warren's ankles as he hands over his keys and accepts his last paycheck. Throughout the awkward farewell, his eyes keep straying to Johnny where he waits outside, leaning nonchalantly against the windowed wall.

Finally, they can leave. Warren expects Minnie to sprint out the door as soon as he opens it, but instead she stops at the threshold and turns, looking back.

"It's strange to be leaving it behind, after everything," she muses, her voice quiet. "If it weren't for this place, we never would have met them. *Any* of them."

Warren follows her gaze, taking one last look at the Blue Wave Laundromat. He sees the inexplicable beach mural with its jumping dolphin, the grimy plastic chairs, the rows of neglected machines. None of it has changed since he started working here. But Warren has.

He remembers cold nights in January. He remembers sitting alone at the cash register for hours and hours with only his daemon for company. But he doesn't remember how it feels to be lonely anymore. He's always had Minnie, but now he has Yolande and Nadia. He has Zoe and Jonas. And he has Johnny. Johnny who found him here, and then decided to stay.

"We're taking the good parts with us," Warren says to Minnie.

They look at each other. Then, as one, they turn and step over the threshold. Warren closes the Laundromat door behind them.

Outside the sky is just beginning to lighten.

Warren exhales a long breath, his eyes falling closed as he raises his face to the dawn. Lucinda comes over to him. She leans against his thigh, and he rests his hand on top of her head. Her fur is warm beneath his palm.

When he opens his eyes again, he sees Johnny standing on the sidewalk a few paces away with Minnie on his shoulder, waiting for him. Looking at him, Warren's chest feels full.

Johnny reaches out his hand. "Ready?"

Warren takes it. "Yes," he says. He laces their fingers, pressing their palms together so there is no space between them. "Let's go."


------


It's a short walk over to Johnny and Zoe's apartment.

Warren and Johnny hurry up the stairs hand-in-hand, shooting each other excited glances like they've just gotten away with something, and tumble through the door into the entryway, where they quickly divest themselves of bags and shoes and jackets.

When Warren straightens from untying his sneakers, Johnny immediately presses himself up against his back from behind. He wraps his arms around Warren's waist and rests his chin on the top of his head, humming contentedly into his hair.

Warren brings his hands up to Johnny's forearms, and leans back into the embrace. He feels like he's floating. He's light as air, held aloft by the bubble of joy in his chest.

"This is familiar," he murmurs.

"I remember," Johnny replies, dropping a kiss into Warren's curls.

"I can't believe I didn't realize you liked me sooner."

"I can't either," Johnny teases, and Warren smacks him lightly on the arm. "Especially since…" He trails off.

"Since what?"

Johnny makes a contemplative noise. "See them?"

Warren instinctively looks toward their daemons. Lucinda is sitting on the carpet in the living room, her eyes gone half-lidded and hazy as Minnie rubs herself along her side the way a cat would, slow and deliberate. Warren watches as Lucinda lowers her head to tenderly nuzzle the spot between Minnie's ears in response.

"Lucinda has never been like that with anyone else's daemon," Johnny says quietly.

"Shane?" Warren asks. He feels Johnny shake his head.

"They're close, but it's not like this. Nothing has ever been like *this*." Johnny holds Warren tighter. "I'll be honest, it scared the hell out of me at first."

"Why?"

"Because it meant this was *real*, not just my own wishful thinking." There is the briefest moment of hesitation, before Johnny adds, "And I wasn't certain I wanted it."
"And now?" asks Warren. He knows the answer— he *knows* it. He wants to hear it.

"Now," Johnny says, directly into Warren's ear, "I'm all in."

Warren's heart picks up speed, a quickening tempo that beats loudly in his ears. He turns around in Johnny's arms and reaches up to cradle his face in his hands. Johnny's skin is smooth beneath his palms, except for the slightest prickle of stubble along his jaw. He's watching Warren with soft, moon-grey eyes, his smile slightly crooked and utterly gorgeous.

Warren has to kiss him. He rises onto his toes and presses their lips together. Johnny's hands come up to fist in his hair as the kiss catches and ignites, fueled by the unresolved desire that has been passing back and forth between them like an electric arc since the moment Johnny stepped into the Laundromat this morning. Warren is practically vibrating with want. He can feel himself hardening in response to the solid line of Johnny's body against his, and it sends heat rushing to his face.

He whines in protest when Johnny abruptly releases him.

"Okay, no, not here," Johnny says, sounding strained. He takes Warren's hand. "Come with me."

Warren follows, his pulse thudding with anticipation as Johnny leads him down the hallway to his bedroom. He lets go of Warren's hand once they're inside, and closes the door. Then he goes to switch on the lamp on the bedside table.

The first thing Warren registers is the double bed with its familiar brightly patterned quilt. There is a big pile of laundry in the middle of it.

"Let me just…" Johnny mumbles, and begins hastily clearing away the laundry, tossing it carelessly onto a chair in the corner that's already heaped with clothing. Lucinda helps him, gathering up some stray socks that have fallen to the floor and sweeping them under the bed with her paw.

While the two of them tidy, Warren takes the opportunity to look around the rest of the room. It's only the second time he's been in here, and the first time he's seen it in the light of day. He sees an over-full garment rack lined up along the opposite wall, with boots and shoes strewn haphazardly on the floor beneath it. There are band posters on the walls, and a full-length mirror with photographs taped all around the edges. There's also a shelved cabinet covered in books, and knickknacks, and a dozen interesting half-finished projects that Warren would like to investigate more thoroughly at a later time.

Not now though.

Now, the reality of finally being alone with Johnny in a room with a bed is setting in, and he has to sit gingerly on the edge of the mattress to disguise his suddenly shaky legs. Minnie leaps onto the bed as well, gazing curiously at her surroundings as she makes herself comfortable nearby.

"Where's Zoe?" Warren asks, plucking at the quilt with his fingertips.

"Probably downstairs. I told him to be out," Johnny replies, tossing one last jumper onto the chair. He meets Warren's eyes. "Is that… all right?"

"Yes," Warren says. It doesn't come out quite as confidently as he means it to.

Johnny notices. He comes to stand in front of where Warren is sitting and reaches for him, circling his wrists with his long fingers.

"Hey. This doesn't have to be anything you don't want it to be," he says. He steps in close and lifts up Warren's hands, holding them to the centre of his chest. "I just want to be near you."

Warren swallows. "I want that too."

Johnny regards him cautiously. "Don't let me rush you."

"You're not," Warren denies automatically. When Johnny's expression doesn't change, he adds, "I won't."

Johnny squeezes his wrists. "You should know, it's been a while since I've done this, and I'm a little nervous."

"You are?"

"Yeah, because it's *you*, and I want to get it right," says Johnny. He's looking straight-on at Warren's face, his attention unwavering. "But I really want this. If you do."
Warren breathes out a laugh, disbelieving. "Of *course* I do."

A smile spreads across Johnny's face, slow and bright like a sunrise. "Good."

"Good," Warren echoes. Then, slowly, his heart pounding like a drumbeat in his chest, he shapes his hand into a fist around the front of Johnny's shirt and *tugs*.

Johnny tips forward, and Warren scoots further back to accommodate him as he kneels on the mattress, bracketing Warren's legs between his own. When Warren fits his hand to the back of his neck, Johnny bends to meet him, slotting their mouths together.

Johnny's hands roam restlessly over Warren's body while they kiss, like they can't decide where to settle, skimming over his hair, his shoulders, the tops of his arms. Warren thrills at the touch, shivering as Johnny runs his fingers down his sides over his ribcage.

He pauses when he reaches the hem of Warren's shirt, and leans back to look at him. "Yes?" he asks, tugging gently.

Warren's mouth goes dry at the thought of Johnny's hands on his bare skin. "Please," he says hoarsely.

Johnny obliges, lifting Warren's shirt over his head. Being the focus of his attention is heady— it always is— and Warren holds his breath as Johnny's eyes rake over him. He releases it, all the air whooshing out of his lungs at once, when Johnny leans in to press a kiss to his bare shoulder.

"Beautiful," he murmurs, nosing thoughtlessly at Warren's skin. "So damn beautiful, Warren. I'm going to kiss every single one of these freckles."

Warren blushes, feeling heat spreading up his chest and across his face. "Your turn," he says, pulling insistently at the fabric of Johnny's t-shirt. "Off, take it off."

"Wish, command," replies Johnny, reaching back to pull his shirt off in one quick motion.

Warren's hands go immediately to his chest, trailing reverently over his naked skin. He slides a palm up Johnny's left arm, pausing once he reaches the colorful half-sleeve of tattoos. He brushes his fingers over them lightly, carefully tracing the outline of the jackrabbit daemon, before moving on to the set of cracked dice. He *understands* that one now, and he takes a moment to appreciate how far he and Johnny have come since those first few winter nights. He leans in to kiss the tattoo, his lips lingering as Johnny sighs above him.

The mattress dips suddenly as Lucinda jumps up onto the bed. She comes to lie flush against Warren's hip, her hair tickling his bare skin. Warren reaches for her without thought. He holds Johnny's eyes as he digs his fingers into the velvety fur at her belly.

Johnny's reaction is instant. He gasps, his hands flying to Warren's chest to brace himself as his eyes fall half-closed. Through the dizzying waves of warmth and want, Warren registers that Lucinda is arching her head back, her ears going flat against her skull as a rumbling growl rips from her chest. Johnny makes a noise too, deep in his throat, his fingers curling on Warren's skin.

Encouraged, Warren keeps going, stroking his hands more firmly. Beyond the display of pleasure, he tracks Minnie, who has been watching them with rapt attention, her body still and tense in the way she gets when she is waiting to pounce on something. She stands abruptly and goes to Johnny, briefly nuzzling Lucinda as she climbs over her to get to him.

Warren sees the moment Johnny notices Minnie's movement, his eyes sharpening with intent. He picks her up in one hand, and uses the other to run a finger along the length of her back.

Sparks of electricity shoot down Warren's spine, even as his breath rushes out of him like he's been kicked in the chest. He lets himself fall backward onto the mattress, gasping. Johnny stays hovering over him, his pupils blown wide as Minnie mewls quietly in his grasp. All Johnny is doing is lightly caressing her back, but it feels as if his hands are everywhere, all over Warren.

"You..." It's difficult to focus beyond the hypersensitivity of his skin, his entire body lit up by the phantom echo of Johnny's touch on Minnie, but Warren tries. "Okay, stop, put her down," he says. "I need—" He reaches for Johnny, stretching upward. "*You*, I need you, come here—"

He cuts himself off with a whimper. Something sparks in Johnny's gaze at the sound, a flare of heat that sets Warren's blood alight as if it were kindling.

Johnny sets Minnie down on the bed, where she collapses in a spent little heap against Lucinda's side. Then he reaches for Warren, palms open and fingers spread, his eyes bright and dark and hot.

Warren rises to meet him, desperate for the weight of his body, the taste of his mouth, for every last foreign and familiar piece of him. Johnny lowers himself so that their bodies are pressed flush together, and Warren experiences an overpowering awareness of every single place they are touching— he is *dizzy* with it.

"I've had some fantasies of my own, you know," Johnny whispers into Warren's ear. "Let me show you one of them."

Then he begins trailing a line of devastating, open-mouthed kisses down Warren's chest. His thumbs hook in Warren's waistband as he travels lower, tugging.

Warren clutches at the bare skin of Johnny's back and holds on for dear life. He feels like he's unraveling, but all he wants is more, more, *more*.

Johnny gives it to him.

------

A chime sounds, rousing Warren from sleep.

He blinks up at the unfamiliar ceiling, struggling to get his bearings, his mind hazy from being woken too soon.

Someone sighs next to him, and Warren's stomach swoops pleasantly as his memories come rushing back. He's in Johnny's bedroom— in his *bed*. The thought makes Warren grin to himself as he stretches his naked limbs beneath the blankets.

When he turns his head on the pillow, Johnny is already looking back at him, bleary-eyed but smiling.

"Hey," he murmurs, drawing out the syllable.

Warren likes the sound of Johnny's sleepy drawl. He could get used to hearing it.

"Hi," he replies, turning onto his side so that they're facing each other.

Minnie yawns where she's tucked between them, cuddled up close to Johnny's chest. When Johnny shifts to wrap his arm around her, Warren feels it like a hand around his heart, not squeezing, but holding, safe and warm.

Minnie lets out a contented purr, and Johnny's smile widens. Warren reaches out to trace his fingers over the gorgeous curve of his lips.

"You have my favorite smile," he says quietly.

Johnny's eyes go soft, and Warren's heart flutters in his chest. *He* did that.

Johnny uses his fingers to brush the curls off of Warren's forehead. "You've said that before."

"I have?"

"Yeah," Johnny tells him. "It made me crazy then too."

He leans in close and kisses Warren once on each cheek, and then on his forehead, before finally letting him taste his perfect mouth.

They break apart when their phones chime again, one after the other, as they both receive messages. Somewhere down by their knees, Lucinda makes a low noise of complaint. Minnie wriggles out of Johnny's arms, pausing only to stretch, long and low, before she goes to her.

Johnny smirks at the disgruntled look on Warren's face. He kisses him again, just once, short and sweet, and then rolls away to pick up his phone from the bedside table.

"Who is it?" Warren asks, too comfortable to even consider moving to get his own phone.

Johnny rolls back, coming to rest half on top of Warren. Warren grunts, but doesn't protest. He wraps his arms around Johnny instead, marveling at the ease of it. He breathes in, inhaling the masculine, sleep-warmed scent of Johnny's skin, and settles his hands low on the base of his spine, holding him in place.

Johnny is looking at his screen. "It's Yolande and Nadia. They want to meet up for brunch at Sol."

Warren groans. The light coming in from the window still has the look of morning, slanting through the half-open blinds to spill in shadowed lines across the floor and the bottom of the bed, so they've only slept for a few hours at most.

"Can't we just stay here?" he complains. "I'll help you make pancakes."

Johnny hums, tossing his phone carelessly onto the mattress. "We have the whole weekend. Surely we can spare an hour for brunch."

"You promised me a week. At least."

Johnny laughs. The line of his throat when he tips his head back makes Warren's pulse jump. Helpless to resist, he rises up to press his mouth to it, and then starts kissing a path up Johnny's jawline.

Johnny sighs blissfully, tilting his head to give Warren more access. "Keep doing that and you can have as long as you want, sweetheart."

Warren's breath hitches. He forces his tone to be casual when he says, "There you go, making promises again."

Johnny lowers his head to meet Warren's eyes. "I intend to keep them."

The words send a wave of happiness cresting over Warren. He raises his hands to cup Johnny's face, as their mouths meet in a gentle kiss.

Minnie and Lucinda are pressed together in a tangle of dark and light fur, making low noises at each other. Warren can sense them both, and their joy fills up every corner of him.

He can't believe he has to leave this bed. How could Yolande and Nadia betray him like this?

A thought occurs. "Wait, stop."

Johnny pulls back immediately. "What's wrong?" he asks, concerned.

Warren shakes his head. "Nothing, it's just... how did Yolande and Nadia know you were back?"

Johnny glances to the side. "Lucky guess?" he says weakly.

Out of the corner of his eye, Warren sees Lucinda duck her head, her ears lowering.

"They *knew* you were coming home early?" he demands, putting the pieces together.
Minnie makes an offended noise. "I can't believe no one told us! They all just let us *suffer*," she grouses.

"We wanted it to be a surprise," Lucinda says, nudging Minnie's cheek apologetically. She turns to Warren. "Didn't you like it?"

Warren softens at her earnest expression. "I loved it," he admits.

"Yeah?" Johnny asks, sliding his palms up the sides of Warren's neck. "What else do you love?"

Warren pretends to consider it. "Hmm, I don't know. Maybe you should ask my *boyfriend*."

Johnny grins, and kisses him back into the pillow. His long fingers drag through Warren's hair, deliberately tangling in the curls of it, as Warren melts into the mattress, his body thrumming with euphoria.

Warren puts his hands on Johnny's hips and holds on tight as he kisses him back with everything he's got. Maybe he can convince Johnny to stay in this morning...

His stomach gurgles.

They both freeze, and then burst into simultaneous laughter. Johnny buries his face in Warren's shoulder, his breath puffing warmly there. Warren tips his head back and grins up at the ceiling as he laughs, feeling lightheaded and giddy.

"So, brunch," Johnny says, once their laughter has subsided to giggles.

"Yes," Warren agrees.

"Coffee first?" Johnny asks. He raises his head and smiles down at Warren, his grey eyes crinkling at the corners. "I know a great place. Best in the city."

Warren hooks a hand around the back of Johnny's neck to keep him close. He couldn't stop smiling if he tried.

"Take me there."

Ingram Content Group UK Ltd.
Milton Keynes UK
UKHW030648220623
423873UK00012B/311